"WHAT DO YOU WANT?"

"What do YOU want?" Pierce's lip curled into a sardonic smile. Suddenly the silver of his blade rippled in the air once again and touched her throat.

Rose forced herself not to move.

The curve of his smile deepened. The blade moved, ripping open the shreds that remained of her bodice. She gritted her teeth, determined not to flinch.

He dropped the blade to his side. "What every good pirate wants!" he assured her, leaning close once again. "Plunder, riches! Pieces of eight! Ships and cargo and hostages. And . . . revenge."

SHANNON DRAKE

BRIDE OF THE WIND

AVON BOOKS  NEW YORK

This is a work of fiction. Names, characters, places, and incidents either are the product of the author's imagination or are used fictitiously. Any resemblance to actual events, locales, organizations, or persons, living or dead, is entirely coincidental and beyond the intent of either the author or the publisher.

AVON BOOKS, INC.
1350 Avenue of the Americas
New York, New York 10019

Copyright © 1992 by Heather Graham Pozzessere
Published by arrangement with the author
Visit our website at **http://www.AvonBooks.com**
Library of Congress Catalog Card Number: 92-93061
ISBN: 0-380-76353-2

First Avon Books Printing: September 1992

AVON TRADEMARK REG. U.S. PAT. OFF. AND IN OTHER COUNTRIES, MARCA REGISTRADA, HECHO EN U.S.A.

Printed in the U.S.A.

WCD 10 9

Prologue

A cannon exploded. With the thunder and boom of the shot, a cloud of black powder mushroomed on the air. The shot fell just short of the *Lady May*. Water gushed up in a cascade and crashed back down. The ship weaved and rocked in the clasp of the sea.

Then the cloud of powder slowly dissipated, and there, before them the root of the menace could be seen. It rose high against the crystal-clear sky. Fluttering, rippling, with each soft whisper or harder gust of the wind, it rose there, stark against the blue of sea and horizon, striking terror into every heart.

The skull and crossbones. White upon black. The pirate flag, flying as proudly as the flag of any nation, and bearing down upon them quickly.

Captain Niemens stood by the helm, his glass fixed on the ship that seemed to cut the waves so very smoothly. He quietly gave the order to his first mate to return the fire, and his first mate shouted out the command. But his shot, too, fell short of his target.

He was outgunned, and he knew it. Perhaps the

pirate had been firing a warning. Still, it was clear that the pirate meant to have the ship.

Captain Niemens studied the flag, for every set of skull and bones was different—just as the men who sailed beneath them.

A shivering filled his heart.

"May I see?"

He started, taking his eye from the glass, looking down at the woman who stood beside him. Again, a shiver seemed to rip right through his heart. Damn the pirate! The captain didn't give a fig for himself, he'd fight the fellow to the very end.

But here was the Lady Rose . . .

To Captain Gaylord Niemens, she was as exquisite as her name. Her eyes were as deeply green as an emerald, her features were more finely sculpted than those of any statue. God had cast her in colors that radiated. Her lips were as red as the flower for which she was named. Her skin was ivory, yet her cheeks were touched with a soft and tempting blush of pink. Against the startling green of her eyes, her lashes seemed like ink while her hair was a rich shade of auburn that caught the sun and reflected shades of gold and copper.

She was tall for her gender, and appeared taller still because she seemed ready to meet any challenge, poised, determined. Surely she had seen the flag. But she was neither shrieking with fear, nor blasting him for what was not his fault, nor sinking down to the deck in a dead faint.

She stood beside him, staring out at the pirate vessel, silent and proud, the green of her eyes enchanced by the deep, rich green of her gown, an extraordinarily fashionable creation with a swirling green skirt, velvet bodice, and silk overshirt. Lace in both black and white trimmed the hem, low, rounded neckline, and sleeves that puffed to her elbows. For all her delicate beauty, she could be exceptionally strong, fierce and fiery, especially in defense of anyone who had been wronged. Her temper could fly quick, but she was fair and intelligent, and unwaveringly kind to those who served her. Captain Niemens knew this because he served her. She had taken over the shipping business from his past master, and Niemens had come to love her. To him, she was beautiful, within and without.

"My dear Lady Rose—" he began.

"Do you know the flag?" she interrupted him, staring determinedly into his eyes.

He nodded. "I think. Yet I might well be wrong. He has not been known to attack English ships, and our colors are flying high and clear."

"The Dragonslayer?" Her cheeks paled just slightly. She gave no other sign of emotion.

Rose felt the first quiverings of terror plunge deep into her. The Dragonslayer. In the past months he had become infamous. No Spaniards or Dutchmen were safe upon the seas. And though the royal word was death to all pirates, it was said that King Charles II relished each and every victory of this high-seas fiend who liked to rob from the Spanish and make himself rich. All manner of noblemen—and women—had been snatched from Spanish vessels. High ransoms had been demanded for their return.

And, of course, the rumors of what else went on once a ship was seized and the hostages taken were absolutely chilling. The Dragonslayer. The very terror of the seas. And he was almost upon them.

"From all I've heard of his flag," Captain Niemens said. He turned to her. "I'll see you to my cabin, milady—"

"No. I've no wish to be locked up like a caged bird. It will make no difference if the action goes badly. I'll see what happens from here!" she protested.

"Milady, no!" he said urgently. "Please, listen to me. Here you could be killed by a falling sail, by an accident of fire from my own men, by—"

"And waiting in the cabin," she said shrewdly, green eyes sizzling, "I will just be skewered by this peg-legged knave!"

Niemens didn't think that he had time to give her a lecture on pirates. Everyone knew about the robbers of the seas, of course, but so much about them was rumor.

And very much was true. For a moment he thought that his greatest charity to the girl might be to run her through with his own sword now, quickly, mercifully. But then again, if this was the Dragonslayer, then Rose would certainly live. The Dragonslayer had yet to take the life of a captive. As to how she would live . . .

He didn't dare dwell on such matters. Rose's father was one of the wealthiest men in the colonies. The Dragonslayer must know it, and thus he was attacking this ship. An English ship.

"Captain Niemens," Rose said softly. "I desire a sword—"

"Fire again!" Niemens gave the command to his first mate, a lean fellow with a graveyard face. He caught hold of Rose's arm and urged her from the gated helm down the three steps to the main deck, and then around and down another set of steps to his cabin, a large, pleasant place directly beneath the helm. He thrust Rose inside, and she spun around, staring at him.

"Captain! I cannot stay here, helpless like this!"

"Please, milady, I implore you. On your honor! Remain here!" he begged her.

Damn him! Rose thought swiftly. He didn't try to

lock her in, he just stared at her with huge brown eyes, like one of the king's spaniels, and trusted in her honor! He didn't understand. If they were taken, she couldn't be seized or murdered without some fight! Captain Niemens would valiantly die for her—but not give her the opportunity to defend herself!

For a bleak moment she remembered that there had been a time when she had been ready to die. The pain within her had been so vast that she would have embraced any angel of death. But that had been before she had discovered just how much she had to live for. And that she had to survive now.

"Captain!"

He closed the door, and she heard his footsteps, hurrying away.

There was another explosion. The ship veered and careened. The second shot had come so very near!

Rose staggered, gained her balance while grasping on to Niemens's desk, and made her way to the brocade-covered seat. She gasped, seeing how quickly the pirate ship was bearing down on them. She could make out the flag now herself. The ship carried a figurehead, too, a woman's upper body with nearly bared breasts and long tendrils of hair curling over and over the exposed flesh. The figurehead was beautiful, and such a contrast to the hideous grimace of the skull on the flag!

She grit down hard on her teeth, trying to assess the pirate ship. On both starboard and port, she was well armed. Rose counted at least ten cannons on each side. Her heart began to sink. She heard feet scampering above deck. An order was called out. "Fire!" The *Lady May* seemed to inhale and tremble as a shot was sent out in return. Rose watched anxiously. The shot fell short of the pirate ship bearing down on them. The reverberations were close now, so close that her own ship began to heave and toss.

"I cannot stay here!" Rose told herself. But dared she fight? She had to return home, she had to . . .

A cry escaped her. It suddenly seemed as if the figurehead from the pirate ship was just about to plunge through the captain's cabin windows! But even as she flew up, determined to be away from the danger, the ship slipped around, ramming into their side. The whole of the vessel seemed to groan and shudder with such ferocity that Rose found herself pitched forward into the desk, then thrown completely to her left where she fell upon the handsome bunk with carved wood head and footboards nestled compactly between shelving.

Clattering and screeching sounds came to her ears as she scrambled to stand. She realized that her ship had been set upon with grappling hooks, and that the pirates were now streaming aboard. She managed to pull herself to her knees despite the tangle of her clothing, but a whimsical gust of wind sent the pirate ship careening against the *Lady May* hard once again and she went flying backward in a mushroom of petticoats, cotton, velvet, eyelet, and silk.

On the deck there were wild cries and the clash of metal. There would be a fight, a horrible fight, and dead men would lay strewn about the ship. And she had to pray that Captain Niemens would be the victor. Yet even as she did so, she thought of the dear dignified captain, a good friend and a fine sailor, but no match for a vicious pirate. She shivered, thinking of his fate.

Yet just as suddenly as the noise had begun, it stopped. There was no long, drawn-out battle.

The world seemed to be silent.

She went still on the bunk, caught upon her knees once again, listening.

And then the door to the captain's cabin burst open.

She gasped, sagging back, for just as she had feared, it seemed that Captain Niemens had not been the victor.

No . . .

The victor stood before her.

The Dragonslayer.

As he was caught in the shadows, with only the faintest glimmer of light coming from behind him, she could see little of him. Tall and dark, he filled the doorway, one hand upon his hip, the other brandishing a sword. His loose-sleeved, open-necked shirt was black as ebony, as were his form-hugging breeches and the boots that rose above his knees. He had, at least, condescended to wear a hat, a tall-crowned and wide-brimmed creation with a single, huge white feather. His features were shrouded, but Rose could see that he wore a black patch over his left eye.

He stood there like an executioner.

The thought sent rivers of icy fear cascading along her spine. She wouldn't be terrified! she promised herself. She would survive this, she would fight it. She wanted to live. She had to return home.

He stared at her long and hard from the doorway. What went on in his mind, she could not begin to tell, for with the light far behind him, he remained nothing but a tall, lithe, muscled menace. The silence deepened. A breeze picked up, suddenly ruffling the feather in his hat and his dark hair.

She tried to untangle her legs from the pile of clothing around her, jerking upon the fabric and at last managing to come to her feet. As she did, she noticed that there was a glittering, razor-sharp letter opener upon the captain's desk.

She made a desperate lunge for it without think-ing that the small blade would not be much of a weapon against the pirate's long and shimmering sword. She simply had to have some defense.

She reached it, clutching it tightly in her hands. But at that moment, the pirate made his move, striding into the cabin.

The door slammed shut behind him.

"I'll kill you!" she promised. "I demand that you leave me be this instant. You'll receive an exceptional ransom for me if you—"

She broke off with a sharp gasp. He had come close enough to raise his sword—and touch her. She still couldn't see his face, for the brim of his hat obscured it.

She felt the blade, and shuddered. The very tip of it pricked the fabric of her gown at her waist. She stared at it, silent, then gasped when he moved it with a startling swiftness—breaking the laces of her gown. Velvet, cotton, and lace slipped apart and she was forced to step back, trying to hold the pieces together while wielding her tiny letter opener against his far greater blade.

"I will kill you!" she said again, holding tight to the fabric. She tossed back her head. "Haven't you listened to a word I've said? My father is wealthy beyond your imagination! He will pay tremendous sums for my safe return. You rogue! I am incredibly wealthy. Do you know who I am? Are you daft? Can you understand English?"

She flew at him, her dagger raised, intending to strike straight for the heart. But no matter how quickly she moved, he was faster, capturing her wrist before the blade could touch him, nearly breaking it. The letter opener fell from her hand and she became acutely aware of the hard-muscled heat of the man as he held her. Then he thrust her from him. He took a step toward her. "No!" she cried out, and lunged for the letter opener. But no sooner did she grasp it than he moved his sword, flicking the tiny weapon away. The letter opener flew from her fingers and crashed against the far corner of the cabin.

Panic rising swiftly within her, Rose began to search for something to throw. The captain's log lay upon his desk, and she threw it first. The dark pirate ducked. She found liquor bottles next. Fiery Caribbean rum went flying, then good Irish whiskey and colonial rye. With each missile hurtled at him, the pirate ducked anew, coming a stride nearer her each time. She wrenched a drawer from the captain's desk, heaving that at him with a vengeance. Yet he advanced, and the next thing she knew, his blade was right at her throat again, and her eyes were meeting the strange glimmer of his within the haunting shadows of his executioner's mask. He pressed the blade closer to her throat, forcing her back.

"Kill me then!" she cried. "You foolish, stupid rogue. Thrust your blade through—" she began.

But he spoke at last. In excellent English.

"Oh, madam! I do intend to thrust my blade through. And trust me, lady, I do know exactly who you are. You would pay me ransom with DeForte money, would you? Oh, lady, I think not!"

The voice! she thought swiftly. The words . . .

He poked his sword against her—but lightly, the touch of his weapon and the insinuation of his tone leaving her to wonder just what blade he meant. But this time the touch sent her sprawling backward. For all her efforts to escape the captain's bunk, she had come upon it again, and now lay on her back, his sword still at her throat, her eyes locked on his.

Her mind . . . reeling.

The voice. She knew the voice. Knew the heated

tension in it, the tenor and the cadence of it, the very rugged depths of it. But it could not be.

And still, her breath caught in her throat. Her heart pounded fiercely. The pain was deep, stealing her breath. Searing, sweeping through her. Dear God, no. Dear God, yes, please.

His sword fell slack for a moment and he jerked off the black patch that had covered his eye, tossing it upon the foot of the bunk.

First her heart soared. Then plummeted. Indeed, it was he. Coal black hair, richly thick and wavy against the strong, rugged lines of his features. Those eyes so brazenly silver and sharp beneath the clean arches of his brows. His cheeks high and cleanly cast, his nose straight as an arrow, his mouth generous, capable of being so grim and merciless . . .

So damnably sensual . . .

Once upon a time he had been the desire of every young woman in London, noble and commoner alike. The king's great friend, his champion in all things, rich, powerful, striking, a hero under fire, quick to laugh in better times. Fair, magnanimous, shrewd, so it had been said, yet she had never really known, for it had seemed that fate had cast them as enemies from the start.

He bowed low to her in mocking courtesy, sweeping his plumed cavalier's hat from his head. "Why, milady! You look as if you have seen a ghost!"

A ghost, God, yes! A man she had believed dead.

The man who had taught her everything she had come to know about passion, hunger, longing, anguish . . . and love. For a moment the fact that he was alive sent a feeling of joy like ripples of silver sweeping through her. She had come to love him, yes. She had felt she had died a little herself when they had said that he was gone. But he was alive, before her now, and it was such an incredible wonder that she nearly shouted out loud, raced to him. She longed to touch him, feel him . . .

No!

No, dear Lord! It was obvious! He knew nothing of the truth, he didn't trust her, he never had. After all this time, he still condemned her!

She felt herself trembling within. She'd never let him know how deeply she loved him! Never!

She lifted her chin. "A ghost? Indeed! One dragged up from the depths of hell!"

"Yes, indeed, lady!" he said softly. "And, Rose, you will find you have awakened a demon!"

She tried to ignore the tone of his voice, tried not to hear the fury and vengeance within it. How she despised herself at the moment, for, before God! after all that had passed, she entered into new realms of agony now. Even as he spoke, she remembered the feel of his whisper against her flesh, the touch of his powerful fingers, the warmth of him, the sweet magic of lying in his arms.

No!

She could not run to him, she would not be a fool. Surely she could not cast away all dignity and pride!

"I thought you were dead!" she said, chin high.

"I am so sorry to disappoint you," he said huskily, those silver eyes condemning her.

"But—the Dragonslayer—"

"Well, I *was* left for dead, you see, my love." The last was anything but an endearment. "But lucky me. I was taken up by a Spaniard with a bone to pick against Englishmen. I was worked and beaten day and night, and made to be eternally grateful for my salvation. Naturally, once I found my freedom . . ." He paused for a moment and added with a biting bitterness, ". . . and once I had disposed of the captain, I became a pirate preying upon other Spaniards."

He had been seized by Spaniards. Beaten. Hurt. Hearing the words brought a new pain to her soul, but she could not reveal it. Not when his anger was so great against her. "This is an English vessel!" she reminded him, careful not to betray her emotions.

"Oh, yes. I know," he said, his voice deep, husky. Then he was bending over the bunk. Close to her. So very close. His fingers wound around the carved footboard of the bunk. At her side his arm was like the steel bar of a prison door.

"But I had word that you were aboard, my love," he said softly, the silver of his eyes cascading over her, bringing new life to her body and causing fierce shivers to dance rapidly down her spine. "Not to mention the fact that it is my own ship!"

"So what do you want?" she cried, determined to inch no farther back, to meet him coolly. Yet she was shaking, and she prayed that her voice would not give her away.

"What do I want?" He pushed up from the footboard, staring at her, dark brow arched high. His lip curled into a sardonic smile. Suddenly the silver of his blade rippled in the air once again, its tip coming to rest at the throat.

She forced herself not to move.

He leaned close again, the curve of his smile deepening.

"Indeed, what do you want?" she repeated coolly, ignoring the sword, meeting his eyes, her own narrowing.

"What do I what?" he said again, very, very softly. The blade moved with astounding accuracy, ripping open the shreds that remained of her bodice. Rose gritted her teeth, but did not flinch.

"I want—what every good pirate wants!" he assured her, leaning close once again. "Plunder, riches! Pieces of eight! Ships and cargo and hostages. And . . . revenge.''

The blade hovered above her. She gathered her pride and anger and shoved it aside. He smiled, dropping the blade to his side.

''You are a fool, Pierce DeForte!'' she said softly, closing her bodice as best she could. ''But be one, if you will. Those who betrayed you are still in England. If you weren't such a stupid fool, you'd know that I was innocent—''

''I believed you innocent once!'' he interrupted. ''And I paid for that bit of stupidity!''

''You still don't see the truth!'' she cried. ''Yet, even if you are a fool, I'll not give away your secret. I'll not tell anyone who you are.''

''How magnanimous of you!''

''Just return me to my father and—''

''Lady, you must be mad!''

''He'll pay you! You just said that you were after plunder—''

''And revenge. The revenge is so much dearer to my heart!''

Revenge! Against her! She wanted to slap the triumph from his eyes, for he was making such a damnable mistake. He had always misjudged her! He deserved to suffer at her hands, certainly not the other way around! She stamped a foot in sudden fury. ''You will let me go! You've no right—''

''But I do!''

His hands were suddenly upon her, drawing her close against him. And for the first time in what seemed like eons, she felt the rippling muscles within his hard, lean body, felt again the strength that had warmed her in dreams. Felt the fury and the tension, the trembling deep, deep within . . .

''Let me go!'' she insisted.

''You know,'' he said, quite politely, though his

grip upon her was still fierce, "you always were headstrong. A little spitfire. Well, my love, this time, strength of will is not going to be enough. Perhaps I will let you go in time. But if and when I do, it will not be for money, but just because I have tired of my revenge."

"You bastard!" she hissed.

He nodded. "That's right, Lady Rose. Count on it. I will deal with you. And I will return to England and deal with the others, I promise you."

"You cannot return to England! You fool! You will hang!"

"Truly, what difference can it make? If I were to hang for murder I did not commit or lose my head for being a pirate? And believe me, revenge is worth any risk. Why, there were times when thoughts of revenge were all that kept me alive. However, revenge will have to wait just a bit. I've business at hand. But fear not. I will return."

He released her and turned, long strides taking him to the door.

"Dammit, you wretched bastard!" she called after him, panic causing her voice to rise. "You are a fool, and you are wrong! I tell you, you will let me go! You've no right, no right at all—"

She broke off, gasping against her will, because he had suddenly, viciously, closed the space between them. His hands were upon her, hard. He was lifting her. Suddenly she was thrown back on the bunk again, and this time he was atop her, straddled over her, staring fiercely down upon her. She twisted, writhing madly for her freedom, raising a hand in her wild determination to strike him.

But he caught her hand, and held it tight, low against the bedding. "Don't tempt me, Rose!"

She fought the sting of tears, the trembling that filled her—and the urge to surrender. Oh, the feel of his fingers against her! She had lain awake so many nights, aching, feeling the agony of loss. Yet that touch!

She swallowed hard, bracing herself. She would not give in to him! Not when his words and heart were so bitter, not when he lived, and despised her so. Not when it was she who should be so very furious with him! She would not surrender.

Even if the wanting remained . . .

"Dammit, you've no right—" she repeated.

"You're mistaken. I've every right!" he roared. His teeth clenched suddenly as he stared down at her. He reached out, and for one fleeting second, it seemed that he touched her with some tenderness, his knuckles just stroking her cheeks. Then he tightened his fingers into his palm, snatching them away. "Have you forgotten that you're—my wife?"

She lay rigid, staring at him. "I have never been able to forget!" she returned.

"Ah, you thought that you were a widow, rich beyond all imagination, eh? Sorry, my love. I am alive."

"Fool, bastard!" she whispered.

"Ah, but husband still!"

They both held very still for a moment, staring at each other. Then, with an oath, he pushed away from her, rising. His back was to her, his shoulders broad and taut, his back stiff, his hands clenched at his sides. He strode to the door. Rose heard it open and then slam shut.

She rolled to her side, curling herself around the stab of pain in her heart.

Yes, she was his wife.

And from the very beginning she had hated him! she told herself.

Hated him.

Loved him.

She leapt up, both panic and fury seizing her with such a force that she was determined to escape the ship, no matter what she had to do to accomplish the feat. She raced for the door, flinging herself against it, then sobbing softly because he had seen to it that it had been barricaded from the outside. He had known that she would try to escape. "God, I hate you!" she cried, slamming her hand against the wood. "I hate you, I hate you . . ."

Her teeth chattered. She wanted to shake him, hurt him. She wanted to wind her fingers around his throat.

He was alive. Dear God, he was alive.

And inside, she started trembling all over again. It was so incredible, so wonderful . . .

He wanted revenge!

He would come back. Soon, she was certain.

Until then, she had no choice. No choice at all, but to wait and pray and . . .

Remember.

Part I

Dreamers

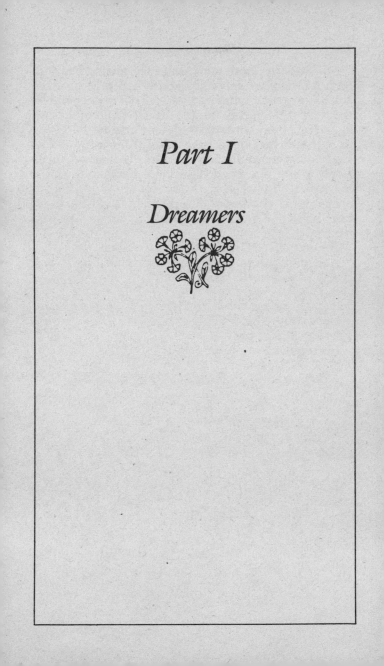

Chapter I

There would be a time, later in Lord Pierce De-Forte's life, when he would remember his first encounter with Mistress Rose Woodbine, the untitled but extremely wealthy daughter of the colonial merchant Ashcroft Woodbine, and realize that sometime on that day, they had all been there.

All of them. He and Anne, and all those who were to betray him.

It all began with Rose . . .

He had been aware, through the intelligence of numerous friends, that Ashcroft considered him to be the most worthy suitor for his daughter. But then, at the moment, almost every matron and proud father in London considered him to be one of the finest catches of the decade. He didn't dwell on that fact or let it inflate his ego. Rather it caused him a good deal of wry amusement, for it had not been all that long ago when the ancient Norman name of DeForte might as well have been mud—not just in London, but in all of England.

Indeed, it had not been that long ago that the current king's father had—with an amazing nobility, not to be forgotten—walked to the scaffold, and there lost his head. In the midst of it all, no matter how dangerous the times had been, the DeFortes had remained completely, almost blindly, loyal to the House of Stuart. At the age of fifteen Pierce had first learned to test his sword in battle, fighting side by side with his good friend, the young Prince Charles. Even when Pierce's own father had given his life in his steadfast loyalty to those he had served, Pierce had determined never to waver. Consequently he had followed his young friend to Scotland, defending him all the way. He had seen him crowned there on the Stone of Scone and then fled with him, going into exile with the landless monarch while Oliver Cromwell held his iron hand over England.

He had risked everything, not just lands and titles, but life and limb as well. Perhaps he had done so because he had been young, brash, and foolish. Perhaps he had done so simply because Charles had been his friend. Perhaps it had even been the adventures they had shared, the good times and bad, the struggle to maintain pride and position abroad. Whatever the reason, he had set his course, and now he was reaping the rewards. Charles had been asked back to England, and he was not a man to forget those who had defended him. He was the king, he ruled a somewhat—no, a very—promiscuous court, but he did so with a certain wisdom and shrewdness, with a wry and bitter humor gained from years in exile. He loved theater, music, art—and beautiful women. And beautiful women loved the king. They flocked to the court. Fluttering mamas and stern papas worried about their daughters, but after the puritanical rule of Cromwell, people were willing to doff the cloaks of respectability and join the handsome young king in enjoying life. Still, Charles was ever careful. The years of deprivation had aged him, given him a reserve that few men ever truly got beyond. Whatever vindictive thoughts he had, he most often kept to himself. He showed bitterness to almost no one and toleration to almost everyone. He was, from almost the first moment he set foot upon English soil once again, a beloved monarch.

Naturally, as one of the king's best and most loyal friends, Pierce found himself the recipient of some of the adoration that fell the king's way. He was tall, well enough muscled, he supposed, and a swordsman of some repute.

Not only that, he was younger than the king, and very rich, since Charles had not only restored his own lands to him, but granted him new properties as well.

And, he thought, grinning, he had all of his teeth, and a full head of hair. He had managed to retain his limbs through the years of fighting. All in all, he determined, he must be a fairly decent bargain.

And Ashcroft Woodbine was a social climber. That fact in itself didn't bother Pierce. He admired the man, and knew a little something about him. Across the Atlantic, Woodbine had done his best to support the wandering young man who had not yet been accepted as King Charles II within his own country. Gifts had often arrived when needed—guns, half-armor, fine swords, and once, even a ship. An orphan, Woodbine had escaped a workhouse to stow away aboard a vessel bound for America. And there he'd worked first for other planters and begun to buy land. His crops had flourished. He had bought more land. He had traded intelligently. He had come from nothing to become a king himself—of cotton and tobacco. He had married the daughter of Lord Justin Renault, and though that old Royalist had gone to the scaffold, Ashcroft Woodbine had managed to make his daughter acceptable to the gentry of England. Of course, reaching for a lord of Pierce's status was quite a stretch, but . . .

Well, he wryly admired the old man for the reach! And he would have been intrigued—at the very least curious—about Mistress Rose, except that he had finally decided, after all his years of wandering, upon a bride.

She was the Lady Anne Winter, and they were very well suited, he thought. Anne was beautiful, wealthy, vibrant, and worldly—indeed they had been enjoying an intimate relationship for quite some time now. He probably should have asked her to marry him by now. He wasn't quite sure why he'd delayed.

Maybe all the years of wandering had caused it. He didn't know. But over the last several weeks, he had spent a great deal of time thinking, and he always came back to Anne. He cared for her deeply. Loved her, surely. And they were so very well suited.

With his mind thus made up, there was really no point in meeting the Woodbine girl.

But he did meet her. The court was at Hampton, and Charles had arranged for a hunt. Pierce was mounted upon Beowulf, an Arabian stallion nearly fifteen years old now but an exceptional horse, one who had carried him through many a misadventure. He was arriving late because he had been waylaid on shipping business, as he had acquired a fleet of six ships since his return to England. A barge had brought him down the Thames from the docks in London, and he had hurried to the stables to see that Beowulf was saddled and ready. He had found the hunt master, and inquired where he might catch up with the king. Riding hard, but certainly not recklessly, he bounded over one of the forest trails.

It was an extraordinary day. The sky was beautifully, endlessly clear. The forest was richly adorned
in brown, the tree branches high overhead weaving
and waving. The air was cool; it felt good against
his cheeks as he rode.

Then, quite suddenly, a burst of different color
appeared before him. He jerked on the horse's reins,
doing his best to avoid the collision, trying to veer
Beowulf to the side. His actions were good and hon-
orable—they risked his own neck far more than that
of the other rider. But the reckless rider had plunged
too swiftly and carelessly onto the trail. No matter
how quickly he acted, they would still collide. He
managed to avoid the main body of the other horse—
and its rider—but still hit the tail end of the other
mount.

Beowulf reared and shrieked, skidding several feet
with the impact. The girth broke, and Pierce found
himself slipped beneath the animal. He held on so
as not to be trampled, then threw himself to the side
the best he could, rolling quickly. Sticks, leaves, and
twigs entangled in his hair and clothing—then a
sudden cold seemed to seep into him. He didn't just
lie upon the forest floor. No. He had fallen by a
stream. If he rolled an inch more, he would find
himself in two feet of cool, bubbling water.

He gasped quickly for breath, deeply irritated.
He'd maintained his saddle in every battle he'd ever
fought, and here, in the middle of the king's own
forest, he had been unhorsed by some reckless
horseman.

Lying upon the ground, panting, feeling the prick
of sticks and stones against his flesh and clothing,
he looked up to see that the other rider was still
horsed, and edging close to him. Then the rider
spoke with a very soft and feminine voice, one that

held just a hint of superiority. ''Can you move, sir? Shall I call for the king's physician?''

Horseman! Horsewoman! It was all the worse.

Yes, he could move! Just what did he look like, some elderly dolt? He pushed up. He was seated in the water, his knees above it, his hindquarters and his feet planted several inches within it. He gritted his teeth, emptying his hat of water, and met his nemesis.

She was not in the least ruffled—he noted that right away. Skeins of deep copper hair, very dark beneath the forest canopy but gleaming gold here and there, were neatly pinned in a heavy braid at her nape, while tendrils and curls escaped to frame her face. An exquisite face, he admitted, startled to find himself mesmerized momentarily by its perfect beauty. It was a face totally unblemished, ivory and rouge, with a small, very straight nose, beautiful full lips, and eyes that seemed like gemstones, even against the green of the forest. Clad in deep green velvet and sitting atop a pitch-black mare, she seemed like some forest sprite, unearthly, stunning—and completely unaware that she was the one at fault.

Rose Woodbine was not quite so unaffected as she was trying her best to appear. She had been in such a hurry . . .

She was late for the hunt, because she had been tarrying in the ladies' solar, dreaming of home while a number of the queen's women had been gossiping about the king's exploits.

She liked the king and the queen, and enjoyed the court. But she wanted to go back to Virginia. She'd been away too long. She wanted to ride over the hills, lie in the grass along the river, feel the sultry Virginia breeze on a warm summer night. In the very worst way, she wanted to go home.

And she had been expecting to do so soon!

But then last week a message from her father had arrived at her school just outside of London directing her to join the king and his court. The message had instantly sent her heart sinking, for she knew exactly what her father wanted from her. "I came from nothing!" he had once told her as he paced their beautiful Virginia ballroom. "And I worked my fingers to the bone, yet all of it would have been for naught had I not met your sainted mother!"

Rose had kept quiet, of course, because when Ashcroft was in one of his moods, it was always best to keep quiet. And though her memories of her mother were dim, they were tender. Her mother had been beautiful, soft, gentle, and she had always smelled sweetly of green fields and flowers. It had seemed a nightmare when she had died, trying to give Ashcroft a son. Rose had scarcely been five at the time, but after all these years, she still missed her.

To give her father credit, Rose knew that he had adored her mother—whether he had married her for her social position or not. He had never remarried. He had buried his desire for a son, but he had determined that he would set his daughter among the aristocracy. Rose simply listened to his tirades in silence.

Then she turned about and did exactly what she chose.

Not that she had really chosen to disobey him. It was just that he intended her to marry some arrogant nobleman, and she had absolutely no intention of doing so. She was going to play the court game, and then she was going to go home! In her favor was the fact that the particular lord her father seemed to have in mind was nearly engaged to Lady Anne Winter—lovely, witty, rich, and sophisticated.

He was hardly likely to change his mind. So despite her father's desires, things could go well. She could be charming at court, Lord DeForte could marry, and she could sail home. On a Woodbine ship. Her father owned several. And when she returned home, she'd prove she was every bit as able to run their shipping business as any man.

There seemed to be one small flaw in her plans, however. Her father had written to an old friend asking him to act as her guardian while she was at court. However, while Ashcroft's letter had been crossing the Atlantic, Lord Bryant had passed away.

His son, Jamison, a young man Rose considered somewhat unsavory, naturally acquired his father's charge.

It was a chilling thought! And her thoughts had made her so late that when her beautiful black mare, Genie, had been brought to her, she had leapt atop her and raced like the wind.

Perhaps she had been racing just a bit recklessly, but so had this awful, arrogant man!

Defensively, she stared down upon him.

"Sir, if you're not all right—"

"I am quite all right, dammit!" Pierce DeForte lashed out. He'd been sitting in the wretched cold water, just staring at her. His temper flared. "And no thanks to you, girl!"

She bristled visibly. "As I've said, sir, I shall be most happy to go for the king's physician—"

"I do not need a physician."

With grace and agility, she slipped down from her mare's back, grimacing as her feet touched the muddy earth. She picked up her skirts and approached him, standing just beyond the water. "If you cannot rise—"

"You're going to assist me from there?" he inquired politely, his tone just barely touched with sarcasm.

"I can send—"

"Girl, you can learn some common good sense and courtesy—and how to ride!" he exclaimed angrily.

"Sir, I do not wish to boast, but I ride with exceptional skill," she informed him.

"You don't wish to boast, eh, yet your skill is—exceptional?"

"It is, sir. I have ridden since I was a very small child. And if you have had the misfortune to discover that you cannot control your mount—"

"My dear child! I was doing my very best to avoid injury to another!"

She sighed, with a great deal of exasperation. "I am not a child! And if you will note, sir, I maintained my position upon my horse while you did not!"

Pierce gritted his teeth. "I just told you—"

"Yes, quite a good excuse, I think," she said sweetly.

"You rode as carelessly as a two-year-old!" he exclaimed angrily, wincing as he shifted and a rock grated against his backside. She stepped closer, still trying to keep her dainty boots and the hem of her skirts from coming into contact with the water.

"Look!" she said impatiently. "I didn't mean to injure you, even if you are an arrogant fool."

"Oh, girl! You do press your luck!" he hissed.

"If I can assist you—" she began.

He smiled, his teeth gleaming beneath the curl of his lips. "Perhaps you can." He stretched out a hand to her. "Perhaps you could reach me?"

She let out a soft sound of impatience, but stretched out her fingers to him.

Perhaps he shouldn't have done it. Charles was

known for his chivalry—and he expected it of those around him as well.

But today . . .

Something about this elegant and brash little chit simply rubbed him wrong. And she could certainly use some manners.

He met her startling eyes, and his smile deepened as her lime-green-gloved fingers touched his. He curled his hand around hers. Very strongly. And he pulled hard.

A startled screech escaped her. His grin broadened as she came near flying over him, landing half atop him, half in the chilly water.

"Dear me, what a dolt I am!" he murmured, suppressing his laughter as she struggled amidst the wealth of velvet and lace of her costume to right herself. She squirmed against him in the effort, and to his surprise he found himself acutely aware of her in a physical manner—not just as a girl, but as a woman. She lay flush against him, and through the barriers of clothing between them, he could feel the length of her legs, the curve of her hip. He could feel the bone of her corset, and above its hard constraint, the soft fullness of her breasts. He was aware of the sweet scent of her, like the petals of a flower, yet with the weight of the woman against him, it seemed to combine with something that was all natural, and very feminine, and completely sensual. She made him think of darkness, of hot fires that blazed in the flesh. For several long seconds he was still, caught up in some trap of the senses, quite simply mesmerized by something lush and compelling within the girl. Perhaps there was innocence in her eyes, perhaps there was not. He was amazed by his reaction to her, annoyed, even furious with himself.

Fool! You've a near perfect woman you're about

to wed! he reminded himself. A woman who loved
him, who came to him, who filled his nights.

And yet he could feel this dark, fierce desire for a
girl he had barely touched. A desire unlike anything
he had known in all his life. A desire created by the
copper flame of her hair, by the emerald blaze of her
eyes. By the weight of her within his arms, her
breasts heaving with the fever of her fury.

He set his jaw hard, determined he didn't feel a
thing for her.

"Oh, you overgrown oaf!" she cried, trying very
hard to regain her balance, and snapping him out of
the curious lethargy that had seized him.

His fingers tightened around her arms. His eyes
sizzled. "Oh, dear Lord, yes, girl, I am so very sorry!
Of course, it's not really my fault if you're incapable
of standing. But let me help you now!" And with
an apparent attempt to right her himself, he flipped
her over, so that she then lay backside down in the
water, drenched, her plumed hat drifting off in the
water, her dark hair coming loose and sodden all
around her.

"How dare you!" she raged, striking out at him.
But he was quick and avoided her blow, catching
her wrists and offering her a wicked, warning smile.

"Alas! I slipped! But you must be very wary of
men who cannot sit their horses. You never know
where else they may falter. I am so sorry—"

Her eyes could surely burn an emerald fire. She
was undaunted, unbeaten, the type who would fight
to the bitter end. "You most certainly are not sorry,
you wretched knave! You did that on purpose!"

"I most certainly did not! We oafs have a terribly
difficult time with grace of movement, that is all. But
if you'll let me try again—"

"No!" Her eyes rippled with a luster that seemed
to reflect from the water. She gritted her teeth then,

staring up at him. "Get off me! I can see that you are quite fine—other than that you suffer from some mental lack that surely has been with you since birth! If you'll just remove your oafish, graceless weight from me—"

He still held her wrists. Her fingers were wound into fists right about them, her lime-colored gloves now deep green since they were so soaked.

"Certainly," he said politely. He stood, dragging her along with him. For a moment again, he was startled to realize that he was holding her very close. Then he released her, determined that perhaps he had taken things just a bit too far, and that he would retrieve her hat in amends.

But the second that he released her, she seemed to turn into a tigress. Her fists pounded against his chest with remarkable strength. He was so taken off guard and so unbalanced in the mud of the stream bed that he started to go toppling over backward again—which was, of course, exactly what she had intended.

"Why, you little vixen!" he cried, and before he lost his footing completely, he reached for her again. She shrieked, trying to escape him, but his fingers wound around her wrists and they plummeted down into the water, this time into the deeper section of the stream, where they both went spiraling down. Pierce came up quickly, finding a boot hold against a rock on the bottom, and for a moment he felt a tremor in his heart, for he had lost his hold upon her, and it occurred to him that perhaps she couldn't swim. He plunged under the water again, catching hold of her skirts. For all his pains, he felt the fevered slam of her fists against him. They staggered to the surface together once again.

"My God, what are you trying to do, drown me

this time? And all because you cannot control your horse!'' she cried.

''Drown you! I was trying to save your fool neck!''

''Save me! Sir, I ride better, and I'm damned certain I must swim better—''

''And swear better?'' he inquired.

She was furious, her cheeks flushed brilliantly with her anger, her eyes even greener because of it. ''Oh,'' she cried out again, then disappeared beneath the surface. She rose, and the next thing he knew, she was flinging mud from the stream bottom at him.

''Why, I'll be damned!'' he cried, amazed and absurdly determined that he was not going to lose a fight—no matter how infantile—with this girl. ''You wretched little brat!'' He wasn't sure what he intended to do, but he ducked back beneath the surface himself, quickly washing away the mud, then took a step toward her. She let out a startled scream and swirled the best and most swiftly she could within the confines of her waterlogged clothing to head for the bank and dry land. His arm came sweeping around her waist, detaining her. Her fingers worked furiously upon his. ''You let me go, instantly!'' she warned.

''Oh! Throw mud at me, and demand your freedom as if you had behaved with the least bit of dignity? Alas! Mud throwing is quite childish, and you, little girl, are going to pay as a child would—''

''Touch me, and you'll be sorry!''

''I'm touching you this minute, and I'll pay no price at all, I'll warrant!''

But he had paid a price. A huge price. The second her eyes had touched his, the minute his fingers had found her flesh.

''You wait, you idiot knave!'' she cried. ''You wait

until the king hears of this! You'll be boiled in oil, hanged from a gibbet—"

"Me! Vixen, someone should wash your sweet mouth out with lye!" he assured her, moving swiftly through the water and dragging her right along. "You wait, my little witch, until the king hears of this—"

He broke off, startled by the deep, rich tones of masculine laughter. He stood still, the exquisite, muddied urchin still held beneath the grip of his arm.

The king didn't need to hear about anything. He had come upon them, accompanied by the Lady Anne.

"The king, my friends, is with you!" Charles announced. "And we are ever so eager to hear all that has happened, aren't we, Lady Anne?"

Chapter II

Charles, attired in crimson breeches with an even more deeply shaded brocade waistcoat over a ruffled white linen shirt, was indeed with them. Mounted on one of his royal horses, he stared down at them with high-arched, dark brows. There was a great deal of laughter about his flashing brown eyes, and had it only been the king to stumble upon him, Pierce might have been richly amused himself.

However, the Lady Anne was by the king's side, elegant and lovely, her golden blond beauty enhanced by the very light purple of her velvet riding gown. She was staring from him to the creature in his arms with a great deal of shock and reproach. He opened his mouth, wondering how he could explain to Anne that the girl was an irascible schoolchild who deserved such treatment.

"This is intriguing indeed," Charles said to Anne, almost as if the two of them were still alone. "I do wonder if they've ever been properly introduced. Let's see, where do I start? My dear little flower, Rose! You must be just a shade kinder and cease referring to this fellow as an oaf. He is one of my oldest and dearest friends, a peer of the realm, Lord Pierce DeForte, His Grace, Duke of Werthingshire. I'm quite sorry. I'm afraid that I cannot boil him in oil and hang him from a gibbet as I might still have need of his sword arm. And, Pierce, my good fellow, this lovely creature is Mistress Rose Woodbine, my guest at court. Though she has a guardian in England, I do feel quite responsible for her welfare, and my wife, most certainly, is equally concerned." He smiled. "Her father, you see, is also a friend . . ."

Woodbine! So this was Rose Woodbine! He might have guessed; he should have known.

He smiled, his teeth grating, then bowed deeply. "Miss Woodbine."

"My Lord DeForte!" It sounded as if she were choking on the name as she said it.

Charles cleared his throat. "Pierce, you might consider setting the girl down!"

She gazed up at him with wicked satisfaction. He smiled in return, unmindful of Anne for a moment. "Certainly!" he assured Charles. He released Rose. Naturally she went sinking toward the bottom once again.

"Pierce!" Anne cried. He strode from the water, looking innocently at her. He could hear Rose sputtering behind him. He smiled at Anne.

"Pierce, perhaps she can't swim, perhaps—"

"Oh, she can swim," Pierce assured Anne. He had reached Anne's mount and leaned against the horse's high flanks, staring up at her.

He could just hear the girl hiss as her head broke the surface of the water. "Nobleman, indeed! Noble bastard!"

He raised his voice. "She can both ride and swim much better than I, and I do assure you, m'lady,

Charles's darling little colonial desires no help from me."

"Miss Woodbine!" Anne called out. "Perhaps he struck his head. His manners are not usually so lacking!"

He was certain that Miss Woodbine was not concerned about his manners. The king had dismounted from his horse, and most solicitously gone to help the girl from the water.

The scheming little social climber was assuredly much more interested in such attention from a king than a duke, he was certain. The fact that she was staring at him with gemstone eyes that seemed to cut pleased him deeply at the moment.

"His manners, m'lady," Rose replied, "seem not lacking, but completely nonexistent!"

" 'Tis the association with colonials, I am afraid," Pierce said regretfully to Anne. Her eyes widened. She'd never seen him be purposely cruel, yet then again, Mistress Rose Woodbine didn't seem to mind in the least being a colonial.

"Pierce!" Anne exclaimed, her huge blue eyes upon him. "What is this? Battle with a pretty little girl! Will you please behave? You'll have everyone talking!"

He gritted his teeth, somewhat ashamed. She was right. But she just didn't realize how irritating this particular pretty child could be.

He looked back to Rose. Her hair was free and wet now, streaming down her back in rich cascades. It fell far below her waist. Anne was wrong, he thought. She was not a pretty child. She was an elegant and exceptionally beautiful woman, very wild and arrogant and headstrong, and she might well be the type to cause an unimaginable amount of trouble. Even soaking wet and totally disheveled, she remained strikingly lovely.

She'd certainly caught the king in her spell.

Pierce smiled suddenly, watching Anne. She was quite right. He had sunk to an absurd level, exchanging insults with this pretty child. "Well, my love," he said huskily to Anne, "I do believe I shall have to forgo the hunt. Your Grace!" he called to Charles. "If you'll forgive me, I shall repair to the castle for a bath."

"Perhaps we should all travel back," the king said, "since I surmise my lovely Rose must also bathe and change."

"How lovely," Pierce said flatly, still staring up at Anne with a half smile. "Let's do all ride back together!"

Anne offered him a stern frown. She was fond of amusement, but she also demanded good manners.

Rose smiled to the king, then left his side to reach her mare. With no assist, she leapt atop the horse. "I shall see myself back to court, thank you, Your Majesty, Lady Anne."

"Oh, no, no, no! We must show this dear little colonial every courtesy!" Pierce insisted. A whistle brought Beowulf trotting over to him. He leapt up quickly on his horse, wondering what demons she had stirred within him. "Let's ride together."

Rose's mare pranced as if she knew her mistress's wild mood. "My dear Lord DeForte! Any more courtesy on your part and I might well freeze to death! I am quite capable on my own, you need not worry—"

"Perhaps I was not quite so worried about you, Mistress Woodbine, as I was about other unwary travelers who might stray upon your path!"

He kneed Beowulf, and the stallion started off at a brisk trot. Rose's mare leapt forward, following. The king and Anne came behind.

They left the shade of the trees and rode into open

fields. Rose gave her mare free rein. In seconds she was racing along.

Pierce was not to be outdone. Not at this. Beowulf deserved the chance to redeem them both. He gave the stallion free rein then, and in seconds he and Rose were engaged in a wild race over emerald green hills.

The king, trotting along in their wake, arched a brow to Lady Anne. She shrugged in return, shaking her head.

"What is he doing?" Charles demanded.

Watching them, Anne shook her head. This was very unlike Pierce. She bit her lip suddenly. They should have married already. They enjoyed each other so thoroughly.

But they were both equally fond of their freedom. He hadn't been her first lover, and she most certainly hadn't been his. They were both rich, powerful, and experienced—and so they had taken their time. Maybe too much time. A shiver suddenly seized her. She was anxious for the night.

Anxious to hold him again.

"You two need to marry," the king commented, as if reading her mind. They were both his loyal supporters. The marriage would be good for him. He meant to be the most tolerant monarch ever—even if, in his heart, he agreed with his father about the divine right of kings. But his father lay long dead, and the pain of all that had been would never die. No matter what his true thoughts were, Charles II would always rule with Parliament, and tolerantly.

It was helpful, however, to have rich and powerful friends. Anne's wealth would make Pierce an even more valuable supporter.

"You're right, we should marry!" Anne murmured. She was struck by how abominably he was behaving toward the Woodbine girl, so why she should feel a little twinge of jealousy, she didn't know.

Yes, she did. They were like a pair of lion cubs, roaring, spitting. But there seemed to be something in the air around them, too. Something that caused the sun to grow warm, the air to shimmer. They might be the most bitter enemies . . .

But there was something like lightning there, too.

Had Charles seen it? No, he was busy musing over Pierce.

"He is a good man," Charles said. "One I call friend with tremendous security!" But then he smiled, shaking his head again. "Amazing, isn't it? There rides the man who often charmed safe harbor for us from the heads of Europe! The man who fought would-be assassins at my back, one of the finest swordsmen in all of Europe. He's determined to outrun her!"

"Oh, and he will," Anne assured him.

Charles's eyes sparkled. He loved racing, and wagering. "A gold piece says she takes him!"

"Oh, I think not!"

"She's an excellent rider."

"Ah, but he is a man, challenged."

"My money is on the girl."

"Your Majesty, you've a bet!" Anne agreed, laughing. She leaned low, nudging her horse with her heel, and started to race herself. Charles, laughing delightedly, followed suit.

When they came into the courtyard at last, where grooms quickly materialized to assist the king, he was smiling still.

Pierce had reached the courtyard first. He had already dismounted from Beowulf. Rose Woodbine was just now slipping down from her mount.

The king slipped a coin into Anne's gloved hand.

"Well, m'lady, he is an exceptional man, we do agree on that!"

Anne nodded, still smiling herself. "But that is quite an exceptional young woman, too, Your Majesty." She hesitated, curious. It was certainly none of her business, but despite the king's marriage, his amorous exploits were the talk of all London. He was a charming man. Charming—and wicked and as determined as the devil when he chose. His eyes were dark and very sensuous, and the way that they followed a woman made her feel special. Perhaps he had cast his eyes upon the American girl, Mistress Rose.

Suddenly Anne found herself wishing that the very beautiful American girl were the king's newest love. It would dim Pierce's interest.

Charles lowered dark lashes over his eyes for a moment, then met her gaze, a secretive smile playing on his lips. "She is not an, umm, intimate friend, Lady Anne, if that is the question that lurks beyond those innocent and beautiful eyes. She's a sweet young thing, really. Totally innocent. And though I may have my failings, m'lady, I'm not a lecher."

"Dear Lord! No, of course! You're the king!" Anne said.

"What is it? What on earth is going on here?" Pierce asked, approaching them, still dripping wet. He had been giving a groom very explicit instructions on how Beowulf was to be rubbed down. Anne was certain that he had scared the poor boy speechless with his stern words, but then he'd pressed a heavy coin into his hands to make it all worthwhile. Pierce was a very demanding man, but generous to a fault. Like Charles, he never forgot the lean days, or what a kindness might mean to someone less fortunate than himself.

"Where is Rose?" Anne asked him.

"I assume the young harridan made straight for her chambers," he said. He was about to slip an arm around her shoulders, but hesitated, grimacing. "Alas! I am a mess. I think I must aim straight for my quarters, too. Forgive me, Your Grace?"

Charles waved a hand at him. "You *are* a mess, m'lord DeForte! Whatever possessed you to go for a cold swim with Ashcroft Woodbine's daughter?"

"Sire, I did not choose to go swimming.'Twas the girl's decision, I swear it!"

The king smiled slowly, shaking his head at Anne, his dark eyes sparkling. "It happens to the best of men upon occasion, Anne. They must all be boys, unwilling to lose a contest."

"There was no contest—" Pierce began, but he could see that the king was laughing. He paused, lowering his lashes. "All right, Your Majesty. You are the king; it will be your way. My love," he said to Anne, "you will excuse me, I pray?"

"Indeed," she replied.

"Between you and Mistress Woodbine, you have quite ended the hunt!" the king exclaimed. "Get away then. I shall go for a walk in my gardens. Join me, Lady Anne? I'll have fair company, and therefore Pierce shall pay for his part in the fracas!"

Pierce, who'd been looking at her hopefully, frowned at the king's words. Longing for assistance washing his back! Anne assumed. Ah, well, she'd been feeling some fine twinges of jealousy. Let him feel the same!

She smiled, linking her arm with the king's. "I think a short walk is in order. I do live to serve my king!" she told Pierce sweetly.

"Umm," he muttered, bending low over her hand. "Take care, my love, how you serve him!"

She ignored him. Charles gave him a smile quite like a wolf who had consumed a quail. He and Anne were both enjoying themselves a bit at Pierce's expense, but then again, Pierce was certainly able to tolerate their teasing.

"Fine then. I shall join you at dinner," he said. "Very clean!" he called to Anne, for she and the king were already moving on. Out of earshot, Anne began to laugh, and the king joined her, and for several moments they traveled the beautiful trails and mazes of roses and flowers set in the gardens. Then Anne, who didn't really want to miss all of the bath, discreetly excused herself, and hurried away to Pierce's chambers.

They were conveniently near her own. Although she was an heiress in her own right, well of age to choose her mate, she shared much of her property with her younger brother.

She sighed, just thinking about Jerome.

He was her half-brother. They had nothing in common, and sometimes he exasperated her badly. Anne's largest inheritance had come to her from her own father, but their mother had been an heiress as well, so Anne and Jerome had jointly inherited some property. Since it brought in a good income, they were forced to manage it together. He was also her blood, she reminded herself constantly. All of the inheritance from her mother's side would go to him should something happen to her; she had even promised her mother when she had lain dying that— should she marry—she would leave half of her father's estate to Jerome as well. Of course, if she and her husband were both to die, Jerome would inherit all her property. King Charles had witnessed her will himself, so she knew that her affairs were in order.

Jerome had nothing to say about the way that she ran her life, but he liked to think that he did. He had his own choices for her as far as a husband went—and she wasn't fond of them.

Actually, maybe that was one of the reasons she felt a certain sympathy for Rose Woodbine. With the death of the elder Lord Bryant, Jamison Bryant was now the girl's official guardian. And Jamison always made her shiver a little. Jerome was always telling her that she should be flattered—Jamison adored her above all women. But there was something about him she didn't like. Jamison was sly, and manipulative. She felt he undressed her each time he looked at her. He would pounce if he ever got the chance— actually, he had already tried to do so.

Maybe she and Pierce had tarried too long, going about so freely, the way that they were. Pierce's parents were both gone now, and the two siblings he might have had died before they had reached the age of one. He owed no one explanations, except the king perhaps, and the king asked for none. Still, for her sake, he was entirely quiet about their relationship.

Anne smiled, hurrying along the hall to his door. When she reached it she looked about, slipping inside. Sometime soon, within the next week, she determined, they would set a date for a wedding!

She closed the door behind her. He was in his bath, his back to her, knees protruding from the water, his dark head with its rich, curling hair just above the rim of the tub. ''Is that you, Peter? I could use another kettle of water here. Did I tell you what that little witch did? She threw mud in my face! The wretched little commoner. Ah, but I could use a back rub!''

Anne crept nearer the tub, grinning. Wretched little commoner, hmmm? She had to admit, she liked Rose herself. The girl might be a colonial, and a bit too independent because of it, but she was also very courageous. Even if she was just a bit jealous, Anne admired her.

"Peter, I'd have some water, please! Talk to me, man. Cat got your tongue, or have you gone daft?"

She knelt down behind him, whispering against his ear as her fingers landed lightly upon his shoulders. "I thought that you might prefer the back rub first. But then again, if Peter is coming . . ."

His hand fell upon hers, locking it against his flesh. "Bolt the door!" he advised her huskily.

She did so. When she returned, he had apparently decided to forgo the back rub. He was standing in the tub, and for a moment she stood back, savoring the sight of his nakedness. There were a few scars on his shoulders, one long one down his back. But to her, they didn't mar his masculine appeal a bit. Pierce was incredibly built, standing perhaps an inch and a half taller than the king. His shoulders were wickedly broad, and his upper arms curved with hard, sculpted muscles earned from years of wielding his sword, ever in his sovereign's defense. His torso tapered to a narrow waist, his hips were lean, his legs long and powerful. And now, as he stood there waiting, grinning at her, what was between those legs was long and powerful, too.

Her heart shuddered a bit. "Now, m'lord, I'll need your back if I'm to—"

She broke off with a squeal, because he stepped from the tub and pulled her into his arms, laughing as he whirled her about. "You're terrible!" she whispered.

"No, I'm wonderful. Give me a chance to prove it."

"I mean you're a—"

"Lecher?" he said, frowning. "A very jealous one. You, m'lady virtue, were walking with the king."

"He was charming," Anne said innocently.

"I shall be more so."

"Hard to prove by the way you handled Mistress Woodbine!"

She was startled by the suddenly dark look in his eyes. "She is a vixen," he said simply, "while you, my love . . . I will simply charm you to tears!"

"Prove it!" she challenged.

A wolfish grin touched his face. Before she knew it, she was naked, feeling the powerful touch of his fingers, the liquid fire of his lips. Here, there, so intimately. The searing tip of his tongue sliding down the valley of her breasts. Lower. Laving upward again. Downward. Downward. Oh!

She gasped, fell back. He carried her to the bed and touched her all over, and then he was with her, one with her, and she was filled with the hot steel of his body, soaring. She was a fool. She hadn't actually run wild, but being mistress of her own fate, she had known several men, all of them fine and brave. But none of them compared to Pierce. None was so sensual, none could sweep her so high that it was near to dying . . .

As she lay with him long, long minutes later, she thought how she'd hate to lose all this. She felt a renewed tinge of jealousy for Rose Woodbine. Maybe Jamison would fall madly in love with his new ward, sweep her off her feet, and marry her.

No. She was jealous, but she didn't really want that to happen!

His arms closed around her. "What is it?"

She leaned her cheek against his bronzed chest.

"I want you to apologize to Mistress Woodbine tonight," she told him seriously.

"What?"

"Pierce, you are a great noble! The king's good friend. You must set an example at court. And I've never seen you behave so badly! Please, apologize to her!"

She heard him set his jaw. She could tell that he wasn't going to apologize. He would do almost anything for her; she knew that. Except go against the dictates of his conscience. The girl had really angered him.

Well, that was good, wasn't it? There was really no need for her to be jealous.

But it was going to make all the rest that she wanted to ask him to do so much more difficult!

"Pierce—"

"Annie, she's a wayward little vixen, and she needs a good switching from what I can tell."

"She's far too mature for a good switching," Anne said with a soft sigh. "She's spirited—"

"She might well have killed someone, Anne, she was so reckless, and—"

"She does ride excellently."

"Umm, and she is completely confident in her own talent. She deserves to be beaten—"

"You beat her this afternoon."

"I was not racing—"

"You were."

"Beowulf was determined," he said defensively.

Anne laughed. She touched his nose lightly. "You bested her. Show some mercy!"

He shook his head, oddly frowning. "I don't think that anyone ever bests her, Anne. Because I don't think she knows when she's been bested. No, I will not apologize to her."

"But—"

He twisted, staring at her fiercely, taking her into his arms. "M'lady, I'll not apologize to her, and I'll not let her get between us again!"

"But, Pierce—" Anne began, pleased.

"But, Anne!"

"Really, you should take pity on the girl."

"And why is that?"

"Well, her father was once very good friends with Lord Victor Bryant, his wife's second cousin, and so he entrusted her into Lord Bryant's guardianship while she was in England."

Pierce frowned.

"But Victor Bryant passed away last month. Which leaves her in the care of Jamison Bryant." She sighed. "He makes me very nervous. He is one of my half-brother's dearest friends, and he's always—oh, I don't know! He's a very attractive man—"

"Aha!" Pierce teased.

She shook her head wildly. "Attractive—but unnerving. I am ever so grateful to be of age, and an heiress in my own right, or else I'm quite afraid Jerome would try to hand me—body, title, and riches!—straight over to Jamison. Honestly, I fear for the girl."

Pierce shrugged. "Her father is still alive. I don't believe young Jamison really has any rights over her."

"Perhaps not. But still . . ."

"Besides," Pierce said, "she probably deserves marriage to some unnerving but attractive fellow." He rolled over, grinning, drawing a line delicately around her breast. "Her father is after me, you know."

Anne smiled slowly in return, smoothing back his dark hair. "So I heard."

"And?" He arched a brow.

"Well, you are quite taken. That is one of the reasons she worries me. She needs a mate, but not Jamison Bryant!"

"Well, don't trouble yourself about her. That would be like worrying about a tigress. All right, then, my love! You keep an eye upon her, as I assume you've already chosen to do."

"I have. But, Pierce, I very much want you to use your influence on her behalf."

"My influence! Anne, I don't know—"

"You should just let it be known that you are interested in the girl, that perhaps she has your—protection. It might well keep her safe."

"From?"

"From the likes of her guardian!" Anne said. "Jamison is very good friends with Jerome. And though he is my blood, my dear half-brother is sometimes capable of a certain . . ." She hesitated. "He loves to plot and trick, Pierce. And at times, he can be evil!"

Pierce laughed. "Evil, eh?"

"His tricks—"

"Everyone plays tricks at court these days. Your brother can be a pest, Anne. And Jamison Bryant is selfish and immature. As to Rose—she's a little witch. She deserves what she gets."

"Pierce, Rose Woodbine is really quite kind and brave—"

"What makes you think so?"

Anne hesitated. "Just a few days ago, my love, Jamison had me rather trapped," she said lightly. It had been worse than that, but knowing Pierce's temper, she had refrained from telling him what had happened when she'd had the misfortune to find herself alone with her brother's friend. They'd all accompanied the king for a ride south, and Jamison had nearly forced her horse off the trail—intentionally, she was certain. But Rose Woodbine had come upon them and immediately sensed her distress. Her riding had been so magnificent that she'd easily pretended to have lost control of her horse—nearly crushing Jamison, and allowing Anne to escape.

Anne touched his chin. "She is an excellent horsewoman, my love. She rode just like a stunning little female cavalier into the fray, and drove off that wicked fellow.''

"What was that wicked fellow doing?"

She waved a hand in the air. "It was nothing, really. I was just in an uncomfortable position. And Rose was very brave and kind in rescuing me from my discomfort. So, Pierce, for me, would you offer her your protection?"

He sighed. "Anne, for you, I would do most anything. She has my protection. And she shall have it with exceptional generosity—if you can keep her away from me!"

Anne kissed his nose. "I shall. Now—"

"Now I want to hear no more about her!"

She raised her eyes to his, but he started to kiss her.

"Let's please be alone for a few moments!" he said huskily. She remained silent, tasting his kiss again. Within moments she forgot all about Mistress Woodbine.

To Pierce's great annoyance, he did not. Even as he lay with Anne, he saw Rose Woodbine's face within his mind's eye. The fantastic wealth of her hair, the color of it! The curve of her lip, the feel of her against him, the emerald green of her eyes, flashing . . .

He shuddered suddenly, startled by the hunger, and then the wave of unease that settled over him. She was just a girl. A pretty commoner, no more, no less. All right, she was beautiful. Still . . .

There was no need for Anne to ever know that he did find something compelling about the girl. Something that haunted the senses, that beckoned, that excited . . .

A feeling of guilt riddled him. He had been making love to Anne while thinking of the Woodbine girl. Wanting her. She absolutely infuriated him!

Yet he could not still this feeling of desire.

He almost groaned aloud.

The girl wanted to go home, he had heard. Badly. She wanted nothing to do with any man, she just wanted to return to her precious Virginia.

And pray God! Maybe she'd manage to do so soon!

Chapter III

He should have been a happy man, Jamison Bryant thought. He was young, good-looking with very pale blue eyes, fine light hair, and a lean, well-muscled body. Yes, he should have been happy, he decided, staring across the room that had so recently been his father's, but was now his own. It was a rich room. Heavy brocade draperies hung from the huge oak bed. Within the confines of an elegantly carved mantel, a fire burned brightly. The entire manor, the Bryant home of Hershire Place, was elegant and warm and opulent. And now it was his. He'd been raised to rule it, he'd been guided, he'd been taught.

And somehow, he thought with a sigh, lightly stroking Beth's soft white flesh, he'd gone astray. He'd never been able to tolerate his noble father. His learned teachers had bored him to tears. He'd escaped his classes to play pranks like setting fire to small logs and tying them to the tails of hapless cats. He wasn't quite sure what flaw had caused him to be the way he was, and for a while when he had been young, it had plagued him.

But then, he thought with a smile, he'd grown older, and discovered that many within the world were flawed. And many of those flawed individuals were so much more interesting than the others.

"You're brooding," Beth told him.

He nodded, smiling down at her. She was a fleshy lass, and he liked that about her. Every single thing about Beth reeked of the farm girl, from her broad hips to her ample bosom and her freckled cheeks.

But she was no simple lass, not his Beth! She had a shrewd way of looking at the world, and she thoroughly entertained him. He enjoyed her because she knew him, knew all his little streaks of cruelty, and even enjoyed them. She knew that he'd never consider granting her even the title of his "mistress," that he would call her nothing but a whore until the day he died. That didn't matter. When he prospered, he saw to it that Beth prospered. She liked rich things. He didn't mind giving them to her. She knew that he thought continually of Anne, and she would have happily done anything to aid him in his pursuit of the lady. She knew that she would always be amply rewarded.

" 'Tis a wretched life!" he told her wearily, lying back beside her.

"Because you can't have the Lady Anne?" Beth inquired.

He grimaced, resting his head against her breast, noting with some dissatisfaction that her middle was broadening even more. He pinched her and she cried out. Then he rolled up to lie on his back, his fingers laced behind his head, his eyes not seeing as he stared toward the window.

"I have always wanted Anne," he said, and it was true. There was something about her blond beauty. She was like a beacon of purity—even if the entire court was well aware she slept with DeForte. Damn

DeForte. And his friendship with the king. And his reputation as a soldier, and as a shipbuilder, and all damn else.

But Anne . . .

He adored her. He worshiped the very ground she walked on. More than anything in his whole life, he wanted Anne. If there had ever been anything decent about him, anything that could actually steer him true, it was Anne!

Anne was someone he could never quite reach, no matter what his station and the title he had inherited. There was something about her . . .

And then there was Rose!

Ah, yes! Rose had it, too. His elegant, headstrong, wayward little American cousin. She was always cool, she walked so straight, she spoke with such a tone to her words. It was in her eyes, her gestures, her dress. He didn't know what it was exactly. It was something that could never really be reached, not quite touched.

Oh, yes! he thought. He was terribly dissatisfied! There was the majestic, elegant Lady Anne, whom he had wanted his whole life, and now there was Rose, the talk of the court, the American beauty. And he was so damned close to them . . .

And yet he was lying here with Beth!

"They're all out hunting today," he said, rising from the bed and striding naked to the window, looking out as if he could see the people he spoke about. "It must have been a very exclusive party. The king, DeForte, the Lady Anne, my cousin Rose, and just a few others!"

"And you were not among them. And so you are unhappy."

He hesitated. "Nothing would disturb me. If I just had Anne."

There was a knocking on the door. Jamison could

hear his father's ancient servant, Crawly, clearing his throat.

"God's blood, what is it?" Jamison thundered.

Old Crawly didn't answer. He heard a peal of deep laughter, and then the voice of his best friend, Anne's brother, Jerome.

"Give the old man a chance, *Lord* Bryant. 'Tis me. Jerome. And I don't give a damn what perversion you're up to at the moment, I've come up with a splendid idea!"

Beth started to hop up. "Oh, lie down!" Jamison told her irritably. It certainly wasn't as if she hadn't been seen in bed by many a man before. He reached to the foot of the bed for his own breeches and crawled into them, strode across the room, and threw the door open.

Jerome grinned broadly at him and stepped into the room. His looks had always struck Jamison as odd. In a way, he resembled Anne. His eyes were very blue, his hair blond. He was slim, his features fine. But his smile was utterly different, cool and bitter where Anne's was warm.

"My dear Beth!" he taunted, bowing deeply toward the bed. Beth scowled at him. Jamison frowned.

"Sorry to interrupt," Jerome said.

"Well, you should be."

Jerome was undaunted. He ambled over to the table where Jamison kept his best whiskey, poured himself a glass, and sat down, propping his feet up on a priceless inlaid table.

"I have the idea of a lifetime!" he said pleasantly.

Jamison arched a brow. "Pray—do tell!"

Jerome chuckled softly. "Well, let's see here, m'lord! I imagine that you've been lying here with poor Beth bemoaning the fact that the illustrious and damnable Pierce DeForte is sleeping with my oh-so-wonderful sister. So let's think about this. Surely, with your wonderfully cunning mind, there must be something you can plan?''

Beth moaned. ''Take care, Jamison!''

''Shut up!'' Jamison snapped. ''What are you getting at?'' he demanded of Jerome.

Jerome shot Beth a smile. ''Beth, we are going to need your help, but I know that Jamison will see that you are well rewarded for any assistance you give.''

Beth arched a brow.

''Tell me about this plan!'' Jamison insisted.

Jerome grinned, swallowing down his whiskey. ''It's really so damned simple! On the one hand, we have the exquisite Rose! Legally obliged to at least pay you some heed. Then we have the object of your dearest desire—Anne. Then, of course, the illustrious DeForte, and finally, my friend, you. Two women, two men. We just have to see that they are all arranged properly!''

''And how do we do that?'' Jamison demanded.

''Are we all in?'' Jerome queried.

Beth nodded. Jamison hesitated. He would have done anything for Anne. Wanting her had become an obsession.

''Yes, we're both in,'' Jamison said at last.

Jerome grinned like a jester. ''This is the plan . . .''

Rose was entirely unaware that she might be the focus of anyone's evil thoughts at the moment. Her own temper had risen to a tempest; and she was too busy ranting about Lord Pierce DeForte to think of her distant cousin.

''Well, now, he can't be that horrid a creature!'' Mary Kate said soothingly as she ran a brush through Rose's long tresses. Newly washed and lightly scented, the long hair felt like silk sliding through Mary Kate's fingers. Though Mary Kate was doing her very best to keep a somber inflection in her voice, she was secretly rather amused. She had been with Rose since her mother's death, and they were very close. Theirs was far more than a mistress-maid relationship, which is why Rose felt free to rant and rave to Mary Kate now about the fury in her heart—all directed at Lord Pierce DeForte.

"I tell you, Mary Kate, God put no more horrid creature upon this earth! You would have thought that I had purposely waylaid the man! And he did soak me with full malicious intent, I tell you! I have never, never in all my days, come across an individual more rude!" She sniffed, whirling around in the chair before the dressing table. Her eyes, ferociously green at the moment, seemed to sizzle with emerald fire. "He is detestable!"

Mary Kate expertly whirled the deep auburn skeins of Rose's hair into a smooth coil at her nape. "He is the rage of all London, you know," she told Rose.

"All London can have him."

"He's one of the king's dearest friends."

"Even such a splendid monarch may be ill advised in choosing his friends!"

"I also believe that your father considers him the most eligible man in England."

Rose waved a hand impatiently in the air. "You know Father, Mary Kate! He simply doesn't understand. And he's certainly never met Pierce DeForte! If he had, he would never think him at all possible as husband material! Oh, I can't believe that he's had me sent here to court to begin with! And set up in such a humiliating position—like a prize racehorse, trying to attract the best stud!"

"Rose!" Mary Kate exclaimed in horror.

"Well, it's the truth!" she cried, her eyes still

green fire, liquid with her fury, and just a trace of tears. She loved her father deeply, but the events that had occurred today had truly brought home the misery of her place here. He wanted her to marry—in England! And all that she wanted to do was go home!

"He has no right!" she said suddenly, staring at Mary Kate. "He spent all those years treating me like an equal! Letting me learn about the ships and the plantation, the people and the crops! Then off he sends me to school—and then to court, where I'm placed beneath the 'benign eye' of Lord Bryant to be 'suitably' wed! And the entire world seems to know that he really wants me to marry that horrible man I met today!"

Mary Kate shook her head. "Rose, I know that your father loves you. I'm sure he doesn't want you to be miserable. He's heard that the king dotes on DeForte, and so—"

"The king is a fool!" Rose cried.

"Hush! That's very nearly treason!" Mary Kate said, distressed, and not nearly so amused anymore. Rose could be very wild and impetuous, and in her anger she might well get herself into some serious trouble.

Rose inhaled and exhaled slowly. "Oh, this is ridiculous! I wouldn't have to hate DeForte and say stupid things about the king if I could just go home!"

Mary Kate frowned. Rose had never really been denied anything. Now Mary Kate was afraid that she was going to learn the lesson of denial in a very brutal manner, for Ashcroft was hardly likely to let her choose her own husband. It made Mary Kate sorry, for she loved the girl deeply.

"Well, there's more to deal with than your father at the moment!" the maid warned.

Rose knew instantly whom Mary Kate was referring to. Lord Jamison Bryant. On top of everything else, Jamison's kindly father had somehow managed to pass away at this most inopportune of moments! Now she was left with Jamison as a guardian. Although he was a handsome enough man, tall, lean, and always impeccably dressed, there was something about him that disturbed her.

"Jamison," she said flatly to Mary Kate. She hesitated. "I don't think he has any real power over me," she murmured, a little uneasily. She inched her chin up a shade. "I won't let him have any power over me. He's a guardian, not my father. He's supposed to see to it that my virtue is kept safe, and he'll never have to worry in the least about that."

Mary Kate, finished with her coiffing, stepped back to survey her young mistress critically. Perfect. He hair was neatly dressed in a coil at her nape, while little tendrils in shades of fire and gold curled softly around her face. Her eyes, certainly her greatest glory, blazed their emerald color in sharp contrast to the deep, dark auburn of her hair. Her gown was a rich blue velvet, the bodice rounded and laced, the skirt gathered twice to display the beauty of the petticoats beneath. It had been whispered that she was the greatest beauty to have come to the king's court, and Mary Kate thought that it might well be true. There were wonderful whispers, too, that the girl would fall into a fairy-tale romance, that the exquisite commoner might find herself a titled lord, and live happily ever after.

Rose didn't want a lord, Mary Kate reminded herself. But then, the good God in heaven sometimes seemed to see to those things people needed, and didn't even know that they desired.

"I think you're ready, my pet," Mary Kate told her.

Rose nodded, still seeming distracted. Then she

blurted out, "Truly, Mary Kate, you should have met him! He's such a lout!"

"Are we speaking now of Lord Bryant or Lord DeForte?"

Rose grinned, wrinkling her nose. "We could be speaking of either. But I meant Lord DeForte."

"Well, I shall try to get a glimpse of him tonight," Mary Kate assured her. "Does he look like an ogre?"

"He—no," Rose murmured. She was surprised to feel a flush rising over her cheeks. No, he had not looked like an ogre. He had spoken like one, but he hadn't looked like one. With his jet hair and amazing silver eyes, he was an exceptionally striking individual. When he had stood by her in the stream, he had been commandingly tall. When he had touched her, she had felt the wealth of power and muscle within him. She had to admit that his physical appearance might have drawn the admiration that seemed to fall his way.

"No, he does not look like an ogre, but if he were to open his mouth and speak, you would know instantly that he was one!" she told Mary Kate.

"Well, I shall keep my eyes open."

Rose glanced at the lovely French clock that sat on the dressing table in her room. "I had best get to dinner. The king will be down soon, and the entire company must sit when he does."

"I shall accompany you down to the hall, and I shall be with the servants, supping, very near, should you need me," Mary Kate said.

They left Rose's room behind and started down one of the long corridors. Rose had stepped on ahead, deep in her thoughts, when she heard a little cry of pain. She swirled around quickly to see that Mary Kate had tripped over a break in the stone flooring.

She started back, but saw that a tall man in a very

fashionable long coat and frilled shirt had stopped beside Mary Kate, bending low to touch her hand and speak softly with her. "Are you hurt there, good woman? Is your ankle well enough for you to stand?"

Mary Kate was fluttering, staring up at the man's face. "I'm—I'm not hurt. M'lord. I can stand."

The man helped her to her feet. Mary Kate continued to stare at him with awe.

And Rose gritted her teeth, seeing that their kindly benefactor was none other than the loathsome man who had been so rude to her earlier. He had yet to see her.

"You're quite all right?" he said to Mary Kate.

Mary Kate nodded dumbly. He started on his way down the hall once again, and so saw Rose. His brow rose curiously, and his lip curled into a singularly mocking smile. "Why, Mistress Woodbine!" He swept her a low, courtly bow. "What a pleasure."

"Oh, I'm sure," she murmured sweetly.

It was anything but—she was very well aware of his true feelings. Yet they were at court, where good manners had to be maintained.

"If you are going to the dining hall, I shall be honored to escort you," he told her.

Rose felt her spine stiffening. She couldn't seem to find words to speak.

Mary Kate found them for her. "Oh, she is, she is!" Mary Kate called out happily. "Please, do escort her!"

Rose cast Mary Kate a stern frown, but Mary Kate seemed to be entirely too enrapt with the man to notice. Impatiently Rose inhaled deeply, staring at Lord DeForte. He didn't wait for her reply, apparently impatient himself now that he had been waylaid by her once again. He took her arm and started down the corridor quickly.

To her surprise and irritation, she found herself growing breathless. "M'lord DeForte!" she murmured. "I can understand our hurry, but we've not all got legs like a horse!"

He slowed his gait. "Ah, but remember! You ride better, Mistress Woodbine. I do apologize. I was certain in my heart that you must race with greater speed on foot as well. Yet how kind! You compare me to a horse! I was so afraid that you might have another animal in mind."

"In truth, I was thinking of some relative of the horse, and that relative the jackass," she said sweetly. "But my father did teach me to be kind."

"Didn't your father ever teach you to mind your manners?" he inquired deeply, his dark head bent, his whisper falling very close to her ear, and bringing with it a startling heat. She discovered that her heart was pounding fiercely and fast, and to her great annoyance, she was shivering inwardly. Her temper seemed to burn whenever he came near her. When he spoke. When he touched her.

But that strange shivering began, too.

"My father would not expect much from me, m'lord, in the matter of extending courtesy to you, if he were only more familiar with your manners."

"Oh, but your father is familiar with me."

Despite herself, she felt a furious flush rising to her cheeks. "I am afraid, Lord DeForte, that due to the king's continued kindness to you, you are a well-known figure. Most Englishmen, in England and abroad, are aware of your closeness to Charles."

"To Charles, eh? You refer to our monarch as just Charles?"

She fought to control her temper. He'd already reduced her to the behavior of a child once; she would not allow him to do so again. "To His Majesty, Charles, the king," she said smoothly.

"I see. So it is nothing but my friendship with the king that might make me—appealing?" he inquired:

She paused, extracting her arm from his, smiling sweetly. "What else could there be?" she asked politely.

He smiled, amused. "Well, I do have a title."

"So does many a fool!" she replied pleasantly. They had reached the doors to the large banqueting hall where the king and his guests gathered for the evening meal. People were flocking around them now, the highest in the land to join the king at the head table, and downward in rank from there—earls, dukes, counts, and barons first, followed by knights and their ladies, and then those whose merchant sensibilities and rich purses bought them entrance to any gathering. It was time for Rose to separate from Lord DeForte. She was surprised to realize that she did feel a brief bitterness, realizing that this man with whom she was carrying on a disturbing war would quickly leave her to join his peers—the very beautiful Lady Anne among them—while she hurried down the long plank tables to sit with the wealthy, but still common gentry folk.

"If you'll excuse me—" she began, but before she could go any further, she realized that she was blocked from a smooth exit away from this man. They had been joined by others.

" 'Tis DeForte! And with your young ward, Jamison!" a male voice stated with amusement.

Rose turned swiftly. She knew the two men who had pinned her into this uncomfortable position. The first, as she had already surmised, was the new Lord Bryant, Jamison, with his curious pale blue eyes. The second man, the one who had spoken, was Jerome Cherney, Jamison's closest friend and gaming partner—and the Lady Anne's half-brother. He had a way of looking at her that made her flesh crawl.

"So the two of you have met!" Jamison said, his glance falling swiftly from DeForte's hard gaze to Rose's eyes. "I am very glad, dear Rose. I shall be able to tell your father that I have done my duty, seeing that you and Lord DeForte become acquainted."

"My dear Lord Bryant—" Rose began.

"Call me Jamison, Rose. We are, in a distant way, kin, you know."

"Jamison then," she said, her voice carrying just an edge of warning. "There was truly nothing my father wished of yours, other than that he keep a watchful—paternal—eye upon me. As your dear father is now deceased, I pray that you not feel responsible for me in any way. I am not planning on remaining in London long—"

"But, Rose!" Jamison interrupted her. "I have indeed inherited my father's charge! And I believe your father intends that you remain here several months now, if not at court, then as a guest at my estate. Your father does not wish you to leave London—alone."

Rose didn't think that she had ever so longed to strike anyone. Jamison was baiting her—and making a fine fool of her before Pierce DeForte. She had never, in all her life, felt so keenly like an object that was for sale—and one that might well have a nick or a mar, since she was an untitled colonial and it seemed that all the world was aware that her father considered Pierce DeForte the finest match she might make. And since there was no real secret about the fact that he and Anne were lovers, it was humiliating that Jamison should put her in such a wretched position.

"Let me just say then, Lord Bryant," she said swiftly, "that I do intend to sail home very soon—and completely alone."

"Now, my dear—" Jamison began.

"Come now, Jamison!" DeForte said sharply, entering the conversation. "I do believe that you're distressing young Miss Woodbine. Perhaps she is upset over the loss of your father. There are those among us who are! And I hardly think, sir, that you've really any say over the girl."

Rose might have been grateful for the quick way that he came to her defense were he not such an arrogant, detestable rogue.

"Oh, but I do!" Jamison advised them. Rose didn't care about any of it anymore. She just wanted to escape.

"Perhaps we'll discuss it at a different time," Rose said. "If you'll excuse me—" she began again.

But this time they were interrupted by the Lady Anne. Beautiful, blond, and elegant—and looking just a trifle uneasy—she descended upon the group of them. "Pierce!" she murmured, coming to his side. Her eyes fell upon her brother, and then Jamison Bryant. "Jerome, Jamison, what is going on here? Rose, you are looking greatly refreshed. Are these knaves giving you some difficulty? You mustn't let them disturb you."

"Thank you so much for your concern!" Rose told her swiftly. "But I am really quite all right, m'lady. I was just trying to excuse myself—"

"But you musn't!" Jerome said suddenly. "You must sup with us."

"I'm afraid that I—"

"You needn't worry about status or position, m'lady," he whispered, giving her a conspiratorial wink. "You'll be with us—and with the very great Lord DeForte, His Grace, the Duke of Werthington. Who would think to challenge him?"

"I have made other arrangements," she tried to tell him, but Lady Anne was touching her sleeve.

"You must come with us, Rose. I'd like you at my side!"

The last thing that Rose wanted to do was dine with Pierce DeForte, yet she found herself being summarily led along with the men and Lady Anne. When they were seated, she was not far from the king, pressed very closely between Jamison and Jerome. She found the meal greatly uncomfortable, for both men gave her the most uneasy feelings, and seemed to assess her with every breath she took. She felt shivers each time she reached for her goblet and brushed fingers with Jamison, and she lost her appetite when she and Jerome reached for the same piece of fowl from a tray offered by a servant.

Thankfully, Charles was holding a spectacular banquet. He sat with his queen, the ever attentive husband, kind and solicitous throughout the meal. But for her entertainment, and his own, and that of his guests, he had gathered a fine group of players. A masque came first, a quick, somewhat ribald play about a husband who had wronged his wife, and tried to come back within her fold. Then a singer sang and played a plaintive tune upon a lute, and when she finished, it seemed that the banqueting was done. From high atop the minstrels' gallery, musicians began to play. The king rose, and helped up his queen, then led her past the tables to the floor. And there he bowed to her, low and courtly, and the two began to dance.

Soon they were being joined on the floor. It would be extremely rude for Rose to refuse Jamison or Jerome if one of the two invited her to dance, and she was poised for the possibility.

But to her relief, Jamison asked Anne to dance. But as she rose, Anne paused, looking back.

"Pierce—" she murmured. She hesitated, and Rose watched her a moment, wondering what was going on in her mind. Then she spoke quickly. "Pierce, you and Mistress Woodbine must join us on the floor."

"Oh, no!" Rose exclaimed swiftly. Pierce merely cast daggers at her—and then at Anne—with his vivid gaze.

But despite his apparent annoyance, he stood to the suggestion. "Come then, Mistress Woodbine," he said. It was a command, not an invitation. She stared at him, feeling a strange cascade of trembling come sweeping down her back.

No, she couldn't dance with him. She didn't want him touching her again. She didn't want to feel his hands, his fingers, his eyes upon her . . .

But Rose had no chance to offer a refusal. He took hold of her hand and nearly dragged her out to join the others who had already lined up for the stylish dance.

It was too late! she thought with panic.

What was too late?

She didn't know. Only that something had begun that day.

Something over which she had no control . . .

Chapter IV

He bowed to her in the proper manner; she fell back in a slight curtsy. The minstrels in their gallery above the floor continued playing.

Their fingers touched, and she moved about Pierce DeForte. So far there had been little held back between them. Rose could see no need to do so now. "You might have refused!" she said angrily.

Dark brows arched. "And what difference would it have made?"

"It would have kept us from one another's company."

He shrugged, silver eyes suddenly sizzling. "It is a dance, Mistress Woodbine. Nothing more."

She smiled very sweetly. "Please, my dear oh-so-arrogant Lord DeForte! Let me allow you to rest assured that I find you quite possibly the most irritating human being I've ever had the misfortune to meet, and therefore, a dance, as little as it might be, is most uncomfortable! My opinion of you can hardly matter, of course, since your own is so very high. But you mustn't feel the least worry over anything

66

you have heard about my father's desires. I would not marry you, sir, were you the last man to walk on God's good earth—solitude would be far preferable. There now, milord. Do you feel less threatened?''

She nearly cried out at the sudden crunch on her fingers. She wasn't sure if he was amused—or furious. "I hadn't known that I was threatened. You seem to be the defensive one, Mistress Woodbine.''

"I am not defensive!" she claimed heatedly. "I just wish to assure you—''

"But I need no assuring.''

If she gritted down on her teeth any harder, they would all break, she was certain. "Could we leave the dance floor, Lord DeForte?''

He smiled. What a fool. She should have never let him see her discomfort. He was enjoying it. He meant to make her suffer. His smile deepened. "The draw of a title truly doesn't mean a thing?''

She lifted her chin. "Not to me, milord. I am anxious for one event only—the day I sail home. Perhaps we are backwoods dwellers, as you people here are so quick to call us! But in the colonies, milord, we have come to judge a man by his actions, by his heart, and by his soul, and not by any title that has come to him by some accident of birth.''

His hold on her eased somewhat. "Ah, so, mistress! What is this fellow's name, he who holds no title but is so noble in action, heart, and soul?''

Startled, she nearly missed a beat. Then she stared up at him, amused herself now.

"There is no man in my life, milord. And though I'm certain that it must amaze you, I much prefer things that way.''

"But they cannot, and will not, be that way," he told her.

Tension swept through her once again. "And just

what can you possibly have to say about my life, milord DeForte?'' she demanded.

''Me?'' Dark brows shot up. ''I don't imagine much—only that you seem to be living in some fool's paradise where you consider yourself as lofty as the king—''

''How dare you!''

''And as you are such an incredible little—brat!—''

''DeForte, there is no reason for you to feel obliged to dance with a brat! Let me go—''

''I'm afraid that I will take great pleasure in trying to explain things to you. Mistress, it is a man's world. Within this world, you are but a pawn. Perhaps your father has neglected to warn you that he couldn't possibly allow you to grow old without providing you with male protection. Without matching your fortune to another, thereby assuring your future.''

Rose's eyes narrowed furiously. Again she tried to wrench from his grasp, but failed. He did not intend to let her go.

''If my father has offended you—''

''Not in the least. I am extremely wealthy, I do carry a title, and I am whole in limb and body. He is a smart man.''

He was so damned arrogant! She longed to tear his hair out! Yet all the while she felt the most curious heat sweeping through her. Anger, certainly, yet more. She wanted to free herself more than she had ever wanted anything in the world, but she was amazed at the forceful power in his touch, the mocking silver in his eyes, and how deeply they warmed her and caused her to tremble. No matter how he infuriated her, he made her feel incredibly alive, ready to do battle on any account, hot, flushed, irritated beyond belief.

"Could we please end this agony!" she demanded.

"I find the music excellent," he told her.

She tossed her hair back, and smiled. Fine. They would continue.

"As you've said, DeForte, I've quite a fortune."

"Your father has quite a fortune."

"I'm an only child. A very rich one. Where lies the difference between Lady Anne and myself?"

He arched a brow high, perhaps startled by the question. Then he smiled again. "Lady Anne has already inherited her fortune. She must answer only to the king."

"And to you, I imagine."

"She does so most willingly."

"Ummm. So you are just waiting to take her fortune into your hands as well?"

He laughed. If he was offended, he certainly hid it well. Then it seemed that his advice was almost tender. Her name sounded intimate upon his lips. "Poor Rose! So headstrong and assured. Some young man will certainly take your inheritance well into hand as well. I pity the fellow! Yet perhaps this would surprise you. I'd be pleased if things could go as you wished."

She arched a brow to him. "You're implying that they will not?"

He hesitated, looking down upon her from his impressive height. There was a brief startling moment when she was certain that she saw a touch of sympathy in his gaze. "Rose, I think that your father has very definite things in mind for you. And Jamison Bryant, being the very thorough knave that he is, will have a full supply of suggestions for your father, since he knows that he will benefit from your marriage to some titled fellow. Maybe things are different in the colonies; I've felt it myself upon occasion. But here, Rose, marriages are customarily arranged when a young woman comes from wealth such as yours.''

Oddly, she felt tears stinging her eyes. He seemed to be speaking from some older, wiser point of view, and she wanted none of it.

''Customarily, perhaps. But you're mistaken. All that I really need is to get home and speak with my father. My father loves me.''

He inclined his head. ''Then I wish you the very best of luck.''

''Oh, I can tell you that you do!''

Silver clouds seemed to slip over his eyes, then rise again quickly. The man was amused.

''They will find you some young swain and you will do well enough.''

''Never! No one will find me a husband! When I marry, it will be for love!'' she said passionately.

He smiled, with a superior look in his eyes, as if she were a very young and foolish child.

''Do excuse me!'' she murmured. ''How can I not realize that only men and women of your ancient years might truly realize the depths of affection!''

He laughed ruefully at that, and for a moment she was again aware that there were, perhaps, reasons for the man's tremendous popularity. When he smiled or laughed, he was indeed handsome. There was the touch of a dimple in his left cheek, his eyes sparked with silver flame, and his mouth curved sensuously.

''Am I so very ancient?'' he asked, and she found herself close to him at that moment, very close, though still within the stylized steps of the dance.

''Incredibly so,'' she murmured imperiously.

''And you would never love anyone so ancient!''

''Certainly not, milord!'' she said apologetically.

"Thank God that there's an ancient lady to return my affections!"

"Oh, indeed! You should thank the good God above us daily for the Lady Anne."

"My, my, Mistress Woodbine! Such an angel's face, to carry such a barbed tongue within it!"

"Ah, but it has been honed by men such as yourself, milord Deforte. The nobility has taught me much."

"Umm, have they? Well, my feisty little colonial, my Lady Anne is most concerned about you. And for her sake, I will accept many 'slings and arrows' from you."

"The Lady Anne is concerned for me?" she inquired, startled.

"Because of your—guardian," he said. He spoke lightly. His distaste for the man was still evident in his tone.

Rose frowned. "But he can't really—"

"I don't know what he *can really*. His father was a fine fellow. Jamison suffers from his very status in life—and from his penchant for gambling. I don't think that he can hurt you, or that he would want to, but he is ever anxious to pay his gambling debts, and you, Mistress Woodbine, are worth a great deal of money."

She shook her head. "Well, my Lord DeForte, Anne need not worry about me. I intend to stay very near the king and sail for home as soon as possible. Just as soon as I can manage it."

"The king feels he owes your father, and he will certainly look to your welfare. But perhaps you should remember this, Rose. He is a careful man, and a tolerant one. But he is the king. Responsible for you beyond Jamison Bryant. If the king decides that you should marry, then you shall. He will command it."

"I will not marry!" she said stubbornly.

"No, you will simply lead poor young lads to distraction and go on your merry way, trying to fool both your father and the king."

"How dare you imply—"

He laughed. "Oh, I'm not implying anything. You will flirt, you will charm, and you will try to have your own way, as you have apparently had for many years. It shall be entertaining to see just where your fate lies."

"It lies in Virginia!" she said furiously. "You should certainly worry about yourself. You're wretched and loathsome and carnal—"

"Very!" he laughed. His smile deepened, and despite herself, she felt a trembling again.

"Dammit, let me go. Don't think about me, worry—"

"I wasn't particularly worried about you. That would be rather like worrying about a clever great cat—my dear girl, I have been touched by your claws. It is the Lady Anne who worries."

Claws indeed! She longed to reach out and scratch him. Ah, if only they were alone! But they were not. She smiled as charmingly as she could manage. "What a pair we do make, Lord DeForte. A great cat with glistening claws—and a jackass."

His brow arched, his lip curved. "Mistress! You called me a horse first, if I recall."

"But we are becoming such good friends, my dear old fellow, that I feel free to speak the truth of my feelings. Jackass it is!"

The music was ending. She suddenly found herself drawn to him, and tightly so. And his eyes were silver flames as they met hers. "You had best be glad that I was not left your guardian. For I would be tempted to pluck your thorns. To wash a child's mouth out with lye, or teach you a lesson in a stable with a switch!''

She struggled to free herself from his grasp, yet could not do so, for his fingers were like iron around her hands. She stared up at him, her own eyes flashing an emerald blaze, her fury held tight in the hiss of her voice. ''Alas! I do thank God that you are not my guardian, nor anything at all to me! Now, my noble Lord DeForte, if you would be so good as to release me . . . ?''

But he didn't. There was a look in his eyes that was extremely obstinate. It wasn't that he was so determined to hold on to her—it was that she was so determined to escape. And he was Lord DeForte, she just a little commoner, a thorn in his side. He wouldn't be commanded by her.

''Let me go!'' she commanded icily.

He waited too long. The music had ended, and men and women were milling about, waiting for it to begin again, talking, whispering, watching them. Rose was painfully aware of the tension and power of his grasp upon her, the heat surrounding her, and the strange lightning that seemed to rip along her spine.

''Let go!'' she insisted. She felt a rising sense of panic and lashed out the best she could, kicking him. Her toe connected with his shin.

She heard the grating of his teeth. The action had been a mistake. She nearly cried out, for she feared that he intended to snap her fingers. He drew her even closer.

''Mistress Woodbine . . .'' he began, his tone deep and furious. But then he paused suddenly. And in those seconds Rose became uncomfortably aware of him in very minute detail. She saw how clean-shaven his cheeks were, and the silver gleam of his eyes, felt the powerful beat of his heart. She breathed in his scent, clean, subtle, masculine. Against her flesh she felt the cloth of his coat, the touch of his fingers—fine fingers, very long, strong, somewhat bronzed from the sun. His breath touched her flesh, and she was startled at the heat it created abruptly within her, a heat that warmed and suffused through her.

"Please!" she heard herself whisper.

And in that same breath, he released her, nearly pushing her from him. Perhaps he had felt it, too. Like a flame, lapping at them both, warning of a fire that might burn painfully and bright.

"Go home!" he warned her. "The very first moment that you can!"

"I am anxious to!" she assured him. "But don't be so certain, Lord DeForte, that I will not do so on my own terms."

He waved a hand angrily in the air. "Mistress Rose, navigating her own destiny. It will not happen."

"But you are so sure that you are master of your own fate!"

"Because I am," he said softly and confidently. "I am well of age, and am a powerful peer within this realm, a place I earned with sweat and blood, Miss Woodbine. You are very young, you are your father's daughter, and you've yet to pay a shilling in dues to life. So take heed."

"I will be mistress of my fate!" she promised him softly. "I will!" She was emphatic because she was suddenly frightened. She didn't know why.

Whatever the sudden feeling of ill boding that came over her, it seemed that DeForte felt it too. "You're in danger here, Rose Woodbine," he said, and he seemed serious, not taunting for once, but truly concerned.

"Lord DeForte, I am no part of your life!" she insisted.

Then she let out a startled cry, alarmed to find herself touched by him again, drawn against him. His hands fell upon her upper arms, and his whisper was harsh and deep. "Dear God, but I pray that is true!"

She braced herself against the force of his hold, once more aware of the tremendous heat that seemed to ripple through her when he came so near. And it was so very odd, for he even seemed to touch her against his own will.

A taunting voice suddenly came their way. "DeForte, if you wouldn't mind unhanding the girl, she is my ward!"

Jamison. He was standing slightly behind her, watching them both politely.

Pierce stepped back instantly, his hands falling from her arms, his eyes still upon hers.

He bowed abruptly. "Indeed, Bryant. She is your ward. Take great care with her, sir. She seems to have found a place in the king's affections, and the Lady Anne and I intend to watch after her as well. Mistress Woodbine, enjoy your evening."

He turned and strode away, tall, dominating the company, drawing many an eye with him.

Rose didn't even realize that her own gaze followed him until she found herself engaged in a dance with Jamison, mindlessly following the music and his steps and being whirled away from a view of Pierce DeForte at last.

The evening had been too much. And Lord Jamison Bryant was eyeing her again in that calculating way of his.

She was weary of it all. The plots, the plans, the machinations. The king was kind, his court was certainly entertaining, but lecherous as well. She wanted no more of it for this evening.

She suddenly broke free from Jamison. "Lord

Bryant, you'll forgive me. I've acquired an atrocious headache. Please, excuse me. I must lie down, and try to go to sleep!''

She didn't wait for a reply, but turned and fled from the gathering, hurriedly making her way along the halls until she reached the room assigned to her.

She found it empty and assumed that Mary Kate must still be with the other servants watching the dancing—and all else that transpired. Rose began to cast aside her own clothing, realizing that she had truly acquired the headache she had lied about.

She slipped into a linen nightgown and crawled beneath her sheets. They were clean and cool. She closed her eyes, willing her headache away.

Her eyes opened again. She stared at the ceiling. She was so very agonized by the pain that pounded against her skull, yet she couldn't sleep. She kept hearing his voice, seeing his eyes, feeling them, silver fire upon her.

Sleep! she told herself.

But she didn't sleep. She had escaped him, escaped his touch—escaped his concern! No. He was haunting her even here. She could feel his touch again within her mind, see the silver of his harsh stare. Hear his words, the tone and cadence of his voice. He had seemed so angry with her.

And with himself . . .

He was horrible. Detestable.

And still . . .

She opened her eyes. Sleep was eluding her. Minutes had ticked by. Maybe hours.

The very thought of him made her feel the heat again. Warm, rushing, rising . . .

She closed her eyes, insisting to herself that she dream of a sweet past, of green hillsides, sparkling, cool waters, the sand on the beach, the fields. Virginia. So beautifully green in the rich heat of summer. Yet no matter how the sun burned down, there would be a breeze from the river, cooling her. She could see the waters of the James in her mind's eye, dark and swirling when a storm threatened, lazily drifting by in the spring with sweet smells everywhere. She had lain in the grass so many times. She could see herself there now.

And then he was there, too. So tall and dark and arrogant, walking her way with that taunting smile. He was in her dream. Coming toward her. She could feel the grass beneath her, the dampness of spring. She could feel it vividly because she was naked. And as he walked toward her, he was naked, too, powerful, bronzed . . .

"Damn!" she swore aloud. "Oh, Lord! Oh, damn!"

Then she winced. The very thought of him had her swearing like a seaman!

She groaned, then buried her face in her hands. How could she be having such horrible dreams? She wanted to forget him, not dream about him!

Mary Kate! She had to find Mary Kate. The woman would rub her temples with cool, soothing water, and ease all the tempest from her mind.

Rose threw off her covers and flew out of bed. A heavy velvet robe lay over the footboard, and she quickly cast it over her shoulders.

She threw open the door to her chamber and looked quickly into the hallway. It seemed deserted. She stepped farther along. There, in one of the secretive little window seat nooks, she was certain she saw movement. Some lovers in a secret tryst? She would hurry by.

She stopped short with a gasp. A man moved into the hallway. It was none other than Lord Jamison Bryant. Very lean, handsome enough with his sharp face and curious, almost colorless blue eyes.

He was not alone. She realized that she had interrupted him deep in the midst of conversation with Anne's brother, Jerome.

Now both men stared at her in the fashion that made her so uneasy.

"Rose," Jamison murmured. "Whatever are you doing out in the hallway at this hour?"

"Is it so late?" she inquired innocently.

"Late enough," Jamison said, surveying her apparel. Her hair streamed over the velvet on her shoulders. She hugged the caped robe around her more tightly.

"I was looking for my maid," she said.

"Oh, I see. Well, she is not about. And you should not be wandering the hallways."

"There can be danger," Jerome advised.

"Well, I will just go back to my room now . . ." she began.

Jamison was walking toward her. Jerome did the same, coming around to her side. She felt trapped between them. It was the same play that had been made on Lady Anne the other day, though this time not on horseback.

What could they do to her? she wondered. She didn't want to find out.

"I'm responsible for your welfare, Rose," Jamison said, frowning. "Perhaps I should insist that you come back to my manor with me."

"I feel extremely safe beneath the king's roof!" she assured him. They were coming closer and closer. She kept backing away. She was beneath the king's roof, she reminded herself. There were guards scattered about. All she need do was scream . . .

Except that they might never give her the chance to scream. They might simply spirit her away.

And then?

Her father wanted Lord DeForte. But Lord De-
Forte wanted nothing of her. So . . .

There might be some wealthy, wrinkled old baron
out there with a tremendous title, willing to pay a
pretty penny just for a bride with youth. One who
wasn't willing in the least.

Such things had happened, she had heard from
the gossip among the queen's women.

"Your headache hasn't confined you to bed?" Jamison inquired pleasantly.

"It's somewhat better."

"I'm ever so glad."

"Still, it is plaguing me. Mary Kate is so good with
a massage at the temple; that was why I was looking
for her."

"Perhaps I should bring you home even now. My
housekeeper is extremely tender with such things,"
Jamison said.

"I'm accustomed to Mary Kate. The hour is very
late, as you've said."

"Rose! I insist—" Jamison said, then broke off
suddenly. He stopped dead still, looking past her.
She continued to back up until she crashed into a
hard chest.

She swirled around.

DeForte. He straightened her back around, staring
at Jamison over her shoulders. "A little late for a
tête-à-tête with your ward in the hallway, isn't it,
Jamison?"

Fury flickered through Jamison's eyes, but he held
his peace. He lifted his hands. "I do agree. I was
just trying to discover myself what my ward was
doing, wandering the hallways."

She felt DeForte's eyes touch her with their silver
mockery. Was he wondering if she had lied earlier,
if she hadn't, perhaps, found some man of her own
choice to meet? And was he curious about just what

kind of assignation she'd had in mind, her hair tumbling down, clad in her nightgown and robe?

She lowered her lashes quickly, biting on her lower lip, wondering why on earth she cared what he thought. Every one of these men seemed to be attempting to destroy her life!

And yet . . .

She felt much safer since DeForte had come into the hallway.

"Perhaps, Mistress Woodbine," he suggested, "you should return to your room. And bolt your door. While we are all here to watch you go safely."

"Yes! Yes," she murmured swiftly. She wanted to cry that it was none of his business, none of any of their concern, that she owed them no explanations.

But she hadn't liked the way that she had been cornered, and despite herself, she was grateful to DeForte for giving her the opportunity to escape back to her room.

"Good night, m'lords!" she cried. DeForte's hands fell from her shoulders as she sped away, her robe and hair flying behind her. As she opened her door, she saw them there, DeForte, Jamison, and Jerome, all watching her.

She closed the door. And bolted it.

Shivering, she raced across the floor and jumped into her borrowed bed.

In the darkness and the quiet, Jamison Bryant stared out at the night, richly dissatisfied. "He doesn't need your fair sister as I do. And the king has given his blessing. We will have to move quickly."

"We will, we will," Jerome assured him. He smiled. "And perhaps it will not be difficult. Rose Woodbine does seem to have distracted DeForte!"

Jamison spun on his friend. "She would distract any man!"

"Indeed, it goes well. Thank God! My gambling debts will shortly see me confined to Newgate," Jerome said tonelessly.

"Ah, no! Anne will never allow her brother, her blood, to be turned over to Newgate!"

"She is weary of lending me money." He paused, looking out at the beautifully full moon. "And if she weds DeForte, he will certainly put a stop to it. He'd be pleased to cast me into a dungeon himself."

"We cannot allow them to marry."

Jerome smiled with pleasure again. "As I said, we must move quickly. Very quickly now."

"Tomorrow?" Jamison asked.

"Tomorrow," Jerome agreed.

A cloud misted silver over the moon.

Chapter V

When Mary Kate brought Rose her chocolate in the morning, her tray contained an invitation to join the king and queen on a hunting party, to commence that afternoon and finish the following morning.

Rose sipped her chocolate, and tossed the invitation aside. Mary Kate immediately sprang upon it.

"Did you read this, Rose?"

Rose nodded dully. She'd had a horrible night. The last thing she wanted to do was spend any time whatsoever with the king, since DeForte would surely be in attendance.

Mary Kate was both incredulous and troubled. "You mean, you don't intend to go?"

Rose shook her head firmly.

"Why on earth not?"

"I don't wish to see—people."

Mary Kate *tsk*ed in reproach. "You mean you don't wish to see Lord DeForte." She began to gather the clothing strewn about the room, casting Rose a sly glance. "Fine. Let him best you, then."

"Best me!"

Mary Kate shrugged. "I'm sure that the occasion will be wonderful. The king is interested in so many things that the people with him are bound to be fascinating! And you'll miss out on the day—because you're afraid of DeForte."

"I'm not afraid of him!" Rose said incredulously. She stared at Mary Kate, then began to laugh. "Make me defensive and I'll go, just to shush you up, is that it?" She said affectionately. Then she sighed. Maybe Mary Kate was right.

And she wasn't afraid of DeForte. Not really. She lowered her lashes quickly. She could already feel a strange fever sweeping through her, just thinking about the man. But she really wasn't afraid. He was domineering, arrogant, and atrociously mannered— but that really didn't have anything to do with her.

And in truth, despite all the things about him that infuriated her, she had to admit that he had come to her rescue last night.

She glanced at the invitation again.

King Charles II was a shrewd and multifaceted man, with a love of art he had inherited from his father, and a fascination with building and architecture. He gathered men and women of many talents around him. The company would be diverse. The party would be likely to include a portrait painter, an astronomer, and numerous friends of the the royal household. The overnight stay would be at a quaint Norman inn deep within the woods.

"So you will go!" Mary Kate said, pleased.

"Maybe," Rose told her.

"It's tremendously exciting. Your father will be so proud!" Mary Kate told her excitedly.

"If I choose to go."

"Refuse the king, and your father might well appear on English soil soon himself, demanding that you wed the first potbellied, balding old sot with a title who will have you!'' Mary Kate warned.

Rose flashed her a quick smile. ''My lord, but you can be as difficult as father!'' She sighed. ''Oh, all right. Fine. And don't you go smirking at me for managing to have your way!'' Rose warned.

Mary Kate walked to the bed and gave her a little hug. Rose hugged her back fiercely. ''Oh, Mary Kate, how am I going to get home? Why did Father put me in this wretched position?''

''Rose, things have a way of working out,'' Mary Kate said. ''They always do. Now, let me see.'' She hurried over to the wardrobe where she had hung many of Rose's things. ''The proper attire . . .'' Mary Kate muttered.

Rose leapt from bed, stretching. ''Mary Kate, do you wish to come along? I'm really quite capable of caring for myself, you know, and the queen will be with the king, so I will be quite well chaperoned.''

''Do I wish to come along! Of course I wish to come along!'' Mary Kate said, her eyes twinkling. ''I don't want to miss a minute of this. Of course, I'll have to miss some of it, since I'll ride behind with the king's servants, but I'll be most anxious to see the inn. In fact, perhaps I'd best go let them all know that you will be coming.'' She laid Rose's hose and boots and riding attire out on the bed, then hurried past her with a smile. ''Dress, Rose! You haven't all that much time!''

Rose smiled. At least Mary Kate was excited. She hurried on out.

Rose stood, frowning, and wondering why she suddenly felt as if an icy finger had stroked down her spine. She shook away the feeling. Mary Kate was right. It should be a nice day. She walked to the dressing table, where a pitcher with fresh warm water and soap awaited her, brought right before the chocolate by a very considerate Mary Kate. She scrubbed her face, and even as she did so, she began to feel ready for the challenge of the day.

Just let DeForte try to be difficult today!

Mary Kate hurried down the hallway, relieved that Rose had chosen to go. She had scarcely left her own corridor when she heard footsteps following close behind her. She slowed and looked back as Lord Jamison Bryant came to her left, and his friend Jerome to her right.

"Good day, milords," she said quickly, wondering why they seemed to be closing in on her so tightly.

"Indeed, 'tis a good day, woman," Lord Bryant told her. "Has your mistress decided to attend the hunt?"

"I believe so," Mary Kate murmured uncomfortably. Why did they both look so sly?

"Ah, then you would be planning on coming along later to attend to her, am I right?" Jerome asked.

"Of course!" Mary Kate said. What did these two rogues have up their elegant sleeves?

They had come upon one of the innumerable nooks in the walls, and to her alarm, Mary Kate realized she was being pressed toward it.

"Now, my lords—" she began nervously.

"Now, my good woman!" Jamison said with a wink.

"I'm afraid that we just can't allow you to attend your mistress this particular evening," Jamison said sadly.

"Afraid not," Jerome agreed.

Mary Kate stared sternly at Jamison Bryant. "But, my young lord—"

She never finished her sentence.

Something was thrown over her head.
And her protest died in her throat.

Rose was dressed and in the midst of choosing
what belongings to take along for an overnight stay
when she realized that Mary Kate had been gone a
long time. She stepped into the hallway, but did not
see the woman returning. She came back into her
room and sighed. Where had she gotten to? If Rose
didn't see her soon, she would have to leave without saying good-bye. But then, she would see Mary
Kate soon enough as the servants' party would certainly reach the inn by nightfall.

There was a tap at the door a moment later. She
threw it open with a smile, certain that Mary Kate
had returned. But Jamison stood there, dressed in
elegant velvet and frills, leaning against the doorframe. "Hello, cousin. I assume you intend to accept His Majesty's invitation to the hunt?"

"Yes."

"Then may I escort you? They are all gathered
outside in the courtyard, near ready to ride. Have
you your things? If you'll allow me, my manservant,
Beckman, is with me, and can carry your belongings."

"I wasn't quite ready—"

"I can wait, Rose."

"I was hoping to wait for Mary Kate."

"You do seem to be losing the woman quite fre-
quently lately," he commented. "Did you ever find
her last night? Perhaps your father should have pro-
vided you with a more dependable servant."

She smiled stiffly. "Mary Kate is extremely dependable."

"But she is not here. And you are invited to ride
with the king. Imagine your father's horror if you

were to refuse His Majesty's invitation because of a tarrying servant!''

"My Lord Bryant, she will not tarry long. You must go ahead, without me. When she returns, I will come along."

"I'll wait with you," he repeated.

Rose hesitated. She would see Mary Kate tonight. And she didn't like waiting here with Jamison.

She waved a hand in the air, moving back from the door. "Fine, Lord Bryant. Your man may take my things. You're right. Mary Kate will come along later."

Jamison smiled, quite pleased. Rose felt a little shudder of unease. She had written her father the moment that she had learned of the elder Bryant's death, certain that Ashcroft would immediately find her a guardian more suitable than Jamison. But though ships traveled swiftly, it could easily be three months before her letter reached her father, and his response reached England. So she'd have to tread carefully, steadfastly going her own way, yet courteous enough to Jamison to make him think she paid him some heed.

"Rose?" While his servant fetched her leather bags, he offered her his arm. She took it, exiting the room, closing the door behind her.

For her part of it, Beth had hurried to a tiny cottage deep in the woods when daylight had just broken.

She had to admit to being frightened, for she had known about Madame Bonnie from the time she had been a child. Madame Bonnie could do things. She could rid a woman of an unwanted child. She could make a man fall in love. She could bring about the death of an enemy. She was a very powerful woman, probably the only woman Beth had ever imagined to be as powerful as a man, and for that, she feared her greatly, and admired her.

Bone chimes hung from the trees before the tiny cottage. There were numerous other telltale signs of Madame Bonnie's vocation as well, and Beth was certain that the woman could be easily convicted of witchcraft. In the days of James I she would have certainly hanged, since he had been rumored to have had a fury against witches.

But Madame Bonnie had bided her time through the old king's rule, and through Cromwell's. The new king, Charles II, was a tremendously tolerant sovereign; all the people said it. He did not hunt down witches. Perhaps he didn't even believe in witchcraft. He was wrong, Beth knew. There was magic. Magic could be bought.

Beth hesitated just a second outside the door. She had only come to Madame Bonnie once before in her life, when she had been young and foolish and had nearly ruined her life by tarrying with a stable hand in the barn. She had used her entire savings to buy Madame Bonnie's magic then. Now she had Lord Jamison Bryant's gold coins, and she could afford to buy all manner of marvelous things.

Before she could knock, the door creaked inward on its hinges. A long, bony finger beckoned to her. "Come in, come in. Speak to me."

Beth entered the cottage. She looked around. Small dead creatures hung from the rafters. Something boiled in a kettle above the fire. The floor was simple earth, the windows shuttered. It was dark and dank, and it smelled as evil as Madam Bonnie looked in her dingy brown dress and robe. Wisps of gray hair framed her face; her eyes looked like pitch-black orbs within the gray-toned pallor of her face.

"Speak up!" Madam Bonnie commanded.

"I need a special potion."

"For what?"

"Something to drug and seduce. Something powerful enough to delude the mind, yet heighten desires as well. Something to trick and deceive—"

"You ask a great deal! An opiate and an aphrodisiac! What you seek is surely dangerous. Dare you dabble so with life?"

Beth inhaled and exhaled quickly. The room seemed to be growing smaller, darker. The smell of the herbs that simmered in the pot seemed to be strangling her.

She slipped her hand into her pocket, producing all of Jamison's gold coins. Madame Bonnie's black eyes sparked. She seized one of the coins and bit down on it, then stared at Beth again. Beth found some courage.

"Give me a potion! It must work! It must. I need enough for three. Something to slip in their wine when they sup. It must cause them to grow weary, to sleep, yet they must all awake later, seduced, willing to allow their minds to believe that they are with the one they love."

"There are no guarantees!" Madam Bonnie warned, a crooked, bony finger pointed Beth's way.

"You must! You must make this happen. My master is a powerful lord. He will see that you hang if you fail—and he will give me more gold to bring if you succeed!"

Madame Bonnie turned away. She walked to the fire and threw some dust from her raw wood mantel on it. It fumed out, sparking, taking on startling colors. Beth watched the colors, amazed.

Drugs, Madam Bonnie thought. The peasant girl wanted magic; all that she needed was the proper chemistry. The wine itself could be a sound base as both opiate and aphrodisiac. All that Madam Bonnie had to do was add the right combination of other concoctions from her extensive larder. She thought for several moments, the colors in the fire buying her time with the mesmerized girl.

Then she began to pick and choose among her vials and stock, mixing a colorless potion before the flames. She made it take time. She whispered incantations and pretended to add a drop of bat's blood for good measure.

Then she gave the mixture to Beth. "Don't forget, old woman," Beth told her, "you will hang if this fails!" But her threat sounded very weak. She was anxious to leave.

Madam Bonnie smiled and pointed a finger at her. "Don't threaten me, young woman! Death is the easiest magic of all!" She began to cackle gleefully.

And Beth began to run.

It was one of the most enjoyable days Rose could remember.

The king and queen behaved as sweetly as any two young lovers, leading the party through the forest.

Several fine bucks were spotted and brought down. The king killed one himself with a fine display of archery.

Another was brought down, Rose noticed, by the never-faltering Lord DeForte.

Rose found the Italian astronomer, Lionel Triolio, a very handsome and charming man, lean and dark, with flashing brown eyes. From the moment he helped her mount her mare, his admiration was alive in his eyes. She rode with him, listening to him explain the way that the stars moved in the heavens, why the moon could be so full and beautiful. His accent was delightful.

Jason Padraic was the architect, a student of Sir Christopher Wren, and he was equally amusing. He had sandy-colored hair, warm hazel eyes, and a most pleasant look of adoration on his face. A Lord Samuel Newburg was also with them, a young count from the Yorkshire countryside. All of them seemed to vie for her attention. She was enjoying herself immensely. Despite the fact that Jamison Bryant followed behind her, the day was beautiful. All that marred it was DeForte. She caught him watching her once with a silver sparkle of mockery in his eyes, and when they chanced to meet on one occasion, she discovered that he mocked her indeed.

"You're acquiring quite a stable of admirers, Mistress Rose. Let's see, a count, a builder, a reader of the stars! Why, imagine, these poor fellows follow at your heels like puppy dogs, seeking some small handout!"

"Would you please go about your own business, DeForte?" she demanded.

He smiled, shaking his head. "The poor fellows! How you do tease and charm!"

"I believe they'll survive," Rose told him wryly.

"Maybe. Maybe not." He was suddenly staring at her in a way that seemed to judge and condemn. "Do you have any idea at all what you do to men? Ah, perhaps you know exactly what powers you possess, and enjoy the tempest you create."

"I'm not doing anything," she responded angrily, uncomfortable with the way that he was looking at her. "The gentlemen are a pleasure, a change from certain people I have become acquainted with at court! They are attentive, courteous, cultured—"

"They are lusting after something far different from a poetry reading!" he advised her. "You are as tempting as a perfect apple, dangling from a low branch of a tree. The very flash of your eyes beckons beyond belief!"

Her temper seemed to soar and snap. She fought

to control it, since she could hardly pitch herself against him and pound her fists into his chest, as she longed to do.

She leaned forward to speak regally to him. "Just what is it, my Lord DeForte, that so irritates you? The court is filled with flirtations! Is there something you want that you fear I will cast too freely to others?"

"Something I want?" he inquired, his brow shooting up. He smiled slowly. "Dear Mistress Woodbine. You forget. I am the Duke of Werthington. If I wanted something, I would take it."

"The great DeForte!" she returned. "Really? I don't think so, sir. As I've told you, I think nothing of titles. Power, my lord, lies within a person! If I wanted something, DeForte, I would have it! Believe me."

A slow smile curved into his lip, and his brow arched high again. "Mistress Woodbine, you are an intriguing creature. A slim little girl, and you think to have the world by the throat! If you wished to wed me, then, you would do so?"

Her heart shuddered suddenly. She was being far too flippant, but he brought out the worst in her. She lifted her chin and gave him a superior smile. "If I wished it, sir, it would be so. But fear not. In all of my life, I have never met a more arrogant, conceited fellow—with or without a title! I would rather wed an ape!" she finished in sudden fury.

She was startled when he came closer, his horse jostling hers, his hand falling upon her wrist. "And I am the arrogant one?" he demanded. He was as angry as she, she realized. More so. Waves of fiery heat seemed to wash off him, cascading over her. She was dismayed by the strange trembling that had begun within her when he had come so close and his hand had fallen upon her. She flushed, feeling color race to her cheeks. He would know, she thought in panic. In a matter of seconds, he would know. He would realize some heat had grown within her, he must feel it now, searing the air between them. He was staring at her in turn, his jaw set hard, not seeming to notice the blush that suffused her face. His eyes caught hers, fell to her lips, to her breasts, then rose to her eyes again, silver anger bright within them.

"Stop it!" she hissed. "Let go of me! I do not need your warning!"

"Don't fool yourself, Mistress Woodbine! A man needs only to see the fire in your eyes to know that he could reach heaven in your embrace!"

"A man?" she challenged. "Any man? You—milord DeForte?"

He seemed startled by the question, then emotions seemed to speed quickly through him—anger first, followed by amusement. "A fair question!" he said, staring at her hard. "All right, Rose. Yes. When I see you, the fire in your eyes, the blaze of your hair, I must admit to a feeling that's definitely carnal! Any man would feel the same. But take care! You will tarry where you do not mean to, and find that you are in trouble."

"How dare you!" she cried. She wrenched free from his grasp. Her mare pranced backward and forward. "I shall always be where I intend to be, milord. Don't concern yourself with me! You've the Lady Anne at your side, milord." She smiled at him sweetly. "But then again, perhaps the Lady Anne will be saved from herself. Perhaps some God-sent fellow will mistake you for a deer and set her free!"

"A deer?" he demanded sardonically. Away from her now, he seemed to find a certain wry amusement in her. "You have made a complete menagerie of me, Rose. First I am a horse, then a jackass, and now a buck."

"I was mistaken," she said swiftly. "In truth you are never anything but a jackass, my Lord DeForte!"

She nudged her horse hard. Her mare went leaping forward, startled by her sudden command.

And she rode on past DeForte, hearing the echo of his laughter in her wake.

Later, when they paused in a small farming village for a drink of ale, she was startled to discover Pierce DeForte watching her again. For the briefest of moments, there was something puzzled within his gaze. Then the curious gleam was quickly shielded. He bowed low to her and turned away, slipping an arm around Anne and walking back toward their horses.

To her amazement and distress, she felt a catch in her throat, then a warmth filling her.

And an aching.

She quickly mounted her own horse. When Jason Padraic asked if he might ride along with her, she offered him a warm and inviting smile.

They came to the ancient inn in the forest. The place had once been a small fortress, and was built unerringly solid, in the Norman way. Long hallways led to guest chambers, and there was a massive hall below where guests could gather. Servants saw to their things while they found places at planked tables in the great hall, with the rotund innkeeper running about, delighted to entertain this royal party. His daughter, equally rotund, with bright eyes and a wide smile, ran about, too, loaded down by a platter of roasted fowl decorated with new potatoes and cabbage leaves.

Rose looked about, wondering whom she should dine with. But before she could move, she discov-

ered Jamison's hand upon her arm, leading her toward a table where the Lady Anne was already
seated, and Lord DeForte was in the process of joining her. Anne smiled at Rose with such welcome
that Rose's protests died in her throat. "Do join us,
my dear! It's been a splendid day, hasn't it?"

"Splendid," Rose agreed, meeting DeForte's
gaze. She took her seat and discovered that Anne's
brother was beside her, grinning her way.

Ah, they had a way of quickly making her lose
her appetite! At the very least, she'd not turn into a
fat goodwife this way!

"Good woman!" Jamison called to the innkeeper's daughter. "Bring us wine here, lass! My throat
is dry and parched. Come, lovely Rose, let me pour
for you! Dear sister Anne, and my Lord DeForte!"

For a moment it looked as if DeForte would protest simply because he disliked Jamison so much.
But Anne, wanting to keep the peace, cast her sup-
plicating gaze upon him, and he winced as he gave
her a barely perceptible nod. "Fine, Bryant, pour."

Rose bit her lower lip, quickly looking downward.
He was so very courteous to Anne! Despite herself,
she wondered what it would be like if he were ever
so tender to her.

Jamison poured the wine, filling all their cups. He
pointed out various antiquities in the room as he did
so, telling Rose that his own home had been built
not long after the Norman Invasion of England.
DeForte seemed uninterested in the conversation. It
was obvious to Rose that he endured Jamison and
Jerome only for Anne's sake.

He managed to down several cups of wine, even
as he murmured to Anne beneath the din in the
room, pretending that Jamison spoke to Rose, and
Rose alone.

Rose saw Jerome watching his sister, then his curious gaze fell upon her. He smiled. She tried to do the same.

Food was brought to the table. She tried to eat. She didn't seem to be very hungry, but perhaps that was because she was drinking so much wine. Every time she looked about the room, she turned back to find Jamison's eyes probing into hers. He'd refill her wine cup and press it into her hands.

The king rose and spoke to the company, dedicating the event to his queen, who blushed and thanked him. Rose wondered fleetingly if she was aware of his numerous infidelities. Perhaps she was. Perhaps she accepted them. She was, after all, the queen. And there was no more tender man than the king—even if he chose to share that tenderness widely!

The room seemed to be growing very warm. She could feel the snap and crackle and heat of the fire in the massive hearth at the room's rear. People were talking and chatting so loudly. A harp player came. The room was darkened, and a puppeteer created a shadow play against a screen. Rose was trying very hard to concentrate. Something was wrong. The room was too hot. She was too keenly, mercilessly aware of everything around her. Sound was heightened. The least bit of light burned her eyes. She could feel the wood plank bench beneath her, even the rustle of her skirts against her. And she was weary. So very, very tired, she could scarcely keep her eyes open.

What was happening to her? She had drunk too much wine, but this seemed to be deeper than that. Then the question faded from her mind. She didn't really care. She was exhausted, she thought, but she also felt wonderful, and light. She just needed to lie down for a while. She had to rise, had to take herself up to bed. There would be a room arranged for her somewhere. Mary Kate would surely be there by now, to help her.

She tried to speak. "I've—I've got to rest," she managed to whisper. She looked to Anne for help, but Anne hadn't heard her. Anne's eyes seemed glazed, peculiarly highlighted by the fire.

"Yes, we need sleep," DeForte said. He looked as strange as Anne and was staring at Rose. For once, he didn't seem to be condemning her. Perhaps it was the wine, Rose thought. Perhaps he had drunk too much, too, and was now feeling the same curious helplessness. For once, though, she thought that she liked the man. His dark brow was knit, he seemed to sense some danger, and he was truly worried for her, a champion ready to assist her. Of course. They were at a table with Jamison and Jerome, and that worried him. But why? Suddenly she couldn't remember. She felt incredibly peaceful and at ease.

"Anne and I will see you to your quarters—" he began. But he broke off, stunned to realize that he could not rise. Even as he spoke, Rose noticed from what seemed like a very distant place that he crashed face-first into the table. Ah, the great DeForte! It should have been so very amusing; she should have enjoyed this. Except that he had fallen in her defense . . .

But she couldn't seem to think or feel herself, except for those physical things that were so very strong, the exceptional heat in the room, the slightest brush of fingers against her flesh.

"I'll take you to your room," someone said.

Jamison! An alarm sounded in her head, but she couldn't heed it. She could scarcely move. She was falling, then being swept up. She heard him saying something to someone, an explanation.

"No," she managed to murmur.

"It's all right, we'll get Mary Kate," he told her. Somehow that made sense. Mary Kate was supposed to be here.

Had she drunk that much wine? The world was spinning. For long moments there was nothing, nothing at all. And then she thought that she heard whispering.

"Don't be daft, the chemise, too. Strip her naked. How else would she be?"

Clothing was being peeled away from her body. She was aware of it as she might have been in a silver mist, in a dream. Mary Kate. Mary Kate was here, helping her into bed. "Mary Kate!" She tried to form the name on her lips.

"Yes, yes," she heard. "Move your arm so, aye, that's fine."

She was suddenly cold. Acutely cold. "Freezing!" she murmured.

"You'll be warm soon enough." She thought she heard a little snigger of laughter. There was a woman with her. It had to be Mary Kate, even if she did look a little strange in the darkness, even if her touch seemed unusually rough.

Moments later she heard, "Are you sure *he's* out for the moment?"

"The witch guaranteed the potion."

"What of Anne?"

"Next, next . . ."

Then she heard nothing. The blackness swirled around her. She slept so peacefully.

Then . . .

She began to dream.

It was a wild, deep, incredible dream. And she was not so cold. She was deeply, sweetly comfortable, resting on something soft, next to something incredibly warm. Something that touched her flesh, that radiated heat, that sent it sweeping into her.

"My love . . ."

She thought she heard the whisper. She was walking on clouds. Silver clouds, by a stream that rippled with silver waters. She could feel the radiating heat, but in the dream, he had not come to her yet. He was walking toward her, naked. Hard bronze muscle rippled in his chest and shoulders. His legs were powerfully built and strong. She tried to look to his eyes, but her gaze wandered back to his body—but it was all right, for the silver mist encompassed him.

"Want you, sweet Jesu, want you. So tired . . . but want you. Always want you . . ."

Arms swept around her, pulling her close. Hands touched her, fingers stroked her. Rugged, callused fingers, masculine hands. Excruciating against her bare flesh. Creating searing tongues of flame to sweep around her . . .

The silver mist dissolved for a moment. It was dark, so dark. She lay in the clouds, but she could see the fire burning in the hearth, so far away.

It was DeForte, she realized. DeForte in her dream. She moaned softly with distress. She'd never even imagined such things as this! Not until she had met him. Then she had begun to discover the feelings. The heat, the aching, the longing for something she had never touched, something that beckoned, excited.

Oh, no. Oh, dear Lord, no. Not DeForte. But it was him. Hard as steel, searing with heat. DeForte, touching her, stroking her. She lay naked with him.

She had dreamed about him once before, she remembered vaguely. Couldn't she dream these decadent dreams about someone else?

Or did she dream about him because, in truth, she longed to be touched by him? To lie like this . . .

No, oh no.

Yes.

His caresses, fingers stroking her. The touch of his kiss, his whisper breathing fire against her. This was enchantment. Ecstasy and desire, an aching, a longing. She twisted, she turned. The hands swept over her. The fingers threaded into her hair. She moved against his strength and incredible warmth. And her body cried out to feel more.

Now his lips were on hers. Demanding. Parting her mouth. His tongue swept forcefully into her mouth, bringing liquid fire. She felt the heat through the length of her. Felt it spiraling down, between her thighs. She moaned beneath the heady onslaught of his kiss, shifting.

His lips left hers, then pressed to her throat, arousing, tasting, feverishly hot, moist. This was a touch that demanded, that seduced, that evoked. Masculine, powerful.

His fingers curled around her breast, caressing the fullness of it. His thumb flicked over the nipple and she nearly cried out. She felt the hardness of his body, sweeping against hers. His tongue fell where his thumb had been. Savored, caressed.

"Oh, no . . ."

Did she speak the soft cry, or did she dream it? Could she possibly be imagining the shaft of fire that shot through her as his mouth fully savored her breast? She stiffened against him, amazed at the flames swirling wildly through the length of her. Her lips parted and her breath rushed through them. From the very center of her being, she felt a spiraling of need. Of desire. Hot, swirling, aching . . .

He shifted. Dark hair teasing her flesh. His hands upon her, his mouth closing around her right breast now. Dear Lord . . .

Distress swept into her for a moment. She had to fight it. This dream was . . . decadent. She could feel the vital heat of a tongue's silky movement around her breast again, the stoke upon her nipple, a suckling there.

No decent woman had such dreams!

But she could not escape this one. She struggled to think, to reason. This could not be right.

No, nothing had ever felt quite so right before. DeForte! Brash, arrogant, hateful!

Yet so magnificently built, so hot and powerful beneath the light fall of her fingers. Just the feel of his thigh thrown atop her created an urgency in the blood, anguish and ecstasy, this incredible tempest. Building with her every heartbeat. Wicked, hot, haunting.

Now his hands were moving down the length of her. Sliding over her waist, her hip. The tantalizing hot fire of his lips followed, pressing a kiss here, there. She moaned, twisting. Her fingers wound into thick, rich hair, feathered over his powerfully muscled, taut shoulders. Her breath escaped her, she trembled violently. The slow trail of his tongue moved low and hot over the flesh of her abdomen. Jesu, but she had to awaken.

She tried to open her eyes. They were too heavy. She tried to fight the feelings. They were too real.

His hands were against her thighs now. Moving higher, becoming more intimate. The length of him shifted against her. She felt his kiss, teasingly, just above her knee. The stroke of his tongue. A caress . . . moving higher, deeper. She inhaled on a ragged breath, her fingers winding into the sheets. This was not possible! His touch was liquid fire unlike anything she had known or imagined, so intimate, so demanding, so impassioned. Molten honey streaked through her, sweeter than she could bear. She fought, twisting, writhing, surging, aiding and abetting the fierce invasion. The tempest that swept her soared higher and higher, coming faster, harder, deeper. She cried out and tried to twist again, feeling waves of sensation crash down upon her again and again. Shocking, violent, sweet, shattering, the feelings washed over her. She lay stunned, amazed at the sweet splendor that had filled her, shaken her, and left her floating now within the silver mist.

Then she was suddenly aware of a great strength wedged against her, forcefully parting her. Her thighs, drawn apart. That weight, dividing her. Her legs were spread. Even in the silver mist, the pain was excruciating. She cried out, but her cry was smothered against the fervent passion of his kiss as his lips seized hers. Pain, fierce and endless, seemed to tear into her. She fought it, trying to twist from the kiss, trying violently to heave his weight from her body. But he didn't seem at all aware . . .

Their bodies were locked, his flesh was taut and slick. She tore at his shoulders, writhed beneath him, trying to avoid the impalement that seemed to strike into the depths of her body like a sword. Each movement seemed only to give him further assistance to enter her more fully, each twist but seemed to lock them ever more tightly together. Tears stung her eyes; she could taste them in her dream, just as she could taste the salt of her lover's kiss against her lips. Dreams could not be this agony. They could not be the sensual ecstasy she had known before. They could not caress and tear the body. They could not . . .

"My love," he whispered. "Easy, my love . . ."

The voice was his, the whisper his. So tender. A sob tore raggedly from her. She could not escape this. She had taken the beauty of the dream. And now there was this, too . . .

"No!" she whispered, and her fingers found the richness of his hair, stroked the handsome planes of his face. In the silver darkness, he was beautiful in his strength and nakedness. Her fingers trailed over his shoulders.

"Yes," he murmured softly, his lips at her earlobe, then upon the pulse at the base of her throat. "Easy . . ." he whispered again, and she felt the force of his movement. So careful. So slow. So seductive.

Her breath caught. The pain was with her still. But something more. Something within her had been touched. He was arched above her then, a dark form with just the ripple of his muscles touched by a golden highlight of fire. The taut length of him shuddered and tensed, again and again. Deeply in, deeply out. Slowly . . .

Then rampantly. Like a shattering drumbeat. So swift, so sure. The pain was fading. Still there. But not so acute, and not so vivid as the new sweet aching that swept through her. Again, his every stroke heightened it. Her lips were dry. She wet them. Her breath came in a rush. She felt the movement, felt the wonder it created within her. She closed her eyes and let her senses take her. Swirling, rising, spiraling. It was coming again, the great explosion of rippling sweetness, the force that swept her, bursting . . .

She was dimly aware of him. His tension was suddenly so great, he might have been composed of steel . . .

She felt a violent thrust, sinking within her so deeply, they might have been one. He shuddered against her, shuddered again, and fell still.

A dream . . .

A dream that lay so heavily against her. A dream that was slick and damp. A dream with an arm that lay across her like an iron bar, a dream that left her feeling spent and exhausted and amazed and incredulous and sore . . .

Her eyes closed. Or had they been closed all along? She didn't know. She saw silver darkening to gray either way. The darkness came completely, and she slept as soundly as if she were dead.

Eons, eons later, she thought that she heard a pounding. A thundering, like fists against wood. Someone calling to her, she thought vaguely.

She tried to awaken.

She felt as if she were struggling upward from some great chasm. Jesu! She had been so exhausted! She could not find the strength nor the energy to move now, she was so very weighted down.

It had been the wine, she thought. And it was the wine giving her such a fierce headache now, such an awful feeling of lethargy.

For long moments she just lay there, barely awake, aware only of the pounding in her head. Dear God. She'd been drinking wine since she was a small child. But it had never, never made her feel like this before.

Blood suddenly rushed through her.

She tried valiantly to move. She couldn't do so. She was still so exhausted, so torn with lethargy. She hurt. Her limbs were sore, her body, her . . .

She wasn't alone. She felt a shifting. She was lying beside another body.

No. Her heart pounded. Thumped. Ceased to beat.

She was lying in bed with a man. Lying on endlessly white sheets. It was cold. The fire in the room had died. A bronzed arm lay draped haphazardly over her naked back and shoulder. A taut muscled leg, richly furred with crisp, dark hair, lay casually over her hip.

A scream rose in the back of her throat. No dream,

it had been no dream, it had all been real. She was lying here and she didn't even know where . . .

But she knew who with.

DeForte!

She heard the pounding again, then a voice she knew well, calling out. "Are you alive in there, my friend? Come now, it's well past morning! Are you all right?"

The door suddenly burst open. Her eyes flew to it. In stunned horror, Rose watched as the king started in, then froze in the doorway.

"Er, well, you must excuse me!" Charles exclaimed, his voice deeply puzzled.

DeForte stirred, grasped his head. Rose nearly screamed out loud in a rising sense of panic. He sat up, magnificently naked, shoulders broad and dark against the whiteness of the bedding. As if he, too, fought waves of darkness, he ran his fingers through his hair. "Your Majesty," he said thickly.

"We'll speak later!" Charles assured him quickly. The king's eyes were on Rose. They swept over her. She stared at him, wanting to protest . . .

Wanting to die.

DeForte's eyes fell on her. "You!" he exclaimed. Then he leapt from the bed.

For a moment he was still. Confusion touched his silver eyes. He stared around the room. It was his room, Rose realized quickly. She was in his room. His clothing was strewn over the large chair before the fireplace; his sword and scabbard were there. He stumbled toward the bed for a moment, disoriented. He gripped the bedpost. His fingers tightened around it, then he pushed away suddenly, furiously gritting his teeth as if he had come to some realization.

And he stared at her again. So heatedly that it was

all that she could do not to shriek and run naked into the hallway.

She had compared him to a horse, to an ass, to a deer. She'd been a fool. He had the wired tension and prowling menace of an enraged lion right now. Mindless of his nakedness, he circled the bed, staring at her, taut, powerful, the muscles in his arms and chest constricting and rippling as he clenched and unclenched his fists, apparently trying to keep from winding his fingers around her throat. He stared at her as if she were the plague in person, sent down upon him. "You!" he repeated, his voice deep and husky. "My God!" he lashed out. "What have you done to me?"

"Me!" Outraged, she found her voice. She leapt from the bed and pitched herself at him with a wild fury, determined at that moment to tear his eyes out. "Me! Oh, you bastard! What have you done to me?" she cried, a vicious whirlwind of energy.

But he was every bit as enraged, and ten times stronger. She lashed out against him, nails careening across his chest. But that was her last blow. She was plucked up from the floor and held before him. His eyes met hers. She became acutely and painfully aware that they were both naked.

"You little witch! You said that you would have me if you wanted me!"

"I never wanted you!" she lashed back instantly. "I hate you, I loathe you, I—"

"What did you do to me?" he demanded.

"Nothing!" she shrieked, panicking, tears pricking her eyes. Her body was touching his, held against his as he lifted her above him, staring at her. He seemed to realize that they touched. That her flesh was against his. He swore suddenly, violently, pitching her down upon the bed, then walking to her with menace. She struggled up and gasped, horrified as she stared down at the bedding, at the proof that, indeed, the night had been no dream.

He leaned over her. "What did you do to me? How did you drug me? With the wine?"

Fire and fury ripped through her. She slapped him as hard as she could, startled herself by the sound that tore through the room. His hands seized upon her again, wrenching up, shaking her. "Don't you ever, ever do that again! I shall make you rue the day that you were born—"

"Get your hands off me! Let me go, let me be! I shall scream and summon the king—"

"The king indeed! That's just what you intended, isn't it, my beautiful little Rose! Well, it won't work! I won't marry you—"

"Marry me!" As tautly and dangerously as he held her, she had to be insanely furious to fight him still. But she did. She was near tears, confused, aching, physically, in her heart, in her soul. Oh, God! She hated him.

"I will never marry you, DeForte! Never! There is no more detestable creature alive! I would rather wed a leper! I despise you! Idiot, this was not my doing! My God, what you've done to me . . . !" Despite herself, her voice trembled. And she was suddenly shaking fiercely. She wanted to cover her face, she wanted to die. She wanted to sink back to the bed and close her eyes and never awaken.

There was a light tap at the door again. A throat was cleared. The king, once again. "Pierce, I need to see you."

Silver eyes sizzled back to her own. She didn't know if he believed her or not. Oh, God, that he could think that this was some kind of a marriage trap! She couldn't bear it.

He set her back upon the bed. Once again his eyes fell to the sheets. She saw the working of his jaw as his gaze touched hers. She scrambled for the covers, anxious to clothe herself. "Understand this!" she hissed vehemently, fighting the tears. "I truly loathe you! I have no desire to marry you. You wretched fool! You have wronged me incredibly! I will never forgive you for this! I am the one who has lost—oh, God!" she cried, remembering the night. "I'd give my eyeteeth to see you hanged. Drawn and quartered. I tell you, I had nothing to do with this."

He turned from her, stumbling for his trousers. He laced them about his hips. Shirtless, shoeless, he cast her one last furious and condemning stare, coming to within a step of where she lay in the bed, his fingers twined into fists at his side.

"Pray that you are innocent! For if I ever do discover you to be a part of it, you will pay dearly, I vow it!"

In a whirl of fury, he strode from the room, slamming the door so violently behind him that it cracked.

Chapter VI

Pierce followed the king down the stairs, and Charles instantly shooed away the servants delivering hot chocolate where he sat before the warmth of the fireplace.

"I've some understanding of what has gone on, I believe," Charles said wearily. "It seems that Lord Bryant has spirited Anne away."

"He's kidnapped her!"

"She is gone," Charles said softly.

"I will find her!" Pierce replied quickly, turning toward the door.

"Wait!" Charles called.

"I cannot wait!"

"Damm it, listen to me! I am returning to the court immediately. When you've cooled down, you will find me there. And take care if you find them. I do not want to see you hanged for murder. You had best control you temper."

He gave the king little heed. Fear and guilt were ruling him now. He had to find Anne.

"Forgive me, Your Majesty!" he said, bowed

deeply, and exited the inn with long strides, seeking Beowulf in the stable. He accepted no help from any groom, but saddled the horse quickly himself, and began to ride.

For endless hours Pierce prowled London and its environs, trying to discover just had happened, his emotions in a tempest.

Once he was fully awake, it became obvious. They'd been duped as easily as a pair of children, he and Anne. He had wakened beside Rose Woodbine, and Jamison had spirited Anne away somewhere—surely with Jerome's help. He was afraid for Anne. He had to find her.

He didn't want to think about the night. He definitely didn't want to remember that he had desired the girl with everything within him. He had gotten what he wanted. She had been all that he had imagined and more, pure magic.

And in the whole of his life, he had never felt more guilty.

Or furious.

Rose Woodbine had told him that *she* would have *him* if she wanted him. Had she decided that she did? Had she been part of the plan, crying innocence now that the others had disappeared?

She would not get away with it! He would find Anne, and Jamison and Jerome, and so help him God, they would pay. They had gone too far.

He rode all through the surrounding countryside. He threatened, bullied, and bribed, leaving many a man shaking in his boots, but he failed to discover where Anne had been taken. They had not gone to the Jamisons' family estate, but he had known they would not. Nor had they retired to either the London manor or the north country estate owned by Anne—and Jerome.

The hell of it was that he didn't even know which

way they'd gone. In all his searching, he found only one young farm girl who could help him, and she had scarcely been three miles from the Norman inn. She had seen five riders encompassed in heavy cloaks, riding hard from the inn during the middle of the night. The girl was too simple to remember their direction.

He would never find them alone, he realized. He was going to have to return to court, and seek help from Charles.

Actually, he had left in such a rage that it was only now, when his exhaustion had overcome his temper, that he realized Charles probably already had men out looking for his wayward subjects.

Bone-weary, in dire need of a shave and a bath, he returned to his quarters at court. He had barely left Beowulf with the grooms when the summons came to appear before Charles—just as soon as he had bathed and made himself presentable.

Sunken into a hot tub, miserable, weary, desolate, he leaned back, feeling a sense of guilt stealing over him again. He prayed that Anne had not suffered too greatly, and he wondered for what seemed like the thousandth time if Rose Woodbine had been used as he had been used, or if she had been part of the scheme. Closing his eyes tightly, he tried to remember everything that they had said to each other. She would have what she wanted, she had told him. And if she wanted him, she would have him.

But she would rather wed an ape, she had said also.

He sank beneath the water, soaking his dark hair and his face, feeling the anguish that tore through his body. Anne. What ill had she come to when he had been dreaming his sweet dream of ecstasy?

Jamison adored her. He would never hurt her. Jerome was the treacherous one, he thought wearily. Jerome had surely planned this.

It didn't matter who did the planning. When he got his hands on the twosome, they were dead.

But they would know that. That's why they had disappeared.

And then there was Rose Woodbine . . .

A peculiar tremor shot along his spine. His fingers curled around the rim of the tub and he dunked his face forward in the scalding water.

He leaned back, inhaling deeply, wondering if some part of his violent rage was not directed straight toward himself. He hated to remember the night. There had been the mist . . .

He had been exhausted; there had been a woman's body beside him. Naturally. Anne.

But it hadn't been Anne. It had been Rose. And he had thought that he was dreaming. But all the while, he had known that it was her. And he hadn't felt guilty during the consummation at all, just hungry.

How he had desired her. The taste and feel and scent of her. The silk of her flesh beneath his fingers, the undulating movement of her hips, and the exquisite feel of the perfect shape of her body. He had admitted to himself just that day that he had wanted her, that despite the sparks that seemed to fly each time they came near each other, or perhaps because of them, he wanted her . . .

Waking beside her had been such a shock. Seeing the king. Seeing her. The length of her. The deep, dark fire of her hair, spread out over the pillow. The perfection of her size and shape, the rounded curve of her hip, the fullness of her breasts, the dark rouge of her nipples . . .

He groaned aloud. She hadn't disappeared with

Jerome and Jamison. Perhaps that in itself should have signified her innocence. But not necessarily.

He lay a steaming cloth over his eyes.

"Uh-hum! Your Grace!"

He heard the words, then the cloth was pulled from his face. He stared into the old, crinkled face of Garth McCandrick, his father's manservant and now his own, though Pierce had spent so much time preferring his privacy that Garth had remained at Castle DeForte, seeing to the estate along with the reeve. Pierce stared at him, startled to see him. He had assumed that the king's own servants had seen to his bath. He was glad enough to see Garth. The man had the warm, gentle brown eyes of a hound. He was one of the kindest humans Pierce had ever met, loyal to the core, and of all blessed things, quiet and soft-spoken, as well as wise.

"Garth, old fellow!'Tis good to see your face!"

Garth shook his old head wearily, stretching out a big linen bath sheet for Pierce. "Yours is worn and haggard, milord."

Pierce's eyes narrowed quickly. "Well, there's good reason for it."

"So I've heard. Good King Charles summoned me, milord."

"Did he now?" Pierce leaned back in the tub, surveying his servant. "Hmm. I wonder why." The king was up to something.

Garth shook his head, stepping back as Pierce lifted his tall, muscled frame from the bath, water sluicing from his body. "His Majesty will surely share his reasons with you, Lord DeForte." He made a *tsk*ing sound, shaking his head again. Pierce thought his jowls shook, just as a hound's would do. "But looking at you, begging your pardon, milord, I'm glad enough that I've come! I'll have you shaved and trimmed in a blink, and ready to meet with His Majesty once again. Your clothes are set out, and I'll await you for a shave in the chair by the fire.''

Pierce dressed quickly, remained silent as Garth ran his razor over his Adam's apple, then explained as calmly as he could that Anne had disappeared along with her brother and Lord Bryant. He realized that he refrained from doing so much as mentioning Rose Woodbine's name, but then, in truth, he did not do so out of hostility, but rather because he was certain that Charles had not mentioned Rose's role in all of this to anyone, and he was not going to do so himself.

"God is your right, milord!" Garth assured him. "And I know, sir, that the king will lend all his aid to your plight!''

"Yes, of course," he told Garth simply. He buckled on his scabbard, loath to be anywhere without his sword, as he had been since the days of war. He set his wide-brimmed and heavily plumed hat atop his head, bowed to Garth, and left his chambers. He strode the hallways, passing friends and acquaintances, and nodding to each, gritting his teeth with the awareness that people whispered as he passed by.

All of England must know now that the Lady Anne had been spirited away, that Lord DeForte was raging like a lion, and that their fairy-tale lives had been ripped apart at the seams.

The king, he discovered, was awaiting him in his own chambers. Pierce hurried there without pausing to speak with anyone. A manservant met him at the king's inner door, and bade him enter. To Pierce's surprise, he found Charles supping at a table drawn up to a window—alone. There was a place set across from him. Pierce hesitated, looking at the empty seat. The king did not always dine with the queen, but when he did not, there was usually someone very charming to take her place.

"Are you expecting a companion, Your Majesty?"

Charles indicated the chair. "Indeed, I am. You, my friend."

Pierce took the chair. A servant stepped forward to pour wine. Pierce's fingers curled around the cup, and he stared at the red liquid. They had all been drugged through the wine, he was certain.

"What have you discovered?" the king asked him.

"Not a damned thing," Pierce said, "Other than the fact that Jerome and Jamison planned this exceedingly well and have managed to disappear completely."

The king arched a dark brow.

Pierce leaned toward the king. "I need your help to find her."

Charles sat back, rubbing his fingertips over the snowy napkin on his lap. He looked at Pierce, hesitating. Then he sighed. "I'm sorry, DeForte. I'm truly sorry to refuse you anything. But there's nothing that I can do for you."

"I don't expect miracles. But you've so many men in your service. They can help me hunt—"

"Pierce! Please, listen to me. Lady Anne and Lord Bryant were married very early this morning in the chapel at Lord Bryant's estate. They were married by Father Curry, the Catholic priest who has long served the Papists who reside about Bryant's estate. From what I can see—whether there was some coercion or not—the marriage appears to be quite legal."

Stunned, Pierce swallowed down the last of his wine.

He shook his head. "They were married without your permission! And you just said it! In a Catholic ceremony. You can see to it that she is granted a divorce.''

''A legal divorce is not easily acquired, even when your king is your loyal friend. I must go through the Catholic Church and the Church of England—''

''Damn the church—''

''Pierce! I cannot damn the church. Any church! Hear me out on this one. I intend to respect our church and all others. When I think of the men and women beheaded and burned in this country over battles because of the church, I grow ill. I cling to the Church of England because I'd not risk my throne to those who've hated the Papists since the days of Bloody Mary. But neither will I have the Catholics of this country ready to see my head roll! They were married in a legal, binding ceremony, Catholic or otherwise.''

''Whether he wed her or not,'' Pierce cried, ''I will go after her! She cannot have gone willingly.''

The king leaned forward. ''I forbid you to go after her.''

''Forbid me! I followed you from England to Scotland to the Continent, Your Majesty. And now you would refuse me—''

''I'd keep you alive, man! If either of those cowardly fools can find a way—and any man can hire mercenaries!—they will murder you in cold blood. And if you manage to find them in your present fine humor, you'll be guilty of murder, and even I might not be able to keep you from hanging!''

''Jesu!'' Pierce slammed a fist on the table. Charles didn't bat an eye; his servant jumped back. Pierce stood. Hands clenched behind his back, he paced before the royal bed. ''What would you have me do? Forget everything, stay here at court, dance and laugh away the hours while Anne—''

''Anne has written to you.''

He turned to the king. "What?"

From a huge pocket in the front of his long brocade coat, Charles produced a letter. It had been sealed with wax, and Pierce instantly recognized Anne's signet in the design upon it. He stared at the king, then ripped it open.

His heart thundered. It was Anne's flowery script. In silence he quickly scanned it.

Dearest Pierce,

Forgive this message! Trust in the fact that I did love you, but life has now changed. I am about to marry Jamison, who had declared his heart to me in a true and honest manner. As my brother so applauds this union, and for peace among the men I love, I am going to enter into it. I pray that you do not seek revenge, for I could not bear any man's death to come because of me. With my highest regards, always,

Anne

Pierce let the letter fall. Had they forced her to write it? Perhaps not. Anne wouldn't want them all trying to murder one another. He knelt and picked up the letter again, studying the writing. Her script was clear and flowing. There wasn't the least waver in her letters. She hadn't been in any pain.

"Do you know what is in this?" he demanded of Charles.

"Knowing Anne, I think that I do. She begs you to forget her, to get on with your life. And that's exactly what you must do."

"Dear God! And let them get away with what they have done!"

"Marriages," Charles said flatly, "are arranged all the time. I will remind you, my own wedded bliss is due to arrangement!'' He hesitated a moment, taking care with his words. ''The Lady Anne is also a mature woman who has known—men.''

''What are you saying!'' Pierce demanded.

Charles sighed. ''Only that she has known many lovers—''

''That gave no man the right to kidnap her!''

''No. But she will manage Jamison well enough. By her own hand, she is reconciled. You can do nothing but create tragedy if you seek to avenge this wrong. And I want you to wed, for the sake of peace and propriety, just as the Lady Anne has done.''

Pierce inhaled sharply. ''Jesu!'' he exclaimed. ''And I am the king's friend! Pray, how does he manage with his enemies?''

''Being the affable and wise monarch I am,'' Charles said shrewdly, ''I will ignore that. Yet you, who swear to be my ever faithful and valiant soldier, are blind! You have torn about the countryside for Anne. A good and noble gesture, and you did love her, Pierce, aye! I am aware of that! I despise what those wretched fools did to you both, but it is done. And I am left with a quandary. There was another injured party in this matter.''

Pierce started. ''Rose Woodbine?''

''Good, good! You remember the girl!'' Charles applauded wryly.

Pierce stiffened. ''She might well have been a part of it.''

''Oh, come!''

''Her father is a shrewd old merchant. He intended to sell her to me all the time.''

Charles arched a brow. ''He is richer than Midas. And she is not an ugly old hag. Indeed, the girl might well be the most beautiful creature I ever saw in court.''

"Then perhaps, Your Majesty, I should take the gravest care not to come too close—"

"You've already come too close. The girl was virtuous," Charles said. He stared at Pierce hard. "As your king, I'm asking you to marry the girl. I cannot afford the scandal that will come about if the fact that you deflowered and deserted her all in one evening comes out!"

"I didn't desert the girl! I—"

"But you did!" Charles said softly.

Pierce sat again, staring furiously at the king. *I will have you if I want you!* Had she or hadn't she been a part of this?

"I've no wish to marry."

Charles watched DeForte, his heart in deepest sympathy. He was not a man who gave his love or loyalty easily, but when he did, he did so deeply and well. Charles knew that he had profited greatly from Pierce's loyalty himself. He closed his eyes, very sorry to cause such a good friend any discomfort, much less this pain.

But he was king. A king asked back to England, after years of wandering the Continent. He'd watched the path that the wretched war had taken, fought for his father and himself. He could remember the very moment that he had heard the news of his father's death, the cold feel of the air against his face. There was so much that he remembered!

And Pierce had been involved with much of it. He knew DeForte, he thought, better than his own brother, better than much of his own family.

He hadn't reclaimed his throne all that long ago. And above all else, he wanted to keep it. And it was definitely a new world, one in which the merchant class was rising, making men like Ashcroft Woodbine extraordinarily important. The king's wandering days had been expensive, among other things.

Charles wouldn't have minded seeing men such as Jamison and Jerome in the tower. But there were always those who would rush to their defense. Many could die over this.

He was weary of intrigue and fighting.

Watching Pierce, he drummed his long fingers on the table. "I have known you most of my life. I have seen you be loyal, generous, and kind to the lowest urchin walking the streets. Yet now it seems that you have forgotten kindness and decency. How can you be so callous! Rose Woodbine was truly wronged."

It was Pierce's turn to arch a brow. "That might well be debatable."

"How so?"

He waved a hand in the air, then leaned low over the king. "That very day, Your Majesty, she assured me that she would always have what she wanted. That if she wanted me, she would have me."

"You think she was involved?"

"There is the possibility."

The king shook his head. "I think not. She has not come to me demanding anything of you."

"The beautiful little innocent!" Pierce exclaimed softly. "She probably knew there was no need!"

The king shook his head. "I am not Henry the Eighth," he said, "and I am certainly not threatening you. But I am asking you, as my friend, as my loyal subject, and as a man who has fought for my throne with nearly as much rigor as I did myself, to marry the girl."

Pierce gritted his teeth. His muscles tensed. Fury, deep, intense, shattering, washed through him. He couldn't marry her; Charles couldn't expect him to.

Then again, it was the only thing that the king could ask him to do. The girl had been under the king's roof, and there was no denying the fact that

Pierce had been with her. Perhaps they had all kept it a secret so far . . .

Jesu, but she infuriated him! Half of the time he longed to strike her.

Half of the time he longed . . .

To touch her.

"You know," he informed the king dryly, "that she claims to absolutely despise me. If she is as innocent as you say, she would much rather wed an ape. She told me so."

Charles waved a hand in the air. "I'm sure she will get over any feelings of hostility. And as you know, most marriages are arranged. Rose Woodbine must be equally aware of that."

Pierce's lip curled. "I'm afraid that she is not."

"She will do as I command her, I am certain."

"Charles, I will not simply forget all that happened!"

"Pierce!" the king persisted. "I am not asking you to forget anything. I am asking you to do what is right."

His spine stiffened. Fine. He would marry her. And he'd lock her in some damned tower somewhere and throw away the key.

"Your wish, Your Majesty, is ever my command!" he said tensely.

"Good." Charles stood. He waved a hand to his servant. "Fetch Father Martin and the papers I've had drawn up. I shall give her to you in marriage in her father's place. Damon there and Lady Bower can be witnesses. We'll have it done this night. Ah, Pierce! You may go for your bride."

"You want me to fetch her? And wed her here and now?"

Stunned, he looked at the king. Charles had started making these arrangements the moment he had learned about Anne, Pierce realized. Why?

Because of Rose Woodbine's father's money and position in the colonies. Charles was a careful king. A king who meant to keep his crown—and his head.

Pierce almost laughed at the irony of it. Then he quickened, tightening his jaw, as a startling jolt seared through him. She was here. Near. And the king intended that they would be wed tonight. She'd be his wife. His bride. Legally. His possession. His to take . . .

Love was lost. Tempest remained.

Was it hunger, was it a wild fury? He stood. "Indeed! Let me fetch my enchanting little bride to be!"

He bowed low to the king, then exited his chambers. Fine. He'd bring Rose Woodbine. In his present mood, it should be quite a wedding.

In the hallway he paused, and laughed aloud, a hollow sound, one filled with irony. It was rich! Dear God, it was all very, very rich! Now he knew why the king had sent for Garth. To prepare his chambers for the bride.

Well, Garth needn't have bothered much here. He was going to find the man and send him back home again.

He wouldn't be staying at court. The moment he had wed Rose, he'd be taking her home. If she had been any part of the plot, she would get all that she had desired. She would be a wife!

Rose set the last of her folded garments into the trunk, then sat down at the foot of the bed. It was beginning to seem like forever since the disastrous hunting party. She had barely seen a soul since then, and she didn't want to see anyone. Except Mary Kate. And she was sick with worry about her, even though the king had promised to find the woman. From what his men had discovered so far, it seemed that Mary Kate had already been put aboard a ship bound for the colonies, unconscious, as someone's ailing and elderly aunt!

Jerome and Jamison had planned this so very well! And DeForte had the nerve to believe that she might have been involved!

She felt a trembling within her, and determined that she would not think about DeForte!

Rose had discovered through a friendly guard that a ship was leaving the London docks that very night for Jamestown in the Virginia colony, and she wanted to be on it. She didn't care if she had anyone's permission to leave or not—she was going to do so!

She rose, determined to find some servant to help her with her trunks, but even as she opened the doorway to the hall, a dark presence appeared like a storm, such a whirlwind of energy that she found herself instantly backing into her room once again. DeForte! As he approached her, she jumped, wary, her temper flaring, every humiliating memory of the hunting trip rushing to the fore of her mind.

"Leaving, Mistress Woodbine?" he demanded, quickly taking in the packed trunks along the wall.

"Get out of here!" she commanded him. Hands on his hips, silver eyes flaming, he took a step closer to her. She jumped back, returning his gaze with wary hatred.

"What the hell is the matter with you?" he demanded angrily. "I've never hurt you!"

"You've never—" she began to repeat, but she exploded. "Oh! Get out! Get out! How could you have the awful arrogance to come here! I don't want to see you, I don't ever want to see you again; I thought that I had made that quite clear!"

"Mistress Woodbine, I don't give a damn what you do or do not want. The king commands you appear before him. With me."

"Why?"

"Why? You are an arrogant little witch. He is the king. And I am to bring you to him."

Rose backed away again. "Why?"

He swept his hat from his head, bowed elegantly low. There was a fever about him tonight. One that made his silver eyes glitter, his every movement charged with lightning and energy. His eyes seemed to impale hers. His piercing stare brought back vivid memories. Awaking with him. Being touched by him. So intimately.

"Why?" she gasped out again.

"There is to be a wedding."

"Whose?"

"Ours."

"Ours!"

"Indeed, mistress! And I am glad to discover that you are not hard of hearing! I'm also glad that you are packed. It will save time."

"Time?"

"We're going home. Tonight."

"My home is across the Atlantic!"

"Mine is an hour's ride south of London."

She shook her head wildly. "What jest is this! You nearly threw me upon the floor in your haste to be rid of me—"

"Never, Miss Woodbine, did I throw you on the floor."

"You threw me on the bed."

"Now, that I may do again."

"Oh! This is a joke, surely! I'll never marry you. Never!"

"Fine. Inform the king. Then we'll be done with it."

She couldn't begin to tell if he was serious or not. All she knew was that it was the most horrible suggestion she had ever heard. It seemed tonight that he longed to throttle her more than ever. They could never, never be wed. They were like fire and oil, ungodly explosive together.

"What of the Lady Anne?" she demanded. She backed away again, for his expression grew dark.

"Anne has married Lord Bryant," he said.

Rose gasped, then stuttered out, "But—but surely she did not do so on purpose—"

It was the wrong thing to say. He only looked more furious.

"The king," he stated harshly, "has said that the marriage will stand."

She stared at him hard, at the rigid tension in his towering frame, at the flames in his eyes.

Oh, God. She felt ill. Anne was lost to him. He didn't want to marry her. But he would do so.

Dear Lord. It would be a living hell.

"I will see Charles!" she declared. Slipping around him, she ran into the hall. He was behind her, following her. She started to run, then realized that she didn't know where to find the king. It didn't matter. DeForte was right behind her. She spun around to see him, and in that moment he caught up with her, taking her arm.

"Don't touch me."

"Don't be absurd. I've touched much more than your arm."

"And I will never forgive you for it!"

"Really?"

She inhaled sharply, fiercely trying to free herself from his hold. "Don't start that again. I warn you, don't!"

He fell silent, then whirled her around. They had come to a door. She gasped, realizing that it was the king's bedchamber. Pierce knocked softly. The door opened instantly and a servant led them in. The king was waiting for her, his arms outstretched. "My beautiful Rose! I hope DeForte has told you that we mean to atone for what things we might this night! I shall give you to Lord DeForte in your father's stead. The good Father Martin here will marry you, Lady Bower will see to your needs, and Pierce's man Garth sees to it even now that Lord DeForte's quarters will be a fitting bridal chamber!"

Rose shuddered. Dear God! It was true. The king himself meant to press this thing!

Because he thought her wronged, she determined. An innocent woman—tarnished, ruined. He didn't understand. She might bemoan the loss of her innocence, but certainly not enough to marry DeForte!

"Your Majesty, forgive me. I greatly appreciate your kind concern. But I don't want to marry him."

"Nonsense. It is your father's desire."

"I don't want—"

"Rose. It is seldom, if ever, that such a nobleman would marry a commoner! You must thank God for your good fortune."

She couldn't seem to speak, the king was so insistent. Her knees were trembling. She was so strong! She could always fight. And now, in a matter that was this important to her, she couldn't seem to wage her battle at all.

"Your Majesty, please! Where I grew up, we really do not think so highly of titles! We were both part of a wretchedly cruel trick. This is a gracious gesture on your part, but I don't want to marry him! Please—" She stared hard at DeForte. If he would only say something!

But he didn't. His teeth were gritted. He still just stared at her. Then smiled. Like a cat with a bird. Oh, he meant to devour her!

"Your Majesty," she began as reasonably as she

could manage. "I am truly well, I wish only to go home—"

"I couldn't possibly allow you to return to your home, my little beauty, no longer a maid and still no man's wife! What would your good father think?"

"I can talk to Father, and Sire! You are the king!"

"Indeed, Rose, I am the king. And I command it!"

She shook her head. Charles had his hand on her wrist, drawing her forward. He lifted a hand, summoning the priest from the shadow of the draperies at the edge of his bed. Then she realized that there was a buxom, smiling older woman in the room, and others. A few of the older ladies, two more servants. They were all coming forward.

She began to feel the jaws of a trap falling shut.

"Your Majesty, I am your loyal subject. In all things but this!" Rose declared. "Please, Sire, I—"

Charles kissed her fingers, smiling assuringly. "Read from the good book," he told the priest. "As short a ceremony as will be binding before God, I think."

They really meant to do this to her. She slipped her fingers from the king's. She turned, meaning to flee.

To her astonishment, the king pulled her back, pressing her toward DeForte. DeForte lifted her and threw her over a shoulder.

"Read!" the king commanded pleasantly.

The priest began to read. Panic was settling over Rose. She pushed against DeForte's shoulders. "Stop this!"

He shrugged. His hold was like steel. "Oh, I am quite resigned to it."

The priest read on, raising his voice over hers.

DeForte lowered her to the ground, still holding her tightly. His hand wound around hers.

The priest was droning on, louder and louder, speaking above her furious words. "Damn you! Why?"

Pierce's voice lowered. He whispered only to Rose. "Perhaps to make you pay!" His fingers tightened around hers. "Yes. I do!" he said suddenly.

"And do you, Rose Woodbine . . ."

"There is nothing to make me pay for! I was the injured party, don't you understand?"

"Mistress Woodbine?" the priest inquired.

"Say, 'I do,' Rose!" Pierce commanded, his silver eyes burning.

She shook her head. "But I don—" she broke off with a scream. A booted foot had hit hard upon her toes.

She looked to her left with amazement. It had been the king's foot. He smiled at her quite pleasantly.

"She does!" he told the priest. "Didn't you hear her? I did, distinctly. That was an 'I do.' Now, get on with the ceremony, my good man!"

A moment later, they were pronounced man and wife. The king had apparently already had the papers drawn up. She found herself signing them. Charles signed them. Her marriage had been witnessed by God and the king. What could be more binding?

How in God's name had this happened? She stared at her new husband. He still looked as if he longed for her throat. No one could be happy with this, not the bride, not the groom . . .

Just her father! Oh, yes, he would be delighted! Somehow the impossible had been achieved for him.

While for her . . .

She had just been married to a man who hated her.

"A wedding toast!" the king cried. "To the greatest of my cavaliers—and the most beautiful new lady within my realm. Long life, strong sons and daughters, and the greatest happiness!"

Wine was poured. She wanted to throw it at all of them, the very charming king of England included! But she could not do so. She swallowed a single sip.

"Pray, lady! One day you will thank me!" the king whispered to her.

She didn't think so.

He kissed her cheek. Someone else did the same. She could scarcely feel anything, she was so numb.

Then her new husband had her hand again. "You will all forgive me. I have made arrangements to take my bride home tonight, and we've quite a ride ahead of us. We thank you all for witnessing this joyous occasion, and beg that you allow us to take our leave."

The king seemed startled. "Pierce, I assumed you would stay here."

Rose looked swiftly to the two of them. She knew instantly that the king wanted Pierce to remain. He was afraid Lord DeForte would still go after the Lady Anne, try to avenge her kidnapping somehow. She felt very much like a pawn. The king might care for her—but she was certain that she had also been given to Pierce just like a bone might be given to a hound. She was to entertain him, distract him.

"Ah, Sire! I would very much like to begin our wedded life where we shall live in our newfound bliss."

"It would be so much nicer to remain here!" Rose cried. She was suddenly very anxious to remain near the king.

At the very least, Pierce would not dare throttle her here.

But his eyes were on her suddenly, burning their silver fire. And his whisper was very soft, for her ears only, when he spoke. "Unless you wish these lovely ladies to strip you, and the king to attend a public bedding, I suggest you agree with me!"

She paled and felt faint. Yes. It was done all the time. All these people might well follow them to Pierce's chambers here, rip away their clothing.

"Come with me. Now!" Pierce commanded.

The next few moments seemed a wild rush. The king kissed her cheek again. They bid the assembled company farewell. They ran through the hallways. He moved so quickly. She was breathless. "My things—"

"My servant will have seen to them."

They were outside in the darkness of the night and he was shouting for his horse. And before she knew it, she was seated atop his great Beowulf, and he was behind her. She began to tremble.

He was taking her away. Away from London. Away from the docks.

Away from the opportunity to escape for home.

"Please!" she whispered suddenly. But he had already nudged the great horse. They were already riding hard into the darkness. She could smell the night, feel the strength of the horse beneath her. And that of the man behind her.

"Please what?" he demanded.

"Don't—take me away!" she said.

He was silent. His arms tightened around her. He rode at a reckless speed, and she felt the force of the wind against her face.

Somewhere in the wild ride, he reined in, caring for his horse if nothing else. He could see in the darkness, it seemed. He dismounted, and she heard the sound of a softly rushing brook. He started to walk the horse through trees and bracken. When he came to the brook, allowing the horse to drink, she slid down from the great animal herself. She turned in the darkness, so panicked that she would have run anywhere.

But his hands were fiercely upon her.

"Where do you think you're going?"

"You don't want me!" she cried to him. "Just let me go, I beg of you! I'll make it back to London. I'll find a ship—"

"Are you mad?"

"I—"

"I'd never let you go in this darkness, in the night!"

"Then—"

"Lady," he snapped incredulously. "Don't you understand? It's over, you are wed! My wife. You will do what I tell you to do, go where I say you will go!"

"I will go home!" she cried. "Somehow I will escape you, and I will get home!"

He arched a brow. He picked her up and set her high atop Beowulf once again.

"Most certainly, my lady, it will not happen tonight!" he assured her. Then he was up behind her again. And they were riding hard.

She saw very little of his great ancestral estate that night, for he seemed to be a man beset by some demon. They rode across a drawbridge and came to a castle that seemed to reach to the night sky. A boy hurried out for the horse, and she was lifted from it.

He drew her into a foyer where a very old and exhausted-looking man awaited them. "My lady!" He bowed deeply to her. "Welcome, we all welcome you wholeheartedly! Your every wish we will try to fulfill.''

"Thank you, Garth," Pierce said impatiently. "It's been a long day. The Lady Rose will meet the household in the morning. If you'll excuse us . . ."

His hand around hers was fierce. He did not escort her up the huge stairway. He dragged her up it.

They reached a doorway to a suite of rooms. Pierce's quarters, she thought. They were magnificent. A massive sitting room led to a bedroom with a huge canopied and draped bed. There was a roaring fire. The bedclothes had been pulled back. There was a sheer gown upon the mattress. There were wineglasses and a wine bottle on a black bear rug before the fire. All these things she saw . . .

Then the longing to bolt came over her.

She was alone with him. Captive at his estate. In his rooms.

His wife.

There was no escape now. No escape. Not the way that he looked at her.

He walked about the room, keeping his distance from her, staring at her. He plucked up the wine bottle and he took a long swig from it, as if it would help.

She was the one who needed the wine! Something to help her endure this travesty.

"You bastard!" she lashed out suddenly. "How could you let this happen!"

"I told you. I am resigned."

"Because you wish to punish me!" she accused him.

He arched a dark brow. "Should you be punished?"

"You fool!" Tears of outrage and disbelief were stinging her eyes. "I will hate you forever, I will make you pay for this! How can you be so stupid! I had no part in it!''

Pierce paused at the anguish in her voice. If she had been part of the trickery, she was a wonderful actress.

''Well,'' he murmured, watching her. ''It is indeed an irony! But you are my wife now.'' He took a step toward her. She leapt back, staring at him with wild emerald eyes.

She shook her head. ''Don't come near me!''

''Don't ever think to command me, mistress! I will do as I please. Your merchant father has managed to sell you. You're mine now.. Legally. You're Lady DeForte. And I will damned well touch you—if and when I please!''

''You'll not!'' she insisted. ''Not again!'' she cried out. ''Don't come near me.''

He arched a brow and came closer. Closer. When he reached out a hand to her, she turned to fly. He caught hold of her arm, sending the wine bottle flying to crash against the hearth. Flames leaped and roared. He jerked her against him and felt himself grow hard and rigid beneath his trousers just as her body came against his, softness and curves and silk.

Damn her! What was it about her that could cause this rise of desire, this tempest of emotion?

''No!'' she shrieked, struggling against him. He held her tightly. She realized the futility of her struggle. She stared up at him, panting like a wildcat.

''We've just been wed.''

''You can't—imagine to do this!''

''Do what?''

''Be man and wife.'' Tears glazed her eyes. ''I hate you, and you loathe me. You think me guilty of horrible things, and I hate you all the more for thinking them! How could you possibly believe—''

''Jesu!'' he exploded suddenly. He stared at her, searching her eyes. To her amazement, his hands were suddenly on the sides of her cheeks, gently molded to her face. ''I don't know what I think or feel at this moment!'' he said huskily. ''What you did to me—''

''What I did to you!'' she cried out incredulously. She struggled for the words to describe her feelings. He was referring to the night they had spent together. The dream.

The nightmare.

''You are accustomed to such things. For you it was nothing. For me it was disaster!''

''Disaster! Oh, madam! I lay asleep. Then there was this startling warmth, the curve of you against me. You swept me from the mists of dreams. You seduced me—''

''Seduced you! I did not!'' Wildly she tried to pull away from him. His fingers were rigid around her arms. She went still, meeting his eyes with hers an emerald flame. ''I would rather seduce an entire tribe of pygmies!''

He paused, smiling. ''You'd rather marry an ape, and you'd rather seduce pygmies? My, you are in a sorry situation, m'lady!''

''Please, let me go home!''

''You are home.''

''I cannot be your wife.''

''But you are.''

''You don't want me—''

''You are mistaken. I do want you. I touched you and found fire. I thought that I had gone to heaven, I was so seduced! And yet you say you were no part of it, and now you play the absolute innocent. I don't know what to think, or what to believe. Sometimes I'm so angry, I could throttle you. And then at other times, I simply want you.''

"Let go of me!" she pleaded. She couldn't bear the way that he looked at her. There was an honesty about him. She was trembling. She was feeling the same sweep of heat she had known in her dream.

"I never hurt you, Rose!" he told her softly. "And I will not do so now. Jesu, I swear, you will want me again, too."

"No! I was drugged!" she told him.

Watching her, he felt a startling surge of desire. Her breasts were incredible and tempting and he could remember the feel of them all too well, rounded, the nipples hardened little peaks. He could remember the curve of her hip, the length of her legs . . .

The speculation in his gaze alarmed her.

"You insisted on this marriage!" she reminded him. "Have the decency to make it one in name only."

He arched a brow, and stroked his chin, as if considering the possibility.

Then he shook his head. "No, I'm sorry. I don't think so."

"We despise one another!"

" 'Tis sad, isn't it?" he said, and walked toward her. She backed away. She watched him; he continued coming forward. She suddenly discovered herself backed against a wall with nowhere else to go.

She raised a hand as if she would strike out in self-defense. He caught her wrist. "You'll not hit me," he warned her.

"I'd take a sword to you if I could!" she vowed.

He shook his head slowly, his eyes dark upon hers. "I don't think so. And I don't think you are quite so wretched as you pretend. Your lips parted to my kiss, and your flesh awakened to my caress. And oh, lady, your limbs did entwine most sweetly with my own!"

"Stop it! It was the drug!" she whispered fervently.

"I think that it was more."

"I will fight you violently!" she promised him.

"I don't think so," he said softly, studying her eyes. He shrugged. "But it won't matter. We are locked in this thing now. Man and wife." He reached out suddenly, pulling her into his arms. She struggled wildly against him, but he held her still, his fingers threading through her hair, tilting her head to his. A protest left her lips, but it was quickly swallowed into the passion of his kiss. He parted her lips to his, the fullness of his mouth. She tried to twist. He held her still. He plundered and invaded the sweetness of her, force becoming coercion, his desire coming alive all throughout him. She tried to raise her fists against him; he drew her closer. He kissed her until the breath was all stolen from her body, until he felt her trembling wildly beneath him, until her hands against him went still. Only then did he lift his lips from hers, whispering softly, "I did not hurt you!"

"I tell you, it was the drug!" she said desperately.

"I don't think so. I think that there is a fire within you, exciting and warm. And I think that I can touch it, find it, stoke it, no matter how you claim to despise me."

"I tell you—"

"M'lady, I've an idea," he said very softly, watching her with his head slightly cocked.

"And what is that?" she demanded.

He let his arms fall from her, and he turned away, walking away from her. Then he turned back. "Why don't we discover what was, and what was not, the drug?"

She didn't reply. She was very still, returning his gaze, framed by the firelight. A dark, hot tremor shot through him as he saw her there. She stood on the huge black bearskin before the fire. Golden light, soft and ethereal, fell gently upon her. It touched the soaring highlights of red within her hair, making the length of it shimmer around her shoulders and down her back like a cascade of liquid flames. The beautiful commoner's daughter. He'd been trapped into this marriage. Was she guilty or innocent? Did it matter? He burned. The whole of him. His throat burned, his loins burned, he shook with the heat of it. Of wanting her. Maybe it was anger. Maybe it was desire. Maybe it was both, and more.

He strode across the room to her. She might have been about to fly. To streak across the room, fleeing from his touch.

But she stood still. Her heart pounding visibly, her chin raised just slightly.

He paused just before her. Not touching her. Waiting. Her scent was as sweet as the rose for which she was named. Her breasts rose and fell in a swift, fascinating rhythm.

And her eyes met his. Emerald, fierce, defiant. She was trembling.

"Was all the magic in the wine? Or may it not exist elsewhere as well? Let's discover it, shall we?"

He reached for her, pulling her hard into his arms. She cried out, startled, her body stiffening. "Rose Woodbine!" He spoke her name harshly, just over her lips. "You are my wife now. What a couple! Here we are, master and mistress of our own destinies! Yet tonight, lady, I will be master! But I swear, I will do my damned best to be tender!"

He swept her up into his arms.

And to their bridal bed.

Chapter VII

She was scarce in his arms before he felt the startling rise of the curious magic again. What was it about her that could make the longing stronger than thought or emotion? He didn't know, and he didn't want to care. He bore her down upon the softness of the bed, amazed at his reaction to the feel of her beneath his hold. But whether she did or did not recall anything about their night together, she clearly did not want to repeat it. Beneath him, she was squirming to rid herself of his weight, half thrown over her

And each time that she moved, she did incredible new things to him.

"Rose!"

He caught her hands. Laced his fingers through hers, and brought them down to the bed by the side of her head. Her eyes met his. The anger was still within them. And more. Something Rose Woodbine always tried so very hard never to show. Unease, discomfort . . . fear?

He smiled, straddled over her, and leaned down

to test her lips again. His mouth claimed them before she could twist or turn. He allowed her no movement, but his kiss was tender, slow, seductive. He lifted his mouth from hers. There was something wild in the emerald of her eyes. Another kind of fear.

She did remember.

"Why are you fighting me?" he asked her huskily.

"This is no real marriage!" she charged him.

"The king himself was there," he reminded her. He arched a brow, smiling ruefully. "What did you think? That you could wed me and go about your own way again?"

She stared at him, then said with a quiet dignity, "You're still in love with the Lady Anne."

A sound of impatience escaped him. Anne. For long moments he had actually forgotten Anne. Rose could do that to him. Rose could fight him like a tigress, and still the silk of her skin, the scent of her, the feel of her beneath him, could make him forget everything. Anne! He closed his eyes. She was lost to him. She was wed to Jamison, and the king had determined that the union would stand.

Well, damn the king. For the sake of his honor alone, he was going to have to find Anne and Jamison. And he was going to have to hear from her own lips that she was reconciled to her marriage.

Later. But not tonight. Before God, he had cared for Anne deeply. But there was nothing that he could do now.

And he had a wife of his own.

His fingers curled ever more tightly around hers. His eyes met hers again. "Lie still," he commanded her.

She moistened her lips, shaking her head. "So our marriage is legal," she whispered frantically.

''You'll still leave to search out Anne. You'll seek out Jamison until you do find him. And he'll be prepared, and you'll be careless because of your fury. He's treacherous and he might very well discover a way to kill you. Then—''

''Then you'll be a very wealthy widow.''

''Or perhaps you will kill him. And then the king will be forced to hang you, or perhaps, due to your position, he'll manage to get your head mercifully lopped off by a good axman!''

''Either way, you'll be a very wealthy widow.''

''But you're still in love with Anne!'' she said in dismay.

Women! They were incomprehensible creatures, and none more so than this freethinking little colonial!

He rose and walked over to the fire, gripping the mantel. His shoulders tightened and strained. He watched the rippling flames, then leaned against the marble.

From the moment he had first seen Anne with her pale and ethereal nobility, he had assumed he would marry her. Now this little piece of baggage—albeit exquisite baggage—was his wife. Maybe she hadn't been part of the game played against him.

And maybe she had.

It didn't matter.

''I will be damned,'' he declared, starting off with his voice low and somewhat controlled, ''if I am going to be locked into this travesty of a contract and not bed the woman forced on me as a wife!'' He roared out the last, control forgotten, pushing away from the fireplace, and spinning on Rose.

She was sitting up, tense and wired like a horse about to bolt.

He swore savagely again, letting his long coat fall

from his shoulders to the floor, then striding for the bed, wrenching his shirt over his head as he did so.

He had never imagined his wedding night would be like this. Even when Charles had *asked* him to marry Rose. He hadn't actually planned very far ahead, but he'd never thought he'd have to force the woman who had become his wife into bed!

He should have been gentle with her, tender.

But it was already too late. She watched him coming, then leapt up on the opposite side of the bed. "If you force this issue, I swear, I shall see that you pay for it!" she cried to him. And so regally! Really, she should have been born a duchess. She could sound incredibly superior when she chose. That grated, made him forget his best intentions.

"I've already paid, milady. And I'll have the merchandise now, thank you!" he retorted. "You are, after all, a merchant's daughter, are you not!"

She gasped, going pale. He was sorry for his words, but they were spoken.

"Rot in hell!" she returned furiously, then spun and ran.

Where the hell did she think she was going? It didn't matter. She wasn't going to get there.

There was no contest. He was in a rare mood indeed and came after her with a startling speed, lifting her up with a forceful sweep, casting her down quickly and impatiently. She panted, rising halfway as he methodically pulled off his boots and trousers, then walked toward her with absolute purpose. Her eyes met his, fell down the length of his body, then rose again. Her cheeks colored to a soft crimson. She would have bolted again, he knew, if the block of his body had not prevented her from doing so. He heard the grating of her teeth as he crawled atop her again, straddling her hips. She rose against him, a gemstone glitter in her eyes, just a hint of tears. Her hands flew against his naked chest with a wild fury. "DeForte—" she began, but he had no tolerance for this new protest.

He caught both her wrists, pressing her back against the bed. "Lady, lie still!" he commanded her, his tone low but brooking no opposition.

She swallowed hard, her eyes locked with his. She fell against the sheets, still staring at him. He released her wrists, cupped her face in his hands, and kissed her lips. Slowly, evocatively. His kiss trailed from her lips to her cheekbone, to her earlobe. To a pulse that beat at her throat.

A little strangling sound escaped her. She pressed her hands against his naked chest again.

"No," he said quietly, firmly, catching them, pressing them back.

Her eyes met his; she delicately licked her slightly swollen lips. She shivered, and her lashes fell over her eyes.

"Just what do you remember?" he asked her softly then. Her eyes flew open, meeting his. "What do you remember of the night? Treachery, ah, yes, but magic, too. The sweetest magic."

"Magic!" she whispered with a strangled sound. "Perhaps for you—"

"Umm, and for you, my love."

"You flatter yourself!"

"Do I?"

"It was wretched!"

"I'll not hurt you again," he said very softly. And in that particular moment, he did not think that she could have been guilty of anything. Her eyes upon his were huge, liquid. Color flooded over her cheeks again. She had not expected him to remember that there had been moments of intense pain for her.

Maybe she hadn't wanted him to remember.

Her lashes closed again. His fingers fell upon the

strings to the bodice of her elegant gown, pulling upon them. She reached for his hands, clutching them in her own. Their eyes met again. His remained steadfast. "You'll not leave me tonight," he warned her gently.

"Perhaps you'll leave me?" she inquired hopefully.

He shook his head, fighting the smile that tugged at his lips. Her hands remained upon his fingers but with little force. He loosed her bodice until it fell free, but found himself then hindered by the linen and bone structure beneath it.

"Women wear far too many clothes!" he muttered.

"Perhaps you'll find the effort too much—"

"No," he countered, "I will persevere against the inconvenience." He tugged upon another silken tie. He didn't realize quite how fiercely he had done so until she swore out at him in a sudden outcry of fury, flipped over by his force. But the offending garment at least came free in his hands.

But Rose Woodbine also slipped free from him, trying to leap from the bed but tripping upon a pile of her own petticoats. She pitched over upon the floor, and he rolled swiftly from the one side of the bed to the other, looking down at her. She lay there stunned, staring up at the ceiling, panting for breath. Then she noticed his eyes on hers and she gave a little cry, trying to struggle to her feet. She was caught in her own clothing.

Pierce smiled, calmly rising, watching her frustrated struggle as he walked the few steps to her and reached down for her. She still tried to wriggle out of his way, but he caught her hands, drawing her upward.

And she was naked. His heart slammed, his breath seemed to cease. He had not realized until that moment just how exquisite she was. Flawless from head to toe, her flesh was ivory silk, her breasts were full and beautifully formed. She was slim and sensually curved, and all the perfection of her body was enhanced by the wild fall of copper hair that cascaded down her back, framing the pale loveliness of her face.

The pulse at her throat beat furiously. She was still ready to run. If he had released her hands, she would have done so.

"Where would you go that you could run to?" he asked her softly.

She opened her mouth to speak. No answer came.

"There is nowhere for you to go," he said.

And indeed, there was nowhere.

He released her wrists, sweeping her up into his arms. Her heart seemed to thunder and her breasts rose and fell swiftly. Her fingers fell upon his chest, and their light touch seemed to set all the fires of hell free within him. "I will be tender," he promised her in a hoarse whisper, "but I will be with you."

He laid her back upon the bed. Her eyes closed. He touched his lips to her throat, his hand cupping and cradling her breast as he did so. He ran his palm over the nipple, then caught it with his mouth, his tongue rubbing erotically over the peak. She shifted against it, another soft sound escaping her.

He slipped his hand low against the length of her body and began a slow movement upward along her leg, kissing her lips, her throat, her earlobes, all the while. She had ceased to fight. She didn't respond, but she didn't fight . . .

And the fascination within him burgeoned and grew. He brought his lips to her breast once again. Slid his tongue around and over it, savoring the way the dark peak hardened to his touch, the weight of her in his hand. He lay down beside her, drawing her to him, stroking her again and again, his fingers running down the length of her spine, cupping her buttocks, rising over her hips, stroking upward on her legs again. He stroked and brushed her belly, her upper thighs, her belly again, creating an evocative circle, then gently brushed the downy fiery red triangle at the center of the circle, his touch light, then more and more intimate, his palm moving while his fingers discovered the crevice and gained entry. Fire seemed to shoot into his own system as he caressed her there, finding a slick liquid warmth, the response she tried so very hard to deny.

He found her lips while he continued to touch her. They parted to his. Her eyes opened as he lifted his mouth from hers. She shook her head, and tried to twist against him, gainsaying his hand. He smiled, thrusting her thigh back, wedging his leg between hers.

"Uh-unh! Lie still!" he insisted again.

A shaking sigh escaped her. He leaned over, his tongue drawing wet lines against her belly. He met her eyes, then sent his own sweeping down the length of her. She was perfection, her flesh beautifully damp and glistening golden in the firelight.

He met her gaze again. Her breath came swiftly from slightly parted lips. She tried to form words again, shaking her head. "No!" was the best she could manage.

"Lie still, my love!"

He just touched her lips with his own. Then the valley between her breasts. Her navel. Then he lowered himself against her. He touched her intimately with just the very tip of his tongue. Very wet. Very hot. She surged up against him.

"Lie still!" he repeated softly, and then he smiled, for he realized that she could not do so anymore.

He buried himself against her. Felt her rise and twist and cry out. His hands braced against her hips. He felt the wild wave of her trembling. He covered her with the length of his body, riding high above her for one long moment, then sliding with a massive shudder into the seductive sheath of her sex. She seemed to wrap around him exquisitely, willing, tight. He shuddered again and again with the little spasms of pleasure that seized him just to feel the enveloping warmth.

Then the desire leashed within him seemed to explode. He caught hold of her, and began to move. Her eyes flew open. Glazed, they met his. She wet her lips, then tried to look quickly to the side. She was exquisitely beautiful with her emerald eyes and wild fiery hair a tangled mass beneath and about them. He wouldn't let her twist away. He curled his fingers into hers, seized upon her lips, and continued to move against her and within her. He kissed her, rose, kissed her breasts again. She gasped, arching against him, her fingers stretched and taut beneath his. The sound of her voice, the movement beneath him, all enhanced the soaring thrust of his desire. He gritted his teeth and cast back his head, willing himself to slow down until he had taken her with him.

Her fingers curled hard into his, she inhaled, the slick length of her body going taut against his. Warmth, like a molten nectar, seemed to surround him, then send him hurtling toward a climax. It was ecstasy. It burst from him and swept into her. Again, again. Shudders swept him. He thrust deeply and hard, once, again, and again. Small after-tremors seized him. He held himself against her until they had shook their fill through him, and then he fell to her side, amazed at the force of the pleasure that had swept him. The wonder stayed with him as the seconds ticked by.

Perhaps not so for his bride. She drew her legs up, turning away from him in a little ball. Frowning, he raised himself upon an elbow, trying to watch her. "I know I didn't hurt you!" he said irritably.

She shook her head in silence.

"Then what in God's name is the matter with you?" he demanded.

"Life!" she snapped back.

Smiling, bemused by the tenderness he felt toward her now, he rolled her back to meet his gaze. There was just the faintest glistening of tears in her eyes now. He stroked his finger down her cheek. "Life! Indeed, 'tis brutal, is it not?" he inquired softly.

She clenched her teeth tightly, meeting his gaze, her eyes searching his. She swallowed hard, then said primly, "I believe I've served as your wife. Could you possibly release me now? Perhaps you'd even be so kind as to allow me to have my own set of rooms? I believe that's a customary thing among the nobility who reside within the framework of their arranged marriages."

Puzzled, he watched her. He knew that she had reached at least one climax that night, and that she was certainly discovering the extent of her own sexuality. Then he thought that she hated him all the more fiercely because he could make her enjoy their physical relationship—instead of just nobly enduring it.

"You're not going anywhere tonight," he told her. Stretching out on his pillow, he swept his arms around her, pulling her against him. The length of her body fit to his, her back against his chest, derriere to his hips, his chin just above her head, the tangle of her hair teasing his nose. She stiffened, her fingers falling against his hand where it lay casually over her abdomen. They curled tightly for one minute, then she realized that he wasn't going to let her go.

"Does this mean that I may have my own rooms?" she inquired.

"Be nice to me. Humor me. Make me happy. I may give you all sorts of things," he told her.

"Be nice to you! You wanted a mistress, not an unwilling bride! But then, you had a mistress—" she began, then broke off in dismay, feeling the tension that riddled his body. She spoke quickly again. "If you would really be decent enough to do anything for me—"

She could still feel the terrible constriction in him as he interrupted curtly, "Give you your own room?"

She moistened her lips, glad she wasn't seeing his eyes. "No. Find out what happened to Mary Kate for me."

"Will that put an end to things?" he queried.

"Can it?" she whispered.

She tried to move away from him. Furious, he caught her wrist and dragged her back. "Damn you, lie still!" he thundered.

She tossed back her hair, trying to use her free hand to pull the bedcovers about her. "What, my lady?" he demanded through clenched teeth. "You think that there is something that I still haven't seen of you?"

She blushed crimson, trying to wrench free from his hold. "I can't understand why I am obliged to stay here even now!"

"Because I may long for a wife again in the night!" he stated, staring at her. "It is amazing how easily a man can rest when he lies down beside a warm, tender—still!—body. Then that body starts to move and it seems to start his fires burning again.''

At last she was still. Very, very still. She lay down beside him, stiffly.

"If I weren't so worried about Mary Kate," she murmured miserably, "I might be able to sleep—still—beside you. I was told that she was put aboard a ship for home. If that is the truth—"

Pierce sighed. "So the king has told me. I've ships out to discover the truth. With my whole heart, though, I believe that your maid is well. She should soon be with your father in Virginia."

"Can you find out for me?" Rose breathed, forgetting herself as she pushed up to stare at him, relief visible in her beautiful features.

A spasm seemed to touch his heart. She was wayward, far too proud. But she loved her servant dearly, and this, somehow, endeared her to him.

"Yes, I will do so."

She seemed to realized that her bare breasts and torso were very visible to him, the way that she sat. She colored again, lowering her head and quickly sliding down to lie beside him. "Thank you," she murmured awkwardly.

He grinned, staring at the ceiling.

"Was I that good?"

"I beg your pardon?"

He laughed out loud. "Never mind. Go to sleep."

"That good . . ." she murmured. Then she gasped out, "Oh!" In a sudden flurry she swung around, a fist pounding down hard on his chest.

"Damn!" he swore, then grasped her wrists and pulled her against him, his eyes a blaze of silver. "Remember, my love, movement causes this great awakening . . . !"

"I will remember!"

She wrenched free from him, but seemed ready

for no more argument that night. She lay beside him, touching him.

But not moving.

He wrapped an arm around her and pulled her tight against him once more. He closed his eyes. Rest. Dear God, he needed some rest.

But Rose wasn't sleeping. She suddenly cleared her throat and murmured, "If you . . ."

"What?" he snapped.

"If you love Anne . . ."

"If I love Anne, what?" he demanded wearily.

"How can you be here with me?" she whispered.

Indeed, how could he? Since he had met Anne, he had never strayed. Not on journeys with the king. Not at court. Not when his friends jaunted from the theater to a night with the city's finest paramours.

He had thought that he had loved Anne. But in all of his life, he had never known anything as overwhelming as his desire for the copper-haired vixen who had become his wife.

He owed Anne! He would have to ride out to find her, to assure himself as to her welfare. But he could certainly never explain the tempest in his heart to Rose. He'd be the greatest fool on earth to ever let her know the hunger she had created with him, the tenacious hold she already had upon his senses . . .

And his soul.

"Leave me be!" he told her, suddenly fiercely angry.

"But—"

He sat up. "No more! You, milady duchess, are my consolation, so it seems! A balm to ease the pain. And above all else," he told her, his temper rising again, "through no great desire on my part, you have become my wife! You claim your innocence in it all—''

''I am innocent! And wronged! And if you were in any way kind, you'd let me return home to Virginia!''

''Oh, my love!'' he said, his voice deep, trembling with emotion. ''You are not going to Virginia. You are home; I've told you that; accept it. Now, leave it be!''

''It isn't—''

''Keep me up much longer, and I swear to convince you that movement arouses me through the whole of the night!''

She inhaled, as if she was about to speak again. She caught the look in his eyes. Her own burned with fury.

But she fell silent.

A little sound escaped her as his arms wound hard around her.

She exhaled slowly. And at long last, lay still.

All that he could feel was the beating of her heart. If he could only sleep . . . !

But he lay awake, his thoughts revolving.

In the end, he realized that she drifted to sleep long before he did. He breathed the perfume in her hair and held the silky softness of her flesh, and knew that he desired her again.

Her breathing was slow and even. She slept so sweetly. Soft and tender in his arms.

What had she done to him? How had she changed him so completely? Bewitched him?

Maybe the passion would burn itself out. Maybe . . .

He swallowed hard. Jesu, he wanted her again. He eased closer to her. Stroked her hair, touched her cheek. There was a touch of moisture there.

Tears. Proud, defiant Rose! She had silently cried herself to sleep.

He kissed her damp cheek, and held her ever more tenderly.

And tried to deny the fact that he had already fallen just a little bit in love.

Chapter VIII

The sun fell upon Pierce's ancestral estate, Castle DeForte. It was a true castle, in every aspect, built along the Conqueror's trail when he had first come to England, a fortress begun of earth and stone to discourage any Anglo-Saxons lurking in the forests after Hastings. Over the years, the place had been greatly modified. As the threat of attack from outside forces had diminished, windows had been created, and the family had used its wealth toward the comforts of the home. Now rich, elegant tapestries covered the cold stone walls. Persian carpets and woolen rugs lay about the floors. Oak and mahogany furnishings were amply upholstered, and stained glass added color and elegance to many of the windows.

DeFortes had survived much through the generations. Through the bloody reigns of the last Plantagenets to the Tudors and into the Stuart days, DeFortes had managed to keep their hold upon most of their possessions. Even when Cromwell had become Lord Protector, even when Pierce's own father had gone to the scaffold for his support of Charles I, the DeForte lands had been left alone. The people themselves would have revolted if Pierce's kind and elegant mother had been ousted from her home, and Cromwell had—with the innate wisdom that had brought a commoner to the rule of all England—chosen to look the other way, and let the Lady DeForte alone. She had quietly maintained the estate, writing Pierce constantly of affairs in England.

He hadn't even known that she was ill until he had returned home in triumph with the king. It was as if she had merely waited for him all those years. She had greeted him in the entryway in the great hall, and then she had fallen into his arms. Fevered, she had talked the night away, stroking his face, telling him that God had let her see him again, and that she could die easy, assuring his father that all was well.

He had the king's finest physicians at his beck and call. But no one had been able to save her, and he had held her in his arms, rocking her, as she had drawn her last breath.

Perhaps that was why he and the king had always been so close. They had both felt the bitterness and pain of losing loved ones in times of great trial. Charles was aware of what the DeFortes had suffered for him. That was perhaps why he was such a friend.

Friend indeed! The king had forced him to marry, Pierce thought.

And he had now spent several days of matrimonial bliss, and if anything, his emotions were even more in a tempest than they had been.

He stared out one of the windows in his counting house, a place that was uniquely his, much more than his immense bedroom suite, for here he kept his books, ledgers, and logs on all the ventures he now engaged in, including his tenant lands, farm stock, and ships. He did business here, and he escaped here. His desk was huge and of oak, solid and sturdy. When he was weary he could cast his feet upon it, stretch back in his chair, and close his eyes. The drawers contained all manner of writing utensils, and a fine selection of liquors acquired from all over the world. Against the wall was a yellow brocade daybed, a gift from the Prince of Orange, Charles's brother-in-law. Some of the paintings on the walls were Van Dykes, gifts to his father from the king's father.

He gazed over this realm that he loved so much, then turned back to the man speaking before him. He was a tall fellow, nearly as big as Pierce himself, with steady brown eyes and a cap of hair to match. His name was Geoffrey Daraunte. He had been born in Bruges, and become a mercenary in many an army. Once, in a skirmish, Pierce had slain the fellow about to slice through Geoffrey's throat. Since then, Geoffrey had been his man.

Pierce had brought him to England because he was intelligent and strong, a good man to have at his back, and one in need of honest employ. He was tenacious and determined, and merciful, all excellent qualifications for a right-hand man.

"The captain of the *Lady Fair*, heading westward, did catch up with the *Yancy* out of London. She reported that there was indeed a woman on board who was a servant to your wife. The seas were rough, so it seemed most prudent not to attempt to retrieve the woman, especially since she will be taken to her home in Virginia. I waited at the docks and just received this information, and of course, my lord, rushed here immediately."

"That's good news," Pierce said.

"Jamison Bryant is really just a fool in all this," he added softly, only a touch of bitterness to his voice. He could speak freely. Geoffrey knew the circle of nobles in which Pierce moved well enough to understand what his master was saying. "But then there is Jerome! I always tried to tolerate him for Anne's sake! I just pray—"

He broke off.

"The serving woman hadn't been hurt," Geoffrey assured him. "Surely the man would not harm his own sister."

Pierce was not so certain. They'd all been such idiots! Once Anne had married Jamison, he gained control of her lands. And now that control would be shared with her brother. Jerome had always been thirsty for power and money.

Jamison had been thirsty for Anne.

It was all a dull ache within him now.

"You've found out nothing more on that matter?" Pierce asked.

Geoffrey shook his head. "I believe, milord, you discovered the best lead the other day when you came upon that small tavern just south of here where the innkeeper mentioned the rider who had demanded food in such haste. It seems that they have traveled somewhere closer to the Channel."

"But where?" Pierce mused softly.

He clenched his fingers into fists at his back as he walked over to stare out the mullioned window to gentle hills that stretched behind it. His home was beautiful. An hour's ride from London, another few hard hours' ride to the English Channel. The landscape was low, but rolling endlessly in a beautiful array of colors, rich emerald fields, purple dottings of heather, yellow sheaves of wheat.

To his absolute amazement, he suddenly realized that the field before him was not empty. A rider, clad in a hooded cape, was starting the climb up the slope that led into the forest.

He couldn't quite pinpoint why the rider appeared so furtive. Perhaps because it seemed that the horse pranced, and paused, allowing the rider a quick look back. Maybe it was the hooded cloak the rider wore. Rider. Damn!

It was his wife, he thought, amazed, amused—and furious. He turned to Geoffrey. "Excuse me, will you. I will return directly."

He hurried out of his office, and out the great entry to the castle. He ran down the stone steps and across the courtyard to the stables, nodding grimly to the groom who rushed up to assist him. "I shall manage on my own, lad," he said, quickly sweeping Beowulf's bridle from a peg on the stall. "Tell me, did the duchess come for a mount?"

"Aye, milord. She said she wanted to see the estate."

The estate indeed! She wanted to see a ship bound for the colonies, he was certain.

"Milord!" the young groom said anxiously. "I beg your pardon if I've done anything foolish—"

"Nay, lad. You've done something foolish." I underestimated her! he charged himself. He didn't bother with Beowulf's saddle. When the horse was bridled, he leapt atop it. Beowulf seemed to know his mood. The horse pranced and thundered from the stable.

She was well ahead of him. His advantage was that he knew the terrain like the back of his hand. And she did not know that he was in pursuit.

Within minutes he had crossed the fields and come to the forest. He slowed his wild gait before a slender trail leading through the trees. Numerous branches were broken off. It was the way that she had come.

He nudged Beowulf to a canter again. The woods were canopied with green, and here the day was darkened and cooled. He rode swiftly until he saw her before him at last. She had paused at a break in the trees, trying to gauge her direction.

Then she heard the snap of a twig beneath Beowulf's great hoof and seemed to panic, nudging her horse hard. She didn't even look back; she couldn't have known that it was him. She began a wild race through the trees.

"Headstrong little idiot!" he muttered aloud, following hard. Thanks to Beowulf's great power and speed, he was abreast of her in seconds.

"You're going to kill yourself!" he roared to her. She glanced his way at last. Her eyes widened. Her horse was panicked, too, and heading straight for a cove of trees. She might be the best horsewoman in all the world, but he didn't think she could possibly have the strength to rein in the terrified creature before she reached those trees.

"Dammit!" he swore, reaching out. She screamed when his arms wound around her, sweeping her from her runaway horse to his own. The mare she rode thrashed on through the trees. Beowulf dutifully pranced to a stop. They would have been fine.

Except that Rose·was wildly fighting his hold, something he hadn't expected, and hadn't prepared for. Together they toppled from the great war-horse. Fuming, swearing, and falling, he still tried to catch her weight atop his own. He managed to do so and they came to rest with him supine upon his back and Rose stretched out atop him.

"What on earth are you doing?" she gasped.

He stared at her incredulously. "Trying to save your life!"

"If you hadn't chased after me—"

"If you hadn't tried to sneak away—"

"I just came out for a ride!" she cried.

But it was a lie. He arched a brow, staring at her, watching her cheeks redden since they both knew that it was a lie.

His lip curled and his voice was light, if challenging. "Just where were you going?" he asked her.

She tried to push away from him. His fingers were laced around her waist, holding her tight.

"To see the sights."

He started to move her. He wasn't at all sure that some part of his body wasn't broken. The whole of it hurt, although he had no intention of letting Rose know that. She'd be calling him ancient again if he wasn't careful.

As he lifted her above him, he heard a jangling. It seemed to come from her side. She took advantage of his assistance, though, and leapt up, instinctively backing away from him. He stood quickly, following her. "My dearest love, what could that sound be?"

"Nothing!"

But he reached her, pulling her into his arms and flipping away the cape. She was dressed in simple cotton, and the jingling had come from her pocket. He reached out and discovered that she was carrying a small pouch in her skirt. She struggled for a second to keep it, then, knowing he would defeat her, surrender the pouch and backed away swiftly.

He jingled it by his ear, smiling at her. "Why, how amazing! This has the sound of a good sum of coins!"

She colored slightly but kept her chin high, her eyes steady upon him.

"It's my money."

"Maybe. Maybe not."

"I'm a wealthy woman—"

"Maybe. Maybe not. I am owed quite a dowry for you. But that is not the point, my love. Just where were you going? To London perhaps? To board the first ship leaving for the New World?"

Her coloring betrayed the truth of the matter. He lowered his head for a moment, fighting the wave of fury—and of fear—that had seized him. Perhaps it was not a match made in heaven, but she was his wife. And in a few days time, she had managed to weave a web of silken enchantment around him. He would never let her go. And when he thought of the dangers she might have encountered in London, unchaperoned, with her face and figure—and a pocket of gold to boot—he felt ill.

"Lady, I should beat you black and blue! Lock you in the highest tower!"

She might have trembled slightly, but she didn't back away. "Why is that, milord?" she demanded icily. "You are free to ride where you will! Perhaps I only wished to take a ride."

"With a pocketful of gold coins?"

She lifted a hand in the air. "They were for the poor. Again you have wronged me!" she cried, a consummate actress. "You dragged me ruthlessly from my horse and now accuse me of all evil—"

"I saved your life!" he snapped.

"You simply cannot accept the fact that I am the better rider!"

"And I'll also not accept the fact that these coins were for the poor!"

"How dare you! I have a very generous nature—"

"Really?" A touch of amusement tinged his voice. Smiling, he stepped forward, catching her elbow. "Come, then."

"Come where?"

"With me, upon Beowulf."

"And where are we going?" she demanded, her beautiful eyes wide—and very wary.

He lifted her easily upon his horse, leaping up behind her. His arms came around her as he picked up the reins.

"I've my own mount. The mare is frightened—"

"Is she? Poor thing. I imagine she'll trot on home."

"While we . . . ?" Rose queried.

"Why, my love, I'm going to help you. We'll give your coins to the poor!"

"But—" she began, and fell silent in frustration. Behind her, he smiled. He suspected the pouch held all the gold that she had with her. Oh, she was rich as Midas. But once those coins were gone, she would be hard put to prove it to any ship's captain.

He made his way quickly through the woods to a small farm village. A tiny wooden church stood in the center of it. Cows, chickens, and goats all moved about small peat fires that filled the air with their rancid smoke. Men and women, so quickly aged, looked after dirty young children while they worked.

From their midst a very young priest all in black except for his collar came walking toward them. "Milord DeForte!" he called in cheerful greeting. "We are honored! What brings you among us?"

"Father Flagherty, I'd have you meet my wife, Lady Rose," Pierce said, not dismounting. He smiled. "She has brought a gift for these good people." He tossed down the bag of gold coins.

Rose watched the pouch fall with dismay. They were the only coins she had. Father Flagherty opened the pouch. His dark eyes widened in amazement. He looked back to her with a gratitude in his eyes that shamed her. She'd lost the coins. But when she looked at the people and all the little children, she realized she had lost them to a good cause.

Pierce had seen to it.

But he had done this only to thwart her!

"Milady!" Flagherty said, his voice trembling. "What kindness, what goodness, that you have the duke grant us this great boon—"

"The gift is hers, Father," Pierce said.

The man's eyes fell on her again. "Thank you, thank you, oh, Lady, the good God bless you—"

"Please!" Rose gasped, wanting to crawl beneath the horse. "Father, you and these good people are heartily welcome to the coins!"

"Come, then, milord, milady, break bread with us—"

"We cannot, Father, as I've business I must return to. Keep well." With that he turned Beowulf, nudged the horse, and they started toward the castle at a trot.

Rose was dead stiff.

"Aren't you pleased, my love?" Pierce asked her tauntingly.

She tried to sit forward so that she wouldn't feel the muscled strength of his chest at her back. *Pleased!* She might have been pleased. She might have cried out that she lay awake at night in tempest and anguish because she found herself so absurdly *pleased* at times.

But she could never explain everything in her heart. The days here were too painful.

He slept with her every night.

And every day he disappeared throughout the sunlight hours.

Looking for Anne, she knew. And though she wished Anne all the very best in the world, she couldn't bear the way she was beginning to *wait*—no, *long*, for the nights, when he returned to her.

A consolation prize! He had said it himself. His heart lay with Anne.

"The coins have gone to those who need them," she responded.

"But truly, milady, that was not your intent, was it?"

"My intent was to ride. And I cannot begin to see why I am not allowed to do so when you spend all of your days . . ."

"When I spend all of my days doing what?" he queried sharply.

"Looking for another woman," she cried out. Then she waited for the explosion of his temper. It didn't come.

They returned to the castle. He rode straight to the stables. The young groom came hurrying out. "Milord, milady's mare came back! We were heartily frightened—"

"Ah, but my lady is well!" Pierce assured him. "She is not very familiar with the area, though," he said lightly enough, but he followed it with, *"and she will not be taking any horses out again for the time being unless she is in my company!"*

Rose stared at him, inhaling sharply. Then she turned and ran for the entrance to the main tower.

"Rose!"

She didn't answer him.

"Rose!"

She reached the doors. He caught up with her at last, just within the entrance.

"Damn you—"

"Am I truly a prisoner here then?" she demanded. His jaw locked. "Am I? Oh, you're hateful!"

She didn't give him a chance to answer. A whirlwind of fury with more tempest than a winter's storm, she hurtled herself against him, a small fist catching his chin and his chest. He itched to slap her, but maintained his temper, both because he could see that Geoffrey, Garth, and other servants were coming into the hall, drawn by the noise, and because the gleam of tears in her eyes somehow caught his heart.

"Damn you, Rose!" he hissed furiously, catching her wrists. "I have looked for Anne, yes! But I also spent time in London sending out captains to ascertain the fate of your maid! I have the answer now. Your Mary Kate is safe, and bound for your father's house!"

She gasped softly, pulling away from him. Her cheeks pinkened just slightly when she realized that Geoffrey at least, and maybe some of the others, had heard them.

Geoffrey was quick to assure her, too. "It is true, milady."

Leaning against the stone wall, Pierce crossed his arms over his chest, staring at his bride.

Garth cleared his throat. "If I'm not needed—?"

"Thank you, Garth. You're not," Pierce told him, his eyes on Rose. His body tightened into knots. They had been here nearly a week now.

Every day he had gone through the motions of tending to his estate and business.

And he had ridden out each day.

But he had spent his nights with her. Each had been different. Twice she had tried to argue with him. Twice she had feigned sleep. Twice she had tried to lie dead still with absolute indifference. Now, tonight stretched before them.

Yet no matter what her manner when he at last came to his bedroom, he always wanted her. No anguish for another could stop the longing that seized him when he thought of her. He had planned the first few days to take her again and again, until the fascination died. But it never did. It refused to fade. Each night it only seemed that the hunger intensified.

Now, as she watched him, her lashes fluttered over her eyes. She lowered her head, then met his gaze again. "You really spent some of that time sending messages out with your ships, searching for Mary Kate?" she asked softly.

"Indeed, madam," he said. He lowered his voice carefully then. "Whatever your thoughts, milady, and whatever your heart, you are my wife. What causes you anguish, I will always do my best to change—even if you do spend your days seeking new ways to deny me my nights!"

She paled. "For Mary Kate, I am grateful," she murmured. "Thank you, milord DeForte!" she cried softly, then tore past him, and up the stairs.

He watched her go, then realized that he wasn't really alone. Garth was hovering within the archway that led down a path to the kitchen, which had once been a separate building.

"I think I will dine now, Garth. In the counting room."

"If I may be so bold, milord," Garth said, clearing his throat, "you might to try dining above the stairs, at the cherrywood table at the foot of your bed. That is where the duchess dines."

Pierce ignored Garth's reproachful tone. Damn them. The whole lot of them. The fools were all falling halfway in love with his wife themselves.

"I'll dine in the counting room," Pierce repeated.

"As you wish, milord," Garth said with exaggerated patience.

He left. Now Geoffrey was staring at him. Pierce threw up his hands. "What?"

Geoffrey bowed to him. "I can see you are in no mood to continue with business, milord. I will keep you informed of any information I receive."

He bowed deeply, and walked out the entryway.

Pierce swore softly. He entered his counting room

and immediately swept up a bottle of his best Caribbean rum.

He barely touched the rich mutton stew Garth brought him, but he did manage to set down the bottle of rum before drinking too much from it. The hour grew late. After a while he rose and went into the great hall, staring up at the broad, curving stairway.

He started up the steps, wondering what it would be tonight. Ah, yes, it was late! She would pretend to be asleep. She would curl when he tried to touch her. Then she would sigh, and grit her teeth.

But in the end, he would take his silent triumph, for no matter how she tried to fight, he knew the signs. He heard the gasps of breath, felt the sweet surging of her body. Rose Woodbine might be trying to fight him and herself, but she was innately sensual and exquisite, and could not deny either of them, no matter how she pretended.

Still, he was weary of the games. He entered the antechamber, closed the heavy old door behind him, and strode through the dark to the bedroom. There was more light there, for a fire burned low within the hearth. The master quarters were huge. His great draperied bed was centered against the back wall. To the right of it, two huge armchairs sat before the hearth, book racks surrounding them.

He strode quietly to the bed, stripping off his long coat as he did so, folding it over a high-backed chair near the door. He sat upon the foot of his bed and pulled off his boots and hose, then stood, puzzled.

She wasn't in bed.

He spun around, wondering furiously if she had been foolish enough to try to escape again.

But just as the thought occurred to him, his heart ceased its frantic beat and his temper came crashing back down. He saw her. She was curled in one of the chairs before the fireplace, wrapped in a long, deep blue velvet robe. Her shimmering copper head hung over the arm of the chair. A book she had been reading had dropped to the floor.

Incredibly, she had been trying to wait up for him. And for once, she wasn't feigning sleep.

He walked over to her, kneeling down beside her. "Rose." He smoothed back the wild fall of her hair. "Rose, you cannot sleep so. You'll awaken with all manner of pains in your back." She stirred slightly. He rose, scooping his arms around her to lift her.

He discovered that she wore nothing at all beneath the deep blue velvet robe. She had bathed and washed her hair, and both her tumbling copper curls and flesh smelled faintly of flowers.

His weariness fell from him like a doffed coat. It was almost as if she had planned to seduce him.

Her eyes flickered open as he held her. They widened with alarm for a moment, then, startling him, they seemed to fall again with a comfort and security. Her arms curled around his neck.

"What is it?" he asked her.

"I don't . . ."

"You waited up," he told her, carrying her to the draped expanse of his bed. Her eyes stayed on his, very wide, as he laid her down.

Yet as he moved away to shed his trousers, she came up on her knees, then slipped from the bed. He turned to her, dropping his last piece of clothing, curious and surprised. If anything, he had been expecting an exceptional freeze from her this evening, after their encounter in the woods.

But she didn't speak. She moved quickly to him. The blue velvet robe hung loose, and when she reached him, twining her arms around his neck, the rise of her breasts against his chest teased, then the full length of her body pressed erotically to his. She kissed the flesh of his chest. She rose on her toes, and her kiss fell against his throat as the taut brush of her nipples raked against him.

Sweet Jesus.

He didn't move. He didn't dare move. She reached up even higher, her eyes just touching his, then her lips forming lightly against his mouth, withdrawing, then the tip of her tongue encircling them.

He swept her into his arms, kissing her deeply, pulling her tightly against him. Letting her feel the hardening rise of his desire against the mound of her sex. The ache to possess her surged through him. He fought it. Fought the urge to sweep her up. He had to see where she planned to go next.

Down his throat. Kissing him. Lightly. That erotic flicker of her tongue. She was experimenting as she went, he knew. Tentative at first, then growing more secure. Her fingers roamed over his chest, fell lower. She followed with the liquid dance of her tongue. She stroked his sides with her knuckles. He waited, catching his breath, all of his being seeming to concentrate in a wealth of desire that pulsed against her.

He slipped his hands upon her shoulders, forcing the robe to fall to the floor. He lightly ran his fingers down the length of her spine, up again, down again. He began to hear the rush of her breath, feel its heat against him. Her head bent low. The softness of her hair rubbed against his chest, his hips, fell teasingly over the fullness of his erection. He groaned aloud, tensing. Ready to whisper that she was a temptress. To sweep her up into his arms, and down upon the bed. But she moved then. Laving him with the heat of her tongue. Going down slowly before him. Touching him, her fingers light and hesitant, brushing against him, curling more tightly. She buried her face against the fur of his belly, then he gasped out

an amazed oath, for he felt the incredibly erotic
flicker of her tongue against him. In seconds, a searing climax exploded throughout him. He swore
again, near savage when he swept her up and into
his arms, staring at her incredulously. She cried out
at the dark tension restricting his features. ''I meant
to please you!'' she whispered. Her emerald eyes
were wild, her body was a golden flame in his arms.

She had given him so much. It didn't matter. He
wanted more. The very feel of her in his arms
brought a sweet aching need to strengthen him
again. Even as he laid her down, he wanted to be
inside her. To drown in her. To be enveloped by
her. His body followed hers. Melded within it. He
closed his eyes and felt a fierce rigidity come pounding into him, and he forced himself to move slowly,
to watch her eyes, to feel her body, and listen to its
rhythms. He held himself above her, watching her
lips, how the breath came and went within them,
how she moistened them. He watched her eyes.
How they opened to his, how she closed them
quickly. And he watched how their bodies met, the
subtle arch of her hips, the thrust of his sex sinking
into her. She began to toss her head, breathing
quickly. Her body suddenly arched violently against
his. A cry escaped her, a gasp, a soft sob.

He cradled her in his arms, finding his own release, gentler than that first, startling explosion, exquisite nonetheless.

He listened to their breathing, loud and harsh in
the silence of the night, fading to normal at last.

He leapt from the bed, striding for the fire, light-
ing a candle to set beside the bed. Uneasily she
reached for her blue velvet robe, sweeping it quickly
around her. Her eyes met his. She bit her lower lip,
quickly looking downward.

Then she cried out, startled when he swept her

up and carried her to the huge chair before the fire.
He sat with her there upon his lap, raising her chin
to his.

"Forgive me. I can't help but being incredibly curious. You wanted my throat earlier. Yet tonight was
near a paradise. Jesu, lady! What warranted that?"

She lowered her lashes. He eased his touch from
her chin and she stared at the fire.

"Your search for Mary Kate. Especially after—this
afternoon," she said very quietly.

"Ah, I should have known," he murmured.

"I didn't mean to make you angry!" she said
quickly, and her gaze found his again.

He exhaled slowly, thinking of how very young
this unwilling bride of his was. And just how exquisite with her emerald eyes, shimmering copper
hair, and temptress curves. If it weren't for the extraordinary guilt. If it weren't for the pain . . .

Yet perhaps there was some kind of a future. For
both of them.

"That was a thank you? Milady, I will have to do
my best to see that you are eternally grateful to me!"

She flushed, her lashes lowering again. "You
don't understand—"

He pressed a finger against her lips. "I do understand."

"Mary Kate is very dear to me. She has been with
me for years." She looked to the fire again. "My
father would be delighted, of course, to give you a
ship for assuring me of her safe return, but I understand that you already have several."

He laughed, gazing into her eyes, and wondering
if she teased him or if she was serious.

"Well, milady, I'm sorry to disappoint you, but I
believe you already owe me a ship or two, and a
great deal of money. I never did heard the exact
specifications, but I understand you were to have an

extraordinary dowry if I married you. But,'' he said politely, ''the thought was there, and I do appreciate it.''

She pushed against him, struggling to rise, soft color swirling to her cheeks. He tightened his arms around her, whispering huskily. ''Ships are fine. But this other thank you gift you decided to give me . . .''

''Don't mock me, please!'' she murmured. ''I just wanted you to know that I was grateful.''

''And I found your gratitude completely enchanting.'' He gently stroked her cheek. Her features were so very perfect, her skin so soft and smooth. ''Tell me,'' he demanded. ''Is life with me so very, very horrid?''

''I . . .''

''The truth, Rose.''

She would not meet his eyes. She shrugged. ''Well, I—I've yet to slit my wrists,'' she murmured, dark lashes falling over the flashing emerald of her eyes.

''My!'' he exclaimed. ''What an incredible declaration of emotion, my lady!'' he teased.

He could well imagine that she blushed, but now her head lay against his chest, and the fire of her hair hid her expression.

He rose, sweeping her off her feet, carrying her along with him to the sweet encompassing softness of the bed.

This time, he made love to her. Tenderly. Completely. Leisurely. Stroking and arousing her. Wanting her hunger to reach unbearable heights, and her ecstasy to reach the same. He wanted to love her unselfishly. Undemandingly . . .

But even in that, he realized, the enchantment enwrapped him again. She awoke the wildest demons within his own soul. And there were things that he wanted from her, things he demanded.

"Whisper my name!" he urged her. "Whisper my name!"

She did so.

"Pierce . . ."

She arched and writhed. Whispered it again. And finally, "Please . . . oh, please!"

His fingers laced with hers and he glided into her, held her hard and firm beneath him. Moments later, her fingers were still curled tightly in his as she reached a volatile climax. He covered the cries of it with the tender fever of his kiss.

He slept well that night, entangled in the fire of her hair, in the silk of her limbs.

Slept, captured forever by the emerald of her eyes.

Chapter IX

"I think that this is the most perfect place in all the world," Pierce told her. He was leaning against a giant oak with branches that dipped over a narrow, bubbling stream, idly watching the water as it danced on its way. The grass on either side of it was beautifully thick and rich and green, the water itself light blue and white where it skipped over the rocks. The foliage around them was encompassing, and though Castle DeForte was just over the rise behind them, it felt as if they were in a strange cool Eden. Gentle rays of the sun fell through the cover of foliage and trees. The light itself appeared to be green and gold in magical shafts. It was a beautiful place.

Rose, seated on the coat he had thrown down for her on the soft velvet grass just beyond the water, hugged her knees to her chest and looked out over the water smiling. She didn't think that she'd ever felt quite so restful, so peaceful or happy.

She set her chin down upon her arms and watched him and felt the warming swell of her heart.

Don't love Pierce DeForte! she warned herself, but

the warning came too late, just as it had been too late the very first time she had silently given in to him.

He was too easy to care for. Arrogant, confident, commanding as he could be, she simply found herself too quickly beneath his spell.

Beneath the spell of a man who wanted her, but loved another woman.

She didn't want to care for her husband, but she did. She definitely didn't want to love him. There would be nothing but pain for her in loving him; that much seemed obvious.

But it also seemed that something infinitely tender had entered into their relationship now. She was convinced that, at the very least, he no longer thought that she had been any part of the conspiracy.

And she wished desperately that she could close her eyes and pretend that the past had never been. Because the present was as sweet and glorious as the cool, clean air that drifted from the water gently swirling by them.

How odd. In so very many things, he was the wiser of the two of them. He was older, far more powerful, stalwart, and incredibly strong, the warrior who had stood by his king in good times and bad.

But he didn't understand. Yes, she still held back. Not the way that she had longed to hold back. For all his greater wisdom in the ways of the world, he just didn't realize that she could never forget that he was really in love with another woman.

The time would come when he found where Jamison had taken Anne. What then? What of the passion and the love she had discovered, even in the midst of their argument? She admitted now that she had been drawn to him from the very beginning, when he had pulled her into the water. Drawn by his eyes. Drawn by the heat and tempest in his hands when he touched her. Drawn by the way that he loved her, so passionately, with no quarter given, with complete demand . . .

And with such startling tenderness.

And since that night when she had awaited him, things had changed. Several days had passed now, but each morning when the dawn broke, he was still with her, stroking her shoulder, her back. Whispering softly. Sometimes ardently. Awakening her.

He sent messages that he would dine with her. He told her when he was going into London for business, and when he would return.

Last night he had spent the night away. But when he had returned in midmorning, he had sent Garth looking for her immediately, asking her if she would be so good as to ride with him.

And he had brought her to this beautiful embankment. He had lifted her down from her mare with tender eyes, touched her lips when she had slid against him.

He had doffed his long coat, and set her on the grass, and now stood by the tree, looking out over the water. Clearly he loved this place. Seeing him here, she felt as if he had opened a bit of his soul to her, and she shivered suddenly, afraid.

"It is the most beautiful place in all the world," he said softly. "When I wandered with Charles, wondering if I would ever come home again, I didn't really miss the castle. I missed this place."

Rose could well understand his feelings. But she smiled dreamily, feeling a tug at her own heart. "Oh, it's beautiful!" she agreed. "Very, very beautiful. But it's not the most beautiful place in the world."

"Oh?" His eyes focused on her with their silver

sizzle. His lip curled at one corner into an amused, sensual smile. "Where, pray tell, my well-traveled lady, might the most beautiful place in all the world be?"

"In the Virginia colony," she said softly.

"A great planter's house. Your father's home?" he inquired.

She shook her head. "It's a place very much like this. My father's house sits on the river, so that his ships may come to dock. But inland from the house is a stream. It runs over flat land, not gently rolling like this, but truly, you cannot imagine the color of it! Nothing on earth is so green, or so very rich. Except in fall, and then you have never seen such shades of gold, deeper than any fire. Red like blood. Oranges, crimsons—it is extraordinary. And the water rushes by cool and incredibly sweet to drink. I know what most Englishmen think of the colonies. That they're wild and savage and barbarian. But it's not like that at all anymore."

He came and sat down beside her, plucking a blade of grass from the ground, idly chewing it. His silver gaze touched her. "What is it like?"

She arched a brow to him. "My home?" He nodded. She shrugged her shoulders. Having had so much to say a moment ago, she was suddenly hesitant. "Well, the main house is really wonderful. Years ago, not long after the first settlement at Jamestown, there was an awful uprising by the Pamunkey Indians under Powhatan. So many settlers were massacred! But after that, the colonists came very strongly against the Indians. They forced them back inland." She hesitated. "Actually, we stole their land," she murmured. "In a way, though, many of them are still with us." She smiled at him. "And many of our people with Indian blood have very blond hair—intermarriage does not take long in a lonely wilderness.''

"Tell me more. Tell me about this great paradise that is so wonderful, you were willing to risk life and limb to escape me and reach it.''

"Pierce, I . . .''

"Never mind. Tell me,'' he laughed.

"There is not so awfully much to tell,'' she said, but smiled. "What we have is called a 'hundred' for a hundred acres, but it's far more than that. Father wound up getting grants and titles to thousands of acres. And he meant to become very rich right from the start, so he hired on dozens of indentured servants, and he enticed them with promises of land to give away. So now, on his 'hundred,' there are hundreds and hundreds of people. He rules like a little king, although he really has no title at all, except that he was very excited the last time I spoke with him because he was expecting to be knighted for his services to the king. That would make him Sir Ashcroft Woodbine. I haven't heard, of course, whether the king has decided to do so or not, but Father would be very pleased. I don't think that it would matter very much in Virginia anyway—the people all call him 'm'lord,' and they scurry about when he is near! He's managed to acquire vast fields of cotton, sugar, and tobacco. He's quite kindly for a tyrant. And he believes in absolute religious freedom, unlike the Puritans in the Massachusetts colony.'' She sighed. "Not that Father is really such a theologian. Actually, he doesn't want to be bothered by such things as religion, and so he tolerates absolutely anything, although the high-standing members of the community do worship at the Anglican church. Father really could be a king, except, of course,'' she added hastily, "that he is such a fierce loyalist!''

She paused, feeling as if she had talked too long

about herself. And given away too much. But he had leaned back upon an elbow, still chewing upon his emerald blade of grass, and still watching her with a silver glitter of amusement about his eyes.

"I can imagine this place you describe. He rules like a king, which must make you a princess. So I can easily see why you were not overawed by marriage to a simple duke!"

"M'lord DeForte, it is just that I lived mainly among simple men. And I found many of them to be uncommonly brave, kind, and considerate of their fellow man. That, in itself, is nobility, I believe!"

"Bravo! Spoken like a true princess," he teased her. "But tell me, do you really believe that Virginia is more beautiful than the stream I offer you here?"

"It would be difficult to choose," she answered him politely.

He looked out across the bubbling water. "I think I agree," he told her.

"You agree! You've seen Virginia?"

He nodded, a smile curling into his lip. "I do own numerous ships, you know."

"And you've sailed on them?"

"Up and down the American coastline. Down to the islands. But I do like Virginia. I agree. What I've seen is exceptionally lovely."

"Oh!" she cried recklessly, knocking his elbow from beneath him with a swift tug of her hand. Unbalanced, he fell flat, and rose swiftly with surprise as she started to leap to her feet. "You've let me run on and on, making a fool of myself!"

"Whoa, milady!" he commanded her, sitting up then, pulling upon her skirt so that she swirled back, falling down hard into his lap. "There was no attempt on my part to make a fool of you! I was curious about your life, that is all. All I knew was that my bride was the most hardheaded, independent creature I'd ever come across. I never stopped to realize how very homesick you must be at times, or that you might miss your father. I remember missing my own terribly after he—after he died. Are you homesick?"

"A bit," she murmured uneasily, caught within his arms on his lap.

His knuckles grazed over her face very softly. "Perhaps my brook is not more beautiful. Perhaps things in the colonies are different—and better. In all of my life, I don't think I ever saw a woman as beautiful as you are, Rose. Green fire in your eyes, copper in your hair. Your cheeks are the most delicate marble, your skin so perfect. And there remains this fantastic innocence about you. Can it be real?"

The breeze rustled around them. The trees shifted and bent. He kissed her lips, easing her back to lie upon his coat on the soft earth. His fingers fell upon the strings to her bodice and he untied them, watching her face. "You once threatened that I would pay for all that I've done to you. Do you still feel so determined?" he asked her.

She kept her eyes locked with his. "You accused me of treachery and tremendous malice," she reminded him.

"Why did you marry me?" he asked her.

"You forced me to!" she cried. "Why did you marry me?"

"I think because I was furious," he told her huskily. "Because I didn't know . . . Why did you marry me?"

"Because the king stepped on my foot," she replied honestly. He laughed.

His hand slipped inside her bodice, his fingers closing over her breast. She closed her eyes, swallowing against the onslaught of sensations. " 'Tis broad daylight," she reminded him.

"Ah, but this is my own little realm!" he assured her. "No one would dare disturb me here. Well, I imagine that you would, but since you are with me . . ." His voice trailed away. His lips touched hers.

But then he was watching her again. "Why did you finally agree to marry me—other than the fact that the king stepped on your foot?"

He was making it very difficult to answer any question. She tried to lie very still, to ignore the warmth that flared through her body. The center of his palm moved erotically over her nipple. She tried to remind herself that she was in the open air before a brook, but the breeze against her cheek only fanned the fire deep within her. He kept touching her.

She kept her eyes closed. She moistened her lips to speak. "There is no other reason. You were determined. The king was determined. I don't think I ever did agree. You all managed that wedding without me."

He laughed. "Not a bad night's work!"

Her eyes opened upon his. "I had no part in the plan, Pierce. I was innocent and wronged, I swear it."

Innocent. She had to be innocent, he thought. No angel had ever appeared more innocent. With her hair spread out upon the grass, her rich lashes fallen over her eyes, her lips so barely parted, she scarce seemed to breathe. Her face was alabaster. Her breasts, spilling from her brocade bodice, were a glimpse of heaven, he was certain. He felt sometimes as if he were falling under an exotic spell when he was with her. As if a mist of enchantment surrounded her. It was so easy to forget the violence and the fury, the things she had said to him, the threats she had made . . .

And the way that she held back. Laughing and tender one minute, pulling away the next. He couldn't help but wonder what went on in her mind. Where her thoughts led. What secrets lurked in the beckoning emerald depths of her eyes.

He pressed his lips lightly to hers. Her eyes remained closed. "I think you said once that I should hang. That I should be put to the rack."

"No," she murmured. "Drawn and quartered."

He smiled. She smelled like roses. The scent mingled with that of the richness of the grass. He shifted his position, slipping a hand beneath the hem of her skirt.

Her eyes flew open. Wide, startled . . . innocent.

"Pierce! We cannot possibly . . ." She hesitated, her cheeks coloring. For all the things that they had done together, the words were still difficult for her. "We cannot make love here!"

"But we can," he assured her.

She tried to push up, looking around. He cupped her jaw, and caught her lips, pressing her back to the earth. A murmur of protest was swallowed into her throat. He kept his lips on hers, his hand beneath her skirt, teasing the flesh above her garters, stroking her thighs. Finding the soft, downy curls of her mound, slowly stroking down the crevice between it. Rhythmically, seductively, he entered her with his fingers. Touched softly, touched deeply. Found the exquisite little petal of her deepest sensation, and stroked and teased and caressed.

"Jesu!" she whispered against his lips. Her vulnerability was incredibly sweet and intoxicating. He barely shifted the extraordinary pile of her skirts and hastily untied his trousers. He impaled her very slowly, determined that she would open her eyes and meet his. She did so, her lashes falling again quickly, her arms reaching up to wind trustingly around his neck.

He could hear the bubbling of the brook behind him. Feel the breeze, so cool against his rising heat. Then there was the touch of the sun upon him, the rich scent of the earth. With the sound of nature pounding in his ears, he made love to her swiftly, headily, hungrily. A great surge of desire filled him, drowned him, burst over him.

Flooded from him.

And again he could hear the bubbling of the brook rushing gently by them. He lay down beside her, tying his trousers at his waist once again, smoothing her petticoats and skirts.

She was magic. In all his life, no one had ever aroused such feelings of tenderness within him.

But did she, in truth, still long to see him drawn and quartered for his arrogance? Or was that sentiment changing bit by bit? He wished that he knew. She was, even in her gentlest of moods, very proud. And independent. Being a colonial had made her so.

As he lay there, he heard someone carefully clearing his throat from a discreet distance.

Rose bolted to her knees, her eyes wild. Pierce pulled his coat from the ground, protectively wrapping it around her shoulders and looking to the source of their interruption.

"Lord of the domain?" she murmured reproachfully.

He smiled. "It is only Geoffrey," he assured her quickly, which seemed to make no difference to her. He rose, catching her hand and pulling her to her feet.

He left her by the brook, his long strides quickly covering the distance between the stream and Geoffrey, where he stood beside his huge gray horse, patiently awaiting Pierce.

Rose pulled the coat more tightly about her, biting her lip and wondering what had brought Geoffrey out here, searching for Pierce. The breeze that had seemed to touch them so gently before seemed bitingly cold now. She watched the exchange that passed between the two with growing concern. She saw Pierce's expression darken, saw him question Geoffrey sharply.

Then Pierce seemed to explode with an angry oath. He turned quickly, heading for his own horse, tethered to a tree branch nearby. He reached Beowulf, and Rose was certain that it was only when he saw her mare that he remembered her existence at all.

"Geoffrey, see to my wife!" he called.

Then he leapt upon Beowulf, and raced back toward the castle.

Rose flamed, humiliated that he would have left her half-dressed, in such an awkward position, and stricken that he had not taken the time to explain or excuse himself.

"Milady . . ." Geoffrey began politely.

"I can see to myself," Rose told him firmly. She gathered what she could of her dignity, and walked past him to her mare. But when she reached her horse, she paused, turning back to him quickly.

"Geoffrey, what has happened?"

He looked down, shifting his feet uncomfortably.

"Geoffrey?"

"*Je ne sais—*"

"Don't tell me you don't know! You just came to get him!"

He sighed. "I don't know if I should tell you, milady," he said unhappily.

"I need to know!" she cried.

He hesitated. "I have just learned that Lord and Lady Bryant are somewhere near Dover."

Rose gasped, and nearly fell back against her horse. She had known that he was determined to find Anne, to assure himself that she was well. And Rose desperately wanted her to be well. Alive and well. And happy.

But now it was over. The foolish Eden she had allowed herself to live in was dissipating into the truth. He would see Anne. Remember that he loved her.

And he very well might try to kill Jamison . . .

"Oh, God!" she breathed. "Why did you have to tell him?"

Geoffrey saw the tears that stung her eyes. His heart went out to her.

"I serve him," he said simply. "He wanted to know."

She fought the tears that threatened to spill from her eyes. "He'll ride down there now!" she told Geoffrey. "And he'll be angry and reckless."

"I will be with him, milady. I swear to you, I will stand beside him."

Rose stared at him blankly.

"Milady!" Geoffrey said softly. "He has to see that she fares well, that . . ." His voice trailed away.

Oh, yes. It was that question of honor, Rose thought wearily. She lowered her head. She didn't want Anne to suffer either; she wanted Anne's blessing.

But she was afraid. Terribly afraid.

How ironic. It was not so long ago that she had told herself she could not bear his touch. Now she did not think that she could bear life without it.

She stared at Geoffrey again, shaking her head. "He can't go," she whispered.

Rose bit her lip, then spun around and leapt atop her horse. She walked the animal slowly at first, then squeezed her knees into her flanks, and raced back to the castle.

She left her horse in the courtyard with a young groom and burst into the great hall. Garth came hurrying out, but she ignored him, racing up the stairs to the bedroom they had shared.

He was stuffing a clean shirt into his trousers, buckling his scabbard around his waist.

She stood in the doorway watching him. His eyes caught hers. Some emotion rode darkly within them, but Rose could not read it.

"Don't go!" she whispered.

"I have to."

"You're still too emotionally involved." She hesitated. "In love with Anne. You can't kill Jamison or Jerome! You'd hang for it! Not even the king would be able to save you. All of England knows how you despise the pair of them!"

He arched a brow to her. A rueful smile touched his lips. "Didn't you want me to hang once?"

"Don't, Pierce!" she implored him.

He was decked out now with a clean coat, his sword, a pistol, and his sweeping cavalier's hat. He strode to the door, but paused there, for she was blocking his way. "I have to go, Rose! By God, I owe her that!"

She braced herself against the doorframe, afraid that she was going to fall.

"You could be setting yourself up for a trap, Pierce," she said swiftly. "You don't really know where you're going. You—" She broke off. She couldn't say the words that were now trying to tumble from her lips. *Please don't go, please, because I am falling in love with you and I want a future for us.*

"Dammit, Rose! You tell me that you were no part of this thing, and so you must understand. Let me by!"

No. There was no sense in saying those words to him.

"You can't kill in cold blood."

"I have never killed in cold blood."

"You have never been in such a fury."

"And what are you now, Mistress Woodbine, an authority on my moods?"

Mistress Woodbine. He had already forgotten that she was his wife.

She curled her fingers around the doorframe behind her to remain standing. "Do as you wish then!" she cried to him.

He hesitated then, watching her face, drawing a hand up to it to cup her chin, and stroke the flesh with the callused pad of his thumb. She tried to wrench away. He caught her. Held her firmly. "Rose!" he murmured very softly. "Rose, you must understand—"

She was trying to understand. Trying to fight her tears. He wanted her, but not enough to stay with her now. She twisted away from him. "Go, milord DeForte! Go, kill Jamison or Jerome, or be killed. Avenge us all—slay someone! *And hang!*"

"Damn you, Rose!" He reached for her. She lashed out, nearly catching his cheek, but he was too swift, and he caught her hand. He pressed her against the doorframe. The coat fell from her shoulders, baring breasts and flesh that spilled from her untied bodice. He held still for a long, slow moment, staring at her. His eyes met hers.

"I hate you!" she whispered, trying so very hard to fight the tears. Everything had been so beautiful. Now everything was lost.

He bowed low before her, mockingly low. "So you have said before." But then he paused. He pulled her into his arms. Found her lips. Kissed her deeply and hard. And surely tasted the salt of those tears she strained so furiously to hide.

"I owe her, Rose! It's a matter of honor!" he whispered.

"No!" she breathed. But it didn't matter. He had pushed away from her.

He placed his hat atop his head. His eyes met hers. He gritted his teeth in pain but turned quickly again without touching her, leaving the room and hurrying down the staircase, calling orders to Garth.

Rose hurried into the anteroom of their private chambers. She closed her eyes, sinking down to one of the daybeds.

Most assuredly, Jamison and Jerome deserved whatever Pierce chose to do to them.

But Rose still couldn't let him die, brought down by some other treachery of Jamison's or Jerome's.

Or hanged by law for murder.

She leapt up, suddenly equally determined herself.

She was going to Dover, too.

Anne paused as she started down the few steps from the stairway to the great hall at Huntington Manor. She tried not to wince, but she did so, lowering her head.

Jamison was already there.

She had tried. Once she had discovered herself duped and wed, she had quickly determined that she was going to accept her marriage. If she didn't, she knew someone would die. If Pierce suspected that she suffered in any way, he would have come for her.

He was married now. To Rose Woodbine. And certainly, even if he was still determined to find Anne as his honor must dictate, he must have reconciled himself to his own marriage. Rose was beautiful. Wild. And Anne had seen the sparks of passion flying between the two when they had not realized it themselves.

Aye, Pierce was wed! But Jamison still walked in fear of him, and Anne was well aware of it. He wanted to return to London, but he dared not do so. And as much as he adored her, Anne thought dryly, he also seemed to miss his paramour. He had once let slip the name Beth, and so Anne was certain that he did have a mistress—and that the woman had assisted them in their treachery.

Once Jamison had wed her, he'd been near frantic to leave London, and had called in some favors owed his father. They had been offered this place that so pleased Jamison, for it was nearly a fortress. She was aware that her husband had hired at least a dozen guards just to watch the place, and that he had alerted his own men at home that they were to keep their eyes upon every movement made by Pierce DeForte.

Jamison was in their host's great parlor, looking out the windows toward the direction of the sea. A coldness stole over Anne. He was a handsome man. Tall, blond, with fine aristocratic features. She should have felt something for him! Some form of pity. She was trying. Truly she was.

He heard her, and swung around to watch her come. It was just morning; he was in one of their host's fine dressing gowns. He already had a cup of whiskey in his hands. He lifted it to her.

"Ah, here she comes! My sainted wife!"

She walked on into the room, ignoring him. There was a carafe of water on a large oak breaker. She poured herself a mug of it and turned back to him. "You say that you love me," she said softly. "If you do, you must stop trying to mock me at every turn. And you can't be afraid."

"Afraid? Of you?" he inquired haughtily.

"All right then. You're afraid of Pierce. Horribly afraid."

Jamison shook his head. "Pierce is going to die."

Cold fear washed over her. "You'll never kill him."

"He'll be ambushed, milady. As soon as he comes here, determined to kill me, he'll be ambushed. It will all be so very—regretful. But everyone knows how viciously he has spoken threats against me!"

Her fingers were shaking. She clenched the breaker before her. "You are a fool. Truly you are a fool."

"I'll get him out of my life!" Jamison cried.

She shook her head. "Jamison, he'll come here eventually. Don't you see? You've got to let me see him, talk to him. Damn you, Jamison, do you know why I married you?"

"Because you were drugged," he said dully.

"Because I didn't want anyone to die!" she insisted. She felt pity for him. And something almost like affection. He had tried. He had tried very hard. She took the whiskey from his hands and set it down. "It's too early to drink. Now, listen to me. I am going to send a message to Pierce and Rose. I'm going to see them alone."

"And . . . ?" he asked, clutching her hand.

"I'm going to convince them that we're doing very well, that we intend to be happy, and wish them well, too. That way, perhaps we can all appear at court again."

"Is that so important to you?" he asked her.

Anne hesitated. It was. Her position was important, as was her way of life.

And she was determined that she could make life work.

"Yes," she said flatly. She smiled. As long as Jerome stayed out of their lives, they could do well enough. "Order us some breakfast," she said. "I'm going to write a note."

Jamison was staring into the fire when he heard her cry out. The sound paralyzed him with fear. He ran out to the staircase to see Anne's body tumble down the long flight of steps like a broken doll.

"Anne!" he screamed. Her head hit the final step and she lay still.

Jamison ran to her and fell to his knees. He swept her into his arms in terror.

She was so very still.

"Anne!" he cried desperately. Her head was rolling peculiarly. He shifted her onto his shoulder.

Then he saw the blood. It ran in a stream all along the bottom step. It was still running silently and crimson from the gash against her forehead.

"Anne!" He screamed her name that time. He shook her. He laid his head against her breast. He laid her down. He touched her cheeks frantically. He tried to kiss her mouth, find life. Blood greeted his lips.

Then the truth came to him. He couldn't claim her, couldn't love her, couldn't hurt her. Neither could Pierce DeForte take her from him.

Because she was dead.

Crying out, he laid her down. The blood was still threading through the angelic gold strands of her hair. Her face was so beautifully still, so peaceful.

"Oh, God!" he cried, shivering.

Now what would happen when Pierce found him? He would never believe that it had been an accident. Nor would anyone else.

He could hang!

But Pierce wouldn't let that happen. When he discovered what had happened to Anne, he wouldn't give a damn about the law. He would find Jamison and take him apart, limb by limb. Hanging would be a mercy!

"Oh, Anne, Anne! Look what we've come to! I loved you, my God, I loved you, I swear that I loved you!"

Grief tore through him.

And then terror again.

DeForte had loved her, too. DeForte had already killed men, endless men, fighting against the Roundheads in the bloody civil war. He wasn't afraid of anything.

I am protected! I've hired guards, I've swordsmen, mercenaries, he reminded himself.

It didn't help. He knew DeForte.

He sat back on his haunches, rocking with fear.

Then he froze, going very, very still.

He could hear footsteps. His guards had failed him! Someone was coming. Hurrying over the stone of the entry.

Coming to the parlor.

To him . . .

To Anne!

Chapter X

Jamison Bryant looked up with terror in his heart.

He stared blankly at the pale man who had been his friend and accomplice in all that happened—until now. The woman in his arms was Jerome's half-sister.

Jerome had been incredibly anxious to take her away from Pierce DeForte, to see her wed to Jamison. He had been interested in the portion of Anne's estate that would come his way. But now . . .

Jerome strode through the entryway, coming to the marble at the foot of the grand stairway, staring from Anne's bloodstained blond head to Jamison where he knelt on the floor with her in his arms. "Holy Mother!" he exclaimed, stopping dead in his stride. His eyes narrowed on Jamison. "What happened?"

"She fell," he said softly. "Before God, she fell. I'd have never hurt her. I loved her."

Jerome stared from Anne to Jamison, still incredulous. His sister was indeed dead. Beautiful, peaceful in death. She had been so very lovely.

He should have felt something. They had never planned on doing away with Anne . . .

But she was dead. And he had just heard that Pierce DeForte had left his estate and was riding hard for the coast. Jerome was certain Pierce didn't, as yet, know where they were staying. The house belonged to an old nobleman who had been very good friends with the elder Lord Bryant, now deceased. The owner of the place was taking some spring waters up by the Scottish border in an attempt to do something about his gout. They had asked for hospitality in deep secret, warning the old man that Lord Bryant's bride had once had a half-mad fiancé who might come after them.

They should be safe for a while. Pierce would find them, of course—they'd hired five burly French assassins with just that knowledge in mind.

But he couldn't let Pierce DeForte find them too quickly.

Jamison was rocking now, holding Anne as if he'd lost his senses.

"I never meant this," Jamison said. "I loved her. I loved her so much."

Oh, God! Jerome thought. Jamison Bryant was cradling his dead wife as if she still breathed. He was losing control.

Jerome grit his teeth. He couldn't let that happen.

He stepped back, still viewing the situation, his mind working quickly. Anne was dead. Regrettable, true. Or maybe not so regrettable.

If Anne hadn't married, all of her estates would have come to Jerome. Now, of course, half of her father's property would fall to the fool losing his mind before him.

Quite unfair.

Jamison was covered in her blood . . .

Could Jamison be convicted of—murder?

Hmm. Perhaps the estates would be confiscated from Jamison if he were convicted of having killed Anne. In a jealous fit, perhaps. Everyone knew about her affair with Pierce DeForte.

But then again, perhaps he would not be convicted of murder. Jamison was sitting on the floor practically blubbering at the moment. If there was ever a trial, it would be Jerome's word against Jamison's. And, of course, Jamison would surely tell the world that the entire plot to kidnap Anne from DeForte and see that Rose Woodbine was left compromised had been hatched by Jerome.

And then there was the matter of Pierce DeForte. The man already wanted to kill them both.

A coldness stole its way over Jerome.

The solution to all of his difficulties lay before him. A very simple solution. One that would solve everything. All the property would become his.

And he would no longer have to worry about DeForte because . . .

DeForte would be hanged.

Jerome wore a sharp hunting knife strapped to his ankle. The blade was always honed. He moved in a shadowy world of cutthroats and whores at times, and it was best to be prepared.

He walked over to Jamison, knelt down besides him. "It's going to be all right," he told him. "Set my sister down."

"He'll rip me to shreds," Jamison murmured. "If DeForte gets near me now, he'll rip me to shreds."

"DeForte will never get near you," Jerome promised. "Never. Set her down."

Jamison leaned over with Anne, setting her gently upon the marble floor.

And while his back was bowed over her, Jerome seized his opportunity. He slipped the hunting knife swiftly from his ankle and plunged it into Jamison's back.

Jamison never made a sound.

He fell, dead and bloodied, over Anne.

Jerome rose, wiping the blood from his blade on Anne's skirt. "United in truth at last, my dears!" Jerome said quietly. He waited for a feeling of remorse to seep over him. It didn't. This was really too perfect. He'd be a rich man, sharing with no one. And he wouldn't even have to be afraid to live and enjoy his new affluence. All he had to do was see to it that Pierce DeForte stumbled upon them before anyone else could do so. All of England knew that DeForte had sworn to kill Jamison Bryant.

There had to be a way to get DeForte here. That should be easy enough. Then, Jerome decided, he'd alert the constable so that Pierce would be found surrounded by the evidence of his guilt. Found and taken.

Now, as to getting DeForte here . . .

Ah, there was the girl! The beautiful little flower who had played so sweetly into their plans before. The girl had defended Anne fiercely once before. Surely she would do so once again.

Ah, yes. This was going to be perfect. Absolutely perfect. All of them out of his life . . .

Leaving his sister and Jamison locked in their last embrace, he strode quickly from the room.

Once she had determined that she was going to follow Pierce, Rose wasted no time in doing so.

From one of her trunks in the bedroom she dug out a few piece of gold jewelry since she had remained bereft of coins. She dressed in a simple cotton gown, finding an encompassing dark green cape of her husband's in his wardrobe. Thus prepared, she raced down the stairs, nearly crashing into Garth.

"Milady! Where are you going?"

"To Dover, or thereabouts, I believe," she told him. "Garth, you must let me pass! I have to follow him." Garth watched her stubbornly without moving. "Garth, I want to keep him from getting killed—or from doing something that will send him to Newgate." He didn't move. "Or to the hangman's noose or the headman's block!"

Garth stared at her a moment longer, then sighed, shaking his old head. "And if anything happens to you, milady, I shall be out in the streets! And at my age!"

She smiled, feeling almost dizzy, then rushed by him.

Garth watched her go, then sighed again, calling to Sally, who ran the kitchen. "Come here, my good woman. The house will be in your care. Seems the mistress has followed the master, and I'm quite afraid that I must follow them both."

Pierce reached Dover by nightfall, but down by the docks, the fishermen and many of the sea salts were still about. Old songs, sung by fellows already deep in their grog, filled the air in a drunken cacophony. Harlots were plying their trade with the sailors coming off the ships. The alehouses were alive with music, laughter, screams and shouts.

Sometimes dark shadows seemed to materialize from the street. Liars, murderers, muggers, and thieves all came to life by night. During the day, honest men held sway here. But by night . . .

Still, Pierce wasn't looking for honest men. He had Geoffrey Daraunte at his back, and his own sword and pistol close at hand. They rode along the seediest street for a while, then Pierce nodded to

Geoffrey and they dismounted, entering the ale-house to their left.

Haze and smoke filled the huge common room, spewing from an ill-vented fire in a far corner and from the New World pipes being smoked by a number of tattooed sailors. There was a stage, and a rowdy wench with ink-dark hair and breasts that spilled from her white cotton bodice was singing a bawdy tune about what Captain Jack ought to be a'doing with his rod. Ale and rum was being rushed about the room by harried serving girls—none of whom seemed to manage to keep all of their clothing on as they passed by the men with their groping hands.

Yet with all that was going on, Pierce felt a change in the room the moment they entered. They were seen, and despite the drab cloak he had worn with its overhanging hood, it seemed apparent enough that he and Geoffrey were not the customary clientele.

Still, he walked on in warily. He found a vacant end of a rough planked table and sat down on one side while Geoffrey sat across from him. He was barely seated before one of the serving girls was there, a pitcher of ale in her hands, a welcoming smile on her face. "Evenin', milords, and to what great honor do we owe the likes of you in this place tonight? Not that you're not welcome, fer ye are! But 'tis rare . . ." She lowered her head and tone and spoke discreetly. "Lookin' for something a bit different in a woman, milords? Fine entertainment you'll not enjoy with your great ladies!" She was a small creature, way too small to carry her heavy jugs of ale. She was freckle-faced, red-haired, and filled with energy. "Whatever ye'd want to pay me, mi-lords, I'd make it worth your while! Ah, Holy Mary!

Ye'd not need to pay me much, ye're whole, ye've fine teeth!''

Pierce reached into the small leather satchel he carried at his waist and produced a gold coin, setting it on the table before him. The girl's eyes went alight. "My lord, whatever your fancy, I can arrange it! Young girls, very young. Young boys. Both. Anything you crave, anything whatever. I'm Molly, and I'm truly at yer service!''

Pierce shook his head impatiently. "I seek information. A wealthy lord and his bride have recently taken up residence near here. They've assuredly been trying to live very quiet lives, but in a place like this, someone must know something. They must have bought goods and services. And they've a friend who is often with them—a friend who might very well have sought some of the sorts of entertainments you mentioned.''

The girl's eyes were still bright, filled with the glitter of greed. "What exactly do you want to know, milord? I can tell you anything that you want to hear—''

His fingers vised around her wrist. "I want the truth, that's what I want. Find me someone who has served them, someone who has sold them fish or other goods from here. Find me a lass who has encountered a gentleman who might brag of his exploits against others.''

She nodded, quickly understanding. "Ale, while ye're waiting?''

"Aye, ale will be fine,'' he agreed.

She produced tankards for them, then nodded grimly. "I'll find what ye're after, I will! I swear it. Fer that gold coin, I'd beat it out of the sea rats, I would!''

Pierce smiled, watching Molly go, making her way

through the throngs of men. He leaned back, swallowing down the ale. For swill, it was not bad.

Geoffrey leaned forward. "What do we do now?"

Pierce shrugged. "We wait." He lifted his tankard. "Enjoy your ale."

He sat back, his eyes half-closed. The sailors were all watching him. Weighing the odds. Did they dare risk attacking him for what he carried on his person? There were so many of them!

But he was obviously a powerful man, and one of great wealth. Did he have a score of armed men waiting for him in the shadows beyond? Worse, was he someone for whom they would be made to pay dearly if he were to disappear among the seedy ale rooms at the docks?

They all kept their distance. Watching. Waiting.

He leaned back, suddenly aware that a ragtag sailor was moving his way around back of him.

He spun, rising, bringing his sword to the man's chin before he could raise his pistol to Pierce's brow. "Drop it, kind fellow. Or I will prove that I am every bit as talented with this sword as you might be expecting me to be!"

The fellow dropped his pistol. He scratched his scruffy chin. He was probably a man of about twenty-five, but he looked twice that.

Life, Pierce knew, could take that toll.

"Don't cut me, my fine lord!" the fellow said. He came closer to the table, taking a wild look about the room. "I think I may have some information for you." So saying, he slid into the seat next to Pierce, and lowered his voice still further.

Rose, not at all certain what she should be doing now that she had come after Pierce, was glad that old Garth had been so determined to follow her. He had ridden behind her for quite some time, but she had quickly become aware that she was being followed, and had set up an ambush for the old man. He had wagged a finger at her—quite respectfully, being Garth—and prayed that she not come so near to causing his old heart to quit beating again. She told him to go home. He refused, reminding her politely that she was a woman alone and therefore very inviting prey. With him at her side, there were at the very least two of them, and really, she had no right to be going about on her own when she was the Lady DeForte. All manner of foul things might befall her.

Rose refrained from reminding Garth that Lord DeForte was recklessly going to the rescue of another woman.

With a sigh she told him that if he must accompany her, then he must.

When nightfall came, she was glad of his company, and keenly aware of just how reckless she had been to start out after Pierce alone. She had never been to the coast here; Garth had. He knew of a respectable tavern where many of the nobility stayed when they found it necessary to cross the Channel. He led the way there, and while she waited on her mare, he made arrangements for her to have the one private room in all of the house. He had also ordered them a meal of the innkeeper's finest mutton and fish, and if Lady DeForte would just dismount from her mare and come in . . .

She did not need much of an invitation. She was famished, if still worried sick. She didn't know how to find Pierce, and if she did find him, she didn't know how to keep him from doing anything rash. But she was here, and she had to think of something.

Inside, she sat before a warm fireplace with Garth. She insisted he sit across the table from her when he would have left her to go and eat in the kitchen with the servants.

"Where is Pierce, do you think?" she asked him.

He sighed unhappily. "Milady, he's down near the docks somewhere, in scurvier company, I daresay, seeking someone willing to talk for gold."

"Then, once we've eaten—"

"Oh, no, milady! You're not going into that area of misfits and vagabonds!"

"I have to, if I'm to find him."

"But, milady, I think that he'll come here afterward. The hour will be late. There will be nothing that he can do tonight. If you'll be patient, he'll come here."

Rose sighed. Garth set down the leg of mutton he had been gnawing and went to stand before the fire, warming his hands.

It was then that Rose noticed someone standing in the entryway, looking toward her.

It was a man. He was dressed like a pilgrim, in gray, with a braid rope about his waist, and a high cowl covering his head. He raised a finger to his lips, then turned away.

A moment later, the innkeeper came in, flushing as he looked from Garth to Rose. Seeing the old man studiously warming his hands, he passed her a note.

She slipped it open. "I am a friend with news, and it is urgent that I see you, but I am frightened. I beg of you, if you would see the Lady Anne again, have pity on me. Go to your room. I will find a way to come to you there."

Rose folded the note again quickly, looking to Garth. He rubbed his hands together, then set a palm against the crook of his back. "I'm too old for this," he murmured wearily.

Rose leapt up. She set an arm about his shoulder. "Indeed, you are too old, and I have been careless of you. Go find your bed. I will retire to my room, and wait as you have suggested.''

He arched a brow to her. She hadn't been Lady DeForte long, but he had learned that she had tremendous willpower and was not usually so quick to give in.

''I should sleep before your door—'' he told her sternly.

''The innkeeper has no room for you in any bed?'' she asked innocently.

He straightened. ''Milady, I am to look out for you!''

She smiled. ''If this is truly the respectable establishment you told me it was, I'll warrant that there is a good, secure bolt on my door. And I've a knife in my skirt pocket, and I'm not at all afraid to use it. Sleep in a bed, Garth, not on a cold floor. I promise you, I will be all right.''

He shook his head unhappily. ''I don't like this, milady. If milord were even to discover that I let you out of the castle—''

''And how were you going to stop me?''

''I should have locked you in a tower.''

She flashed him a warm smile. ''Not in this lifetime, my good man! Now go, you have been loyal and true. Go to sleep. I am going up to my room this very minute.''

''You do so swear?''

''Before God, I swear that I am going there now.''

He turned away. A tinge of guilt seared through Rose. But she had cast away any semblance of propriety or reasonable behavior when she first determined to pursue Pierce. She simply had to follow any lead whatsoever to Anne's whereabouts.

She turned and hurried up the narrow stairway that led from the public room below, easily finding the chamber allotted her. As she had suspected, there was a heavy bolt for the door.

She walked in and bolted it behind her. It was not so bad a place. The bed was not huge, but adequate for a couple.

Perhaps it even lacked bedbugs.

She started, nearly crying out, leaping away from the door. There had been a knock upon it.

She stared at the door from a distance. "What is it?" she demanded softly.

"My Lady DeForte! It is urgent that I speak with you. In private. Now!"

She hesitated. She had her knife, but she walked to the fireplace and picked up the poker. "Who are you?"

"A friend; though you might not believe it, it is God's own truth. Please, in His name, I beg you! Open the door. The Lady Anne's very life may be at stake."

She hesitated, then slid back the bolt, stepping away quickly again, her poker held fiercely in her hands.

The gray-clad pilgrim entered. He started to close the door behind him.

"No!" she warned him quickly.

He lifted his hands, agreeing. "Just don't cry out when you see my face!" he warned her. "If Pierce's loyal old hound of a servant finds me, we might all fail at this!"

"You know Garth—" she murmured, then she gasped, for he threw back his cowl and she did nearly scream.

It was Jerome.

She lifted her poker, ready to use it. "You vile snake!" she hissed. "How dare you come near me! How dare you express concern for your sister, how dare you show your face! Pierce will kill you, you fool!"

"Let him kill me!" Jerome cried softly. "Aye, lady, yes, I wronged you. Hate me, hate me deeply. But listen to what I've got to say, I beg you!"

She longed with all her heart to smash the poker over his head.

But she had to let him talk.

"How did you find me?" she demanded curtly.

"I was going to try to speak with you at Pierce's estate, but before I could begin my journey, I learned that Pierce was on his way south—and that his wife had followed him. I know this place. I thought that you might have come here."

"What do you want from me?"

He sighed, and folded his shaking hands before him. "I want you to get to Pierce. He has to go for my sister. Oh, my God, Rose, I never knew just what I was doing! Jamison used to spend his days and his nights crying to me over Anne. He loved her so deeply, he was so enamored of her, that it was pathetic to watch! All right, yes, it was also for selfish reasons that I was willing to help him spirit her away. He offered me money. But I feel that I have been kissed by Judas! My God, Rose, I have been wretched—wretched!—watching what has happened. He is a monster! He is horrid to her. The way that they fight, I am afraid that he will kill her."

The poker lowered slowly in Rose's hands. Jerome's face seemed nearly white. He was very close to tears himself, his pale blue eyes seeming like glass in the firelight.

God. Shivers seized her. She closed her eyes briefly. Poor Anne.

She felt ill. Her knees had gone incredibly weak.

"What can I do?" she whispered miserably.

He had been pacing before her. He went dead still.

"You have to find Pierce for me. I can't go to him. He'd kill me before he'd listen to me."

"With good cause."

"You have to tell him what I've told you."

"And then?"

"He has to rescue Anne from that monster! Pierce is a far more powerful nobleman than Jamison Bryant! He could rip Jamison to shreds. He can seize Anne away from him! Oh, lady, listen to me, please! Perhaps I have destroyed all your lives, and perhaps it is too late to set them straight again. But he has to get Anne away from Jamison. Every minute now we take a great risk. You see, she compared him to Pierce, and he nearly lost his mind. If Pierce can just rescue her before he hurts her, I can take her to France. We have family there. A divorce can be arranged. You have to help, Rose. Don't you see, he will kill her!"

"And Pierce could well hang if Jamison is killed in this rescue attempt."

"Never! Because I would be there."

"How can I trust you?"

"How can you risk Anne's life so callously? You have to trust me."

Rose tried to brace herself. Her knees weren't going to hold her much longer. She stumbled backward, and luckily found a seat upon the foot of the bed, clutching one of the posts.

"You have to find Pierce," Jerome _____ "You have to find him, and tell him to g___

"How?"

"Ah!" Jerome said. "Dear Lo__ forgotten such an important p___ know where they are. Exact___

His eyes were still glaze___ was a redeeming featur___ sister.

She swallowed hard. She couldn't bear this. Pierce could be risking his own life. He could be lost to her . . .

"Tell me where they are!" she murmured.

And Jerome smiled, fervently kissing her hand. "Thank you, Rose! Thank you, oh, thank you! Bless you."

She pulled her hand back. "Don't! I will tell him for Anne's sake. But I will never forgive you. Never. For as long as I live."

He nodded, lowering his head.

And she didn't see the smile that tugged at his lips.

Pierce sat in the hazy tavern, listening to the man who had come to give them information. "One of the girls who has gone for the night was telling me about a fellow paid her richly just a few nights back. Said he was gloating all evening, saying that he had finally found his fortune. She tried to get him to sleep the night with her, but he said there was a very fine manor nearby where he'd be going, just on the outskirts of the city. The owner is off, and the place has been taken by friends, a young lord and his lady."

"What manor?" Pierce demanded.

"I do not know the name. But 'tis not far, I am certain."

The man was still talking, but Pierce's attention had been caught elsewhere.

There was another new arrival to the tavern. Someone who had come in an encompassing cape with a low cowl.

His cape. His cowl. A curious dark green, one that ld recognize anywhere.

God's name . . . ?" he began.

knew. Rose. She had followed him

here. Incredulous, he started to rise, then swiftly sat back down. He hadn't been in the least worried about the place's seedy clientele until this moment. If some of these fellows got a good look at Rose . . .

He was going to thrash her! he decided. Dear God, the fool girl, what did she think that she was doing? Why in hell had she followed him?

He gazed at Geoffrey, who as yet was unaware of the danger. "Give this fellow his coin," he told Geoffrey. "I think I've seen another bearer of information." He stood, circling around the crowd.

Rose, in her voluminous cloak, had come to a stop, staring at the singer who was now busy crooning about men's "members."

He came up behind her, his arm encircling her. She started to scream, but he whispered quickly in her ear. "Not a sound, milady! What would you have, a riot in this place? Me attempting to slay a dozen men for your honor?"

She swirled around, facing his fury. "I've got to speak with you!" she assured him.

He gazed down at her. The cape and cowl did little to hide her exquisite beauty. There was going to be trouble if she was seen.

"No, milady, you'll not speak to me now."

"It's about Anne!" she insisted.

"Rose, I've got to get you out of here!"

A drunk stumbled into them. Rose's hood fell back. Her hair was displayed in all its fiery splendor, her face with its perfect features and alabaster skin.

"Who's the new 'hor?" someone cried out.

"Jesu and damnation!" Pierce swore, sweeping her swiftly behind him. "Geoffrey!" he called out. His friend was already up, and heading his way. Pierce drew his sword, a warning to those who were closing in around him.

"The hell with the gold pieces!" someone cried out. "The girl is worth a treasure!"

A broken-toothed sailor surged forward, brandishing a sword, murder in his eyes. Pierce was compelled to cut him down. The others backed off for a moment; behind him, Rose cried out, stifling the sound with the back of her hand. Served her right! Pierce thought angrily. She had caused this mess by being where she should never have been.

"Let us pass out of here!" he cried in a ringing voice. "There'll be more dead men on the floor, I assure you, if you don't!"

"He can't fight us all!" A gray-haired, broken-toothed wretch called. "Charge him, fellows, charge him one and all!"

But fortunately for Pierce, those fellows the man commanded were not of a mind to listen. Some surged forward, and some did not. Geoffrey was at his side, Rose behind him. He and Geoffrey began to parry the thrusts that came their way, backing toward the door with each new onslaught.

From the corner of his eye, he noted a fellow coming fast behind him. He braced for the attack.

But no attack came. Rose had plucked a chair from the floor and crashed it over the fellow's head.

This was no delicate flower, his wife, he determined. She was a rose indeed—with prickly thorns!

A breath of fresh air touched his neck. They had reached the door. He thrust Rose strongly outside, then slammed the door behind them. He threw her up atop Beowulf, mounting behind her. Then he spurred his horse, and they raced through the streets, Geoffrey coming behind him.

He didn't rein in until they were far from the tavern on a quiet street close to the more respectable inn tavern where Rose had taken her room.

Then, when he did, he leapt down from Beowulf, dragging her with him.

"What in the hell did you think you were doing?" he demanded, shaking her furiously.

She stared at him in return, teeth gritted hard. "I had to find you!"

"To stop me! Well, you can't stop me! And you nearly got yourself raped!"

She paled at that, but her chin lifted. "I haven't come to stop you!" she cried out. "I came to tell you that I know where Anne is—and that you must find her and get her away from Jamison just as quickly as you can."

Pierce froze. "How do you know where she is?"

"Jerome found me. He was in a horrible state, stricken by what he has done!"

"Why?"

She hesitated, searching out his eyes.

"Why, Rose?" he roared.

"Because Jerome is afraid that he will really hurt her. Because . . ."

His fingers tightened around her shoulders. "Why?"

"She has made comparisons between the two of you, it seems. And Jerome is really afraid for her life. He thinks that Jamison might be furious enough and jealous enough to—kill her."

"Oh, God!" he breathed.

"You have to be careful!" she whispered, tears stinging her eyes. "Very careful!"

"Where is she?"

"Huntington Manor. It is just—"

"I know where it is," he said wearily. "The king found refuge there once. Come. I'll want you safe, and I feel that I must hurry."

"I've a room at the inn. Garth is with me."

Garth would be, Pierce thought. He was served by good and loyal men.

"Come."

He set her upon Beowulf, feeling all her softness, inhaling her sweet scent. He mounted behind her, his arms around her.

He rode back to the inn, and dismounted with her. Geoffrey remained with the horses while he swept Rose up, and walked her into the inn, and up to the bedroom.

Despite his need for haste, he laid her down tenderly upon the bed. Her eyes searched his out with a liquid, emerald fire. Enchantment.

No, no enchantment. He had come to love her. He had taken her innocence, he had forced it. And she had taken something from him in return. He had fallen prey to the beautiful copper skeins of her hair; he was forever entangled within them. The sight of her, the scent of her, would be with him always.

"I have to go," he said.

She nodded. She reached out her arms to him. He kissed her lips tenderly.

"Pierce!" she cried softly.

"Aye, Rose?"

"Come back to me. Please, please, come back to me!"

Chapter XI

With Geoffrey hard on his heels, Pierce rode for Huntington Manor. It was a solid hour's ride, but for once in his life, he gave Beowulf no thought, nearly riding the fine stallion into the ground.

When they reached the outer walls of the manor, there was no one about. Pierce could see a light in the gatehouse, but no one answered his call when he beat against the gate. He looked at Geoffrey worriedly, realizing that a growing sense of disaster had followed him all the way here. He surveyed the walls of the estate. They were brick, but ancient, and there were handholds he could use to scale over the top.

Letting Geoffrey hold the horses, he did so, nearly slipping once, gritting his teeth to find a hold on a chipped brick. By the time he reached the top, his fingers were torn and bleeding. He ignored them.

When he jumped to the ground below the wall, he saw that the manor house was strangely quiet. He unbolted the gate, pushing it open for Geoffrey to ride through. "The house!" he told Geoffrey anxiously. He turned and started to walk toward the door. Then he walked faster, a great unease stealing over his heart.

He started to run.

He came to great, heavy oak doors and lifted a hand to pound upon them. He didn't need to do so. The doors swung open the moment that he touched them. He entered into a silent foyer, then saw the marble entry with the grand stairway far at its rear.

He had been in such a hurry. Now he didn't want to go any further. There was no one within the house, it seemed. No one came to challenge them. There was nothing but silence.

He drew his sword, and carefully started down the entry, motioning to Geoffrey to wait. Slowly, with near silent treads, he made toward the stairway.

There, his sword fell heavily to his side as all strength deserted his arm, his body, his soul. His breath caught in horror, and he stared unmoving at the couple entwined on the floor.

No! The word was silent, but it screamed and screeched in his heart and mind. No . . . this could not be.

"Sweet Jesus!" he cried out then, finding motion at last. He sheathed his sword and nearly flew the few steps to Jamison and Anne where they lay on the marble. Frantically he pulled Jamison's body off Anne's, half expecting the man with the bloodied back to come to life again.

But Jamison fell to the floor, his pale, sightless eyes staring to the ceiling. There was no doubt here, no trickery. Jamison Bryant was dead.

As was Anne.

Beautiful Anne, sweet Anne, gentle Anne. He took her into his arms, mindless that her dried blood stained his cloak. He smoothed back her golden hair, touched her lifeless cheeks. Then a rage filled his heart and he held her close, encompassing her against him. "My God, my God!" he whispered to her. "What have they done, Anne? What have they done?"

Vaguely he was aware of hurried footsteps coming toward him. He couldn't really hear, couldn't reason. He held Anne. Death had taken her, in all her youth and beauty. He should have come sooner. He shouldn't have slept nights.

Oddly, her delicate features were touched with an expression of perfect peace. No one could hurt her now, no one could touch her.

"Milord!" It was Geoffrey, speaking to him anxiously. "Riders have come through the gates. I cannot see the pennants in the darkness, but I think it is the lord constable with an arrest party. Milord DeForte! We must leave."

"I cannot leave her!" Pierce stated.

Geoffrey came to his knees beside him. "She is dead, milord. She rests with the Father, and there is nothing you nor any man can do for her now! Milord, you must come away with me." He sighed, for Pierce didn't move. "Milord! They will think that you slew them! You made so many threats against Jamison Bryant! Someone has summoned the lord constable! Jesu, listen to me! We must ride away from here. You will be taken by the law. The king himself will not be able to save you. Milord, we must be away from here!" He paused for a moment, seeking the right words. "Milord, how will you avenge her cruel death if you hang from a gibbet yourself? How will you ever find the true murderer, how will you bring the truth of it to the light?"

That moved him at last. Pierce began to rise slowly, laying Anne down with all the tenderness and anguish in his heart. No, he couldn't do anything for her.

Not anymore. He should have defied God and the

king to come for her before! He should have slain any man in his way, he should have risked hanging, burning, the very fires of hell! He should never, never have let this happen, fallen for this treachery. But then, there had been Rose . . .

Agony ripped through him. Rose, who had sent him here tonight. Rose, who had defied him. Rose, who had slowly slipped her way into his life, into his heart. You will pay, she had warned him. You will pay.

She had sent him here tonight. She had met with Jerome, and she had sent him here. But so cleverly. *Don't go! Don't go!* she'd said.

Then she had told him exactly where he had to be!

Rose! Ah, yes! Just when he had believed in her innocence, in the wild emerald beauty of her eyes. Just when he had begun to admit to himself that the enchantment had gone deeper than a searing desire. Just when he had begun to realize that he wanted and needed and . . .

Loved her.

Ah, God. She had sent him here. To find Anne. And now the lord constable was coming.

"Milord!" Geoffrey cried again.

Pierce tightened his shoulders. Anne's soft hair fell over his fingers. He clenched his eyes tightly. He had to go, had to run. But this was wrong. Riding away from her. He hadn't killed her. He hadn't even killed the fool Jamison!

"Please, please, come away!" Geoffrey urged him.

Pierce nodded, but he moved slowly, like a man in a daze. Geoffrey caught hold of his arm, trying to make him move faster.

"Come, milord, come!"

But they had scarce left the house behind when

they were accosted by the riders who had come through the gate. There were six of them, including a man Pierce knew well, Thayer Harrison, the lord constable, a man who had served both Charles I and Charles II, a man Pierce counted as a good one. He was old and gnarled, a dignified soldier with straight carriage and very gray whiskers.

But Geoffrey was right. He could not let himself be taken. Any man in the country would be convinced that he was the one guilty of the horrible murders.

Two men were already off their horses, racing into the house. Pierce backed away carefully, his sword drawn.

"If this comes to a fight, go," he said softly to Geoffrey. "Go—the very second that I give you a sign!"

"Go!" Geoffrey exclaimed. "I'd never leave you, milord! What manner of man would that make me?"

"One alive and ready to come to my assistance should I call upon you at a later time! When it comes to a fight, you may help me along. But when we reach the point where it is nobler to ride and fight again, then we will part ways, and you will ride home to Castle DeForte, and await me."

Geoffrey started to protest, but Harrison's men had come out of the house. "Jesu, he's killed the woman as well, milord!" one fellow cried. "There she be, all crumpled upon the floor, bathed in blood!"

"My God, DeForte!" Harrison breathed.

"I'm innocent, Harrison!" he cried in return. "I have been set up here, framed for these murders!"

"You threatened the man time and time again! You swore to have his throat!"

"His throat. Never the lady's. I loved her once."

"And jealousy drove you to this!"

"I am innocent, Harrison. As God is my witness, I swear that I am innocent."

"Then come before the king. Prove your innocence."

"And how will I prove my innocence from Newgate or the Tower?"

Pierce stiffened, and spoke calmly, quietly—and with deadly warning. "I'm afraid I must pass by you. I've no wish to hurt any man, but I'll not die here, not tonight. I intend to prove the truth of this. And I must live, and live free, to do it. So any man who comes against me now must be forewarned. I will kill for my freedom. It will be to my everlasting sorrow, but I swear, I will kill if I must! Lord Constable! Do not send these boys against me!"

Thayer Harrison shook his head unhappily. "I cannot let you go! Don't be daft, man! 'Tis my job to bring you in, you know that, Your Grace!" He let his sense of propriety fall for a moment. "Pierce, there are six of us, my good friend!"

Pierce lifted his sword high to the night. "Justice will be my guardian. If you would fight me, come. Try to take me."

The first man surged forward, trying to strike him a single hard blow. His blade met Pierce's, then flew quickly to the far corner of the yard. Two of Harrison's soldiers rushed him next. They were brave, but nothing more than inexperienced pups, and he disarmed them easily, both hands on his swords, swinging around to catch their blades before they could reach his flesh. Yet even as he battled the two, he could see from the corner of his eyes that the next two approached while he was thus engaged. Geoffrey joined the fight, lunging at one fellow's stomach and sending him sprawling, and the last of them fell upon his downed companion.

Pierce rushed quickly to Beowulf, leaping atop

him. Harrison swung his own mount around, ready to take on Pierce himself. Pierce was not about to harm the old man. "I'll definitely not kill you, you old war-horse, for it would break my heart. But I will not be stopped!" he cried to Harrison. Swinging back, he crushed so hard against Harrison's mount that the animal staggered back and fell, and it was all that Harrison could do to avoid the legs and weight of the animal.

Pierce sheathed his blade and rammed a ball into his pistol while Harrison struggled to rise. He fired a shot into the air, and the men's mounts went racing into the night.

Buying him time.

He urged Beowulf close to his floundering friend. "I didn't do it, Harrison. I swear that I didn't," he said, calming Beowulf, who continued to prance since the sound of the shot had spooked him. "Believe in me!" he cried.

Then he gave Beowulf a free rein. He lifted a hand to Geoffrey.

They rode together until the darkness had nearly swallowed them.

Then Pierce rode in one direction, and Geoffrey in another, and any man, at that distance, would be hard put to say just which man had ridden which way.

"Good God, Lord Constable!" one of the young soldiers cried, scrambling to his feet. "Jesu! He is incredible with that sword. He must have been a great cavalier indeed! How sad that he has come to these awful murders."

"Hmmph!" Harrison declared, dusting himself off as he came to his feet. He pushed aside the young officer, Alwin Anderson, and entered the manor house.

In the parlor, he felt his heart surge to his throat

as he knelt down beside the Lady Anne. What sweet beauty to die this way! He looked to Jamison next and scratched his cheek, rising.

He walked outside.

"What about Lord DeForte?" Anderson asked. "Do we ride for him now? Which way, milord?"

"Oh, you bloody fools!" Harrison, addressing them all. "Don't be so bloody anxious for the taste of his steel. You are unhurt now because he chose it so."

"But, milord!" Anderson said sadly. " 'Tis murder!"

"Murder, yes! But I'd stake my life it was not murder committed by Lord DeForte," Harrison declared.

"But he threatened Lord Bryant, we were told to arrest him and my orders—"

"I'll warn you, young man, so you'll be prepared. I fought the Civil War with DeForte. I've known him in war and peace. He did not kill Bryant."

"How do you know?"

"Because in all the years I have known him, he has never stabbed a man, friend or foe, in the back. Nor would any fit of jealousy in all time have caused him to do the Lady Anne so ill. Now, we will find him. And I'll convince him he must come before the King. All in good time. But for now, for mercy's sake! Someone go cover the sweet Lady Anne, though God knows, she'll never find warmth again."

Rose had spent most of the time that Pierce was gone pacing the room. She could picture so many different things happening! Pierce, finding Anne, sweeping her into his arms, vowing to take her away.

Then, too, she could see Jamison coming upon the

two of them. Anne would step back in horror. And the men would fight. And the . . .

Jamison could not best Pierce! She was certain of it. So he would kill Jamison. But perhaps not. Jamison was never alone. He would have trained men-at-arms with him. Perhaps Pierce would see Anne, and try to reach her, and Jamison would attack him . . .

She couldn't keep thinking about it. It would drive her mad.

She sent down for a carafe of wine. She drank deeply from it, praying that it would calm her nerves. She dug into her bag and found a comfortable white sheath to wear as a nightgown, then changed into it and lay down on the bed, trying to rest. But she could not.

She sipped some more wine, and began to pace anew.

Finally exhaustion caused her to stop. She curled into a chair before the fire, watching the flames. He had hurt Anne. Jamison Bryant had hurt Anne so cruelly that Jerome had come to her—and so to Pierce—for help. And Pierce loved Anne.

But he had told Rose that he would return to her . . .

Her head rested upon her arm; she closed her eyes. And in time, she must have dozed.

For when she awakened, he was there.

She wasn't sure how she realized it at first, he was so very still and silent. But she turned, and he had come into the room, and watched her now with his back toward the door.

"Pierce!" she cried, startled, as she had just awakened.

"Aye, Rose!" he murmured, his voice deep. Husky. Shaking with some emotion. He watched her. He didn't make a move toward her.

She leapt up. She rushed to him, anxious to see

if he was injured in any way. "You're here!" she murmured, throwing her arms around him, then moving her hands down his back first, and then his chest. She was so worried about his limbs and body that she never realized just how still and cold he stood against her touch.

"You were not expecting me to be here?" he queried at last.

"I thought that—Anne—did you find Anne?"

"Oh, yes, my love. I found Anne!" he told her.

"But you came back here?" she whispered.

"Oh, yes, I came back here. You didn't think that I would come back, did you? Admit it!"

She stared at him, still trying to fathom his emotion. She shook her head. "All right. No, I didn't expect you to come back. But I wanted you to! I swear that I did!" she whispered, wondering at the tempest in his eyes. She backed away from him, suddenly and painfully aware that his mood was very strange, one she had never know before.

"Ah, Rose! Rose . . . Rose."

Abruptly he took a step toward her. His hand clenched her shoulders, and pulled her tight against him. Her head fell back, her eyes met his. He was smiling, but it was not a smile to give her much comfort. "Rose!" he murmured. His knuckles stroked down over her face, almost mocking in their very tenderness. He cupped her cheek, lightly kissed her lips. Then his hand fell against the soft bodice of her nightgown, his fingers clenching inward to a fist, and he wrenched downward, tearing her garment in two. Stunned, Rose cried out, staggering back, fumbling to catch the two pieces of the gown in her hands and hold them together. But he was walking toward her with a studied determination . . .

Still smiling. But oh, the smile was frightening! It seemed so cold. As cold as . . . death.

"Ah, don't leave me, my love!" he murmured. "After all, you did not think that I would return, but here I am. Returned to my very beautiful bride. And you are beautiful, my fragile flower! Exquisite, haunting . . . seductive, bewitching. All that innocence!"

There was no escaping him. He was before her again, catching her wrists, squeezing them so that she dropped the torn ends of her gown. "Sudden modesty does not become you, milady. I've a deep yearning to see all the glorious beauty that so bewitched me from my senses!"

"What are you talking about?" she demanded, growing frightened. In truth, she had never seen him like this. His words were soft, very soft. So soft that they held a tremendous menace. "You're frightening me! You've ripped my gown, I'll not—"

"I'm just so very glad to have returned to my devoted, caring bride!" he told her. "I want to remember you. I want to remember the emerald in your eyes. I want to remember the fire in your hair. The full red beauty of your lips. And more, of course." His hand fell over her breast, curving over it, the fingers shaking but stroking her seductively. "I want to remember the feel of your breast in my palm, its fullness and beauty, the ivory-colored mound against the rouge of its crest. I want to remember the way that you look, my hands on your hips, and my lips against your throat. I want to remember being with you, dying a little with you, drowning in the innocence of your eyes . . ."

He had backed her against the bed. She fell upon it, still stunned. She had been too startled to fight him at first, but now she felt a strange fear and fury sweeping over her. What was wrong with him? Dear God, what was he saying, what had he found out?

"Pierce, let me be, let me up! What is it? What are you talking about?"

"Innocent to the very end," he said flatly. His knee thrust between hers where she had fallen on the bed. She tensed instantly, trying to fight the weight that parted her. It was impossible. His rigid strength was implacable. She had never felt quite so vulnerable. "Stop it!" she cried to him.

"Ah! But you wanted me back, dear wife! I'm your lord husband." He leaned over her, his eyes meeting hers. The hard, muscled bulk of his body was a massive power that kept her forced there no matter how she tried to struggle against him.

"Pierce, stop—"

"But you want me, my love! Sweet Jesu!" His hands held her head, his fingers dived into her hair. They fell to circle around her neck. "Do I strangle you, or pray that the violence can burn from my body to yours? Ah, lady, you craved me back, remember?"

"Not like this!" she cried, near sobs, pressing against the rock-hard bulwark of his chest. "Not like this!"

"But, lady!" he persisted. "I have never been anything but tender!"

"No, damn you, Pierce, no—"

His lips found hers. Her fingers, clenched into fists, still pressed hard against his chest. She tried to twist from his demanding touch, thrashing her head. He caught it between his palms. His mouth molded over hers. His tongue teased her lips. Pried them apart. Entered deeply into her mouth, stroking, playing, seducing. The kiss was achingly exotic, deceptively tender. It lasted forever. Until its sweet nectar had entered unbidden into her limbs. Until her breath had been taken, her will quelled. She had felt this touch too many times before to deny it . . .

Her fists went still against his chest, but her heart continued to pound wildly. She felt the strange, leashed passion of his kiss, and wondered desperately what was going on in his heart and mind. His hand left her cheek. Fumbled swiftly at his pants. His tongue moved over the rim of her lips. She was briefly aware of the touch of his fingers between her thighs, then the force of his body joining with hers.

She cried out, but the cry was strangled within her throat. She tried to twist from the sudden, startling invasion, but there was no escaping. He pinned her with his body, with his mouth. With a kiss that continued oddly tender, yet growing ever more passionate with the swift, near savage rhythm of his body. She would not catch the fire! she promised herself. Would not, when he had taken her with so much anger! She would not give in . . .

But his lips pressed hungrily to her throat. His ragged breathing brough a wildfire burning against the lobe of her ear, the hollow of the throat, her neck, her breast. She did not want to make love to him. A sob escaped her, for she could not deny him. Oh, her heart and mind still strived so valiantly to do so! But hot liquid magic swirled from her body, seared between them, adding a succulent fuel to all the fires that burned. Brightly, swiftly, savagely. He stiffened like steel against her, touching inside her so deeply, she thought that she had died. But stars burst instead. She began to tremble with the fierce spasms of climax that seized her. He fell against her, hard, sweet-slickened, breathing deeply.

His fingers moved just slightly through her hair. Then he pulled them away, as if he had singed them. He righted his clothing.

Then he rose, pushed away from her with a vengeance. Left so bare, so cold, so vulnerable, Rose curled swiftly inward, sitting up to watch him with amazement.

"Ah, yes, lady, I will remember!" he vowed to her. "I will remember your treachery to the very end!"

Stunned, Rose sprang up, her flesh burning, her sense of betrayal acute. She wrapped the remnants of her gown about her, hugging it to her breasts, incredulous as she accosted him.

"What treachery! Before God, I don't know what this is about! Remember . . . what?" Tears burned her eyelids. "I swear to God, you arrogant bastard, you have wronged me . . . used me! Are you leaving? Did you find Anne—?"

He was walking toward the door. "Oh, yes! I found Anne."

"Then—?"

He spun on her, a whirlwind of fury. "As if you did not know! I found her dead!" he exclaimed furiously.

"Dead!" Rose gasped, the color draining from her face.

"Aye, lady, dead! Dead and cold upon the floor, the red of her blood entangled with the gold of her hair."

"Oh, my God! Then Jamison—"

"Jesu, Rose! You sent me there! Sent me there to find her, sent me into a trap! And I blamed that idiot Jamison! Well, that damned fool lies there dead, too. It was you and Jerome! You sent me there so that the law would find me there with Anne and Jamison tied together in their last unholy embrace!"

She couldn't comprehend the horror of what he was saying. Anne. Dead. It couldn't be.

And Jamison? Jamison was dead, too? No, it was not possible. What had happened? Jamison had killed Anne in his jealousy? But Jamison was dead, too. How?

Jerome.

The coldness settled over her.

She had sent Pierce to find it all. She had urged him to go there. She had met with Jerome.

Her teeth were beginning to chatter. He thought that she had been in on it. Oh, God! He thought that she had known that Anne was dead. That she had sent him to discover her.

"Oh, you bastard!" she breathed. "How could . . ."

But her voice trailed away. She understood the emotion in him at last. It was anguish, agony, the deepest pain and wrath imaginable.

Suddenly they both became aware of the sound of hoofbeats, coming loudly from the streets below. He stared at her, a dark brow rising. "Come to me here, eh, my fine, sweet Rose? Rich, milady, 'tis rich! Come back to me—isn't that what you said? If I wasn't taken at Huntington Manor, you could use your gentle wiles and see that I was taken here!"

She gasped. "No!" she cried out. But he was already drawing his sword. "Oh, you fool, no!"

There was the sound of footsteps, rushing now, on the stairs leading to the room. Numerous footsteps.

The door burst open.

Rose shrieked, wrenching the sheets from the bed. A young man surged into the room, his blade bared. Then it seemed that a full score of men came behind him. "He'll not hurt you, milady!" the first man called to her. "Thanks to your hasty message, there's a score of us here, and we'll bring him down, I swear it!"

"Message, eh, milady?" Pierce queried, his silver gaze finding hers swiftly.

Then he shoved at the door with his foot. The oak

slammed back heavily, knocking over the men who had come for him.

He dragged her brutally into his arms. "My turn, milady. You'll pay for this! By God, you'll be made to pay for this!"

"No!" she cried in fear and fury. "I—"

He thrust her savagely from him. The men were scrambling to their feet, charging after him once again. The screech and clatter of metal became an awful cacophony as Pierce drew his sword and parried and thrust with the men. He clutched the large chair by the fire, throwing it hard upon his attackers. They fell back briefly. He leapt for the window, ripping the draperies from it. He paused, ready to plunge down to the street below.

One of the men nearly caught him in the back with his sword. "Pierce!" she cried out.

He turned, slicing the man's arm in the nick of time.

His eyes met hers for just a second. Then he jumped.

She heard him fall into the street below.

"After him, men!" came a cry. And a savage melee broke out, the soldiers falling over one another in their haste to follow Pierce.

"No!" Rose shrieked. "Leave him be! Leave him be!" Heedless of her half-naked state, she followed them, tripping and stumbling down the stairs and out into the coolness of the street. Shouts arose, and she followed them through the shadowy darkness. She raced barefoot and freezing along the dirt roads, down to the wooden docks, following the men.

Pierce was in front of them, pausing now and again to parry with one of his attackers, slicing an arm here, a wrist there, making them drop away, injuring them, besting them . . .

But slaying no man.

Oh, God, couldn't they see the truth?

No, for they had him racing down the dock now, coming closer and closer to the edge, closer and closer to the black abyss of the water. He barely had room to stand. They were upon him like flies. And he fought them still.

Then a great roar sounded. For a moment his blade was raised very high. The moonlight glinted upon it.

"Justice!" he thundered, and the depth and fury of his voice seemed to reverberate in the night.

Then he turned, and plunged into the icy blackness of the cold waters . . .

And Rose screamed.

And screamed, and screamed . . .

Hours later, they told her he was dead.

Several men had plunged in after him, but they hadn't been able to drag him up. It was just as well. He had been a great and powerful man.

None would have relished his hanging . . .

There was a sorrowful older man there then. He had come unhappily upon the scene. He had set his cloak around Rose's shoulders, and had seen that she was taken back to the tavern and seated by the fire. He gave her whiskey, and forced her to drink it, and the fiery liquid gave back some life to her body.

He could not be dead.

Not when she had fallen so deeply in love with him.

Hate him! Hate him! she cried to herself. Hate him, for he never believed in you. At the very end he believed that you had betrayed him.

The thought was agony.

But someone said that she had sent the message, assuring the lord constable that if he failed to take

Pierce at the manor, he would find him at the tavern.

Jerome.

"Perhaps it is best," the kindly lord constable told her gently, forcing her to drink more whiskey.

No, no, it could not be best. It was horrible. Anne was dead. Jamison was dead. Pierce was . . .

And Jerome was alive.

She would kill him, she vowed, trembling. She would find a way to prove his guilt. It would be a reason to live.

But not tonight. Tears welled into her eyes again. She drank more and more whiskey. It burned, it hurt.

Not like the hollow place in her heart. Not like the emptiness that seared inside her . . .

"He was innocent. He loved Anne," she told the lord constable.

His hand curled warmly over hers. "Aye, milady. He was innocent. Perhaps he was guilty of passion, of arrogance, of life! But he never killed the Lady Anne, nor Lord Bryant."

"I will prove it!" she vowed, tears in her eyes.

"Aye, lady. In time," he soothed her. "You should sleep now. Rest."

But she stared into the fire for hours. And then, at dawn, she began to sob.

He was really dead. Pierce was gone.

Chapter XII

Somewhere in the darkness, he entered into a great void. The water had been frigid, freezing him, stealing sensation from him. He couldn't feel his limbs, his body; he couldn't even feel his soul.

Then came the blackness. Neither life nor death meant a thing in that black void. It was total, encompassing, enwrapping . . .

A thud against his rib cage brought him from it. Then all the pain and the anguish of the night came rushing back upon him. He felt the vicious cold of being sea-soaked in the chill night air. He felt the weariness in his arms, the burning in his lungs from the water he had gulped and inhaled. He felt the salt that clamped over his flesh and filled his tongue.

And he felt a blade, prodding his ribs. A small blade. The kind used by a fisherman. Sharp enough though to slit his fish.

Someone was talking. Someone who thought that Pierce was still unconscious. ''He's someone important, 'e is, Jake. Take ye a look what clothing 'e's wearing. 'Tis fine stuff, that fabric of his breeches! His shirt is silk.''

"Then we can claim a ransom for him, Billy!"

Pierce allowed his eyes to open a slit. The salt stung them, and for a moment he was blinded again. He remained perfectly still. He felt the heavy rocking of the vessel he was on. A fishing boat, he thought. One that was out very late.

With a curious twosome aboard.

Perhaps a twosome who looked for wrecks, and salvage.

"Aye, 'e's a rich one!" the man named Billy mused. He was middle-aged, Pierce determined, once the stinging had faded and he could see. His face was peppered with white and black whiskers, like a man who shaved upon occasion, but could never quite decide whether he did or didn't want to do so. He was lean, and as hungry-looking as a shark.

"So a ransom, maybe," Jake said. Jake was younger, but meaner-looking. He was dark and sallow, clean-shaven himself, but with a nasty scar slashing across his left cheek.

"Or maybe . . ." Billy said.

"Maybe he's a traitor out here like this, or some such thing. Maybe the king or some sheriff or law official would pay a great sum for him! What do you think?"

"I think we should steal his coins and shirt and throw him back overboard! Maybe we shouldn't be getting rung up with this one; 'e's a powerful-looking one, 'e is!"

"Throw him back over—to drown?"

"Aye, man, that is the thought!"

"Then how do we start 'ere?"

"Get his trousers!"

Pierce heard them, and prayed for strength. When

the first set of hands fell upon him, he tried to bolt up, smashing a fist against Billy's jaw.

"Jesu and the Blessed Virgin!" Billy cried out, falling back.

"The mighty lord's near dead!" Jake retorted, enraged. He stood above Pierce with one of the oars waving in his hands. "I'll crack his skull, I will!"

He couldn't possibly move fast enough now! Pierce thought. He'd already fought all he could fight this night. No more. He had thought that he'd drowned, that he'd already come to meet death's sweet harbor.

But not, it seemed, before he suffered more pain!

He tried to roll. The boat was small. The oar cracked down and he did roll. The wood caught his arm.

Oh, God! He could still feel pain, Jesus, but he could still feel it!

"Finish him off! Finish him off!" Billy encouraged Jake.

But before the oar could fall again, the small boat was rammed hard.

Jake tottered. The oar went flying from his hands. Pierce watched him fluttering his hands wildly, almost as if he could fly. Then he pitched over into the ink black water.

Pierce tried to rise. They had been rammed by another small boat, but not a fishing boat. This was a small boat cast off from a larger ship, a trim shadow in the night out in the deeper water.

"*Hola!*" Someone called in the night.

She was a Spaniard, Pierce thought. A Spaniard, hovering in English waters . . .

"Speak up there, English!" a heavily accented voice cried out. A dark-mustached face came into view. Pierce saw it there; he tried to speak. His head was ringing again. He fell back, welcomed into the warm embrace of the dark void.

Later, he awakened again. He was slumped into a hard chair. Candlelight shone around him. He opened his eyes slowly. The light hurt.

He was in a chair before a heavy desk in a captain's cabin, facing an immaculate Spaniard with dark hair and eyes and a pale face with a pointed chin.

"So, English, you are with us again. Who are you?"

Pierce moistened his dry and cracking lips. "Who are you—and what are you doing with a Spanish warship in English waters?"

"We're not at war!" the man said quickly. "So who are you?"

Pierce shook his head. "It doesn't matter."

The Spaniard stood, shaking his head. Pierce realized that men were standing behind him, awaiting the captain's order.

The captain came around and leaned against his desk, staring at Pierce. "So, you are dressed finely, but you will not tell me your name! You are a cutthroat, a pirate, like those others?"

Pierce shook his head. "No."

"You are worth quite a ransom?"

"No."

"Then you are a pirate, no better than the others."

"What did you do with old Billy?" Pierce inquired politely.

The Spaniard smiled icily. "He is sleeping with his friend, warm in the darkness of the night—in the embrace of the sea. So, my friend . . . what do I do with you?"

"I am no pirate!"

"But a man with a past nonetheless. And one who knows that I have steered this ship into these waters . . . hmm."

"Kill him!" One of the men suggested. "He is no different from the others."

"Oh, but he is," the captain said, tapping an elegant silver letter opener against his cheek. "He is very big, and strong." He smiled, leaning close to Pierce. "He can earn his life on this ship! Shackles on his feet and wrists, and he will be a willing worker! Maybe then, sometime, he will talk. And if not . . ." The captain shrugged. "Then we can throw him to the sharks later, when his work is done!"

The captain had come too close. Pierce found a spark of life indeed. The man leaned low, smiling cruelly.

Pierce knotted his fingers into a fist and slammed it against his pointed chin. The captain staggered back, swearing, blood dripping from his mouth and nose.

"Take him!" he commanded his men. "Take him and shackle him. And whip him for that. Tie him to the mainmast, and give him forty lashes, just as our Lord was given. We will teach these Protestant infidels to find faith again!"

The Spaniards set upon him. Too many of them. He fought them off, but he had no strength. He thought he might have broken a bone or two in the fight, but in the end he was subdued. Bucking and straining against the hands on him, he was dragged out to the mainmast and tied to it.

His shirt was ripped from his back.

Then the blows began to fall . . .

Blessed Mary, death would be a mercy!

But death would not come. The blows did. Again and again.

And with each blow, he saw her face.

Heard her name.

Rose . . .

He didn't feel them all. On the thirty-second lashing, he passed out, entering into sweet oblivion once again.

He was very near death. For days on end, he slipped in and out of consciousness, feeling sunlight, seeing darkness.

Some kind soul fed and bathed him when his fever rose too high. Someone fed him gruel.

Then angels came. Angels in white robes. Angels who whispered. One angel, a naked angel. Walking to him, whispering his name.

Rose. Rose cloaked in the fiery splendor of her hair alone, Rose beautiful and sleek and satiny soft, if he could just reach out to touch her. Rose, with her innocent smile, with her emerald eyes touched by the glaze of tears.

Rose, reaching out to him, whispering to him. "Come back to me. Come back to me . . ."

Come back—and the law had been waiting.

Rose . . .

The angel vision faded away. He was in hell, and someone was laughing, cackling.

Then that, too, faded.

Someone, indeed, saw to it that he was shackled, for as the moments of consciousness came more often and lengthened, he could feel the cold steel against his flesh.

Then one morning he awoke, and the blackness was gone. He was alive. Sound and alive, and past the fever.

Alive, but oh, God!

He was quick to discover that he had fallen into the pit of an ungodly hell on earth!

Jesu, how had he come to this?

And the name came to him again.

Rose . . .

"Come back to me . . ."

And he had come back, and in that time, someone had sent a message summoning the law. Someone. Who else but Rose, who had pleaded so sweetly that he return?

"The hedges are coming magnificently, don't you think?" the king asked.

Rose, still aggravated by all the time that it had taken her to get an audience with the monarch who had once claimed to be her friend, had a difficult time finding a polite response.

She felt she'd had a fair amount of time now herself to try to accept everything that had happened. At first there had been nothing but anguish. Then there had been numbness, and then the pain once again. Then she had walked the floors in torment. He had thought that she had conspired with Jerome. That she had planned to send him there to find Anne and Jamison dead. And he had also thought that she had sent a note to the lord constable, assuring him that if he failed to arrest Pierce at Huntington Manor, she would hold him until the law was able to find him.

He'd had no belief in her. None at all. He had died believing that she had betrayed him. She was furious with him. She wanted to see him again just to shake him and tell him how wrong he had been. Then her anger would fade, and the pain would be there. No matter how angry she was, or how furious he had been the last time they had met, she had fallen in love with him. And so it was the pain that remained.

And now she was absolutely determined to clear his name. He had been innocent of murder. She was going to prove it, somehow, no matter how long it took.

The king had put off seeing her, and now he didn't seem to want to talk. But she knew that he wasn't really so involved with the highly manicured garden. He stopped to touch a leaf here and there, but when he paused and looked back to her, his sparkling dark eyes appraised her studiously. "Rose?"

"Your hedges are magnificent, Your Majesty," she said softly. "Your masques are always wonderful, your love of art is surely applaudable, and England is deeply blessed to have a monarch so devoted to the sciences. But as to the matter on which I have come . . ."

He nodded, and turned and walked along the row of hedges again. He could be so very charming, so lulling when he chose. Gentle, sensual, still young, and so quick to smile. "You attended the services for Anne?" he asked her quietly.

Lady Anne had been interred in Westminster Abbey very near Queen Elizabeth's royal tomb. Charles has ordered it so. He had ordered a magnificent marble sarcophagus to be crafted for her, one made from a death mask that would forever do her gentle beauty homage.

"Yes. I attended the services. I understand that Jamison was interred at his family's estate."

Charles nodded. He had made Anne's burial place his private concern. Everyone knew that Jamison had displeased the king; it was not surprising that his remains had been sent quietly home while Anne had been laid to rest with tender care.

"Ah, yes! Both are buried, and may God have mercy on their souls!" the king said. He strode back to her, linking his arm through hers. "There is nothing else to be done, Rose."

"But there is!" she told him passionately. "Pierce has been cruelly accused—"

"Pierce is dead!" he said bluntly, then he softened. "Milady, I have avoided seeing you to give me time to search for him in hopes that he might have survived. I'm afraid I must assure you that he did not."

Tears welled into her eyes. She had cried so many times over the past weeks that she had thought her eyes forever dried. Yet the king spoke the words with the same bitter sadness she felt herself, and for the first time, she realized how deeply others felt his loss as well.

"Dead—but innocent!" she insisted.

Charles stopped walking, gently swinging her around to meet his eyes. "Rose, you must face what happened. I don't believe myself that Pierce killed Anne in a rage of jealousy. I believe that fool Jamison did so, not even purposely, perhaps. Maybe Anne's death was an accident; who knows now? But there she lay, dead, and Pierce came upon them . . ." His voice trailed away. "And so he slew him. He threatened to kill him. He vowed to do so."

"It could have happened that way," she argued, "but it did not! Jerome was the murderer, I know it! He sought me out, using me to get Pierce to ride to Huntington Manor! Your Majesty, it was as cunning and heinous as everything else he planned. Who gains from these deaths!" she cried. "Jerome! You know that Pierce didn't kill Jamison! He would never stab a man in the back!"

He sighed. "Rose—"

"I tell you—"

"Rose!" He squeezed her fingers and she fell silent, her eyes downcast. "Rose, look at this as a court of law would. Pierce made the threats. Yes, Jerome came to you. He warned you that Jamison was hurting Anne. But then Pierce came upon the scene. And then . . ."

"And then he still didn't murder him in cold blood!" Rose cried.

"I don't believe it myself, Rose. But Pierce is not here to tell us the truth."

"That is why we must speak for him!" Rose implored. "Your Majesty, I have carefully kept silent, for fear of endangering my servant, but I have a man in my employ who was with Pierce when he rode to Huntington Manor. He saw that Anne and Jamison were dead before they ever arrived."

"Ah, yes, the elusive fellow who fought the lord constable with your husband," Charles murmured.

Rose was startled. Then she realized that she had underestimated the king. Pierce had been his very good friend; he had loved him like a brother. He had certainly demanded that no stone be left unturned in determining what had happened. He had known about Geoffrey, and perhaps he had even known that she had been determined to keep the man in hiding for his own welfare for the time.

"His name is Geoffrey Daraunte."

"I know Geoffrey," the king said. "He was with me in Europe, along with Pierce."

"Then you'll know that he's telling the truth—"

"I'll know, Rose! I'll know! But the only way to clear Pierce would be to bring him to trial. And he's dead. So I would be left with Jerome, the aggrieved brother and brother-in-law of the deceased, and Geoffrey Daraunte, a foreigner, to argue before English peers. He is dead, Rose. If he were to magically spring back to life, I'd still have to see that he was arrested and brought to trial. Perhaps we could prove Jerome guilty. I don't know how. Pierce left behind a cloak covered in blood. The evidence against him is damning."

"It is just what you see!" she whispered. And she couldn't help thinking about the things that Pierce had seen that night. Betrayal. From her. When she had been innocent. Jerome had used them both.

And now he was free.

And very, very wealthy as well.

She prayed suddenly, fiercely, that God would send a lightning bolt striking down from the heavens to sizzle him to ash. But that wouldn't happen, she was certain. God seemed to make justice something very hard to come by.

"Rose, I am deeply sorry, but Pierce is dead. We need to let this lie for the meantime. Perhaps, later, when the scandal has somewhat died down, I can do something about clearing his name. He was never convicted, and I'll not allow anyone to confiscate his estates. Though I imagine that you'll want to go home now, you'll retain all the rights to Castle DeForte. Will it matter if this lies quiet for a while?"

Rose inhaled and exhaled on a shaky breath. "Aye, Your Majesty, it matters! I'm going to have his child. He must be declared innocent! A daughter could be forever tainted when she sought to marry if this charge is left hanging over her head. And a son! He could be shunned by his peers. Please, Your Majesty!"

Charles sighed. "Rose, I will do my best. It will take time." He kissed her forehead. "Go home. Go back to that savage wilderness you call home and love so very much. I will stand as godfather for your child when it is born, and no one will say a word ill of the little bairn. I will do my best to clear your husband's name. But be patient, Rose. It was a lesson I had to learn in a very cruel fashion all those years ago when I wandered Europe because of that jackal Cromwell!"

She lowered her head and nodded. She would have to put her trust in him for the moment.

She longed to run out and drive a sword straight through Jerome's treacherous black heart all on her own. But she couldn't do such a thing. Jerome had appeared, head bent and grieving, at Anne's funeral. When she had tried to accost him, he had begun screaming to the crowd that she was a murderer's accomplice. It had only been Geoffrey's quick thinking and amazing speed that had saved her, for he enfolded her in his cloak and nearly dragged her to their carriage.

He was a good man, she knew, and she had clung to his support through these long, awful days. Garth, who had seemed like death himself after Pierce had fallen, had also been her mainstay.

The three of them, she and Geoffrey and Garth, had made their way like wraiths through the castle, none of them knowing how to live anymore.

Then she had slowly roused from her lethargy and noticed the subtle changes in herself. She had missed her time. Perhaps . . .

Then she had been positive.

She had been wretchedly sick. And there were other signs.

Life began to matter again. She wanted her child, his child. And she was willing to fight again. She was determined that she would never be naive again, she would never be used.

She might never be happy, but she would be strong. The incredible new life she carried within her had given her not just life, but fire.

Garth had dropped ten years with her announcement. And as she watched the old man move about the castle with a spark to his stride and a new rumble in his voice, she knew that he was imagining a little boy, one who would be just like Pierce.

She hoped, for Garth's sake, that it would be true. But if the babe was born a girl, then Rose was determined that she would know from the very start that she had been born a duchess, that she was powerful, that she must never be tricked . . .

Never be hurt.

But that was all for the future.

The king was asking her to be patient now. He meant to be godfather to her child, and she was suddenly convinced that he also meant to see that Pierce's name was cleared. Charles II was a charmer and diplomat; he valued his throne greatly, and he was not beyond doing the expedient thing.

But he was also a good man, Rose was convinced. One who believed in the ties of loyalty. He would keep his word to help her—when the time was right.

She couldn't ask for more.

He took her hand suddenly, pressing his lips to her knuckles. "Rose! My beautiful little colonial flower with all the thorns and bristles! Take heart, have faith! I will help when the time comes."

She bit into her lip, lowering her head. She nodded.

"And now, I am enchanted, as always, to have you in my company, but I've a long and tiresome day before me. My brother James has all manner of woes to set before me, I've promised to speak with members of the Royal Society on earth-shattering scientific discoveries, the Spanish ambassador is demanding an audience, Edward Hyde, my chief minister and my brother's father-in-law, wants an hour of my time, and I have promised dinner to my wife and a rousing game of tennis to Lord Walton. My brother bested me in my last yacht race against him, and I've a mind to see to my vessels at the royal shipyard. Ah, I can see it in your beautiful eyes, Rose! I am thinking of yachts, while you are filled with righteous fury. First, you must remember that it is a sport I introduced to this country myself. Secondly, it is part of life, of living, to go onward. So if you will forgive me, little flower . . . ?''

She swallowed hard. Little flower. For a moment the king had reminded her so much of Pierce!

''You're staying with us awhile at court, I hope?''

She shook her head. ''Just the night, I think. I am not feeling very well, and prefer to be home. At Castle DeForte. And I will be sailing home soon, I think. Since Pierce will not—will not be with me, I think that I would like to have my child in my father's house.''

''I can well understand,'' Charles assured her. ''But for the night then, Lady DeForte, I think that you'll find your quarters here warm and well prepared for your visit. Tell me, though, is this man of yours here with you, Geoffrey Daraunte?''

She nodded.

''Waiting for you now?''

She smiled slowly. ''Just at the garden gate. In case I needed him. To swear to all what he saw on the night that Anne was killed.''

Charles nodded. ''Send him to me on your way out then, please, milady.''

Mystified, Rose agreed. She curtsied to him, murmuring a swift ''thank you'' for his time, turned, and hurried along the trail to exit the garden. Geoffrey was waiting just beyond the king's guards. ''He wishes to see you,'' she told him, puzzled.

''I will swear to him—'' Geoffrey began.

''I don't think he has any doubt about your honesty,'' she said, frowning slightly. ''He knows Pierce was innocent. He has promised to help me, but . . . but he has also warned me that it will take time. It doesn't matter. I will give him time. I will give him a year. If he hasn't done something by then, I swear I'll—'' She broke off.

"You'll what, milady?" Geoffrey queried.

She shook her head. "I'm not sure. Trap Jerome somehow.'' She shivered, quickly sweeping her lashes over her eyes, not wanting him to see her distress. It still hurt her so very badly that Pierce had died hating her.

"I shall go to the king immediately, milady. And if you've any need for me, I shall be near.''

She nodded, and hurried from the garden to the hall, making her way quickly to the room she had stayed in when she had first come to the castle. She was about to try the door when she heard Garth call out softly. "There you are, milady. I'd seen to it that your things were prepared for the evening, then I began to worry that I had not seen you.''

She shook her head. "But where—''

"My lady! Your late husband's quarters are granted to you now, of course.''

"Of course,'' she murmured. She followed Garth in silence.

Fires blazed warmly in both chambers of the suite. She stared about, then carefully, calmly, thanked Garth for his kind service, and said that she needed to rest. She lay upon the great bed in the room and stared at the fire.

Memories flooded back. Silent tears slipped from her eyes. Tonight! she told herself. Tonight she would cry, she would let the tears come. And then no more. She had to think of her child. She would clear the babe's father's name, she would find vengeance somehow!

But first she would go home. Go home to Virginia, and there lick her wounds, and find strength again.

But for the night . . .

The flames flickered in the fireplace. Her tears continued to fall.

And her memories continued to haunt her . . .

Geoffrey Daraunte had not seen his monarch closely since the day they had returned to England from the long years abroad, when Charles had been greeted joyously by the English people, invited back as king. But Charles had a strong memory, and when Geoffrey fell quickly upon a knee, Charles was equally quick to raise him up again. "Your Majesty!" Geoffrey declared fervently.

Charles smiled slightly at the passion in Geoffrey's greeting. He'd always liked the French.

"Rise up, old friend!" Charles told him. "I am not a man to forget the past, and I'll not forget your service to me. Now, tell me—"

"When we came to the manor, they were dead, Your Majesty, I swear it."

"And you were with Lord DeForte every moment?" the king queried.

Geoffrey faltered. "He bid me wait at the door—but he did not kill either Lord or Lady Bryant, I swear it, Your Majesty! He hadn't the time, nor the disposition. May the great God above us—"

"Geoffrey, Geoffrey!" the king murmured, stopping the flow of passionate denial. "I believe that Pierce was innocent; you need not convince me. I know that he did not kill Bryant."

"You know—"

"Any man who knew Pierce DeForte knows that he did not kill Bryant. Ah, yes, it was possible that he might have! I feared it, feared it greatly. But he didn't do it. He'd not have stabbed the devil in the back, he'd have made the man face him."

Geoffrey stared at the king, puzzled. "Then—"

"In time we'll manage to prove the truth. I want to know whatever else you know about that night."

Geoffrey shook his head, more confused than ever. "My Lord DeForte commanded that we ride in different directions. He meant to return to his lady, I see now. I rode north, toward Castle De-Forte, and so some of the men ordered to arrest him followed me in his stead. I had prayed earnestly that I had given him some time. But they found him eventually. Some men say that she summoned the law herself, but that is not the truth, I'd swear it, Your Majesty—"

"I'm not doubting the Lady Rose's loyalty to her lord, either, my good fellow. I want to hear more."

Geoffrey shook his head. "But I wasn't there, Your Majesty. He fought the men who were ordered to take him. He bested them, but he did not take their lives. He bested them all, but there were just too many. And then . . ."

"And then?" the king encouraged the man.

"Then he perished in the water."

The king stroked his cheek. "But his body still hasn't been found . . ."

"You think that he is alive?" Geoffrey demanded. His voice was so rich with hope and anguish that Charles wished he hadn't spoken. "Don't ever say such a thing to Lady DeForte. Don't give her such a thread of hope to cling to. But . . ." He shrugged, then patted Geoffrey on the shoulder. "Very little is impossible in this world, my friend!" he said. "But if you do discover the Lord DeForte alive some-where, warn him that he is a fugitive in this country. Warn him that Jerome is smart, and that he is more— he is evil. Warn him to move very carefully, to keep his head very low if he is in England, or if he returns to England. And if you should ever discover that he is alive, you may tell him one more thing."

"And that is, Your Majesty?"

Charles paused just a moment, his hand set lightly upon one of his boxwoods. Then he glanced at Geoffrey. "Tell him that his king loves him well, and has not forgotten him, or forsaken him. Tell him that for me."

"Oh, aye! Your Majesty!" Geoffrey, warm and effusive once again, fell down upon a knee, this time kissing Charles's hand.

"Up, my good man!" the king commanded him. "And not a word about this to the Lady Rose, do you understand?"

Geoffrey rose. "Not a word! And I will serve you, Sire, I swear it, until—"

"If you would serve me, look out for the Lady Rose. Keep her from trouble. Now, that is order enough for any man."

Chapter XIII

The captain's name was Roderigo Suarez de la Luz, Pierce learned, and an English pirate had seized a ship his father had been aboard years before.

Roderigo's father had never returned from that venture, and so the captain had taken his revenge by plying the English coastline for Englishmen to seize and set to work upon his own vessels. He was, for all appearances, an honest merchantman. And he did trade. Cloth and metals from the finest craftsmen in Europe to the Americas, exotic fruits, rice, tobacco, and cotton from the colonies back to Europe. Along the way, though, if he happened to come across a foreign ship, especially an English one, he trained his cannons on her, boarded and burned her, and ransomed the crew and passengers, if any survived.

Pierce never saw any of the action that took place during those encounters. He was always locked below deck in a small, stuffy storage room. He could smell the smoke and feel the heat of the flames.

He could even hear the screams of the dying, but

there was nothing he could do except throw himself against the door that was bolted from the outside. It was his prison. He shared the hellhole with three other men, Jay Chanbee, taken when his ship went down off Bermuda, and Sean Drake and Joshua Townsend, both bought from abductors on the docks by the English coast. Jay was an older man with a brown, weathered face and a near stoic acceptance of his present misery. Both Sean and Joshua were sturdy, healthy youths who had set out to port to seek adventure. Signing on with Roderigo had not been their idea of how to travel the seas. Sean's hatred for Roderigo had grown to an obsessive level, but Pierce, who had learned that Roderigo was exceptionally fond of using a lash against his prisoners, felt his own loathing increase daily. When they weren't forced to man the anchor or the sails, they were kept chained in their small prison, the four of them, living on what scraps the cook cast them, sharing one bucket for the necessities of life, and breathing the stink as the endless days passed.

Working the ship kept Pierce's muscles honed; his growing friendship with his fellow prisoners helped him keep his wits.

There was only one man with any decency amongst their jailers. He was Manuel Vaquez, the cook's helper. It was he who had kept Pierce alive through the first awful weeks, and it was he who did his best to see that the prisoners were fed bread that was not too filled with weevils. He succeeded in convincing Captain Roderigo that the prisoners must be allowed to dump their own waste, lest the entire ship smell like a garbage barge and some awful infection catch hold and kill them all.

Despite his murderous disposition, Roderigo was a fanatically clean man, very aware of his personal appearance, and certainly much more determined on

cleanliness than many an Englishman Pierce knew.
It was thanks only to Manuel, he thought, that any
of them had survived.

How odd. He had always thought that he would
die with a sword in his hand. Now he seemed fated
to rot to death in a stinking cell that wasn't a full
eight feet square.

But on one exceptionally hot night when they
sailed off the coast of Bermuda, fate took an unexpected twist.

He had already been shoved back in his prison
after the day's endless work, but Sean, Jay, and
Joshua were still abovedecks. Moments later he
heard shouts, and he knew that a ship had been
sighted. Then Sean was thrust back into the hold,
trying his best to flail at his jailer.

"It's an Englishman! Another bloody Englishman! I can see her flag flying, I can see her figurehead!" he cried, despairing. He fell against the wall,
sinking to the floor. "Christ above us! I can see her
bloody name! She's the *Princess of Essex*, straight out
of London harbor."

Every muscle and cord within Pierce's body be-
gain to tighten and burn.

The Princess of Essex . . .

She wasn't just English. She was his own damned
ship!

"She's mine!" he told Sean.

"What?"

In the countless hours he had shared with his fellow prisoners, he had eventually told them not only
his real identity, but almost exactly what had happened to him—leaving out only a few details regarding Rose. So, though Sean frowned for a moment,
he quickly realized what Pierce was telling him.

"She's your ship? You own her?"

"Aye, and I might well know her captain and her

officers!'' he said bitterly. He slammed his shackled wrist against the wall. ''Those butchers will slaughter them, just as they have done with so many others.''

''How do we stop it?'' Sean demanded broodingly.

At risk to their own lives, Pierce thought. But in the dim light in the hold, he could see that Sean was smiling recklessly.

''We might well die!'' Pierce warned him.

''What kind of lives are we living here?'' Sean asked.

Pierce mulled over that for a moment. It was one thing to risk his own life—he was certainly presumed dead at the moment anyway. But the others' lives were not his to gamble with.

''They'll have to bring Jay and Joshua back,'' Sean said.

''We'll both have to be ready.'' He hesitated a moment. ''Have you ever killed a man before?'' he asked Sean.

The young man shook his head. ''But neither had I ever been abducted and beaten and enslaved before!'' he said angrily. ''Tell me what to do, and I will do it.''

''Speed is going to be essential. And you don't have to strangle the fellow to death, just be damned certain you've got him unconscious. I'll take the sailor with old Jay, and you deal with the one with Josh. Get your chains around his fast and twist, cut off his breath before he can summon help.''

''We'll still be shackled.''

''A good, strong sword can free us,'' Pierce assured him. ''Look to my lead. I will not let you down,'' he vowed. He prayed that he could keep his word.

God had to be with him tonight. And if not with

him, with the innocent men aboard the *Princess of Essex*, sailing her way through the sea, so very unaware of the pending disaster.

They heard the first boom of cannon before the hold door opened. For a moment Pierce feared he would lose his balance with the sudden list of the ship, but when the door opened, he quickly saw that Jay was being delivered back to the hold, and Josh right behind him. He bunched his muscles and leapt forward, aware that his own life and the fate of many men rested in their first reckless attack.

His arms locked around the man trying to thrust Jay forward. The man inhaled to cry out. Pierce wound his chains tightly around the man's neck and he let out a gasping sound instead.

"*Qué pasa*—" the second man began.

He went no further. Sean was neither old nor experienced, but he was quick and intelligent and had long been abused. He whipped his arms and chains quickly about the sailor, and he, too, was dragged down. In seconds both the Spaniards lay silent on the hold floor.

"We're launching a mutiny?" Jay said incredulously. "The four of us against . . . how many of them?"

Sean was ignoring his friend. He leaned down, wrenching a cutlass from one of the Spaniards' scabbards. Awkwardly he gave it to Pierce. "As good a sword as I can manage, Lord DeForte. Free me, and I will serve you as long—or as short—as I may live."

Pierce met his eyes and smiled crookedly.

He swung the cutlass hard. Metal crashed against metal. Sean cried out with delight as the chains binding his wrists were broken. He fell to the floor, lifting his feet to offer up the second set of chains that bound him.

"Well, by the saints! I imagine I'm in on this as

'tis!'' Jay declared. "Have mercy, DeForte! Give me leave to take a sword against these Papist swine!'' Within minutes, Pierce had them all freed. Jay swore that he'd return the favor, he was experienced with a blade. Pierce thought himself a brave man, yet the temptation to close his eyes while Jay wielded the cutlass was strong.

Yet in minutes, he, too, was free. He knelt by the Spanish sailors, taking their arms. He kept the cutlass and a pistol, passed a knife to Jay, a second pistol to Sean, and a finely honed dagger to Josh.

The others were looking to him for guidance now.

"Even with the cannon firing, we have to bring them down one by one, lock them in here. If the *Princess* is engaged in battle, so much the better. Her captain is Judson Becker, a fine old salt if ever there was one. He'll lead these bastards on a merry chase!''

"There's just one thing, DeForte,'' Sean began, his dark brown eyes steady on him. "In England you're dead. And if you're not dead, you're supposed to be dead, and some fellow aboard that ship, even though it be your own, might well want you that way!''

Pierce hesitated. "I know my captains, but not all the men. With luck, I'll not be recognized except by Captain Becker, and he'll be aware of my need for secrecy. First, we've got to best these Spaniards! We have to survive tonight to worry about tomorrow, right?''

"There's a movement!'' Jay warned.

There was a clatter of footsteps as men came down the steps leading to the hold. "Ortega!'' someone called. Pierce nodded to the others. He slipped out into the darkening hallway.

The sailor seeking Ortega wasn't expecting trouble. Pierce cracked him hard on the head with the butt of the pistol he had taken. He was a big man, but he slumped down instantly. Pierce dragged him to the hold. He motioned with the pistol for Sean to follow him.

They crept just above deck. Night was falling, so the shadows were with them. Men were rushing around to arrange another volley of shot from the four cannons facing the English ship on the horizon.

Things went remarkably easy at first. Pierce slipped behind one man, and tossed him overboard. Sean took down a second, and together they dragged him down the steps and to the hold. Jay and Josh crept behind them on the next run. A man for a man. They repeated the process slowly, surely, until they had managed to send at least eight of the butchers overboard and imprison another ten below.

The battle with the *Princess of Essex* was heating up. Shots were hitting near the Spanish ship.

Roderigo was on deck himself, walking up and down, jutting his sword into the air, swearing at the incompetence of his men.

Sean had come up behind one of the cannoneers when Roderigo swung in his pacing. He saw Sean and stopped dead still, his eyes narrowing.

"*Madre de Díos!* You insolent dog! You'll die here and now before another cannon roars!" he swore.

But Pierce had seen Roderigo. He leapt forward, blocking the way between him and Sean. "You'll take me on, Roderigo! Me. A man. You'll not fight a boy young enough to be your son."

Roderigo lifted a brow. "I'll kill the boy with no remorse. He is English, yes? But I'll see you die first, if that is your wish. As you please, English!" he cried.

Pierce leaped forward, feeling the deck with his bare feet. He circled Roderigo warily, watching for the man's first thrust and parry. It was swift, well aimed, and strong, just as he had suspected.

But he thrust back with the same force, amazed that after so long, much of what he knew was coming back so easily. He attacked aggressively, driving Roderigo against the captain's cabin, and nearly skewering him there.

But Roderigo seemed unafraid of death, and he parried quickly. Pierce leapt upon the steps to the helm, followed hard by Roderigo. He skirted around the mast, and slashed through the canvas. He jumped high to avoid Roderigo's wild swipe at his feet, hearing the swooshing of the sword as it barely missed his flesh.

Roderigo came for him again.

From the corner of his eye he saw that the two ships had come hard together. The Spaniards were crying out, throwing grappling hooks over the *Princess*, but doing so slowly, awkwardly, at a loss with their captain so viciously engaged in his private war.

"Take her!" Roderigo screamed in his native tongue. "Take the English vessel!"

But Sean leapt quickly to the rim of the portside deck, calling out a warning to the Englishmen aboard. "My friend has near slain her captain! Take the Spaniards, my good men, take these wretched bastards!"

Roderigo swore viciously. He made a wild lunge at Pierce.

It was the opening he had needed. He lifted his blade. Roderigo impaled himself upon it.

The battle did not take long then. Half of the Spaniards were already locked in the hold, some had found graves in the briny deep, and the captain and crew of the *Princess* were quick to give their full support to the fight.

When he saw that it was over, Pierce quickly retired to Roderigo's fine captain's cabin. Sean followed him.

"They've none of them gotten a good look at me," he said. He rubbed the dark stubble of his chin. "And if they did, I don't know what they'd see. Find Judson Becker for me. Send him to me."

"Aye, milord!" Sean agreed.

Moments later, Becker was standing before Pierce. He cried out gladly, embracing him. "By the rood, milord, but we thought that you were gone! I have never been so thankful to see a man—"

"Wait, please, my friend. Tell me, what has happened in England?"

Becker stepped back, a small man with a trim mustache, dark, soulful eyes, and a square, determined chin. "Well, milord, they still claim as how you are a murderer. But those who knew you, including the king, they say, believe in your innocence. God love you, Your Grace! Any sane man knows that you couldn't have done it!"

Pierce crossed his arms over his chest. "My estates, were they confiscated?"

"No, milord. All was left with your wife, Lady Rose."

His brow shot up. "So she inherited my property and title as well! Tell me, does she come to the docks often?"

Captain Becker shook his head. "I saw her but once, milord. Ah, a beautiful creature, she is! She came to me sweet as could be, said she meant to return in time and take the business in hand herself. Said she knew ships well, because her father was a merchant, you see. For the time being, she just wanted to go home. She were so pale and sad, milord. Truly grieved."

Grieved indeed, Pierce thought, but he kept silent. "So she left England."

"Indeed, milord, quite some time ago. She has gone to her father's house, in the Virginia colony, so I understand."

"Thank you, Captain Becker."

"What will you do, milord?"

"First, I'll ask that you tell no one that you've seen me."

Becker crossed himself. "I swear it before God!"

"Then you may ask among your men for a few who are willing to take on a curious enterprise. I'm going to seize a few ships—foreign ships, of course. Spaniards! Promise an even share of any prize, and freedom on any isle any time a man may choose. I believe that I will need a new identity. Perhaps I have already acquired one."

"But, milord! Risking your neck on the high seas—"

"My neck is already forfeit, if I am discovered before I am ready."

Becker nodded gravely. "God go with you, milord. I'll hand-pick the men to serve you."

He gripped Pierce's hand strongly, then turned and exited the cabin.

Pierce stared about himself.

It was a fine ship. The captain's cabin was a little elaborate for his taste, but the vessel was sleek and trim, strongly armed with twelve guns.

It wasn't a bad ship to claim as master.

A bottle of amber Caribbean rum sat corked on the desk. Pierce picked it up, pulled the cork, and drank from it deeply. God, it was good! It burned him, it made him shake. It made him realize that he was alive. And free again. He and the others had bested a shipful of men, and they were free. Masters of their own destinies once again.

He had so very much to do in life . . .

But he had to bide his time. He couldn't behave

foolishly or rashly. He had to take great care with every move he made.

Sean burst in upon him. "The Spaniards who have survived have been given over to Captain Becker. He'll take them back to England to stand trial."

Pierce nodded.

"However, Manuel has asked to see you. He wishes to join us."

"Send him in."

Sean returned with Manuel. The cook wasn't humble. With his chin firm in the air, he reminded Pierce that he had saved his life. "And now I am your man."

"He's a Spaniard!" Jay warned, joining their group.

Pierce assessed the man slowly. "A Spaniard, aye. But a good man, and that's what's important. Besides, he's an exceptional cook."

Josh, keeping an eye at the door as the English adventurers from the *Princess of Essex* joined them, looked from Pierce to Manuel.

"Milord DeForte, just what are you planning on doing?"

Pierce folded his hands behind his back. "I'm going to be a pirate for a while, I think," he murmured. "I believe I'll lift a few Spanish cargoes in return."

He walked around behind the handsome captain's desk, sat, laced his fingers behind his head, and thumped his boots up on the top of the desk. "I think that I will go all the way. I will be a gentleman of a pirate, of course. I will ransom all my hostages. I shall need an earring for my left lobe, I think. Manuel, can you see to a small piercing job?"

Manuel looked at him as if he were losing his mind, but shrugged. "*Sí*, as you wish!"

He grinned at Sean. "And a patch, I think. A black eye patch, a gold earring, high black boots. I'll need a great plumed hat, of course, but I'm sure I'll find one among Roderigo's things. I shall become the ultimate pirate."

Sean and Jay exchanged glances. "To what end, milord?" Sean asked him, "Forgive my impertinence, but we've come to know you here! You're an Englishman, an honest one! How will this help to prove you innocent of the changes?"

Pierce cast his feet back to the floor and stared at Sean. "This . . . will buy us some time. I'm going to wait. Patiently. As long as I need to wait."

"Until?" Jay queried him.

"Until I hear that the Lady DeForte, Duchess of Werthington, has taken to the sea." He paused a moment. "Until I have set my hands upon her! Then and only then will I discover a way to reach England. And once there, my good lads, I will be exonerated and have revenge, or die in the effort!" He lifted the rum bottle he had set down at the desk. "To you, my fine lads. To a pirate's life!"

Sean took the bottle from him, raising it. "To a pirate's life!" he cried in turn.

The bottle was passed from man to man, and returned to Pierce. He lifted it once again and looked at the amber liquid. "And to you, Rose!" he murmured. He swallowed down the burning, healing rum quickly. "Manuel, can you manage me a bath at sea?"

"*Sí!*" Manuel cried, delighted to be asked something that he could do. "A bath. You'll be as good as new, Lord DeForte!"

As good as new . . .

Yes, he was free! He was sound in body and mind.

Strong, and growing stronger with each moment of freedom.

Now all he needed was time.

And he had time . . .

Indeed, it was all he really had in the world.

"I blame myself and no one else!" Ashcroft Woodbine assured his daughter. He was *Sir* Ashcroft Woodbine now, as the king had made good on his promise and knighted the loyal merchant. But it hadn't changed her father any, Rose thought. He hadn't needed a title to be master of his realm, and he was playing the master now, pacing before the huge hearth at their manor on the James.

He was ranting on, but Rose found herself curiously detached. She looked around the fine parlor with its cherrywood tables and beautiful upholstered sofas and chairs. Things here were elegant. Parts of her house were finer than Castle DeForte, for some of it was very ancient and worn, and Ashcroft Woodbine's world was wonderfully new and rich. Still, she had always loved home. Because despite its newness, there was a warmth of it. Ashcroft had always filled it with his own vivacity and energy.

She felt almost tender toward her father now. He was blustering on and on, his jowls wiggling, his green eyes ablaze, his long legs eating up the room.

"I wanted too much for you, I did, daughter. He had the seeds of greatness in him, so I was told. And it turns out the man may be a duke, but a heinous murderer as well!"

She must have said it a hundred times already, but Rose sighed. "He was innocent, Father. I know that he was innocent!"

Ashcroft stopped pacing and strode across the

room, bending on a knee before her and taking both her hands in his own. "Now, daughter—"

"Now, Father!" she countered, and she forced herself to smile, even though the world seemed to be weighing very heavy on her heart right then. "I'm telling you, he was innocent. Eventually I'll prove it to the king, to you, and to God above, I swear it!"

Ashcroft studied her grieved, passionate features. "You'll find another man to love, Rose, I swear it. Take time now, and you'll find another—"

"You didn't!" she reminded him firmly.

He looked down at his fingers. "You're home, and I'm grateful for that. However, if I had ever had a chance to get my hands on his high-and-mighty lordship, I'd have skinned him alive."

"Father, he was—"

"Innocent, I know. Forgive me, Rose." He shook his head. "You're hurt, you're suffering deeply now. But time will help you. And you can just stay here forever, you know, sweet child. This house will be yours one day, and the fields, and the ships—"

"I can't stay forever, Father. Pierce's child, my child, will still inherit his father's title and property. Father, I have to see to it that he has property left to inherit when the time comes. And I have to see that he has a name to be proud of in all the years to come. I have to prove his father innocent."

"Yes, well," Ashcroft murmured. "You're home now. With me. And we've time."

"Plenty of time," she said softly.

His eyes brightened suddenly. "And I am going to be a grandfather! I can't wait for the child! I'm going to teach him everything I know about ships—"

"And if it is a girl, Father?"

"Well, I taught you, didn't I?"

She smiled. "You did. Then you sent me off to England."

"To catch a nobleman," he said with an unhappy sigh. "I do blame myself!"

"Well, don't," Rose informed him. "I . . ."

She was about to tell him that her marriage had had absolutely nothing to do with being obedient to her father's will. She wisely refrained from doing so.

"Circumstances were simply what they were, Father."

"Ah, but you're still Lady Rose now!" he said, pleased with the sound of it.

How very little it mattered! Rose thought. But it did please Ashcroft, and so she was glad.

And being home was good. It was so different from Castle DeForte.

And Mary Kate had come here. In the privacy of Rose's room, she had told her about the horrible way Jamison and Jerome had tricked and treated her. "Rose, I awoke from a knock on my head halfway across the ocean, so it seemed. Oh, those awful men!"

"Well, Jamison is dead," Rose told her wearily. "And Anne."

"The poor woman!" Mary Kate said, crossing herself.

"And Pierce!" Rose barely whispered.

"There, there, my little love, there, there," Mary Kate had said. She held her against her broad bosom and rocked her. "Your man is gone, but you've the babe to come! You must remember that, always. And the babe will be a part of him, a flesh-and-blood part, to hold and love. It will come right, you'll see. Give it time."

Rose gave it time. She wandered down to the

stream one morning and sat there watching the absolute beauty of the land, and she remembered telling Pierce about the place, that it was more beautiful than his special spot in England. And in the green grass beneath the blue of the sky, he had made love to her . . .

Then Geoffrey had come upon them, discreetly interrupting them. And from that moment on, they had rushed headfirst toward disaster.

She leaned back against a tree, her eyes tightly closed, her jaw locked, anguish tearing through her. She wanted Pierce back. Wanted to feel his arms around her. Wanted to breathe in his scent, feel his lips, his body, entwined with hers. For a moment the pain was so great, she could scarcely bear it. She forced herself to breathe. She was going to have his child.

The months passed quietly while she waited. Then the morning came when she felt the first twinge of pain. It would be slow, Mary Kate told her. Babies took time. First babies took a lot of time.

Ashcroft sent for his favorite doctor, a Jewish physician who had found tolerance with Ashcroft—since Ashcroft belonged to the Church of England for political expediency alone. The doctor, Abraham Golam, was skilled in ways that few men could imagine, and Ashcroft had valued him from the moment they had first met.

Abraham was the only man he would allow near Rose once her pains began. Rose seemed very frail to her father, and he had been worried long before the onset of her labor, though he had kept his fears to himself.

Abraham calmly ignored Ashcroft. Rose, he knew, would be just fine. She might appear fragile, but she had a steely strength.

When the pains first started, Rose was delighted. She was at the end of her waiting. She had felt as large as a ship for months, and though she already loved the little creature that kicked and turned within her, she was weary of the weight she carried, and ready to cradle her progeny in her arms.

But as the hours wore on, she was not so delighted. The pains were terrible, and they grew worse with each passing minute. Abraham came to see her.

"The babe won't come!" she whispered miserably to him, her face bathed in sweat, her hair soaked with it.

"It's not so bad yet!" Abraham said cheerfully. Then he smiled. "I'm afraid that it gets worse."

"Worse!" Rose cried, staring at Mary Kate. Mary Kate, of course, shrugged. She'd never had a child.

The pain was intense. So intense that she screamed—and passed out. It was oblivion. But soon another pain seized hold of her, this one bringing her back to consciousness just as the other had stolen it from her.

Rose was amazed at the way she began to rail against the world. She couldn't begin to understand how anyone had ever convinced women to have children. Mary Kate tried to explain to her that no one had ever really done that, it was merely the way things were. Rose forgot, just for a while, how much she wanted her baby. Mary Kate opened her mouth again and Rose swore at her. Abraham tried to tell her that Mary Kate was helping all that she could. But Rose used the very best—or worst—language she could think of against the doctor then.

Morning came and passed. Night, too. It was almost morning again. She was nearing the end of her strength.

"Come now, milady, you have to push. You have to help me."

"You're supposed to be helping me!" she charged him.

"I am trying to help you."

"If you really want to help me, you should just shoot me!" Rose informed him. Mary Kate lowered her lashes quickly against the smile that curved her lip. The doctor flashed her a quick grin. Rose was still fighting, despite her words.

"Oh, the babe will not come!"

"Aye, Rose, it will!" the doctor assured her.

And then she screamed, because the head pressed through and the pain was fantastic. "Again, Rose!" She found the strength, and pushed. It was over at last.

"What is it?" she cried weakly.

"A boy!" Mary Kate told her. Rose could dimly hear a frail cry.

Her son! Her child. And . . . Pierce's.

Mary Kate wiped the baby and brought him around. Rose stared at him with wonder, reaching out her arms to take him. He was magnificent! So tiny, but so fine and beautiful! Red and squalling and waving his tiny fists and feet . . .

Love, like sweet waves of warmth and fire, came sweeping through her. Hers . . . this precious life. A strong boy. His fingers were already wrapping around hers hard while he screamed against the injustices of the world he had so recently entered.

She checked him quickly.

"Oh, Mary Kate! He has all his fingers and toes!"

"Yes, love, that he does. He's beautiful!"

"Oh, thank God, thank God!" Rose whispered. "Oh, I'm so very, very happy . . ."

Happy, but she burst into tears.

Pierce should have lived to see his heir.

Aye, he should have been with her.

Pierce . . .

She blinked away her tears. She had lost Pierce, but now she had his son.

She would be strong. So very, very strong!

For she would protect him, and his rights, with the very last breath in her body!

Chapter XIV

Rutger's tavern near the Jamestown docks was a place where all manner of seamen gathered. Some honest, some not so honest. Some gathered there to share a glass of ale.

Some gathered there to gossip.

And some to learn.

Sean and Jay entered the place arm in arm, tottering just a little, as if they'd already started on a few measures of rum. The room was filled with smoke from the hearth, and from the dozens of pipes being smoked around the room. Pork fat sizzled over the fire, many a voice was raised high. It was a fine enough place. Those who came with dishonest purposes never once thought to cheat the tavernkeeper, or to make trouble on the premises. There was too much business to be done there. Honest men and thieves alike, they did not hesitate to draw up next to one another.

Jay, the more worldly of the twosome, indicated a short planked table where there was space still available. There they found seats with a few old sea salts, and in a matter of minutes, Sean, with his easy charm, had them talking.

"What do you hear of England, friend?" Sean asked one of the whiskered fellows. "It's been some time since I've been home. How fares our king?"

"He's well and good," the first of the bewhiskered old fellows, a man named Sam, told him. He lifted his tankard of ale. "To His Majesty! Charles the Second of England."

"Aye, we'll drink to that!" Jay agreed affably, then frowned, seeing that his companions' tankards were running low. He lifted a hand to the barmaid. "A pretty coin for ye, miss. See that my friends have another pint of their brew there. And I'll see to you."

The girl rolled her eyes, but seemed to like Jay and Sean well enough—she managed to roll her hips against him and lean low across him to serve him.

Sam's friend, an old Highlander called Duff, thanked them for the ale. "What ships have you been sailing on, friend?"

"DeForte ships."

"Ah, you're working for the duchess then?"

Sean glanced Jay's way quickly. "The duchess?"

"I thought ye'd said ye'd been serving on DeForte ships?" Duff, the grizzly old Highlander, said with a seaman's dour suspicion.

"We've been at sea a long time!" Jay murmured. "Serving just one captain. Hey, we're the crew! We obey orders from the captain and the first mate. If things are changing back home in England, we've yet to hear tell of it!"

Jay spoke earnestly, and with a grain of truth. Duff, a briny old sailor himself, understood about following orders.

"Well, lads, ye should know. She's taken over. The Lady DeForte has taken the business into her own hands. What, man, ye don't even know who ye been working for?''

''It's—uh, good to hear that the duchess is still in command, that's all,'' Jay said quickly, smiling and then casting a stern eye at Sean. ''God bless us all then, the duchess must be doing well herself!''

''Ready to head back to England shortly, so they say. There's a rumor about another wedding. In fact, the duchess is to leave here come next Monday on the *Lady May*, looking to make port in Bermuda to do business with Sir Harold Wesley. Why, she's a power, so they say! Took up in Virginia where her father left off, and took up in England doing just fine by her husband's property. Though she be lucky to have that property. The king does have his weakness for beautiful women, so they say!''

Sean leaned forward. ''So you think the king should have confiscated DeForte's property from his widow, eh? I'd always thought the fellow should have been vindicated! From what I hear say, he was not the man to stab another in the back!''

''Who's to say? The evidence was piled against him, that's what I heard. He was found with the bodies by the king's own men. Maybe he is a murderer.'' Sam shrugged. ''Maybe, maybe not.''

''Maybe not!'' Sean insisted, dark eyes flashing, starting to rise from his chair. Jay dragged him back down. ''She's leaving here on the *Lady May*, eh! That's a DeForte ship, isn't it?''

''Aye.''

''Who's her captain?''

''You looking for more work? What ship was it that you were on before you came here?''

Sean hesitated. Jay plunged in quickly. ''The *Lady of Windsor*,'' he said, giving the name of another DeForte ship he had seen, just arrived in the harbor that afternoon. ''She's going to be staying a spell, so I hear. She needs a few repairs. We are interested in working another ship. I like DeForte ships. An honest day's pay for an honest's day work.''

"Then you might try the *Lady May*. She's being taken out by a Captain Niemens, a fine fair fellow, been with DeForte since Lord DeForte returned with the king, I've been told.''

Jay rose, dragging Sean along with him, and dropping a gold piece on the table. "Well, if we're to start finding work on another ship, we'll be needing a good night's sleep!'' he told Sam and the Highlander.

"You just take care!'' Sam called after him. "There's some mean pirates out in these waters. Keep your powder dry and your eyes sharp, no matter who you sail with!''

Jay would have kept on going. Sean drew to a halt. "Pirates, eh?''

The old man nodded. "They say there's one they call the Dragonslayer who's creating havoc on the seas. The Spaniards are afraid to leave their docks! A lady and her duenna were kidnapped right out of Cartagena, so I've heard. The Dragonslayer! Men downright tremble when they hear the name!''

"They tremble?'' Sean said, a broad smile curving into his lip. Jay punched him in the back. He sobered quickly. "But I heard that he doesn't attack English ships.''

Sam wagged a finger at him. "With a pirate, laddie, you never really know. Just keep your eyes out on the sea! Ye never know when such a one as that may tire of Spaniards and an occasional Dutchman and start on the English! There's never been a ship to wrest with him and come out of it unscathed! There's been word that the king will send the whole Royal Navy after the fellow soon, but then, the king has been saying that for months now, since the fellow first took to the seas. I can tell you, our good King Charles isn't sending anyone after the fellow—not when he continues to relieve Spaniards of their New World gold. Seems he's just robbing from *capitáns* who were really nothing more than thieves themselves! Mind yerselves just the same. These waters can be treacherous!''

Sean smiled. "Thanks for the warning, old fellow! If I ever meet up with that Dragonslayer, I will be forewarned!''

Minutes later they were out walking along the shoreline at the mouth of the river until they found their longboat. Sean rowed hard. Jay chastised him. "Now, we went for information, not to give it!''

Sean smiled mischievously. "And we got the information! I didn't give away a thing.''

"You grinned like a sleek cat when that old fellow spoke with awe of the Dragonslayer. What is he going to think?''

Sean laughed. "Who cares! We did get information. And what information!''

It wasn't half an hour later that they reached their own ship, brazenly anchored not far from the land itself. Josh and Manuel helped them climb back aboard, and then they hurried for the captain's cabin.

Sean knocked upon the door.

"Come in!'' Pierce bid them.

He was seated behind his desk, his hat upon the foot of the captain's bunk, his black patch flipped up so that he could read his ledgers easily. If anything, Pierce DeForte had strengthened as a pirate king. The sea-reflected sun had bronzed his skin darkly. Hard work on the ship, and harder work besting his adversaries, had given him rippling muscles tightened like drums. Even seated, he was a powerful force of a man, his silver eyes sharp as they fell upon his men.

They had served him well. Just as Sean had promised, he had served him faithfully along with Jay and Josh—and Manuel.

And the others, the men who had come from his own ship, had set out on the high heels of adventure. None of them knew his true identity. His companions from the Spanish ship had called Roderigo the dragon when he had used them so cruelly; it was therefore natural that Pierce came to be know as the Dragonslayer.

Every man who served him was granted a share of each ransom he collected. He was an extraordinary seaman, but then he should be, having once been the owner of a whole fleet of ships. They hadn't lost a fight yet.

And they hadn't let a single Spaniard escape. Every man had his value, Pierce knew, and they had grown very wealthy demanding ransoms.

They were also somewhat famous for their cavalier treatment of prisoners. There was one Spanish beauty who had cried when she had been returned to her father.

He had earned his reputation as a fierce fighter upon the seas easily enough. But since they were so careful of human life, he began to fear his very reputation for fairness would work against him one day.

So he picked upon one poor Spanish captain and tied him to the mainmast. He told him all the fine, exquisite tortures he could think of, walking slowly around the man with his arms folded across his chest. He could have put his eyes out with hot pokers, he told the man. Or have lashed him, cut off his fingers one by one and fed them to the sharks, and then give the frenzied fish the whole of him to finish off. But he was going to let him live. Just so long as the *capitán* let it be known to others that the Dragon-slayer would not hesitate to do these things.

It worked like a charm. Before Pierce knew it, his reputation was made.

Maybe he voraciously raped his women prisoners, viciously plundered the ships, and heinously murdered the seamen.

Who could really say?

Now Pierce pushed his ledger aside and idly held his quill between his thumb and forefinger, leaning toward them. "Well? Tell me the news. I crave to hear it! Have I been cleared in England?"

Jay shook his head sadly. "No, milord, I'm sorry." He was silent for a moment, then he cleared his throat, hedging.

Pierce sat back, amazed at the strength of the bitterness that washed through him. "I'd have thought my dear wife—or should I say widow—might have seen to the clearing of my name for her own benefit! If she wasn't in league with that wretched Jerome . . ."

"Milord," Jay reminded him wisely, "that's still not to say that the lady was involved in any way!"

Sean wasn't so generous. "She's taken over your ships, milord!" he said incredulously. "She's been here in Virginia, running your business from this side of the Atlantic!"

The quill snapped between his fingers. Jay jumped back.

"Well, milord, she's doing a good job of it, so it seems."

"Well, now, that is consolation!" Pierce murmured. His voice tightened. "So tell, gentlemen. How can I get to her?"

Sean smiled. "Ah, this is the good part. She's leaving next Monday on the *Lady May* for Bermuda. Seems there's some talk of another marriage—"

"What?" Pierce snapped.

"Rumor, rumor!" Jay said quickly, looking at Sean with a certain amount of exasperation. He decided to finish the story himself. "She's to do business with a Sir Harold Wesley. I've heard of the man. He has a big plantation on Bermuda. All we know for sure is that she's going there. Now, if something more is to happen once she gets there—"

"I don't think so," Pierce interrupted softly, sitting back in his chair, his eyes flashing silver. Dear God! After all this time! He was almost there . . . almost touching her.

She'd plagued him night and day in his memory. She had become an obsession.

All this time! Nothing else had haunted him like his remembrances of her.

And now. Now he was so damned close . . .

He smiled. Oh, God, it was going to be sweet! He was going to savor it! The little witch hadn't even tried to clear him! She'd been biding her time in Virginia, playing mistress of what had once been his life!

"Nothing more is going to happen," Pierce said firmly.

Sean scratched his chin. "Milord, 'tis hard to tell—"

"No, my friends, it's not hard to tell. Nothing is going to happen in Bermuda. Because she is never going to reach Bermuda! Gentlemen, I swear it!"

Monday . . .

He had waited so long. He had bided his time so carefully, making good use of it. Waiting, waiting . . .

But his wait was nearly over.

The blood burned inside him. Then he eased back. So old Niemens was the captain on the *Lady May*! He smiled suddenly. It was a slightly cold smile.

But then, he had always heard that revenge was best when taken cold.

* * *

"I don't like it! I don't like it! I do not like it!"
Ashcroft Woodbine said firmly.

His daughter appeared not to hear him.

"I think that it will be quite easy to make Sir Wesley see the benefit to our shipping his goods from his estates on the island," Rose told her father, leaning low over a ledger book, a small frown knitting her brow. "He is ill prepared to deal with the volume of cargo he is beginning to produce. Between the Woodbine ships and the DeForte fleet, we've all the traffic he could desire." She sat back, studying her father. "Father, we don't want him going into the shipping trade himself! He might take away our business, but if we convince him to stay with us, we'll just add his to ours. I'm sure I'll be able to make him see that clearly."

Ashcroft sighed. He'd always wanted to involve Rose in his business. Now she had her own DeForte ships—and she was very nearly running both businesses! Well, she had a fine head, and she was good at it, but he still worried about her. "Daughter, have you heard a word that I've been saying? I don't like you sailing alone! There are pirates in these waters—"

"Our ships have their own guns. And all I've heard tell about lately is this Dragonslayer. He attacks Spanish ships, Father. Please. Am I not right about Sir Wesley? We must have his business before he begins to take ours away from us!"

"Oh, aye!" Ashcroft stroked his chin, watching his daughter. She had the logic of it. And she was exceptionally beautiful when she was so involved with a project. It seemed the only time that she really came alive, except when she was with his grandson.

She was certainly involved with this project. He

had wanted her to be so. Good friends had told him
not two weeks ago that Sir Harold Wesley had built
himself a fine plantation on the island of Bermuda.
Not so close as Ashcroft would have liked, but he
thought that it would do. The other things he had
heard about Sir Wesley had been equally appealing.
He was a sound businessman, well liked by the king,
wealthy in the extreme from his enterprises in the
colonies, and more. They said that he was young
and handsome and charming, devoted to his
younger brothers and sisters, and in need of a wife
to help manage his estate.

Ashcroft wanted to see his daughter married
again. Once she married, of course, she would lose
some of the DeForte prestige; but with the birth of
her son, she had become the "dowager" Duchess
of Werthington anyway. The little scamp dragging
upon her skirts and trying to stand on his own was
the nine-month-old duke himself, Lord Pierce
Woodbine DeForte, tenderly called Woody by his
daughter, and then by all those around them. She
had an aversion to calling him by his given name,
almost as if she could deny his father's demise and
shame by keeping silent.

Thank God the fellow had served the king so
wisely in his time, Ashcroft thought, for it might
have been easy for the crown to have confiscated his
estates and title with such charges as those which
had been leveled against him. But as it stood, little
Woody would one day be a great duke.

Ashcroft sighed. Aye, life would be good for his
grandson. He would have the DeForte fortune behind him, and his own as well. He loved the little
scamp, and he was anxious to watch him grow.

But he was deeply concerned for his daughter. He
had tried to tell her that he needed help with his
business to bring her out of her depression in which

nothing had seemed to matter but Woody. So he had begun to teach her about her ships, and she had suddenly bitten hold of every piece of information he gave her. Too late, he realized, she was going to use it all when she returned to England. Not long after her return, she had written to a man named Garth back at DeForte Castle, and through him, she had begun to grasp the reins of the DeForte estate. Now, he knew, she was planning on going back to England just as soon as Woody was one year old. Ashcroft didn't want her to go.

He wanted her to marry again. He had discovered, in a very painful way, that titles were not nearly so important as happiness. He didn't want her returning to England, he wanted her much nearer. He wanted to see her laugh again, her emerald eyes sparkling.

He had originally been very encouraged about this voyage to Bermuda. She would surely entrance Sir Wesley, and if Sir Wesley was as young, handsome, and charming as they said, he might just be the man to entrance her in turn.

Except she was so very involved in the business! It might prove unattractive to Wesley to see a woman so very concerned with finances.

"Perhaps I should be going with you," Ashcroft said. "I could explain some of these things more thoroughly. I've been in this all my life, daughter, while you've just come into it lately."

Rose sat back, pulling little Woody up onto her lap. The child immediately reached out chubby little fingers to find whatever he could upon the desk. Rose quickly pushed aside the important papers and reached for the wooden rattle her father had whittled for the child from a piece of hard wood. He had dropped seeds into it and sealed it over, and it made a fascinating noise when the child shook it.

He was a handsome boy. His eyes had remained blue-gray with a touch of silver, and he had a headful of curly dark red hair, even at his young age.

Rose nuzzled her chin against her son's soft head and smiled. "Father, there's no need for you to go. I know exactly what I'm doing."

"I know that, daughter—"

"You also know that Harold Wesley is seeking a bride. You're trying to do some matchmaking again."

Ashcroft stiffened with great dignity. "You forget!" he said, wagging a finger at her. "I am the kindest and most understanding of fathers. I could have signed papers to marry you off without giving a fig about your feelings, and instead—"

"Instead you sent me to England to catch a duke. And somehow I caught him by default, but he is lost to me now. Father, you've got your grandson! And you know that I'm going back to England the very moment I feel that Woody is ready. And you are very welcome to come with me. I have to handle matters for the husband I no longer have before trying to catch a second one!"

Her eyes were sparkling again. He was glad of it. Perhaps there was hope for the future. "Bah! You've no intention of finding another husband, Rose!"

"Not now," she agreed softly. "Father, I have to—"

"Aye, aye! You have to prove DeForte innocent! Why now, girl? The king has left you alone! My grandson will receive his full inheritance. The world will forget if you just let it lie!"

She shook her head. "The world will never forget, Father. If you think so, you have been hiding away here in your little kingdom in the colonies far too long. And I'm convinced that Jerome killed Jamison, if not the Lady Anne as well. And he is living extremely well, Father, or so Garth has written to me, using up his sister's funds! How could I let that man get away with murder and everything else he did to all of us?''

"How do you plan to prove him guilty?" Ashcroft asked.

She sighed. "I don't know as yet. I will have to figure out just how to trap him once I've returned to England. There will be a way. God will see to it; I know that He must.''

Ashcroft sighed again. He stood. Little arms suddenly lifted from Rose's lap to him. Serious blue-gray eyes studied his. "Granpa!"

Oh, how this little scamp could catch his heart! *Granpa.* It had been the first word Woody had said, right after he learned to mouth "Mum." Actually, it was all that he really said at the moment, but it was all that he needed. Ashcroft reached down for the little boy, taking him into his arms. Immediately he started squirming. He was ready to get down. Ready to crawl. Stubbornly determined to walk.

"She wouldn't let you down, and you thought that I would, eh, my fine boy? Well, you might be the great arrogant duke one day, but for now, you'll obey your grandfather!''

Watching him, Rose smiled. In seconds Woody had managed to wriggle his way back down, and was using Ashcroft's leg as a prop to try to stand and walk.

He was a very determined child.

So much like his father . . .

"Well, Sir Woodbine," she said, "I'm sailing to Bermuda, and I'm sailing alone. Is there anything else you'd like me to say to Sir Wesley?''

"No, daughter," he said, watching her. Then he wagged a finger at her fiercely. "You may sail alone because I have given you permission to do so!''

Rose smiled, looking down at the desk again. Ashcroft looked down to his grandson, tottering at his feet, then over to his daughter, a secret smile curling her lip.

When had he lost control?

That night Mary Kate watched Rose with her baby, the two of them playing on a fur rug before the fire in Rose's beautiful room. Ashcroft's was truly a fine house. At great expense he had imported all manner of beautiful glass from Italy, and beautifully draped windows looked right over the river. Rose's room was huge, with a fireplace that seemed to take up an entire wall, but though it grew cold here, Rose's room was always warm because of the draperies and furs set about it. The one that was before the fire was big and white, a bear taken in the far North.

Ashcroft had paid a great price for it, too, Mary Kate knew.

But Ashcroft would consider the price worth it, Mary Kate thought, if he could just see his daughter and the boy now. Rose was in a soft cotton bedgown, as was Woody. They rolled and stumbled and played together, laughing. Firelight caught the magic red in Rose's hair, and then in her son's.

The hour was growing late. The babe needed to be put in his bed. "Come now, Rose!" Mary Kate chastised gently. "I've got to get him to sleep. It will be hard on me once you've gone if I can't get him to bed as I should now."

Rose sighed, hugging her son closer to her. "I don't know if I should leave him for so long, Mary Kate! It's true enough that he's sipping from his cup and eating quite well, but he still needs me!"

"He's nursing less and less, which is a godsend," Mary Kate said flatly. "Keeping up with him is a rare drain on the body, it is! Now, you'll not be gone for more than two days. It's a fine way to start weaning him completely."

"Yes, but how will he do—"

"I'll see that he has plenty!" Mary Kate assured her. "Why, the young duke there is so proficient with a cup, I expect to see him swilling down a whiskey with your father any day now!"

Rose laughed at that. God, it was good to hear her laughter.

"Maybe you're right," Rose agreed. She sighed. "I've just never been away more than an hour or so, really, riding about the estate."

"And it's time," Mary Kate said firmly.

"It's time because it is almost time to go back to England," Rose said firmly. She bundled up her son and stood, determined to give him a good feeding that night. She could begin her weaning in the morning.

Mary Kate watched her affectionately. "Do you remember, love," she said softly to Rose, "that long, long ago we spent an evening with you ranting and raving and telling me what a wretch Lord DeForte was?"

Rose, closing her eyes as she leaned back, just beginning to feel the marvelous sense of warmth and comfort she did each time her son latched on to her breast and tugged gently, stiffened instead.

"Yes, I remember."

"But you came to love him, didn't you?"

"Yes."

"Then, Rose! Give love a chance again," Mary Kate entreated softly.

They didn't understand, Rose thought. They just didn't understand. She wanted to give love a chance . . .

It was just that she couldn't forget. And somehow, she knew that love just couldn't be as good again.

She had to find a way to prove Pierce innocent. To clear his name.

Perhaps that would be the only way that she could ever really live again, much less love.

"We'll see, Mary Kate, we'll see." She pretended a loud yawn. "I'm exhausted. Woody can just sleep with me, Mary Kate. No protests, please? You'll manage just fine tomorrow, I know you will." She closed her eyes, feigning a drowsiness she didn't really feel. But though she loved Mary Kate, she wanted to be alone.

She held her baby close. She closed her eyes, wishing they would all leave her alone. No matter how she tried, she could never forget Pierce.

And she didn't want to love again. Not when his memory still haunted her, night and day. The pain, the betrayal, the anger . . . and the love.

She lay awake late, and remembered.

Morning came swiftly for her. She cuddled Woody, played with him and nursed him, then turned him over to Mary Kate's care.

"He'll be fine!" Mary Kate assured her. " 'Tis you I'm worried about! I should be with you," she said with a cluck of disapproval.

"I'm a widow, and a barracuda of one, so I've heard," Rose said with a slight smile. "Father is terribly concerned that my business acumen is going to destroy my chances for another marriage—no matter how much wealth he manages to bestow on me!"

Mary Kate sighed. "Rose, it's truly not proper that you should be alone—"

"I was alone a long time, Mary Kate," Rose assured her. "Sir Wesley is considered a complete gentleman, and I'm certain I'll be well chaperoned in his home.''

"We were tricked once," Mary Kate said.

"And I am much older and wiser now," Rose assured her.

"Not so much older!"

"Then infinitely wiser!" Rose paused for a moment. "No one will ever trick or force me into anything again. I swear it!" She hadn't realized how chillingly intent she felt until she heard her own words. She smiled quickly to break the tension. "I'll be fine, Mary Kate. And I never could leave Woody behind if you weren't going to be here." She hugged Mary Kate. "We'll all be together when we leave for England soon."

Mary Kate nodded. Rose offered her one last smile, then turned to head for the door.

Curiously, Rose stopped for a moment. The strangest sensation of icy cold suddenly seemed to wash over her.

She shouldn't go out that door . . .

The feeling was so fiercely frigid that for seconds it seemed she could neither move nor even breathe. She fought it.

She had things to do, had to live!

"Rose?" Mary Kate inquired worriedly.

"I'm fine, Mary Kate. I pray you, take care of the boy!"

Then she fled quickly. The carriage that would take her to the docks was waiting below.

It was a beautiful day.

There was nothing to fear.

Nothing . . .

The morning dawned clear and beautifully cool. Pierce leapt up to the decking on the bow of his ship and stood, feeling the ocean breeze ripple around him and the sun beat down upon his face. Legs strong and slightly apart, well attuned to the roll of the sea, his hands upon his hips, he stared westward. His white shirt whipped and rustled against his arms and chest, caught by the breeze.

He stared upon the horizon, his patch lifted as he squinted against the reflections cast on the ever-moving sea by the sun. There . . . a speck on the horizon.

Then he heard the lookout, calling down from the crow's nest.

"There she be, Captain! There she be! The *Lady May*! Sailing our way, direct in our path!"

"Aye, there she be!" Pierce repeated softly. "There she be." He turned, calling his order to Jay as first mate, who would shout it out to all the crew.

"Prepare to fire! Then we wait till she's just in range. Fire wide, fire off! We need to grapple her and reach Niemens. Remember, she's one of our own. 'Tis not a fight we want. Just the ship. The *Lady May*.

"And the Lady Rose," he added softly to himself.

His wait was nearly over.

Oh, yes.

So very nearly over!

Part II

Schemers

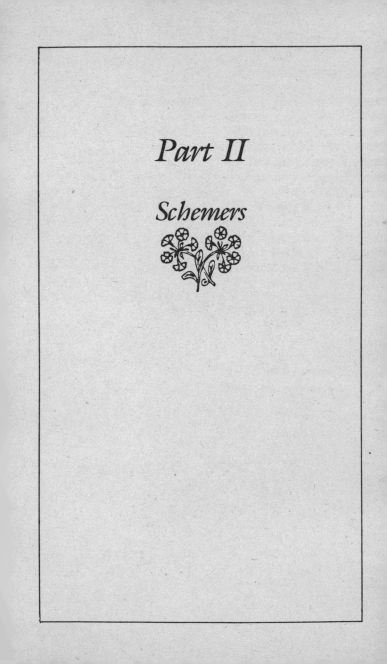

Chapter XV

"Fire!"

The first shot exploded. Pierce watched as the cannon flared, the ball soared, and the water plumed up, hot and white. His shot fell short. He'd intended it that way.

"Get me the glass!" he called to Sean. Within seconds he held a spyglass to his eye, and looked out across the rolling sea to the *Lady May*.

His heart seemed to crash against his chest in a fervor, then go still.

She was there, at the helm, with Niemens.

Ah, Rose!

A trembling swept through him. She had changed little. So very little. Beautiful, passionate, her copper hair catching the sun, she was arguing with Niemens.

Ready to take on the pirates herself, he was certain. Well, that was Rose. Ready to do battle. Some things did not change. She must be frightened. But she didn't look it. She was determinedly telling Niemens something—probably that she was going to re-main on deck.

"Don't let her do it, old boy!" Pierce muttered out loud.

Then he smiled with satisfaction. It didn't appear that Niemens was going to do so. He was appar-ently pleading with Rose, begging her to go below. Smart fellow, Pierce thought. A command would have kept her right where she was standing. An ab-ject plea from the heart might bring her around.

A cannon exploded very near his own ship. White water rained up over him. "Return fire!" he called. "Yet keep it a warning shot!"

Aha! Niemens was going to see to this himself. He took hold of Rose's arm. Her green skirt swirled behind her. Niemens was leading her from the helm, and down to the master's cabin.

Pierce smiled again.

Right where he wanted her.

Now . . . all he had to do was take the ship with as little damage as possible.

The *Lady May* took a shot at him again. It fell just short of the portside deck. The ship rocked and rolled wildly, but Pierce held his stance. "Two vol-leys!" he called to Sean. "One to her starboard, one to her port. Then bear down, and let her know we mean to grapple her!"

The shots were fired at his command. Even as the reverberations died away, his pirate ship was being expertly steered around the *Lady May*. It appeared for long seconds as if the figurehead would jut right through the *Lady May*'s deck, but then his ship came flatly broadside her.

"Grappling hooks," he ordered.

Then he slipped his patch into place and pulled his plumed hat low over his eye, determined that no man aboard the *Lady May* was going to recognize

him until he was ready. He slipped his sword from
the scabbard at his side and leapt down from the
bow to the deck. Some of the more adventurous fellows from the *Lady May* had prepared to jump from
her rigging and sides the moment they had seen they
would be boarded. Those fellows were already engaged in battle, swords clashing with Pierce's men's
blades, determined that they would fight for their
lives. Pierce quickly deflected a blow himself, sending the fellow's sword flying. The man hopped back,
eyes wide, afraid for his life. Pierce stepped on past
him, his voice rising above the shouts and cries and
clashing of steel. "Good fellows, I want no blood-
shed on this ship! Stop the fight. You've proven
your courage. But I tell you, my men will slay you
to the very last man if you force a fight. We've not
come to do murder, nor to take anything that is not
rightly mine. Now, pay heed! I've need to speak
with Niemens, and then he'll speak with you—and
good fellows, I'll warrant that there can be peace
between us!"

There was a silence. Then someone called out,
" 'E's a bloody pirate, ye fools! We can't give him
Captain Niemens!"

"I swear to you—on the Dragonslayer's honor,"
Pierce said, bowing deeply, "that no harm will come
to the good captain!"

There was another hesitation. How could he blame
them? No man had ever looked more the pirate, for
his left lobe sported a gold death's head, his patch
lay over his eye, his loose shirt and form-hugging
trousers were black as night.

He swept off his hat to them. "Gentlemen! On
my honor!"

Before anyone else could speak, Niemens stepped
forward. "I'm Captain Niemens. As you've yet to

seize an English vessel, I'll trust in you. Come into my cabin.''

''Your cabin is occupied. Come into mine.''

'' 'E's not going to your cabin!'' another sailor called out. Sean started forward, drawing his sword.

''Easy!'' Pierce warned him. ''Remember, these are our friends!''

''No one is your friend, my lord, that you can guarantee! No one but those who sail with you now!''

''Niemens will serve me, you will see!'' Pierce said softly. It didn't matter. The man who had challenged Sean had moved back, and Niemens, sprightly for his age, was leaping over the rails between the boats. He had barely approached Pierce when a startled gasp of recognition escaped him.

''Captain!'' someone roared, alarmed.

''It's fine, my lads, it's fine!'' Niemens called out. He clapped Pierce on the shoulder, leading the way to the captain's cabin himself. ''God in His infinite wisdom, Your Grace!'' Niemens exploded. ''You're the Dragonslayer? You? Well, by God, and I wonder if His Majesty Charles doesn't know. He's made no real effort to see that you're apprehended. My God! You're supposed to be dead—''

''Ah, but I'm very much alive!'' Pierce returned softly. ''Can I count on you?''

''To the grave, milord!'' Niemens swore with dignity.

Pierce smiled. ''I didn't do it, Gaylord. Before God and the angels, I swear it. I'm an innocent man.''

''I am your man, sir!''

Pierce glanced toward the *Lady May*. ''What of your crew?'' he asked him anxiously. ''Some of them might know me. Some are assuredly new. What of their loyalty?''

"They'll obey me, I'm certain. Depending, of course, on just what it is you plan!"

"Tell them that I'm taking command of the ship in the next few hours, that I've guaranteed you safe passage after, and that I'll speak with them shortly. Give me just a minute to see my wife. You see, I've come for her, Gaylord. But that's for later. I need just a second with her, and then I'll explain my purpose to the men, and win their cooperation, I warrant."

Niemens nodded. If there was a way, Lord De-Forte would find it. Niemens personally knew every man serving under him. He knew their tempers and their loyalty. He could depend upon them, and he couldn't imagine a one of them who would want to turn the Duke of Werthington in to the authorities in London.

Especially knowing that he was the Dragonslayer, who had given such grief to so many Spaniards!

"I shall go tell the Lady Rose—"

"No, no. Thank you," Pierce said politely with a smile. "I'll go see the Lady Rose." He smiled. "Gather the men on deck. Sean and Jay will follow, just to guard my back until I'm certain all the fellows are at peace."

Niemens nodded. He called out his orders to the men, guaranteeing them that the Dragonslayer would reveal his purpose in a moment, that they were not to fight. They were not, after all, Spaniards.

Pierce leapt over the barriers between the ships, trusting his back to his loyal friends. He quickly strode to Niemens's cabin.

And there he held for a moment. Rose. Just what would she be doing? Heat seared through him. After all this time! This was it.

Revenge.

And all that he wanted to do was touch her again.

He grit his teeth, feeling a rush of fire and steel sweep through him. He kicked upon the door savagely.

And there she was.

For a moment, he stood there in the doorway, drinking in the sight of her. The green of her gown emphasized the emerald of her eyes. Her cheeks were flushed, her lips deeply red against the ivory of her face. Her hair was wild, loosened from the pins that had held it while she had been tossed about the cabin by the wild sway of the ship.

Her face was still every bit as perfectly beautiful as he had remembered. As classically drawn. Her eyes were as wild, as challenging. Her person . . .

Her waist was every bit as trim. Her breasts . . .

Were heaving. Spilling from her gown. They'd grown.

Ummm . . .

The tension in him tightened and wound in a spiral.

She returned his stare, her breasts heaving from exertion, fury and fear mingled in her eyes. She had yet to recognize him, he thought, and he didn't know if that fact amused or angered him. Caught in the tangle of her skirts, she tried to free herself and rise. Jerking upon the cloth, she managed to stagger to her feet, still keeping her eyes locked upon his.

Then he realized that she wasn't quite staring at him anymore, not steadily. Her gaze had slid to the captain's desk where a letter opener lay.

Like lightning she moved, leaping upon the blade and spinning around with it in her hands to stare at him with sheer defiance again.

The letter opener. Against his sword?

Oh, Rose! he thought in silence.

He strode into the cabin. Even as he did so, a fickle

wind picked up. He was so accustomed to the pitch and roll of a ship that he simply balanced with it. Rose teetered precariously. The door slammed shut behind him.

They were alone. At last. At long, long last. Even at this distance, he could smell the sweet scent of her. It curled around him. Beckoned. Taunted.

''I'll kill you!'' she cried out suddenly.

Rose. Sweet, sweet Rose!

''I demand that you leave me be this instant. You'll receive an exceptional ransom for me if you—''

Enough. He took a stride nearer her, smiling as he lifted his sword, just touching it to her waist. She broke off with a gasp. She stared down at the blade, silenced at last.

Pierce smiled. Ah, yes. Revenge. The green gown with its black and white was a true piece of art. With stunning dexterity he lifted his razor-sharp blade, breaking through the laces that tied the bodice together. Her breasts seemed to spill fascinatingly forward. Damn, he just didn't remember them being quite so full or tempting. There was an awful pulse beating in his head, a terrible ache ripping at his body. Suddenly, and with all his heart, he wished that he were a truly dreadful pirate. He'd like to have his wife then and there, naked before him, before the pounding exploded all sense and reason within him.

She stepped back hastily, her letter opener waving menacingly before her. ''I will kill you!'' she promised, trying to hold her gown together. She tried to parry his sword with her small weapon, her chin going up, her eyes ever more emerald and defiant. ''Haven't you listened to a word I've said? My father is wealthy beyond your imagination! He will pay tremendous sums for my safe return. You rogue!

I am incredibly wealthy. Do you know who I am? Are you daft? Can you understand English?"

Did he know who she was! Oh, yes, yes!

Rose, ever wild, ever defiant. So determined and reckless and filled with fire. She flew at him, her little dagger raised and aimed straight for his heart. He caught her wrist, his fingers winding with a furious trembling pressure around her. She gasped, trying to breathe, drawn close to him.

And her fragrance filled him . . .

His fingers wound tighter. A soft cry escaped her at last as the letter opener slid from her fingers. He pushed her from him; she cried out a sharp "No!" and lunged for the letter opener once again. Damn her! When she caught hold of the little weapon again, he knew that she meant to use it, that it was time to end this play. He caught the little blade with an upward thrust of his own, sending it flying.

She was not defeated. Before he could take a step toward her again, missiles began flying his way. The log, a bottle, anything she could get her hands upon.

He came toward her, ducking them, warding them off. He neared her, and lifted the sword to her throat again. He pressed gently, forcing her back. Damn those eyes of hers! They were still so wild, so defiant. And in the shadows and smoke she still hadn't recognized him!

"Kill me then!" she cried. "You foolish, stupid rogue. Thrust your blade through—"

"Oh, madam!" he cried, breaking his silence at last. "I do intend to thrust my blade through. And trust me, lady, I do know exactly who you are. You would pay me ransom with DeForte money, would you, lady? Oh, lady, I think not!"

He laid the sword more flatly against her, a mocking smile curling his lip. He pressed the sword lightly again. Despite her valiant efforts, she sprawled backward to that very spot where he had first seen her, at the foot of the captain's bunk. She lay there, panting, staring at him incredulously. Something widened her eyes. Ah, yes! Now she'd heard his voice.

And now she would know.

He stared at her hard, but couldn't fathom the swift flickering of emotions in her eyes. What would they be? The last time he had seen her, she had been in the act of betraying him. Was there fear within those stunning emerald depths? A fear even deeper than that with which any maid would meet a pirate known as the Dragonslayer? Or was the gleam there that he had always known? Defiance, still, defiance against all odds.

Pierce jerked the black eye patch from his face, tossing it to the foot of the bed. He bowed low to her in mocking courtesy, sweeping his plumed cavalier's hat from his head. He fought the rise of his temper.

And that of his near-overwhelming desire just to touch her, to have her . . .

Had she missed him? At all? Just a little in the darkness of the night?

"Why, milady! You look as if you have seen a ghost!"

"A ghost? Indeed! One dragged up from the depths of hell!" she cried.

Apparently she hadn't missed him.

"Yes, indeed, lady! And Rose, you will find you have awakened a demon!" he promised.

She continued to stare at him incredulously, her eyes gemlike in their luster. Then she cried out, "I thought you were dead!"

"I am so sorry to disappoint you," he said harshly.

"But—the Dragonslayer—"

"Well, I *was* left for dead, you see, my love. But lucky me. I was taken up by a Spaniard with a bone to pick against Englishmen. I was worked and beaten day and night, and made to be eternally grateful for my salvation. Naturally, once I found my freedom—and once I had disposed of the captain—I became a pirate preying upon other Spaniards."

"This is an English vessel!" she reminded him quickly.

"Oh, yes. I know." How dared she! It was his own damned ship. He bent over her, dying a little to touch her. Wanting to wind his fingers around her throat.

Wanting to taste her lips . . .

He gripped his fingers tightly around the carved footboard of the bunk.

"But I had word that you were aboard, my love," he said softly. "Not to mention the fact that it is my own ship!"

She chose to ignore that.

"So what do you want?" she demanded fiercely. So that was it. After all this time, after discovering that he was alive . . .

Hadn't she planned for his death?

Hadn't she . . .

Or had she?

Why wasn't she making some furious bid to claim herself innocent? He wanted to grab her, shake her, demand to know the truth.

Niemens was waiting. The men were waiting. No matter how fierce and furious his passion, this would have to wait.

Yet . . .

Was she trembling? What was the emerald glitter in her eyes, almost like tears?

"What do I want?" he repeated softly. He gritted

his teeth, touched the air with the silver of his sword and brushed it against her throat once again.

He leaned closer against her, his lip curling into a mocking smile. But she wasn't daunted. Not Rose.

"Indeed, what do you want?" she repeated. Ah, but she could be ice!

"What do I want?" he said again, very, very softly.

If only she knew. At that moment? To touch her, ah, just to touch her . . .

He moved his sword swiftly, with great care and precision, slitting the remnant of the bodice of her gown. He groaned aloud to himself, wondering just what in hell he was doing.

Making a threat . . .

Making a promise.

Proud and unwavering, she didn't flinch. Her green eyes met his.

"I want—what every good pirate wants!" he said, smiling mockingly again, yet unsure just who he mocked. He wanted both to stroke her cheek with the greatest tenderness . . .

And to enclose his trembling hand around the exposed mound of her breast. It was lush, it was tempting . . .

It was huge. His last work with the sword had nearly stripped her of a bodice, and he could see the rouge crests of her nipples, too, and even they had seemed to darken and grow.

Making that pulse begin to beat again in his temple, in his loin.

"Plunder, riches! Pieces of eight! Ships and cargo and hostages. And . . . revenge!" he gasped out harshly.

He heard the merciless grating of her teeth. She coolly dared to shove his blade aside. He dropped it, watching her still. "You are a fool, Pierce De-

Forte!'' she hissed softly. ''But be one, if you will. Those who betrayed you are still in England. If you weren't such a stupid food, you'd know that I was innocent—''

''I believed you innocent once! And I paid for that bit of stupidity!'' God! After all this time, revenge was his at last, and all he knew was anguish! He had learned to believe in her after they had wed. He had come to be certain that she had not been in on the plot to kidnap Anne, that she had been as innocent as he in all that had transpired.

And then he had found Anne dead. And even when he had returned to Rose, the soldiers had come. And one of them had cried out that Rose's message had brought them rushing there after him, seeking him where she would hold him until they came . . .

She was innocent, she claimed. Dear God in heaven, how could he believe in her again after that!

''You still don't see the truth! Yet, even if you are a fool, I'll not give away your secret. I'll not tell anyone who you are.''

''How magnanimous of you!'' he cried in amazement. Did she think that he would just sail away now, and enjoy his life as a pirate? Maybe. Maybe she didn't realize that he had come for her first, before dealing with Jerome and anyone else who had aided the man in any way.

Rose was calmly continuing. ''Just return me to my father and—''

''Lady, you must be mad!''

''He'll pay you! You just said that you were after plunder—''

''And revenge. The revenge is so much dearer to my heart!''

She stared at him, emerald eyes blazing. Oh, truly, she had not realized her position yet. She twisted her jaw, gritted her teeth, and stamped a foot furiously. "You will let me go! You've no right—'

"But I do!"

He hadn't meant to really touch her.

Not yet.

She was too distracting. The rich firmness of her breasts was suddenly pressed against him. The silk of her hair teased his hands. Her eyes were liquid, looking into his.

God, he wanted her right then and there!

"Let me go!" she demanded.

Let her go . . .

"You know," he said, "you always were headstrong. A little spitfire. Well, my love, this time, strength of will is not going to be enough. Perhaps I will let you go in time. But if and when I do, it will not be for money, but just because I have tired of my revenge."

"You bastard!" she hissed to him.

"That's right, Lady Rose. Count on it. I will deal with you. And I will return to England and deal with the others, I promise you."

"You cannot return to England! You fool! You will hang!"

"Truly, what difference can it make? If I were to hang for murder I did not commit or lose my head for being a pirate! And believe me, revenge is worth any risk. Why, there were times when thoughts of revenge were all that kept me alive. However, revenge will have to wait just a bit. I've business at hand. But fear not. I will return."

He had to let her go! But he couldn't seem to tear himself away.

At last he did. He released her and turned blindly toward the door.

"Dammit, you wretched bastard!" she accused him, her voice wild. "You are a fool, and you are wrong! I tell you, you will let me go! You've no right, no right at all—''

No right!

Oh, God! He had all the right in the world! Now he really couldn't wait to get his damned hands on her again.

Don't touch her! he warned himself.

But he did. He was back before her. Trembling. He lifted her with scant control, fury, hunger, a tempest, driving him.

He threw her back upon the bunk and straddled her, staring down at her, feeling her, hating her, wanting her.

Loving her.

She was a wildcat. She twisted and bucked and tried with all her might to slap him. He subdued her with a rigid determination.

"Don't tempt me, Rose!"

"Dammit, you've no right—" she repeated.

"You're mistaken. I've every right!" God! He reached out to touch her cheek. To feel its softness.

He snatched his hand away. He had to remember that night at the docks in Dover. Come back to me, she had told him.

And he had come back. After finding Anne dead and fighting an army.

He had wanted her that night, too.

"Have you forgotten that you're—my wife?" he demanded furiously.

"I have never been about to forget!"

"Ah, you thought that you were a widow, rich beyond all imagination, eh? Sorry, my love. I am alive."

"Fool, bastard!" she whispered.

"Ah, but husband still!"

Her eyes glittered as he stared into them. He could feel her trembling. Was it fear? Anger?

Something more?

Aye, she had made denials now. But what could he believe?

He was still an outlaw in London. She was running his shipping business.

He pushed away from her. He had to get out! He strode swiftly for the door, opened it, slammed it in his wake.

He leaned against it then, his eyes tightly shut. She would try it any minute, seeking to escape.

He turned, wedging his sword against the doorframe, making it impossible for her to open it.

Then, seconds later, as he had known she would, he heard her fling herself against it.

"God, I hate you!" he heard her cry, slamming a fist against the door. "I hate you, I hate you . . ."

The last was a heart-wrenching sob.

He stiffened, feeling a new anguish sweep into his spine. He'd wanted revenge. Ah, yes. He could have it now.

But suddenly the taste of it did not seem so sweet in his mouth. The sound of her cry brought a new pain ripping through him.

He didn't want revenge.

He just wanted his wife. He wanted the tempest of love.

But he wanted the sweet peace of it, too.

Chapter XVI

Rose lay upon the bunk fighting the wild pounding of her heart. *He was alive!* No matter what else, the sheer joy of seeing him swept through her. She kept reminding herself that she should be furious with him, that she had never betrayed him, that she had never done anything but fight for him. He didn't believe her. She had no idea what he really intended. And Jesu! She could not give in to him in any way unless she could make him realize the truth.

But he was alive, and she just wanted to touch him, hold him . . .

The door suddenly opened again. She sat up quickly, alert and wary.

It was Pierce. He had returned.

He stepped into the captain's cabin, letting the door fall shut behind him with a definite click.

With the patch off his eye and his plumed cavalier's hat gone from his head, he was very much the man she had known before. He walked across the cabin with a natural grace, well honed and physically muscled and sleek. He was darker now, his skin sun-browned to a deeper bronze. His eyes, if anything, were sharper, more a sizzling silver.

He was the same man . . .

And yet he was different. He had fought battles before. But he had fought open battles in which he had ridden beside his king.

Things had changed now. He had fallen victim to treachery. He had been seized by a Spaniard. Tormented by him.

He came across the room, his eyes upon her, but he did not come near her at first. He took a seat behind the desk, eased his booted feet upon it, and leaned back, watching her with his condemning gray stare. Then he smiled slowly, a smile that was chill, and sent shivers along her spine.

"Well, Rose, we are, at long last, alone and with time to share! And just imagine! There will be no one to beat upon that door, seeking my arrest!"

She controlled her temper through that, sitting as regally and as decently as she could manage with her ripped bodice. "What have you done with Captain Niemens?" she inquired icily.

He arched an ebony brow, staring at her. Then she tensed, nearly jumping, for his feet fell to the floor and he rose, approaching her swiftly. She inched back upon the bunk. His arms created bars about her as he braced himself, leaning against the wall behind her. His face. So close. She could see the burning silver in his eyes, feel the warmth of his breath, and the hair-trigger tension within him.

"Worried about the good captain?" he inquired tauntingly.

"What have you done with him?"

He pushed away from her, and began to stride across the cabin. He reminded her then of a caged cat, but he had created the boundaries of his own cage. He came to a halt then, leaning against the desk, half sitting upon the edge of it.

"You're forgetting, my love, this is my ship. Before my, er, demise, Niemens was one of my captains. For many, many years. And it was so amazing. Captain Niemens was glad to see that I was alive, my love."

That could easily be the truth, she thought swiftly. But what of the crew? She had heard the cannon fire, the screeching of the grappling hooks, the awful clang and clash of steel.

"What of the crew?" she whispered. "I heard the fighting."

"Well, milady, I couldn't announce my true identity until I was close to Niemens! I did have to seize the ship, you see, but I am pleased to tell you that I was able to convince the sailors to send the good captain quickly to a parley. I took the ship without the cost of a single life."

She raised her chin. "Then what is your plan?"

"We are sailing to England," he told her.

"England!"

She leapt up. She forgot the disheveled state of her clothing. She couldn't possibly go to England, not now. She couldn't leave Woody. She shook her head vehemently. "I cannot go to England!"

"Milady, it seems you have not realized your position here! It isn't your choice. It is my ship. Even if it were not, I am still the man who seized it. We will sail where I choose, milady, and nowhere else!"

"You don't understand!" she told him. She closed the distance between them. "You can't do that, you just can't! My father—"

"Your father!" he snapped back. "The illustrious merchant Ashcroft Woodbine! I understand that he had you headed for Bermuda, and there to snare another unwary suitor! Ah, let's see, the man was

Sir Wesley, I believe. Really, Rose! Your father was failing you. He would take down a duchess to marry a simple 'sir'?''

She didn't think. Yet even if she had taken the time to, she would have done the same thing, no matter how blindly stupid her actions were. She struck him. Swiftly, surely, with fire and menace.

And there was a wonderful, if brief, feeling of elation that filled her then, for her blow was quick and sure. Her hand connected loudly with his cheek. The blow left her fingerprints upon it.

Elation was quickly lost, for she saw the deep-set fury in his eyes and then found herself drawn against him, swept into his arms. Struggling fiercely, she flailed against him. "Let me down, you—pirate!" She was distressed that she couldn't think of anything more heinous to label him. "Put me down. This instant.''

She was down. Facedown on his lap, and he seemed to be fighting with the massive swirl of her petticoats. "Since the day I first met you I thought that a really sound switching would serve you extremely well. If I could just get through this tangle—''

"Don't!'' she shrieked, pushing up against him. His hands were merciless.

She bit into his thigh.

He swore violently, then wrenched her around. The dress he had partially ripped began to tear apart completely, leaving her exposed and vulnerable. His hands upon her were punishing and cruel, his eyes were alive with fire. The violence in him was frightening, and she found herself whispering for mercy despite her very best resolve.

"Please! Pierce! Please!''

The violence suddenly left him. He released her, sitting back up on the bunk, watching her from the corner of his eye. "Damn, Rose! Don't tempt me then!"

She lay near him, panting. She tried to struggle up, inching away from him. His eyes roamed over her torn bodice, over her breasts. His voice was husky. He reached out a hand to her. "Come here, Rose."

She shook her head, near tears, gritting her teeth.

"Come here!" he said again. "It has been a long, long time!"

"A long time," she repeated.

"Give me your hand."

"No!"

One of those jet brows of his went up again, a sure sign that his temper was rising. She didn't care.

"Rose, you're still my wife."

"Aye, but a widow a long time now, as you've noted! One you mock and rage against and refuse to give quarter to! If you think that I'll jump, milord, at your beck and call, you've quite another think coming. So far you have done nothing but manhandle and insult me—and my father. I'll not come anywhere near you, I swear it!"

"You're my wife!" he insisted, his voice harsh.

"Then perhaps you would care to apologize, and if you do so with enough humility, I may eventually decide to forgive you."

"Forgive me!" There was surprise, as well as thunder, in his tone. Then he smiled, though the curve of the lips over his teeth wasn't at all friendly. "My lady, I can only pray that you begin to make up to me all that you have done!"

She inched farther to her side of the bunk, her eyes warily upon him. "Milord, I tell you again—I did nothing! Try as I may, I don't seem to be able to get that through your very thick skull. So, milord, as it stands, I shall scream blue blazes if you put so much as a finger upon me. I shall make such a horrible racket that even your pirate crew will rush in here, demanding that you release me!"

He smiled. "Oh, I don't think so, Rose. A number of my pirate crew served with me aboard the Spaniard's ship. Were I to strangle you and feed you bit by bit to the sharks, I don't think that they'd interfere a whit!"

"What about Captain Niemens! And this crew!"

"I don't give a damn," he told her politely.

"But—"

"Captain Niemens knows that you're my wife. Every man jack out there knows it."

"How can you want someone who hates you?" she cried desperately.

A brow arched again. She hugged her knees to her chest, trying hard to keep her distance from him. But he leaned against her. He reached out, just his forefinger moving gently over the angle of her cheek. "Do you hate me?"

"I must!" she snapped back. "To have done all those things you accuse of me doing!"

"Prove me mistaken," he said softly.

"Prove me guilty!" she cried.

The tender stroke of his finger stilled. " 'Come back to me, Pierce!' " he quoted from that awful night. "How clearly I remember those words. And how clearly I remember what I discovered at Huntington Manor, and what happened once I returned to you!"

"I hadn't the least idea that Anne was dead!" she told him furiously. "I'd never have sent you there had I any suspicion! Jesu, how could I know that the authorities might be coming after you?"

"How indeed—unless you were in league with Jerome? You did meet with Jerome. You told me so."

"You are insidious!" she whispered fiercely,

afraid that her tears would fall any second. She was choking. "You can say things like that, and then think to command my emotions!"

"I think," he said, "that it has been a long, long time!"

"A long time! Indeed! And I am much older and wiser now! I'll not pay for sins I've not committed! If you lay awake nights, dreaming of revenge, take your revenge. Bring out your whips—cut me into bite-size pieces for the sharks!"

"How strange!" he said softly. "I had dreamed of just such a revenge. But something else was always there in the dreams, too!"

"And that was . . . ?"

"Wanting you! Rose, you know me! I will have you. Come to me!"

She shook her head wildly. "You accuse me of horrible things, seize the ship I'm upon, and command that we go to England! Then you think that you can command my surrender! Well, you can't do it. And I will not go to England, I cannot go to England! And I will not be seduced or taken by you, I will not fall prey to your talents or expertise—"

"Or hunger?" he asked softly. The sudden, deep tenderness in his tone seemed to rip cruelly through her, far worse than any threatening roar or thunder. Oh, God, yes, it had been a long time. And she, too, had lain awake so very many nights, remembering, wanting him. His touch, the sound of his voice, the feel of his arms around her when she slept.

She stared at him, amazed at what he could do with his voice, his eyes. He demanded, then he invited, but it didn't really matter what he did, because, from the beginning, he meant to have what he wanted.

And he would.

He didn't wait for her to offer her hand, he found it. She hadn't the chance nor the breath to do anything other then gasp out a small protest before she found herself cradled in his arms, on his lap, the two of them in the center of the bunk. Then he was staring down at her, the silver in his eyes a fire that touched and warmed her blood. She still longed desperately to fight him. But the absolute hunger and passion in his eyes touched some cord deep inside her. She wanted to cry out again. She opened her mouth, yet only a gasp came from it.

And then it was too late. His mouth crashed down upon hers. Fevered, urgent. And seductive. She fleetingly tried to keep her lips sealed to the prod of his tongue. How foolish. He breached that barrier easily. Skimmed her lips, her teeth, and played with her tongue, moved within her mouth, touching, seeking, delving, a kiss so totally erotic, it swept away reason. She knew that she couldn't, mustn't, respond.

But neither could she deny him. She closed her eyes and felt the ecstasy of his heat against her. Breathed in the scent of him, savored the taste of him, and the feel of his arms around her. She could not respond . . .

But it was so wonderfully good. She had thought him dead, and a part of her had died. He lived, and now magic was alive inside her once again. She knew so little, yet she knew that no other man could have his passion, his tension, his vital drive. No one but Pierce . . .

His mouth rose from hers, but his eyes seared into her own. Her lips felt damp and swollen as she stared into the silver fire of his gaze. She shook her head, denying all that she felt. Desperate. He had to believe in her.

''No, Pierce!''

His lips lowered to her throat, his fingers pressing back the torn fabric of her bodice. His lips touched her collarbone, found the pulse at her throat. His tongue trailed a burning line from that pulse to the valley between her breasts, then his hand cupped over a mound. She shifted, fighting the fire that the tender caress of her flesh aroused within her elsewhere. She closed her eyes, gritting her teeth.

No . . .

But oh, God! It had been so very long! And he was whispering so softly against her flesh. "My love, you've changed . . ." His voice, his whisper, the hot feel of his breath against her flesh . . . all were so erotic! She would not give in! she promised herself. But his words were washing over her. She was adrift already in a sea of sensation. She had to stop him soon, or she would be lost.

Aching. Wanting . . .

A kiss fell on her breast. "You've changed and grown and . . . my God, the feel of your flesh, the taste of it, the sweetness . . ." His words left off. He groaned softly, his fingers lightly curling around the globe of her breast, his tongue dancing lightly over the crest, then the fullness of his mouth settling over it, bathing it, warming it, sucking upon it.

"Dear God!"

Suddenly his dark head shot up, his eyes, a thousand blades of steel, were cutting into her with dark fury and amazement. His arms, still around her, tightened punishingly, and she nearly cried out.

Yet he hadn't mean to hurt her. Not then.

"You taste of—of milk!" he said incredulously.

She felt herself redden from her cheeks to her bare chest. She struggled to rise against him, but his fingers were threaded through her hair and he held her tightly.

"Yes, yes!" she cried. "I taste like milk! It happens when a woman has had a child!'' she continued in a whisper.

She didn't know if he was going to toss her from him, or crush her in the fury of his embrace. His face lowered against hers.

''Whose child?'' he demanded fiercely.

''Oh, how dare you!'' she shrieked. ''I have absolutely had it! I'll take no more insults from you, I swear it! Beat me, rape me, throw me overboard! But no more of this!''

He still stared at her. To her amazement, his touch was not half so brutal. He leaned back, as if he needed the support of the wall to remain straight.

''Mine?'' It was barely a whisper, ragged and hot.

''Yours!'' she cried in return.

His fingers tightened upon her. ''You swear it?''

''Oh!'' she cried out in renewed fury, struggling to rise. But she had never felt him more rigid, more merciless, in all her life. ''Swear it! You ask me to swear it! You don't believe a word I say no matter what, so why in God's name would I swear? Let me go! I'd far rather *jump* to the sharks then endure another moment of this!''

But he wasn't going to let her go. The silver eyes were still burning into hers.

''A boy or a girl?'' he demanded.

''It's none of—''

''A boy or a girl?'' he roared.

''A son,'' she murmured.

Suddenly she could have broken free. He was barely holding her.

''Mine? I have a son?''

She shoved at his chest, determined that she was going to be free at last. He didn't fight her. She rose, fleeing to the desk, coming around it to put the bulk of it between the two of them. But he still seemed too amazed to come after her.

Or perhaps it didn't matter. If he did want her, he needed only to stride around the desk. And he knew it.

"A son?" he said again, and it was barely a whisper. "And he's alive, and well?"

She didn't want her heart to warm the way that it was doing. She didn't want to forgive him for anything until he had begged for her to do so.

He shook his head, as if he still couldn't quite comprehend the situation. "How old is he?"

"Nine months and a few days," she told him grudgingly

Then he stood. Rose backed away nervously, but he wasn't coming for her. He pulled open the bottom drawer of the desk, then the second drawer, and there he found what he was seeking. It was a liquor bottle. He started to reach for one of the tin mugs beside it, then muttered something unintelligible.

Then he swallowed down a huge draft from the bottle, shuddering all the while that fiery liquor burned its way down his gullet.

"A son," he mused again. Maybe he'd been counting. And maybe he'd realized that the child most probably had to be his.

It seemed the best time to strike her bargain, Rose realized, and she spoke very quietly to him.

"You see, I can't go to England with you. I have to go home. He is still so young. I can't possibly just leave him."

"You left him to come on this voyage!" he reminded her sharply.

"I was returning immediately."

"Ah! And what about Sir Wesley, the very eligible husband material?"

"I assure you, milord DeForte, I was traveling on

business! I had one husband, and that was certainly enough grief for me for a lifetime!''

''Ah!'' he murmured.

''I have to go home to Woody!''

''Who?'' he demanded sharply.

''Woody. The baby.''

''You named my son—the future Duke of Werthington—Woody?'' His words were incredulous.

She sighed. ''His name is Pierce Woodbine DeForte. We call him Woody.''

''Woody.''

''I can't go to England!'' she persisted.

''His home is Castle DeForte!'' he snapped.

She bit her lip, swiftly lowering her eyes. He was definitely in the position of power right now. Whether she still wanted to crack a bottle over his head or not, she was going to try to control her temper.

''I told you, milord, he is only nine months old! I always planned to take him to England. I really didn't wish to risk the health of a very small babe on so long a voyage. I just wanted him to be at least a year old before starting. If you don't believe me, you're welcome to ask Captain Niemens. He was going to be my captain when I was ready to bring Woody. And if you doubt—''

She broke off. Geoffrey could have told him! Geoffrey could have told him about the endless hours she had waited for the king, and then all the time she had tried so hard to see that Pierce's name was cleared.

But Geoffrey wasn't with her. He was with Garth in England; the two of them were caring for Castle DeForte, the ships, the English estates.

''If I doubt what?'' he snapped.

She shook her head angrily. ''I've nothing more to say to you!''

He leveled a finger at her. "You, milady, will have plenty more to say to me!"

But with those words, he was striding out of the room once again. She tried to follow him, running after him. "Pierce!"

He spun around, stopping her. "What do you think you're doing, trying to run out on deck half-clad like that?"

She stood dead still, her temper soaring. "Oh, this is rich! You tear my clothing to shreds, then accuse me of improper behavior? Oh, my God, it would serve you right if I were to strip to the bone and go dancing out on deck!"

He caught her wrist and pulled her to him. "Make such a threat again, milady, and you will be out there, naked, tied to a mast, and trust me! You will be feeling the sting of a cat-o'-nine-tails!"

"You wouldn't dare!" she charged him.

"Don't tempt me! I dare almost anything these days, my love!"

"Don't tempt you! My God, Pierce! My place in heaven shall be assured just for what I have endured from you!"

"Really?" he inquired, coming close again for just one minute. A smile curved his lip. "Saint Rose, is it? Well, you can rest assured that there is much, much more you're going to endure from me!"

He forced her back, and left the cabin.

"Damn you!" she cried after him. "Damn you!"

Pierce strode out on deck, barely hearing her. He still couldn't believe it. In all his long days of captivity, and in all the time he had sailed as a pirate, he had never imagined that he might be a father. A warmth filled him. A trembling shot through him. A son. Woody. Woody! What a name for a titled lord!

He smiled. Well, then again, the future duke was only nine months old. Maybe the name was all right.

He closed his eyes. She had had his child. Well, that was the way of things.

His stomach turned in turmoil. Again, she was claiming her innocence. And so self-righteously! If only he dared believe again . . .

Sean came striding up to him. "Captain! Do we sail straight for England now?"

"What?" he looked blankly at Sean.

"Do we sail for England?"

He shook his head. "I have a son."

"Milord?" Sean looked puzzled.

Pierce laughed suddenly, catching both Sean's shoulders and giving him a hug. "I've a son. I need to retrieve him. I'll tell her—no, I won't. Sean, go to the cabin and . . ." He paused. No! Rose was barely dressed. He cleared his throat. He was the only man who'd be going back to the cabin now. "Find out from Niemens where milady's trunks are. Bring them to me. Quickly. I need to speak with her just a moment longer, then I'll deal with the crew. Hurry now."

Sean nodded. "We'd best hurry, milord! There's another ship's sails appearing far out on the horizon. I can't tell what her flag is, but I thought we had best begin to outrun her before she comes close."

Pierce nodded gravely. "I'll hurry."

Sean returned with a heavy trunk very quickly, and Pierce returned to Rose.

Rose was in a tempest. He had to go back to Virginia! He had been amazed to hear that she'd borne him a child, but pleased. Didn't most men want sons?

Especially men who might hang if it was discovered that they weren't dead already?

She strode to the desk herself, lifted the liquor bottle there, and took a huge swallow. It wasn't rum, it was whiskey, Scots whiskey, strong and potent. She felt it burn through her body, all the way to her soles. It was good, it was warm, it was sustaining. She took another long swallow, shuddering with it. She had just set the bottle down when he burst into the cabin again. Standing in the doorway, he watched her set the liquor bottle down with just a twinge of guilt.

"Ah, so you've acquired a taste for the rough stuff, eh, milady?" he murmured.

"I'm certain, milord, that given time, you could drive me to drink heavily!" she informed him.

"I don't think that saints are supposed to imbibe quite so freely," he told her with a touch of amusement. Another warm shudder ripped through her, but it had nothing to do with the liquor, she realized.

It had to do with the fact that he was alive.

"Even saints have their bad days!"

"Well, my dear saint, swig away. Your day is going to get worse!"

She realized then that he was carrying one of her trunks. It had been left on deck when they had first boarded, though she would have been given the captain's cabin for the voyage sometime during the day.

Pierce set the trunk down on the floor. "You'd best find something decent to wear."

Rose sat stiffly at the edge of the desk, staring at him. "You wouldn't have me striding off the ship with your handiwork so displayed?" she asked sweetly.

He walked over to her, hands folded over his chest. "Well, milady, I can tear the rest of the garment to shreds if you choose. We pirates are wonderful at such acts!''

She felt some of the blood rush from her face, but she tried to hold her ground. "So I have heard. So you've managed to practice ripping up gowns in these many months?''

"Actually, due to the new information that you have given me, I had intended to wait until later to do any more ripping on yours. When I had time. Lots of time. To make it very slow, and enjoyable. But if you don't feel that you can remove this gown by yourself, then I shall just simply have to make the time now—''

"I can change the gown, thank you!" she told him swiftly.

"Do so. Quickly.''

"Are you going back to Virginia?" she asked. "I demand that you tell me now!''

He arched a brow high. "Oh, my love! You seem to have missed something here! I am the one making the demands!" he told her. "Now, get dressed!''

With that, he slammed his way out of the cabin again.

"Damn you!" she swore furiously when he left. Was he or wasn't he going to take her home?

Could she take the chance that he would?

She was ready to burst out after him when she realized that she did want to be dressed. She plunged quickly into the trunk, giving little heed to what she chose to wear at first, then pausing.

She found the simplest cotton gown in the trunk. It was a blue day dress with a little fringe. She shed her petticoat, her plan taking shape in her head. He hadn't locked her in. She was going to dress, and escape out on deck. With any luck at all, she could find a way to free one of the dinghies and escape . . .

Where?

To another ship.

It was a wild plan, but it was possible.

She closed her eyes in anguish. She still couldn't believe that he was alive. But she couldn't allow him to take her away from Woody!

The second she was dressed, she hurried from the cabin. To her amazement, no one noticed her at first. Every sailor aboard the ship had gone mad, so it seemed. They were all rushing about, pulling in sails, listening to the orders that were being shouted out by her husband.

What in God's name was going on?

She couldn't take the time to wonder. She ran quickly portside and looked to the rigging that held the dinghy in place. Oh, God, she could never manage it! Yes, she could. She could leap aboard the little boat, then inch the ropes down bit by bit. It would take time, but they were all so involved with their work that they wouldn't notice.

Did she want to do this? she wondered in agony. Lying awake all those nights, praying, remembering . . .

Don't think, jump! she commanded herself.

She did so, just as she heard cannon fire. She screamed, landing in the boat, and feeling it rock and sway wildly.

''The Spaniard's shooting at us, Captain!'' someone called out.

Oh, God, no! A ship had come upon them. Another ship had arrived, with all the ocean to choose from!

And it was a Spaniard, hurtling more cannon fire at them!

''Fire now!'' Pierce roared in reply.

Still careening, their ship returned the Spaniard's fire. The little dinghy began to swing madly. To

Rose's horror, it swung with such a vengeance that she was flipped wildly out to sea.

She hit the water hard, as if it were a wall, then went spiraling deeply down into it, encompassed by icy blackness. Her lungs burned. She fought the water, treading against it. The light! Oh, God, where was the light of day?

On the deck of the ship, Pierce carefully watched the Spaniard's maneuvers. She hadn't realized that she was up against two ships! he thought. She had seen the pirate flag of the *Dragonslayer* and she had attacked, not realizing that there was an English vessel right beside her. Not at first. She had seen it, and she had begun to shoot wildly.

They could take her easily, Pierce knew.

But dammit, he didn't want a Spanish ship now! He wanted to get to Virginia, retrieve his son, and sail on to England.

"Fire two!" he roared out, and once again the cannon slammed. Another echoed from his nearby pirate ship, for the crew had not as yet had a chance to take her very far.

Then he heard it. The wild cry of warning from his own ship.

"Man overboard! Man overboard. Man—oh, no! Captain, *woman* overboard! The Lady DeForte!"

Rose!

What the hell was she doing? he wondered furiously. She was out of the cabin—

Trying to escape in the middle of the Atlantic Ocean!

Fear plunged into his heart. "Call the orders!" he shouted to Sean. Rose! After all this time. After wanting her so long. Dying for her a little each day . . .

After learning that she had borne him a son . . .

He raced across the deck, catching hold of the rigging and swinging to balance upon the wooden rail. He saw the swirl in the water where she had plunged into the depths. He arched, and dived cleanly after her.

Cold embraced him. The salt water stung his eyes. He swam hard and deep, searching for her until his lungs threatened to burst. He came to the surface, gasping in air for another dive. Then he saw her head, bobbing just feet away. She was trying to swim back toward the ship. "Rose!" he shouted.

Her eyes met his. Emerald and as wild as the tempest of the sea.

Then, between them, a cannon ball went ripping into the sea. A cascade of white water exploded. It fell, and he saw her no more.

"Rose!" Treading the water, he roared out her name. Desperately he swam to where she had been, plunged beneath the water.

In the darkness, his arms came around her. He dragged her up with him, forcing her head above the surface. She choked, then gasped. He clutched her chin, keeping her face above the water. "Hold on!" he told her desperately. "Hold on!"

A dinghy had been lowered and was now lapping through the water toward them. Sean was rowing hard. He pulled back on the oars, bringing the boat around. He reached out, and pulled Rose in while Pierce crawled aboard of his own power.

He grasped his wife immediately, sweeping her into his arms. She lay with her back against his chest, her eyes closed. He chafed her wrists, stroked her cheeks. "Rose! Rose!" She was breathing, no longer choking. Her eyes flew open.

"Jesu!" he whispered with fear, his hand upon her cheek, twisting her face, meeting her emerald eyes. "What the hell did you think that you were doing?"

"I didn't think that I was doing anything!" she gasped. "I—"

"You'd kill yourself to escape me!"

"I wouldn't—"

"You almost did!"

"No! I was only jumping into the dinghy! I would have been fine if you could have managed to pirate only one ship a day!"

"I'm not attacking the Spaniard, Rose! The damned Spaniard is attacking me!"

"Serves you right for being a pirate!"

"If you hadn't tried to escape—"

"If you'd just told me that we could go back for the baby, I wouldn't have been trying to escape!" she cried.

Sean suddenly cleared his throat. "Perhaps you might continue this discussion later, milord. It seems that we still have problems at the moment."

They did have problems. They had come alongside the Spaniard. The men had taken her cleanly and were transferring the hostages to the *Lady May*.

"Take milady," Pierce quickly told Sean. "Jesu!" he sighed in exasperation. "No patch, no hat, nothing!"

"The naked pirate!" Rose muttered.

He cast her a warning gaze, leaping for the rigging as the dinghy reached the ship. It was all right. One of his men had his sword and hat ready as he leapt over the railing and came upon the deck. Manuel was there, ready with the patch. Except for the fact that he was dripping wet, he was the Dragonslayer once again.

He strode before his hostages, a group of dons and their ladies on their way to Cartagena, so the *capitán* told him. He was an old man, very straight, with a curled gray mustache. He looked dead ahead while he answered the questions put forth to him by Pierce in Spanish. "Why did you attack these ships?" Pierce demanded, perplexed.

"I sought the advantage of first fire," the *capitán* told him.

He was about to give the man his usual speech and send him on his way, but even as he opened his mouth, he heard a soft entreaty.

"Dragonslayer!"

Rose stood behind him. Her sea-soaked gown hugged the perfection of her figure. Her eyes were enormous, and the great wealth of her hair hung upon her, darkened by the water. She was still stunning. Beautiful beyond belief.

"Milady!" he snapped, his teeth grating. "If you'll let me handle my affairs—"

"Please!" she begged, stepping forward. "Please! Let them go!"

What the hell had she thought that he intended to do with them? Then he wondered wryly if she could possibly have believed the rumors that he had purposely started himself.

Jesu, he just wanted out of this now!

And he didn't want to think about innocence or guilt or betrayal. He just wanted his wife.

He lifted his sword. He smiled. He bowed gallantly to her. "As you wish, milady." He turned back to the Spaniards, and his men. "Set our guests aboard their vessel once again. Let them go."

The old *capitán* understood his English. He looked from Pierce to Rose, then rushed forward, dropping to his knees, kissing her hand. "The Virgin will bless you, milady! God will bless you—"

"Yes, yes, yes, she's the saint of all saints!" Pierce said irritably. "Now, go! Before I change my mind!"

They was a scramble of footsteps and noise behind him. The old *capitán* hurried away. Pierce stared at Rose. He walked toward her slowly. Her eyes met his. "Thank you," she said softly.

"Are you really grateful?" he asked.

She nodded.

"Grateful enough to stay aboard the damned ship?"

She smiled just slightly. "You saved my life. Only because of the cannon ball," she said quickly. "Otherwise, I swim very well—"

"And you ride very well, too?"

Her lashes covered her cheeks. "You know, Pierce," she said very softly, raising her eyes to his once again, "I did plow into you that day on the hunt. It seems like forever ago, doesn't it? But now I can admit it. I was guilty of that. But of nothing else. I had no part in Anne's kidnapping. And upon my son's life, milord, I swear that I sent you to Anne with my heart raging with both jealousy and fear. I didn't want to lose you, but I didn't want her to die. Jerome tricked us all—you, me, and even Jamison. For all that has happened, I am heartily, bitterly sorry."

His heart slammed against his chest. His hands clenched hard. For so very long he had lived with the fury in his heart . . .

And now all his resolve seemed to crumble to dust, and blow away in the soft, salty breeze.

She didn't wait for an answer. She turned, striding wet and dripping—and dignified still—back to the captain's cabin.

He turned to Sean, who had been silently awaiting his orders.

Sean smiled. "She really is beautiful!" he said, and added quickly, "Milord!"

"Sail for Virginia, my friend," he said, and went striding after Rose.

She stood at the captain's desk, shivering. Pierce

quickly stripped the blanket from the bunk and wrapped it around her shoulders. She pulled uneasily away from him, watching him.

"You have to change," he said. "Then you can prepare your story for your father."

She moistened her lips, still wary. "We are returning to Virginia?"

He sighed softly. "We were always returning to Virginia, Rose!"

"I've no intention of lying to my father."

How could she wind his heart around her finger so quickly and then be so damned stubborn? "Then you'd best change your intentions. I don't want to have trouble with him," Pierce said irritably.

"All right, fine! What am I going to tell my father?"

"You'll say that you met up with another ship at sea. A DeForte ship. You were warned that there has been some trouble at the castle, and that you are needed to sign papers so that the title and land can come to your son. It's urgent that you get to England immediately, and so you're going to leave first thing in the morning on the *Lady May*. Captain Niemens will still be your captain. The crew is prepared to take the ship. We'll need provisions for the longer voyage, but with your father's influence in Virginia, he will manage to have that done immediately."

She didn't reply right away. She stared down at her trunk. "We can just tell my father the truth," she suggested. "He—"

"No!" Pierce snapped quickly. "I do not trust men easily!"

"Nor women!" she reminded him. "If he catches you as it is, you might well find yourself hanged!"

"Then you had best be an angel, my love. Because I've acquired some very loyal friends as a pirate. If anything were to happen to me . . ."

"What?" she demanded.

He smiled. "Do you really want to find out?"

She arched a brow. "Fine, milord DeForte. I shall be as careful as I can manage that no one discovers your identity!"

He paused a moment, watching her. He had meant to leave, but he didn't. Then a sudden, startling rush of emotion flowed from his voice as he spoke. "I fell in love with you, Rose," he said softly. "Did you know that?"

Her breath caught. No. She felt like collapsing. Had he ever loved her? Really loved her. Had he believed her? Did he believe in her even now? Had her words at last changed his heart?

"I loved you!" she whispered hoarsely. Tears were forming in her eyes. She fought to keep them from falling. "I thought I would go mad when they told me that you had died." Passion suddenly filled her. Her tears were starting. "You wronged me again and again! How could you! How could you have believed that I would be in league with Jamison! You owe me an apology! You should be begging for my forgiveness—"

"Rose!" he cried, striding to her. She was in his arms. His lips touched hers. Warm, wonderful, so filled with power and desire and naked excitement. She longed to have him kiss her forever. She longed to feel his hands upon her.

"Milord!" There was pounding on the door. "Milord DeForte! We approach the harbor closely now."

He pulled away from her, his eyes burning into hers. "We will have time later!" he said hoarsely. Then he turned, leaving her.

She quickly shed her wet gown and donned another, her heart and mind a tempest.

Pierce didn't return. Not until they had nearly

come into port, and then he stepped into the cabin for a moment only.

"We must take care here, Rose! I'm warning you, my love!"

As if he might still have some doubts?

"Oh, I'll not give away your identity!" she told him.

"I didn't suggest—"

"Neither have you begged my pardon!" she cried.

"Rose!" He pulled her up against him. "There's just a night here we'll be apart. And when that night is over, we'll have time."

Damn him! He was hardly humble!

He urged her toward the door to the cabin. She exited it, meeting Captain Niemens's pleased gaze almost immediately.

" 'Tis a miracle!" he told her.

"Oh, yes! A miracle," she agreed.

"Captain, since I must be but a poor ship's hand here, would you be so good as to escort my wife to her father?" Pierce asked softly.

"Indeed, milady!" Niemens bowed low to her. Rose smiled, and on his arm, she walked the gangplank from the ship to the deep-water dock.

She saw Ashcroft right away. Someone must have warned him that the *Lady May* was returning to her home port. Wearing a worried frown, he stood at the far end of the dock. She cried out softly, leaving Niemens and her husband as she raced down the wooden walkway.

Let him wonder! she thought. Oh, she was so ecstatic that he was alive, and her heart was filled with the wonder of things that lay in the future. But damn him! He did owe her a very serious apology! Let him worry just a little bit about what she might say to her father! So he was the one with the power! Hmmph!

Damn him! So she was to go home, and spend a night in torture, waiting. And he'd just join his fellows and head for a tavern and drink the night away, and God knew what else.

She had nearly reached her father, but he didn't have a chance to speak at first. Ashcroft was full of questions. "What happened, daughter? Are you all right? The crew? What's happened? I've been a wreck since the ship was first sighted, wondering what's gone on. You're not hurt in any way?"

She shook her head firmly. Behind her, the sailors were coming off the ship.

"No, Father, I just met another DeForte ship on the way out and discovered that it was bearing messages for me. I have to get to England quickly to ensure that Castle DeForte and Pierce's possessions pass smoothly to Woody. I'm very sorry about Bermuda, Father. It will have to wait."

Ashcroft shook his head. "As long as you are well. England, though. I don't like the idea a bit. Not a bit." He was frowning, looking over her shoulder. "Now, who's that young fellow?" he demanded.

Pierce had come off the ship. He was standing just off the gangway, talking to the sailor he had called Sean.

This was it! Her father had given her a wonderful plan. Fallen perfectly into her lap, here was the opportunity she had awaited!

Rose raised her voice so that Pierce could hear, and to her amazement, a story quickly came to her. "That fellow? The one with the shifty eyes? Why, he's—a convict. Sold into labor, he's to serve Captain Niemens for seven years, so I hear. 'Twas a way to keep the fellow out of Newgate."

"A convict!" Ashcroft said.

"Oh, yes. But his crime was nothing so serious. He stole food. Since Captain Niemens always sees to it that men eat well, he was quite certain that this one would not be a danger to himself or other men."

Her father, a compassionate man despite any front he tried to keep up, shook his head. "Imagine! Seven years labor for stealing bread!"

Rose lowered her voice. "He's not that nice a fellow, Father. Don't feel too sorry for him."

"What's his name?"

"Ford," she said quickly. "Peter Ford. Actually, Father, I had been thinking that you might want to take him with us for the evening, and put him to work at the manor. There are numerous things I need done." She lowered her voice. "That way, Father, he will be less of a trial for Niemens. He won't have to worry about the man getting carried away in a tavern, and not being able to hold his grog!"

Ashcroft was frowning. "Will he be safe for you to travel with tomorrow?"

Safe? Not in the least!

"Oh, yes, of course. He stole bread, Father. That was all. Captain Niemens is very fond of the fellow, so he must be redeemable."

Her father nodded to her. "Fine then, daughter. We'll help Niemens out." He raised his voice—calling to Pierce. "You, you there! Young Master Peter! Come here, my good man. Take my daughter's things, and load them onto our carriage. I'll let Niemens know you're doing an honest night's work for me, and see that you're well fed in exchange. Indeed, there might be a gold piece in it for you. Something to save for the day when you've earned your freedom! I'll go speak with Niemens immediately."

"Oh, no!" Rose cried. "I'll do it, Father."

She ran back to Niemens. He was standing with Sean. She offered them both a beautiful smile.

Oh, she was going to relish the night!

"I had to make up a story about my husband for my father, Captain. He saw Pierce and wanted to know about him. I told him that he was a convict, working off his sentence for stealing bread. Father has decided to have him serve us for the night, so don't be afraid when he disappears."

"But, milady—" Niemens began.

"I had to do something!" she cried innocently. "Oh! Father is waiting. Don't worry! We'll be ready to sail, first thing in the morning!"

She hurried back to her father, smiling benignly. Ashcroft lifted the heavy trunk himself, nearly throwing it into Pierce's arms. "My boy! You can manage that much better than I can!"

Pierce caught the trunk, gritting his teeth. Rose smiled with narrowed eyes, and in turn, Pierce cast her a heated, warning gaze, but there was very little that he could do. She lowered her eyes demurely, her smile still in place.

She managed to fall behind with him as they walked toward her father's carriage.

"Having difficulty as a servant, my lord?" she inquired sweetly. "I imagine you had a much different evening planned. I am so sorry! But what was I to say to Father? I had to keep your true identity a secret!"

His silver eyes lit upon her in a way that made her shiver. "I've no difficulty in carrying a trunk, milady."

"Ah, yes, but there will be so much more for you to do once we reach the house!" she said quietly. "So very much more for you to—endure at my hands!"

"Just remember, milady, that whatever you give, I will be delighted to return to you, tenfold."

"Rose?" he father said, calling to her worriedly.

"Threat—or promise?" she challenged Pierce.

He lowered his head to her. "Whichever! Bear in mind, my love, that very soon I will no longer be threatening, but carrying out my every promise!"

Tremors shot through Rose. She returned his gaze determinedly.

"I've still got tonight!"

"Oh, aye!" he told her.

Rose spun around then, hurrying forward to join her father.

Oh, yes! She had tonight! A smile curved sweetly into her features, and she almost laughed out loud.

Tonight the power was hers.

Chapter XVII

By the time they reached the house, Rose was in her glory.

It was going to be a very enjoyable experience to have him beneath her power for a change tonight. She could really do almost anything. After all, what could he do to her at her father's house?

She had a night. A full night . . .

And Pierce was going to have a taste of his own medicine. She was going to make absolutely certain that it was a long, long night!

She started by insisting that a number of the stalls had to be cleaned, really cleaned. She stayed out of Pierce's sight, of course, giving the orders to their head groom. When that was done, there were all manner of harnesses to be polished and oiled.

Her father would have given him a room in the attic, but Rose saw to it that the head groom gave him a pallet in the straw in the loft of the stables.

A man his size, engaging in heavy work, would certainly work up an appetite. In her father's little kingdom, everyone ate well. Ashcroft was a generous man, and he had a wonderful cook named Lucy.

Lucy was especially kind to the downtrodden. If she heard that Pierce was an ex-convict—a man incarcerated for stealing bread alone—she would shower him with the very finest foods available from her kitchen.

Maybe she had made him too sympathetic a man. She should have said that he was a horse thief.

But she hadn't. And when she slipped down through the arbor that led to the kitchen, she discovered that she was already too late.

Pierce was in the kitchen now, hauling water for Lucy. "We'll be needing lots of it tonight, young man. Her Grace, the duchess, is returned unexpected, and she'll be wanting her hip tub and all. The houseboys will see to that, if you'll just bring the buckets of water. Why they have you doing all this work when the sun is set, I'll never know!" Lucy said with a *tsk*ing sound.

"It doesn't matter," Pierce told her quietly, dropping down to slip the buckets of water he carried on a shoulder brace to the floor. "I've a mind to keep busy."

"Well, now, they're usually the finest of the gentry, the master and his daughter," Lucy said with a sigh. She was plump and round and rosy.

And it was most obvious that she was finding Pierce charming, and enjoying every moment that she watched his muscles ripple over his task. His white shirt was open from his throat to the center of his chest, revealing crisp, dark hair matted sensually against his sun-colored flesh. He was certainly different from their usual houseboys and grooms, and it was plain that Lucy was simply fascinated by him.

"Don't you worry, young man. You go ahead and attend to all these tasks they've set ye to! I'll see that when the time for your supper comes round, it's wonderful juicy pork chops and my own special greens.''

Pierce doffed his plumed hat to her, thanking her politely, his amused smile flashing across his face.

Rose bit her lower lip, determined he wouldn't be enjoying pork chops.

She managed to come back to the kitchen later. There was a pile of bone and gristle lying on a plate by the hearth. Lucy had probably left it to make soup. Rose saw the tray waiting to go out to the stables where Pierce was working.

It was a simple matter to exchange plates. And when Lucy came upon her, standing by the table, she smiled. ''Lucy, I am going to miss you!'' She hugged the broad cook while one of her little maids picked up the tray to head out. ''England is not so bad a place, except that no one there can cook half so well as you!''

Lucy gave her a pleased grunt and hugged her in return.

Rose was gone for several long moments before Lucy found the good meat by the fire. Then she stroked her chin, and wondered if the cooking flames weren't getting to be a bit too much for her.

In case Pierce was too near finishing with his first tasks, she hurried down to find the head groom, Randolph.

''Randolph, it has come to my attention that a number of the horses are in need of a serious grooming,'' she told him. ''I think the young convict should deal with them.''

''Milady, you've already set him to a number of tasks—''

''Ah, but I'm certain he's a man who would do well with horses. Start him on Blaze.''

Blaze was nearly seventeen hands high.

And as ornery as the devil.

That was all right. Rose kept out of sight while Blaze was brought out, and Pierce was instructed to groom him. She clapped a hand over her mouth, watching from one of the stalls, determined that she would not laugh. Blaze was a match for any man. He pranced and shifted and kicked. It was a good thing Pierce knew horses. He swore at Blaze, but managed to keep control of him. Still, giving the horse a good brushing and cleaning his feet was a task he would not forget soon. Hmm . . .

Then again, he might do it again soon!

She waited until he had been given two of the mares and three of their huge draft horses to do, then she made her appearance known. She didn't glance Pierce's way, but walked along the stalls with Randolph. "Oh! The others are fine, but I'm afraid that Blaze just won't do! He must be brushed again. And what of his feet? Have they been cleaned?"

Randolph shook his head. "My lady, it's getting very late. I'm certain the horse—"

"Will not do," Rose said with a sigh. This time she remained in full sight while Blaze was brought around and Pierce was called back from stall cleaning to see to him again.

She was delighted by the aggravated expression on his face and the flash in his eyes when they touched hers. "Once more, Peter, if you will. I'm afraid my father demands perfection, and the job you've done on Blaze here is lacking."

Pierce stiffened, but offered her a deep bow. Randolph had moved on. Pierce, a horse brush in his hands, came under Blaze's neck. "And I demand, Duchess, that a stop be put to this," he warned her.

She smiled sweetly, remembering his earlier words to her. "I am so sorry, milord! You seem to have missed something here. *I am the one making the demands now!''*

He flashed her another warning stare. ''Tonight. One night!''

Was she pressing her luck? If so, she couldn't quite help it. She called to Randolph again.

''Peter really does do excellent work—and so quickly! When he's finished here, Randolph, let him have his dinner break. Then there's a small patch of land I want tilled—''

''Tonight, milady?'' Randolph said.

Rose gazed innocently at Pierce. ''Oh, it has to be tonight! You see, I'm going to have some very special flowers planted in my absence.''

''The poor fellow will be working all night,'' Randolph said softly. Pierce's eyes remained on hers.

''Yes, he will, won't he?'' she murmured. And smiling regally still, she waved a hand in the air. ''Come, Randolph, I'll show you where he needs to work next.''

That should take care of her husband! she thought.

Pierce finished with Blaze while she was walking with Randolph. The head groom excused himself to tell Pierce that he might take his dinner break.

To put the final touches on her triumph, Rose heard the clatter of the cover from Pierce's food tray while she stood by the edge of the stables.

He had discovered his ''pork chops.''

Randolph returned to her. She thanked him for seeing that everything was done, and then turned to hurry back to the house.

Pierce, sitting on the rough wooden bench by the door to the stables, heard movement. He rose.

And he saw his wife, swiftly running back to the house.

He looked down at the gristle upon his plate.

"Your turn will come, my love, I promise it!" He smiled himself, hands on his hips, as she slid inside the front door. He started to laugh.

She wanted her vengeance, too. Ah, well! Maybe she deserved it. He had been so dead-set determined that she had betrayed him! He had never really stopped to think that Jerome, who had already proven himself capable of anything, might well have sent a message to the lord constable himself, or in Rose's name. Ah, but then, it was true that she had called him back to where he had been taken.

But then, he had never stopped to imagine that she might really have loved him.

A slight trembling seized him. Dear God, he thought, give us a chance this time! Give us a chance!

He looked to the house. His heart seemed to burn in his chest. His son was there.

One night be damned!

Tonight he was getting into that house! Prudent or not, he'd see his son.

All the torment that Rose was putting him through did not ease her own night. She was back with her Woody, delighted to be holding and hugging him again. But she was afraid to tell Mary Kate the truth, though she couldn't possible leave for England without her!

She was also worried that she had made a terrible mistake, because if Mary Kate were to take a walk outside the house that night, she might well see Pierce and call out his true identity.

And although Rose had claimed Pierce innocent, her father might just want to see him brought to justice. No, that wouldn't be a problem; she could reason with her father if need be. But there were others around, and she had learned that everyone could not be trusted!

Oh! And it was going to be agony to part from her father. She didn't want to leave him again. England was a long, long way away.

And so, while she thought that Pierce was surely busy working his powerful fingers to the bone, she sat with her father, trying to make light conversation. "Daughter, you're really working that poor convict fellow," he told her. "And I can't keep him off the captain's ship tomorrow. Do you think we should let the young man sleep?"

Rose waved a hand in the air. "Don't worry, Father. The head groom gave him a place to sleep in the barn loft. I'm sure he's finished with his tasks by now and will sleep well enough." She hesitated a moment. "I'm going out back for a moment to see the river," she said softly. She was leaving. She didn't know when she was coming back. She wanted to look out over the night, over the moon falling upon the water, and feel the night breeze brush her face.

That place was out there. That pretty place by the water that she had told Pierce was the most beautiful in all the world. They should have seen it together.

She thought that her father would protest. But he didn't.

"You do that, daughter," Ashcroft told her.

He watched her go, keeping his seat until the rustle of her skirt had faded away. Then he leapt up, and hurried out toward the stables.

Pierce dug the last patch of ground from the plot by the side of the house, leaning upon the shovel. He wasn't quite sure what she had meant for him to feel—this was her one night, and bless Rose! She had tried to make her best use of it.

A convict! How quickly she could invent a tale. And how ironically close to the truth it had come.

He glanced up at the house. He'd been watching it for quite some time now. He'd seen her moving about earlier at one window, then he'd seen a heavier-set woman moving in the same manner, and he realized that they had both been walking with a baby.

His son. Something warm that made his fingers begin to tremble swept through him. In all the long days and nights he had never imagined that Rose might be bearing a child, his child.

But he knew now, more fully than before, that he had fallen very deeply in love with his wife, and therefore, the rub of betrayal had been all the greater. There had been the sweetest satisfaction in seizing the ship . . .

And then there had been the doubt. Rose was so passionate in her denials! And she had spoken to him so plainly and honestly.

But he had spent so many months living because he had longed for revenge. There had to be justice in the world, somewhere!

There was. Rose was innocent. Jerome was guilty. And he had to prove that, somehow. Outlaw, pirate, as he had become.

He swirled around suddenly, hearing movement behind him. Instinctively he raised his shovel, ready to fight if necessary.

It was the master of the great colonial estate himself, Ashcroft Woodbine. He didn't shrink or duck away as he eyed Pierce's shovel. He knew that Pierce wasn't going to use it against him.

Pierce let the shovel fall, watching the man carefully.

"Peter, eh?" Ashcroft said to him doubtfully.

"I beg your pardon, sir?"

"Peter, my arse!" Ashcroft said.

"Sir, I—"

"Convicts just don't have the look of you, man. I've seen one or two in my day, and they haven't your build—or your arrogance."

"Sir, I've—"

"No, my boy, it's not in anything you've said or done. It's in the way that you walk, in the hold of your shoulders. Just looking at you, I'd have to say that you were born to the nobility. You've had a hard time of it along the line, but it seems you've taken charge of your own destiny again. Peter— Pierce. You stopped the *Lady May* at sea, eh?"

"Yes," Pierce told him quietly.

"So you're the infamous Dragonslayer!"

"We never hurt a captive, sir. I had to see that a few rumors were started, or else we would have found ourselves in difficulty. A pirate has to be credible, you see."

Ashcroft Woodbine was smiling, a fellow with a fine enough sense of humor. "The Dragonslayer. And I never imagined! Now, I don't mean to say that I didn't think you guilty right along with half of England when I had heard all that happened. But Rose said that you didn't do it. She says that she knows that you didn't do it, just because she knows you."

He lowered his head. She had been defending him all the while that he had been seeking his revenge. "I am glad, sir, that you seem to believe her."

"I trust in my daughter—Your Grace."

As he should have trusted her, Pierce realized. "You'll not betray me then, sir?"

"Betray my only son-in-law? Oh, I think not! But England, son. Are you daft? You and Rose could live here, right here! It's an empire, son, one that will fall to Rose—and you—one day as it is!"

Pierce smiled slowly. "Well, I thank you, sir. But this is still an English colony. Some man seeking to climb a political ladder would one day stumble upon me and seek to set a noose about my neck. I've got to go home. And prove my innocence."

Ashcroft looked at him for long moments, then nodded slowly. "Well, now, a man can understand that, I'll warrant."

"You'll not stop us leaving?"

Ashcroft shook his head. "I chose you once as a man I would most desire for my daughter because I had been told of your position, your person, your youth—and your loyalty to the crown. Now, milord DeForte, I am glad that I chose you for the man that you are. I'll not stop you, though I will lie awake many a night worrying! Keep her safe, Pierce De-Forte! I charge you with that."

"I thank you, and I'll do that, sir."

Ashcroft frowned, looking toward the barn. "What was all this manual labor today? Has my daughter a bone to pick with you, milord?"

Pierce shrugged, smiling. "Women. They do enjoy power."

Ashcroft grinned. "You've yet to see the bairn, eh?"

Pierce felt his heart thunder in the most curious way. He shook his head painfully.

"He's a fine boy," Ashcroft said. "Befitting of you both. He was born alert and handsome, he was!" Ashcroft chuckled. "Perhaps it was well enough you weren't around the day he arrived. Rose had a few fine words for all of us, and I think she might have saved the choicest for you!"

"Oh, I'm sure she would have!" he said softly. His glance veered toward the house.

"Third window," Ashcroft said, clearing his throat. "There's a trellis up to the second floor, first balcony. Now, you don't want to be going through that window—it's mine. But if you follow the rail along to the third window, you'll find Rose's room. I'm sure that a man in your physical condition can manage it well enough. Oh, you might want to keep my name out of this, but I think that Rose has had her fun for the evening. The stalls are spotless. Besides, I can't help but imagine that you were going through that window with or without my blessing, eh, milord?''

Pierce smiled slowly. ''The idea had crossed my mind, sir.''

Ashcroft grinned. ''Good night then, milord DeForte.'' He extended his hand. ''It was good to see you face-to-face. I'm sure we'll meet again.''

''Sir, it will be my greatest pleasure,'' Pierce told him, accepting Ashcroft's firm handclasp.

Then his father-in-law took the shovel from him. Pierce grinned again, and started through the jasmine-scented night for the trellis that would lead to the second floor of the house.

And his child.

And his wife.

The babe was sleeping in his cradle when Rose came up to bed. The nursery was right next to her own room, and Jennie, the Irish lass who often helped look after him, shared a fine room with Mary Kate just to the other side of it. Between them, they were wonderful. They took such good care of Woody that it made life easy for Rose.

She was determined that both Mary Kate and Jennie were coming to England with her. It didn't matter if Mary Kate recognized Pierce once they were aboard the ship. As long as they were out of her father's house, and no trouble was created.

She touched Woody on the forehead with a fingertip kiss, then closed the door to the nursery, and walked into her own room.

Mary Kate had seen to it that she had been drawn a bath in the big hip tub, and two hot kettles still burned for her on the rod over the hearth. She walked straight to the fire, sighing with pleasure as she dumped one kettle of water into the tub, then stripped off her clothing carelessly, allowing it to lie where it fell.

She had just sunk into the water when a strange sensation seized her. A sensation of being watched. Her breath caught in her throat.

She realized that she wasn't alone.

Staring out across the room, she discovered him there.

She nearly screamed.

She'd left him enough work for hours! He should have been exhausted, he should have been sleeping in the hay in the damned barn.

But he wasn't. He was stretched out upon her bed, relaxed, somewhat concealed by the draperies that hung fashionably from the bed. He was leaning upon an elbow. Lazy. Completely comfortable.

Waiting.

And now staring at her naked form as she bathed.

"What are you doing in here!" she hissed.

He rose. Graceful. Easy. And he strode over to the tub, kneeling down by her side, his silver eyes touching hers.

"You brought me here."

"Not to my room!"

"Ah, yes, but I finished with those charming tasks you set for me!"

She lowered her lashes. "I had to make my father believe my story!"

"Like hell!" he murmured swiftly.

"You shouldn't be here!" she warned.

His fingers dangled in the water, then he smiled at her, his silver eyes alight: "I thought you might have further tasks for me."

"Such as?"

He walked to the fire and plucked up the second kettle of water. "More water for your bath?"

She jerked up her knees while he added the steaming water to her tub. "Thank you," she murmured warily. "That's—fine."

"Then there's your back."

"What?"

"I thought you might want your back scrubbed."

"Really, I don't—"

But he was on his knees, behind her. A searing heat shot through her as his hands plucked the sponge and soap from the water. He lifted her hair, then slipped the soap over it. Slick. Slow. Oh, dear Lord, it had been such a long time. His very touch awakened the most incredible sensations. Everything within her seemed to come alive. She felt the tips of his fingers. The warmth of his breath. She was ready to scream. To slide down in the water . . .

"I think you're finished for the night," she told him quickly.

"I think I've just begun."

"It's time for you to go to bed!"

"My thought exactly," he murmured huskily.

"Pierce!" she cried softly, just a little desperately. "You shouldn't be here!"

His very sensual touch went still for a moment. "I had to see my son!" he said.

She flushed, looking down at his brown hand where it hovered so very near her breast.

"How did you get in here?" she insisted.

He didn't reply. His voice was hoarse when he said, "What did you think, Rose? That I would play this game of yours, and not think to see my son?"

"You would have seen him tomorrow morning!" she said.

"I've waited too long for too many things," he told her. "I have no more patience."

"But—how did you get in here? This is too dangerous!" she told him.

"I don't care about the danger, milady." She twisted, facing him where he hunkered down beside her. A touch of a smile curved his lip. "Well, my love, Woody has a headful of copper curls. But he has DeForte eyes, beyond a doubt!"

A flash of anger sizzled through her. "You've seen his eyes, you've been up here long enough to waken him? You need to get out of here! You'll have time enough to torture me later. Now, I don't know how you managed to get in here, but it is time for you to slither your way back out!"

He shook his head slowly. "Not a chance, my love!"

She pointed a finger at him. "You listen to me— Lord DeForte! I will not endure your accusations and your insinuations—"

"What now?" he demanded. "I have commented on my son!" She saw suddenly that he was shaking slightly. She had never seen him do so before, and realized swiftly that his emotion was for his son. He didn't doubt her. He was still amazed to find himself a father.

"Jesu, lady! Perhaps it is nothing to you! But if you think that a man can discover he's got a son and not seek to see him, then you're mad. Perhaps you counted fingers and toes already. I was not here, and therefore had to come up and do so myself!"

She inhaled swiftly. "You've—held him?"

"Indeed."

The audacity of the man!

He *had* awakened Woody. And then put him back to sleep?

"He didn't—cry?"

He arched a brow. "Well, admittedly, he was not pleased to find a stranger before him. But your serving woman was easily able to assure him. She bade me sit with him, and rock before the fire."

Rose gritted her teeth. How did this man always land so very cleanly on his feet?

"Mary Kate found you in here?"

Damn Mary Kate! The woman had always been a fool for Pierce DeForte!

"Oh, yes, but don't worry. She knows the importance of secrecy! She was charming. Just charming! She understood that I had to see to my child and my wife." He smiled pleasantly.

Then suddenly he reached for her in earnest. A squeal of protest escaped, but she swallowed it down quickly. Strong arms came around her, sweeping her drenched and soaking from the water.

Naked and wet, she was held against the hot steel of his body, staring up into his eyes.

"And, oh, my love, it is time to see to you!" he promised.

He walked to the bed with her. Her elegant bed. He set her upon it, spraying droplets of water upon it. He started to draw his work-torn and dirtied shirt over his head, his intention now indisputable.

She opened her mouth to protest.

But a trembling rushed through her. Hot . . .

Hungry.

And suddenly he was down beside her, steel-tight arms around her. And he whispered, "Would you protest, my love?"

"Yes!" she lied.

"Even if I begged your pardon in the most humble of ways?'' His silver eyes met her with the wild challenge.

She could not move her lips.

''I've yet to see you humble!'' she whispered. Did he mean it? Did he beg her pardon, believe in her completely?

''Imagine it then,'' he warned her with a tender smile. ''For I have waited oh, so long, and can wait no longer!''

His lips touched hers, and the fire and aching of a lifetime seemed to explode into flames of longing within her.

Imagine . . .

Oh, yes.

For at long last, this was real.

Chapter XVIII

It might have been different if she hadn't lived with memories and dreams so long.

Vivid, evocative dreams. Dreams in which he kissed her lips. In which the hot, sensual stroke of his tongue moved over her throat, teased her nape, her earlobes, her throat again.

Dreams in which the rugged force of his body moved down upon her own in a bold, slow rhythm, his hands cupping her breasts, his tongue bathing them. Dreams in which he moved against her, fresh and fragrant from a bath, then licked her dry. His kiss, his lips, his tongue upon her belly. His fingers upon her thighs. Delicately pressing upon the copper-downed mound between them, finding the cleft, dipping inside . . .

Dreams . . .

Except this was no longer a dream, no longer a memory. And sensation had never before been so vivid, or so sweet. He was a talented lover, had always been a talented lover, and so he quickly found the most sensitive, erotic bud within her. Touched and stroked with the slow rhythm of his fingers. Delved down with the searing heat of his tongue.

"No!" she protested, her head thrashing. But he'd never given her heed before. He did not intend to start doing so now.

And the words he had said before were so very true. It had been long time. A very long time. The magic was growing within her. The spiraling magic. Rising like jasmine on the night wind, sweeping through her, taking a hot, fierce control. Her fingers bit into the muscles of his shoulders, tugged into his hair. She thought that she would explode, die in a cataclysm of shooting silver stars. It would end, she would reach that Eden, those searing moments of sweetest human ecstasy . . .

He held her back, his weight shifting, parting her, coming atop her.

She was hot and slick and very wet, yet so incredibly tight. He thrust into her, then was startled by the cry of pain that escaped her. She cut it off quickly herself, burying her face against his damp chest. He silently swore at himself, realizing that she had not made love since the birth of their child.

"Easy, my love, I'd not hurt you. Ever . . ." he whispered hoarsely. He cradled her closely against him. He allowed himself to move fully into her, and held there very tightly for long moments. A little shudder escaped her and he began to thrust anew. His lips found hers, her collarbone, her breasts, even as he moved. His whispers fell against her flesh.

"Jesu, how I have waited for you! How I have died without you! No punishment, no labor, was more cruel than my abstinence from you . . ."

Her arms wound around his neck. Her back came off the bed in a wild arch, and he realized that she was moving with him, eager to meet his thrusts. He rose above her, watching as their bodies meshed.

Then he closed his eyes, and the tension, the hunger, seemed to rip through him. He moved like mercury, aching, so aching, desperate to have the ache assuaged. God, this was it. So long, so very long he had waited . . .

Then a climax, fierce, violent, burst upon him. He tried to fight the waves of it washing over him, anxious that he had brought her to this sweet point along with him. But the fiery tremors shot through him again and again, and he was powerless but to drive sweetly homeward into her feminine sheath. And when they had subdued, he fell to her side, still trembling. He pulled her into his arms, and felt her resist, but it didn't matter. His voice shook when he whispered, "My God, my love, but that was good. By heaven, I swear, I waited far too long."

She remained silent. He rose up on an elbow to look at her. Emerald eyes, just a touch glazed, returned his stare. His eyes didn't remain upon hers, but stroked warmly over the body he had just loved so thoroughly. She had changed so little. Her breasts had swelled. Her nipples were deep, dark, dusty rouge, evocative even now. Perhaps her hips had gained an attractive half an inch. Two tiny little hair-thread lines trailed from low on her abdomen into the fiery dark red down of her mound.

He stroked a finger down her body, tenderly, from the fullness of her breast to the base of her abdomen. "Dear God! I missed you!" he murmured. He touched one of the little lines. She stared at him, then caught his hand.

"What now? My love, if I was not tender enough—"

Her lip curled in a subtly wise smile. "When will you understand!" she said softly. "Oh, you are good! You're experienced, and you're powerful, and you know it very well! But—"

"Ah, yes!" he said softly, his eyes glittering in turn. "I haven't groveled at your feet for a hundred days like a supplicant for ever having doubted you!"

"Doubting me!" she exclaimed. He pressed a finger quickly to her lips, and she spoke in a whisper once again. "You damned well deserve to grovel! You didn't doubt me. You accused me of everything!"

"Rose!" he hissed in return. "I am trying to beg your pardon. But how would it have looked to you?" he demanded heatedly.

"Well, milord, I will tell you this! I am innocent. I have been cruelly and pathetically wronged since I found myself awaking in your bed that morning. I never, ever plotted with anyone to marry you, I never desired to marry you. And I certainly never wished Anne's death! Nor yours, nor the agony I went through that night, or in the months that followed. So, my lord, you are right. I am your wife. And fool though I may be, I am delighted to see that you are alive. And you do have the power to demand what you want, to take me or ignore me, but if you wish a response from me—a total, freely given response—then . . ."

"Then what?"

"Well then, you definitely do need to do a little more groveling!"

His muscles were tensed like wire. His teeth were gritted, and he seemed to be fighting some awful battle with himself. "Dukes do not grovel!" he snapped out.

"This duke had best learn to do so!"

"Oh, really?"

"Oh, really!" She snatched up her sheets. He just as quickly snatched them away from her.

"What are you trying to cover now?" he demanded, pouncing upon her.

Jaw hard, hair spread wildly beneath her, she stared up at him. Her mood had swung again. "Don't look at me so!" she pleaded suddenly, startling and confusing him.

"Rose, you are exquisite," he told her, puzzled. Was she disturbed by what was almost invisible? She had never been more beautiful to him. "Rose, you have given me a beautiful son. And you are still the most stunning woman I have ever seen."

She shook her head. Puzzled, he lifted her hardset chin. Her eyes, green fire, met his. "My Lord DeForte!" she said in a husky whisper, heated in the night. "I know you, I married you."

"And what does that mean?" he inquired at a total loss to understand.

"Would you get up, please! Your weight is killing me!" she murmured.

It was a lie, a ploy, he was certain. But for the moment, he obliged her anyway.

"Tell me what you're talking about, Rose!"

"It's still my night!" she hissed back. "My turn! You're in my father's house! You had no right to come to this room, and you've still managed to come in and—and—"

"Claim all that is rightfully mine?" he suggested.

"You are an incredibly arrogant man!" she told him, sitting up, inching away from him, pulling the covers chastely to her chest.

"I want to know what you're talking about!" he persisted.

"All right!" she lashed out. "Ah, let's see! You were given up for dead. But you survived. Then you were picked up by Spaniards, and . . ."

Rose paused for a moment. She didn't doubt that story, and a catch seemed to form in her throat even as she spoke. Her fingers had moved feverishly up and down his back just moments ago.

And then had touched the welts left by the Spaniards' cat-o'-nine-tails.

"Yes, I was picked up by Spaniards," he said impatiently. He crawled from the bed and stared down at her, naked and lithe in the fire-cast shadows. "Pray, go on."

"But then you fought your way free," she said softly. "Free to become a pirate king—the Dragonslayer."

"Do continue."

"That was a while ago. Several months, at the very least!"

"At the very least," he said.

She felt a flood of color come to her face. "Well, then I am quite certain you didn't actually wait for me."

He smiled. A broad, deep grin that made her long to slap his handsome face.

"My love! It's quite unbelievable. You're jealous."

"I don't care to be one of many," she said primly.

"You're jealous," he said smugly. He strode across the room like a fantastic beast, at ease with his muscled frame, and with his nakedness. He paused, looking out the window, hands on his hips. He spoke softly.

"Well, if you are jealous, you needn't be," he assured her. "I was a pirate king, and I did have many opportunities. It was the damnedest thing about a few of my hostages! They seemed to *want* to be ravaged by a pirate. It was all that I could do to hold them off and maintain my reputation!"

Rose stared at him, her eyes widening. "You are a conceited rogue!" she informed him.

"Not really. Some of my hostages were nearing

eighty, and trust me, they were sorely in need of a good ravaging, but not from me.''

''You didn't touch another woman in all that time?'' she queried softly, incredulously.

He paused, then decided to be honest. ''Once,'' he murmured. ''I had made myself nearly ill hating you, blaming you—wanting you. And she was young, and very pretty. And a whore.''

He sat upon the window seat, looking over the elegant walkway that led to the front of the house.

''Just—once?'' Rose said.

''Once.''

''Why?''

''Why?'' he repeated. ''I told you, I was bitter—''

''No,'' she interrupted, her emerald gaze steady on him. ''Why just once?''

Why indeed? Why not be honest in this, too? ''Because,'' he answered quietly, ''I discovered that there was no satisfaction in another woman, no sweet pleasure, no reward. I should have been fulfilled; I was empty. I told myself it was the anger.''

''And was it?'' she murmured.

''No.''

''Just once . . .'' she repeated.

''Just once!'' He was giving away enough of his heart!

But it wasn't enough for her, oh, no!

''Why should I believe that?'' she queried. ''You were deeply in love with Anne, but the very night we were married, you were determined to make love to me.''

He lifted his shoulders in a shrug, ''Rose, if we are confessing all, then I must confess this. I did believe that I was in love with Anne. I did care for her deeply. But . . .'' He hesitated, then continued tenderly, ''From the moment I first saw you, I wanted you. Even that wretched day when you un-horsed me—''

''And you half drowned me!''

He shrugged. ''Even that day, I was captivated. In all of my life, there has never been anyone like you.''

Rose was careful, looking downward, feeling an unbelievable joy race through her. ''But you did think that you loved Anne. And you still managed to make love to me.''

He groaned. ''I think that any man might *manage* to make love to you.'' He sighed. ''Rose! Anne and I were right for one another. She was inde-pendent, very wise and mature, experienced, and—I haven't lied about that—I cared for her greatly. But I don't think that I ever really knew what love was until I met you. Until I held you. And once I had fallen in love with you, well then . . . nothing on earth could ever equal you, my love.'' He pointed toward the nursery door. ''I swear on his life that all I have said is true,'' he said very softly. ''Is that enough?''

She bit into her lower lip, watching him, pulling the covers to her breast. She was trembling so that she could scarcely bear it. She wanted to throw her arms around him, but she was still afraid to believe the wonder of the night.

''You love me?'' she whispered softly.

''Milady, I do.''

She trembled, ready to hold him, to forgive him. But it remained her night. She was still determined that he would make amends.

''And you only slept with another woman once?''

''Once, Rose! I've said it—''

She threw back a lock of her hair. ''Then,'' she murmured very softly, ''since I have been a saint, I shall only have to cheat on you once in retaliation!''

She leaned back, still secretly smiling. It hurt her. She couldn't bear the thought of him with anyone else. But it had been so long ago now. And in that night, he had discovered that no other woman could be her.

"Oh!" She gasped suddenly. It was a loud gasp. He had startled her, coming so swiftly from the window seat, just like a panther in the night. His hand fell over her mouth at the sound that she made, and her eyes widened as his eyes burned into hers and the weight of his body pressed her down.

"Don't even think about it!" he warned her, lifting his hand from her mouth. She looked into those silver eyes, so close above her as he straddled her hips now.

"Think about what?" she said blankly.

"Retaliation. In any way, shape, or form."

She smiled slowly. "And why not?"

"I would beat you black and blue and pull every hair from your head!" he warned her. "And kill the man, of course," he added as an afterthought.

"You're already in trouble for murder!" she reminded him.

"So what would another one matter?"

Her eyes shimmered their emerald fire into his. "Don't say that!" she cried to him.

He pushed away from the bed, rising to stalk the shadows once again. He paused at the window seat, one knee upon it as he stared out at the night.

Dear God, but he had been a fool. All those months, thinking that he needed to seek revenge against Rose! Sometimes he had been a fool for the right reasons. He had been a fool when he had fought for Anne, when he had felt the pain and anguish for her. Anne, poor beautiful Anne! He'd owed her any foolish battle he might have fought, because they had cared for each other!

But then . . .

Dear God. He'd lived. He'd survived, albeit cruelly at first. Now there was so much ahead!

And he was still an outlaw. Still an accused murderer in his homeland. He had to prove Jerome guilty, himself innocent. There had to be a way.

He was a lucky man. God had been good to him. He had Rose. For all that had been taken from him, he had Rose. Beautiful, fiery, passionate.

And despite everything, she loved him.

He might well have lost her in his hatred and bitterness.

His hands were trembling. He clenched them tightly together to keep them from doing so.

He had Rose. And miracle upon miracles, he had his son.

He rose from the window seat, stretched, seeking to stop the trembling within him. It did no good. He walked back to the bed.

He stared at her, kneeling down beside her there. Rose watched him with wary emerald eyes. He took her hand, and gently kissed the backs of her fingers. Then he turned her hand, and kissed the palm. He looked into her eyes.

"Forgive me!" he said softly. His eyes caught her with a glimmering light. "I shall try very hard to learn to grovel."

"What?" she demanded in a whisper, a delicate copper brow shooting high.

"Forgive me!" he repeated, smiling ruefully.

She reached out, touching his cheek. "A duke would really grovel, for me?" she whispered softly.

He nodded, pulling the covers from her hands, stretching his length down beside her again, drawing her close and into his arms.

Stunned, she allowed him to do so. She felt the warmth flood from him into her. Felt the tenderness of his arms cradled around her.

"God, Rose, for months all I did was go over and over everything that had happened. I should have trusted in you. But Jesu, it was a bitter time!" he said. "You sent me to Anne—I discovered her dead, and the authorities after me because Jamison was dead along with her. Apparently someone had cried murder. You bade me come back to you, and I did so. And there they came after me again."

"But—"

He pressed a finger to her lips. "Not to mention the fact that there had been this rumor your father had determined that I would be your husband."

"You must know—"

"Ah, but see, I had begun to believe in your absolute innocence! I had believed that you cared for Anne. I had come to . . ."

He paused. Confessions. He had never confessed so much of his feelings to anyone.

"I thought that I had been duped once, and then that I had been stupid enough to be duped a second time!"

She stared up at him, swallowing hard. He was laying out his heart to her. She began to speak in a sudden rush.

"Truly, it was never so terrible! I think I might have been afraid from the first that I could too easily want you. But I was afraid to do so when I believed that you loved Anne, even while you slept with me."

"No part of me could be elsewhere when I slept with you!" he told her softly. "Though guilt did plague me. I had you, you see. And God knew what Anne was going through."

But time and distance still separated them. There were only so many things that he could bring himself to say.

"We were all set up easily!" Rose murmured bitterly. "By Jerome!"

"Ah, well, Jamison was in on it, too, at the time. And they certainly had other help. We have yet to discover the whole truth. But I will have my revenge against Jerome," Pierce promised in such a voice that made shivers rip down Rose's spine.

"Pierce!" she cried softly, turning in to him, searching out his eyes. "I know your anger. I can't know all that you went through, but I feel your hatred and your bitterness. I longed to kill him at Anne's funeral. To cast all caution to the wind and leap across the abbey to cut his throat. But Geoffrey kept me steady, for it would have done no good! Pierce, you can't come to England seeking only to cut his throat—"

"I will kill him," Pierce said, his arm cast back, his gaze upon the ceiling.

Once again, the way that he spoke was absolutely chilling.

"You're missing the importance of my point here," she told him swiftly. "You can't kill Jerome at all! You have to prove that he is guilty of the crime, and that you are innocent."

His eyes shot to hers like mercury. "Jerome has to die!" Once again, she felt as if she could not reach him at all.

She caught hold of his fingers, dragging his hand to her cheek, gently rubbing against it. "Milord! He has to die by justice! He tricked us all with cunning. We must trick him back with cunning. Fury and righteousness will not serve us well at the moment." She smiled, tenderly kissing the roughness of his hand. "Treachery will!"

He sighed, then smiled, watching her. "I hadn't intended to go marching right in, announcing my arrival to the king. I always meant to try everything in the world to prove myself innocent."

"Thank God," she murmured.

"And then call him out and kill him if all else failed!"

"We can't let it fail!" she cried. "Pierce, I lost you once. I cannot do it again."

Her voice stirred him deeply. Touched the guilt in his heart for the way that he had misjudged her. Touched the longing in his soul that had lived there day and night for so very long.

He rose on a elbow, bending low over her, brushing her lips with his kiss. "I will not leave you again," he promised her.

"Then—"

"We've a long ocean voyage to plan our revenge," he told her.

Again his lips touched hers. The taste was nectar. He cupped her cheek, and kissed her again. Then he watched his fingers move over her breasts and her belly. His eyes met hers.

She shook her head.

"What now, my love?"

"Well," she murmured, "I *am* upset about the other woman."

A sharp oath escaped him.

"And," she added regally, "you think that I am supposed to forgive you that easily! Think of all the torment that you put me through! I think I said something once about the fact that if I were ever to forgive you, you must grovel for a hundred days, upon your knees, and you did say that you were willing to grovel—"

"I certainly did mean to try! I never said a duke had the ability to grovel easily."

"And duchesses do not give in easily, either!" she promised.

"You want me on my knees again?" he demanded.

"Well, yes, I would enjoy it, I believe."

"Fine!"

He was down upon his knees. But Rose realized too late that it was not to grovel.

"Forgive me!" he whispered, but there was the lightest touch of laughter in his words. And before she knew it, he had caught hold of her ankles, jerking her down to him, her legs parted around him. And he began to touch and caress her, making love very slowly and determinedly to acutely sensitive regions of her body, her breasts first, her belly, her upper thighs, between them.

She protested at first. Murmuring that he was not exactly offering an apology. But she swiftly forgot what she was saying.

Because he loved her, and had never really loved anyone else. Because the sweetest of sensations were ripping hotly through her and because she could not bear the pain/pleasure anymore.

She tried to rise against him. Touch him. Stroke his arms, his back. Touch his shoulders. She nipped into them gently with her teeth, washed over the breadth of them with her tongue.

Met his eyes, and smiled.

And died a little when he sank into her, part of her again.

And as he did, his whisper touched her ears. "Forgive me, my love!"

And it was enough. She forgave him with all her heart.

Moments later, they were still entangled, gasping

for breath, content to lie close within each other's arm. She felt his silver gaze and she smiled. "Well, you are almost forgiven," she told him primly.

He grinned, pulling her closely. "Almost! You had best take heed, Duchess. That's as far as I've groveled in all my life."

"You've a very different manner of groveling," she assured him.

"You didn't like it?"

"Oh, I did, I did!" she whispered. "Still, something a little more traditional, like your head bowed upon the ground, would be nice."

"If I bow my head upon the ground," he warned, "you'll be on the ground, too."

She lay her head against his chest, smiling in the shadows. They hadn't broken his arrogance. She didn't think that she minded so terribly.

His fingers moved through her hair. Then his hands were on either side of her face. "Once again! With all my heart, lady, I do beg your pardon!" he said fervently.

She inhaled sharply. She met the passionate silver in his eyes. "With all my heart!" she said softly. "I give it."

He scooped her into the tender caress of his arms. "Rest then. We've an early morning ahead of us, and the dawn is nearly breaking."

She lay against him, the softness of her hair like silk over his bare flesh. Her cheek rested on his chest, and the ruffle of a copper lock tickled his chin. He smoothed it back. "Ah, Rose! How I longed to be with you," he murmured. "In all my life, I swear, I've never known greater beauty, inside or out."

He paused.

"Rose, I love you," he murmured.

He waited for her response, but received none.

He stretched awkwardly, trying to look down upon her.

She slept. Her lips parted, curled into a small smile, her face so very beautiful, and so peaceful. She hadn't heard what he had said.

He smiled tenderly. He let her rest.

They had a long voyage ahead of them. A voyage into truth.

Chapter XIX

Rose had never imagined that she could be so happy, so content.

The weeks at sea had been beautiful ones. The weather had held for them, clear and balmy, and during the long days it was wonderful just to sit out on the deck, lazily feeling the sun and the breeze caress her cheeks. In all her life, she had never been on a more beautiful voyage.

Maybe the sky had always been so soft blue, maybe the ocean equally as cobalt, perhaps even the sun had shone so brightly before.

Or perhaps the sun that now touched her was different, and different because of Pierce.

When he was aboard a ship, Rose thought, he was her captain. He had given that duty to Niemens, but every morning he was at the helm right along with Niemens, and they did little but discuss the sea and sailing every time they came together. They were old friends, Rose realized, and she was happy.

She was happiest, however, to see Pierce with his son. She had never imagined that a man like Pierce—

all muscle and fierceness and business—could be so exceptional a father. He loved to lie in the great bunk in the captain's cabin with his little one crawling on top of him. He would pick Woody up, dangle him above his face, and have him shrieking with laughter, time and time again. He was eternally patient helping to mash little bits of food for Woody, and he didn't seem at all disturbed when little bits were spit into his face.

Had she not been in love with him, she could have forgiven him anything anyway, just for the look in his eyes when he watched his son.

So upon the high seas they had those wonderful days, lying together in the sun while Mary Kate and Jennie saw to Woody, and playing with him themselves.

Then there were the nights, and the nights were exquisite. When the sea was velvet blackness, and only the dim candle and lantern lights of the ship filtered down upon them. Then she would watch him come into the cabin.

She would watch the clothing fall from his broad shoulders and to the floor.

And she would begin to grow warm and tremble, waiting, anticipating . . .

And he would come to her, his naked flesh burning against her own, and hold her, and make love to her.

Bit by bit, he talked about the awful days when the Spaniard had held him.

Bit by bit, she told him about the anguish of thinking him dead, of pleading with the king just to see that his name was cleared, of finally deciding that she must come home, and there find the strength to return to England.

In each other's arms, in that velvet darkness, they shared many things.

"Father was really wonderful," Rose told him. She sighed. "My father is a good man, a truly good man. He didn't come up with all those tasks for you, you know."

"Of course not. You did," he told her with amusement.

She leaned up on an elbow, seeking his eyes in the darkness. "And, Pierce! I've a surprise for you!" she said. "Father did know! When we were leaving, he kissed me on the cheek, and then he winked and told me to warn my husband to take care!"

Pierce folded his hands behind his head. "I've a surprise for you!" he told her, smiling, his teeth flashing very whitely in the night. "Your father knew long before we left! He sent me up to your room."

"No!"

"Yes!"

"Oh! And you let me think that—oh! I should tear your hair out, right now!" she informed him in an indignant and lofty tone. "I should—"

"Yes?" he inquired huskily.

"I should do terrible things to your body!" she cried.

But he was laughing, and she was in his arms, and his voice was very deep, and husky, and sensual, and it alone sent a shower of hot tremors shimmering throughout her. "Come, my love, do terrible things to my body. I'm waiting, and ready!"

And she quickly forgot about her father until the next day, as it turned out.

And then they discovered that a ship was following them. It was Pierce's ship, the DeForte ship he had taken himself, with his own crew aboard.

And amazingly, Ashcroft Woodbine was aboard that ship, too. Pierce gave no pretense of not knowing his father-in-law. He looked sternly at Ashcroft as the man waved and demanded to be taken aboard the *Lady May*.

"What do you think you're doing, man?" Pierce demanded.

"There won't be a thing wrong with a father escorting his daughter back to England," Ashcroft said firmly. He wagged a stern finger at Pierce. "You're dead, you must remember. I can do some protecting of Rose that you cannot! And, my fine fellow—you can't go marching straight into England as you are."

"I don't intend to go as I am."

"Then how do you intend to go?" Rose queried, worried now herself.

Pierce rubbed his chin. "I'm going as a monk."

"A monk!" Ashcroft hooted.

Pierce stared firmly at his father-in-law. "I will follow Rose off as a brother from the Llewellyn Monastery, returning from a trip abroad, spending time now in the DeForte household. The cowls worn by the brothers are hooded. I intend to grow my beard the rest of the time that we are at sea, and I should pass well enough."

"Aye, if they don't get a good look at your eyes!" Ashcroft said.

"It won't work!" Rose insisted.

"It will work, because I'll be staying out of sight," Pierce promised her.

She was still very worried. Ashcroft joined them on the *Lady May*, leaving the other ship to return to Virginia to await further orders.

They discovered that Ashcroft had bribed Pierce's crew with land grants from his own holdings if they could just get him to the *Lady May*. With a pleased grin, he informed Pierce that the whole lot of them were now colonials.

In bed, Rose, still very worried, tried to hide her fear. "I think I like you much, much better as a servant," she told him, trying to laugh. But then her voice grew grave. "I could order you to clean stalls and groom horses all day long, and then you'd never fall into any danger."

He kissed her lips. "I will be careful," he promised her. "Honestly, Rose. I need to follow you to court. I need to discover what has happened in my absence. But I will be careful, I swear it." He drew her hand to his heart. "Hear the beat!" he whispered. "I swear it—for you!"

But she was afraid. The weeks on the water had been bliss.

Too soon, they approached England, and sailed the ship around to London by the Thames.

To Rose's relief, they rode first to Castle DeForte. There, in the darkness of night, they arrived. Garth and Geoffrey and all of his household greeted Pierce with a stunned amazement.

"Old friends, it is me, I assure you!" Pierce said softly.

The two men were like blubbering infants, first skinny old Garth hugging him fiercely, then massive Geoffrey doing the same. All of the servants greeted Pierce with a love and loyalty that warmed Rose's heart.

Then Geoffrey and Pierce closeted themselves in Pierce's accounting office so that Geoffrey could tell Pierce anything he knew about Jerome's activities.

Ashcroft made himself right at home, finding himself a suitable room—as the grandfather of the new little Pierce DeForte. Her father, Rose thought, was having the time of his life in a way.

Yet he was also worried about her, and she knew it. She loved him dearly for that worry.

She tried to get Woody settled, but found that she

was going to have some trouble there. Mary Kate and Garth were firmly at each other's throats.

"I've had the young milord DeForte in my keeping for nigh unto a year now!" Mary Kate informed Garth loftily. "I shall see to his sleeping arrangements!"

"You do as you wish in your heathen colonies, woman, but in England the Lord DeForte has his own room, and that's the room the lords have always had and always will have!"

"Heathens! Man, the babe is not quite a year old! Now, there's a fine nursery right off the lord's bedchamber where it seems Their Graces sleep—"

"Where do you bloody think they'd sleep, woman?"

Rose decided that she had best wave an olive branch of peace between them. "I do think that Woody would be best in the nursery right now, Garth," she said gently. "Just for a few months more? That way Mary Kate or Jennie can attend to him quickly in the night, and milord DeForte need not awake."

She had decided it best not to tell him that Pierce had never seemed to mind waking himself to walk with the child when he cried in the night.

Garth sniffed, and then left them to it.

She told Pierce about the argument when he finally came to bed that night. He laughed, and said that he was glad she managed to solve it without ruffling Garth's feathers too much. Then he sobered and told her, "Jerome has been living quite nicely for himself in the past year. He has already gambled half of Anne's estate away, and I assure you, it was a lofty inheritance. He bemoans his sister's death at every opportunity," he told her, his voice growing hot with anger, "and is quick to tell anyone who will listen that I am a terrible, cold-blooded mur-

derer. That I killed Anne and Jamison in a wild
fury.''

Rivulets of fear danced along Rose's spine. He had
been hurt so deeply!

On the sea, they had found happiness.

Here, in England, she could feel it slipping away.

She wanted to throw herself against him, to keep
him with her—cleaning stalls if that was what it
would take to keep him safe!

But she could feel again the anguish of all that
happened. It seemed to lie atop them.

Between them.

He had to clear his name. As much as she wanted
to go forward and forget the past, she knew that
they could not do so.

Nor could she keep Pierce from seeking his revenge. All that she could do was help him as she
could.

''What do we do?'' she asked.

''We wait.''

''For what?''

''For the king to summon you to court. He will do
so. And, I warrant, he will summon Jerome just the
same. And Jerome will come, because he will surely
be convinced by now that I am dead. And that he
can never be proven guilty. And I imagine he will
be delighted to be near you, tormenting you with all
he has accomplished.''

''How can we prove him guilty?''

''I don't know yet. I will find a way.''

''And until then?''

He stroked her hair. ''Hold me!'' he told her
softly. ''Come into my arms, and hold me.''

Gladly, she did so.

Just as he had expected, Rose was summoned to
court within the week. Her father and her servants

were welcome to accompany her. The king wanted to see his godchild, the little DeForte who had been baptized through proxy in the colonies.

"So it is time to go!" Rose murmured.

"It is."

There was nothing she could say that would dissuade him. They left for London, Ashcroft, Mary Kate, Garth, Rose—and her new mentor, Brother Peter from the Llewellyn Monastery.

Rose had to admit that Pierce looked like the monk he was portraying. The brown cloak he wore was encompassing and had a hooded cowl that fell very low over his forehead while the robe's collar stood tall, hiding the lower portion of his face. Pierce had grown his beard, and his cheeks and chin and lip were concealed in the deep richness of it.

All that gave away the man was his eyes, and he promised Rose that he would keep them in shadow.

Still, on the day when they came to see the king, Rose could scarcely breathe as she walked down the long hallway with her party behind her. Charles was not alone when he greeted her. The royal family was at rest in one of the quieter drawing rooms in his private quarters. With him were the queen and his brother, James, James's wife, Anne, and Anne's father, Edward Hyde. The king had been sitting; he rose to greet Rose, catching her hands, kissing both her cheeks in the French fashion that was often his way.

"Lady DeForte! We are glad to welcome you home, and we are most anxious to see the babe, are we not, my love?" he asked his wife warmly.

The queen, ever gentle, joined him, fascinated with the DeForte heir. She gazed longingly at Rose. "He is a fine child. And a son!"

"Thank God!" Rose said.

The king inspected the boy, then looked up. "Ah!

Sir Ashcroft Woodbine!'' He shook Rose's father's hand warmly. ''How good that you have come to us at last!''

Rose had never seen her father speechless. With some amusement, she watched his face grow crimson, and his lips work with no words escaping from him. But Charles was looking past him to the monk in his brown robe. He arched a brow to Rose.

''Your Majesty!'' she said, trying very hard to keep her nervousness from her voice. ''This is Brother Peter from the Llewellyn Monastery. He was at my father's house in the Virginia colony, and asked passage to London with us. I have brought him here since he has been teaching me a great deal about world history.''

''Ah,'' Charles said after a moment.

Brother Peter bowed low and gravely to him. ''Your Majesty.''

''Yes, well, er, welcome to my court then, too—Brother Peter.''

And so it was over then, the moment that Rose had been dreading. Charles gave her Pierce's old rooms, and Brother Peter was assigned other quarters. While Garth went away to prepare them and Mary Kate disappeared with Woody, Rose was left with her father and the royal family for several minutes.

Thank God, her father managed to talk at last. He spoke about Virginia with a passion that was rousing, and he captivated the king. Rose was grateful, since she seemed to be entirely out of conversation herself.

She was able to retire at last. She paced Pierce's elegant quarters for long hours, then gave up and crawled into bed. She must have dozed, because when she awoke, she nearly screamed. She was not alone.

Pierce had come to her. Naked, he loomed over her in the darkness.

"Did they teach you this stealth in the monastery?" she demanded.

He smiled, caught bronze and rippling and beautiful in the firelight. "The monastic life has been too much for me, I fear."

"You shouldn't be here! What if you are caught, coming or going?" she demanded.

"I won't be caught," he promised.

"Milord, you are a monk!"

"By day—never by night," he promised wickedly.

She smiled. There was no choice. He was determined.

Later, when the fire burned low, she curled into his arms. She slept again.

When she awoke again, he was gone.

She didn't see him all that morning and was worried sick. The king was involved in a tennis match, and the court came out in full measure to watch him.

It was then that she first saw Jerome.

He was elegantly dressed in silk breeches and a long coat, fur- and velvet-trimmed. His garters, too, were silk, his shoes ornamented with jewels atop the toe. He seemed sleek, still lean, still very blond.

And his eyes, when they touched hers, were still watery, almost so pale a blue as to be colorless.

He smiled, seeing her, even as the rest of the crowd watched tennis balls fly between the king and the Duke of York.

Jerome bowed deeply and mockingly to her. Then he disappeared into the crowd.

Dinner that evening was in the great hall. Mary Kate helped Rose dress, for which Rose was grateful. She still hadn't seen Pierce, and her stomach was in wild knots. Garth arrived when she was nearly ready. Rose looked at him hopefully. "Have you seen him?" she demanded.

He shook his head. "Milady, he made some discovery from a kitchen maid this morning, and left here soon after. I have not seen him since. But you mustn't be afraid. He knows what he is doing!"

"If he is recognized, he will be thrown into prison!" she cried.

Both Garth and Mary Kate put their fingers to their lips. Rose inhaled and exhaled swiftly, then nodded. "Yes, all right! But, Garth! You must find me when you see him. Immediately. Please?"

"Yes, milady, yes!"

Mary Kate set a brush through her hair one last time. Just as Rose turned to go, Woody began to fuss from his little bed in the outer room. Rose instinctively turned.

"Allow me, milady!" Garth said primly, and went to pluck up the little boy.

"Go on now, go on!" Mary Kate ordered. She gave Rose a little shove for the door. Rose went, then paused, looking back. Mary Kate had gone to stand beside Garth. "Why, you old coot! I think you've got the knack of it at last!" Mary Kate said, and with affection.

Rose stared at the two of them for a moment, surprised. A smile curved her lip. Garth? And Mary Kate? It seemed that something was growing there.

Stranger things could happen, she told herself. Then she hurried from the room. She had to appear normal! Even if Pierce had disappeared, even if she could scarcely walk.

Her father awaited her in the hall.

For a moment she remembered when she had first come here. She remembered looking to the head table where the nobility was invited to dine.

And now she belonged at that table. A shiver

seized her. Ah, but the things she had discovered. Happiness could be had by any man, commoner or noble, and it could not be achieved with either power or status. Happiness existed in the heart. It had to be held and cherished . . .

"Milady Rose!"

A handsome young man she should have remembered paused before her, taking her hand. She tried to recall his name but could not. "Ah, milady, we are glad to see you back!" he said. He was fairly tall with a handsome head of rich brown ringlets. "The king has arranged dancing this evening. I hope that you will be so kind as to give me the first dance."

"I—" she began, moistening her lips.

Her father stepped up behind her, rescuing her. "Lord Yerby! A pleasure. I am Ashcroft Woodbine. I'm afraid my daughter is still in mourning, and will not dance for some time yet. Were she able, I know that we would both consider your request a most pleasant one."

Yerby bowed gracefully, accepting Ashcroft's edict. "Milady!" He kissed Rose's hand, and then disappeared into the crowd.

"Father!" Rose murmured, giggling. "When did you grow so eloquent?"

He seemed very pleased. "Perhaps it is a shame I was such a successful merchant. I might well have been a true talent on the stage!"

Rose smiled. She was glad to take her father to the high table for dinner.

Yet during the meal, she suddenly felt a tiny piece of meat stick in her throat. Pierce had made his appearance. He was down with other clergy members, far from the noble table. He seemed animated, though, enjoying a discussion with a young priest. Rose felt her temper flare. She had been so very worried. And he seemed to be having the time of his life.

When the meal ended, she excused herself to her father. She found young Lord Yerby and smiled at him bewitchingly. "I think, milord, that perhaps one dance might be proper enough."

His eyes lit up. As the music and stylized dance began, his fingers touched Rose's. He smiled and spoke to her softly.

She flirted—just a little.

And she was very surprised when the king claimed the next dance with her. He asked again how she had been, and complimented her on Woody. Then, his dark eyes ablaze, he demanded, "And now, milady. You've been here a full day—and you've yet to begin your demands that I clear your husband's name."

"I do demand it!" she said swiftly.

He smiled. "Jerome is here. Ah, the stage is set, is it not?"

"I don't know what you mean, Your Majesty."

He smiled crookedly. "I think that you do. If not, perhaps you should avoid dancing with any other young swains. Elsewise, my dear, I think that the dark-frocked Brother Peter there is going to strip off his robes and throttle someone! Now, if you'll excuse me . . ."

Smiling, he left her.

Rose bit her lower lip. He knew. Or he was guessing. But he was keeping their secret.

She refrained from dancing anymore, instead escaping to her room. She changed, looked to her sleeping son, and chatted with Mary Kate nervously.

Midnight came. Mary Kate went to her room. Rose waited.

At one, Pierce slipped into the chamber. He strode

to her angrily, sweeping her off her feet. Breathless, she stared at him.

"How was the dear young pup, Lord Yerby?" he demanded.

"You disappeared!" she challenged him.

"And you forgot me so quickly! Alas, I have failed you. Let me imprint myself upon your memory one more time!"

The fire crackled. His lips touched hers. The flames seemed to leap into her.

Later, she whispered that she had never forgotten him.

And she never, never could.

"But where did you go?" she demanded.

He lay back, staring at the ceiling. "I went to see an old witch-woman in the woods."

"What?" Rose cried.

"Shush!" he warned her, then drew her to him, whispering softly, "I managed to get one of the maids here gossiping. She said that Jamison had a mistress, a plump, pretty thing named Beth. It seems that she has been ill over the loss of Jamison, but believes he was double-crossed by the man he was helping."

"Jerome?"

"Indeed. The maid didn't know where to find Beth, but she did know that she sometimes went to an old witch-woman in the forest. She gave me directions."

"And you went to see the witch."

He nodded. "With a little persuasion, she admitted to me that Beth had come to her for a potion. A very special potion. One to steal reason—and enhance the senses."

"The drug! The drug we were all given, you, me—Anne!"

He nodded bitterly. "Aye, that drug!"

"Well, do we go to the king?"

He shook his head. "All I can prove now is that we were all drugged."

"Then . . ."

He touched her cheek. "We wait. The old witch-woman intends to get word to Beth that Lady De-Forte is looking for her—and intends to pay for whatever information Beth can give. Now, you must listen. I have to be there when you meet with Beth. Somewhere near you. When you receive the message, you must find me. Immediately. Promise?"

Rose nodded. A ripple of pure unease tore down her spine.

"I don't want you hurt!" he warned her.

"Nor do I want you hanged!" she cried softly.

He kissed her lips tenderly. "They won't catch me!" he promised, and she had to be happy with that.

"When will the message come?"

"I don't know," he told her, then repeated softly, "We wait!"

The message came far faster than either of them had imagined. Garth brought Rose a breakfast tray in the morning. There was a small note upon it.

"Where did this come from?" she asked Garth anxiously.

"Milady, a young maid I did not know rushed up to me in the hallway. She said that it was from a friend, and that it was important."

Rose's fingers trembled. There was no seal on the note. The paper was of a poor quality.

She lifted the flap. "Milady. Meet me in the rose garden. This afternoon at three."

There was nothing more.

Rose looked at Garth. "We have to find Pierce and tell him," she said.

He nodded.

Once again, she waited through long hours for Pierce to make an appearance. She lingered in the hallways, speaking with other wives. She went down to the river to watch a rowing match, where she cheered and waved and tried very hard to appear as if she were a widow adjusting to her fate. She started to tell her father about the note, but then determined not to.

As the day wore on, she became more uneasy. In the very early afternoon she suddenly summoned Mary Kate. "I want you and Garth to take my father and Woody back to the castle."

"And leave you alone?" Mary Kate said, horrified.

"I'm just afraid for Woody suddenly."

That caught Mary Kate's attention. "Beneath the king's very nose?" she said.

"We were both kidnapped beneath the king's very nose!" Rose reminded her.

Mary Kate grew silent. She sighed, loudly. She huffed for a few minutes. "All right, milady, but His Grace, the duke, may not like it."

"His Grace, the duke, is simply in no position to question my decisions," Rose said gravely.

Mary Kate was easy to manipulate compared to her father. Ashcroft didn't want to leave her, and wasn't going to. Not until she convinced him that his grandson needed him, and she had Pierce. And every man in London knew that her father was with her in England now, to chaperon her. She could never remarry, not without his permission, and the king's.

Garth balked at leaving, too. "I've still not been able to find His Grace!"

"I will find him, Garth. Please, I want my son safe."

By the time her family had left the castle. Rose left her quarters herself, nervously pacing the hallways. She was just turning the corner to return for a cape when she saw a dark figure leaving her rooms. She flattened herself against a wall, watching with amazement.

It was Pierce . . .

It was not Pierce!

Her heart raced. She closed her eyes. She was so very, very glad she had sent Woody home!

She opened her eyes then, determined that she must follow the dark figure. But as she turned the corner again, the figure disappeared down another hall. She ran, but by the time she reached the next hallway, it was gone.

A clock began to strike. It was a quarter of three.

Time to go to the rose garden.

Rose hadn't known quite what she had expected, but not the pretty plump and bosomy woman who awaited her nervously there. She was just a bit coarse-looking, and her eyes were hardened, but there was a look of desperate unhappiness about her that Rose knew only too well herself.

"Beth?" she asked softly.

The woman looked around her. "Yes, it's me."

"I'm Rose DeForte—"

"Yes, yes, milady, I know who you are! I made you who you are!" She stared at Rose defiantly. "I stripped you and put you in his bed. So there now, you are the duchess. If you tell the law, though, I'll deny it, I swear it! You should be grateful, you—"

"I didn't come to see you about that. I want to know what you know about my husband's innocence!" Rose said firmly.

The woman squinted her eyes at Rose. They could

suddenly hear a party of others laughing softly as they walked through the garden.

"Your husband didn't kill Anne; I don't believe it for a moment. Nor did he kill Jamison. I'm certain of it. That bastard Jerome was the one who came up with the plot. He was always after his sister's money. I can't prove that he killed the two of them, but I can testify to the fact that it was him planned the way for Anne to be wed to Jamison. I don't mind going to Newgate if I take him with me!"

Staring at her, Rose realized suddenly that the woman had loved Jamison.

She, too, wanted revenge.

"Perhaps it would mean something . . ." Rose began. "But still, the murder, how can it be proved?"

Bess held back for just a minute. "There was a maid at the manor that night. She's never said a word because she's been so terrified. Gossip often runs freely among servants, milady. This maid heard what happened at Huntington Manor when the Lady Anne and Jamison died."

"Oh, my God!" Rose breathed. "And she'd testify to it?"

"If she knew she was protected by someone as powerful as you, milady."

"My God, yes!" Rose whispered. But even as she stared at Beth, the woman's face went white. Rose suddenly sensed someone behind her.

She spun.

Dear God in heaven. Jerome was there.

"Beth! Giving away our little secrets!"

He stepped past Rose. He moved so swiftly that Rose didn't even see his blade.

Not until he had sunk the long knife deep into Beth's chest. Blood spilled over her worn cotton bodice.

Rose opened her mouth to scream. The sound

didn't come because Jerome had spun on her, smiling, the bloodstained knife against her own throat. "Milady! I had thought to take your son to assure your silence. But the little dear is gone. How sad. I will have to take you."

She shook her head. "Pierce is alive!" she whispered. "He'll come for you."

His pale eyes sharpened. "I don't believe you!"

"It's true."

He started, just as Rose did, as they both became aware of voices. "He killed her! I just saw that man kill the woman! Lord Neville!" someone screamed.

He'd been seen, Jerome realized. For the briefest second, panic flashed through his eyes.

Then he grabbed Rose's hand. "Come on!"

"No! You can kill me here and now! I won't come!"

"Fine, my great lady!" he thundered. To Rose's amazement, he sheathed his knife instantly. She opened her mouth to scream again.

His hands closed around her throat. Squeezed. They pinched away all sound.

He was a strong man. Far stronger than she had ever imagined. She fought him wildly, desperately. It didn't matter. She couldn't dislodge his hands.

And she couldn't breathe . . .

She pitched over into his arms. And he was able to make away with her quite easily.

Pierce had discovered the information regarding the maid from Huntington Manor from another source, one of the young girls serving in the court kitchens. As a monk, he had managed to spend time in the kitchen with the servants and had let it be known that he had some powerful friends who were still seeking the truth about the murder of Jamison and Lady Anne. The girl had hesitated, then looked in his eyes.

And she had decided to trust him. She had sent him to the other young maid from the manor, the very girl who had heard all that happened that night.

She had taken up work in a London bakery, determined to stay as far away from the nobility as she could.

He was able to win her confidence at first because of his monk's robe, and because her friend had referred him to her. Though Pierce felt guilty about the disguise, he had no choice. He wooed her into talking, swearing that he would see that she received a goodly sum of money, and more important, protection from the king himself.

"Otherwise, you will not be safe until Jerome is dead," he told her.

"Oh, God!" she cried. Tears formed in her eyes. She started to shiver. "I should have gone to De-Forte himself, but he died that night, you know."

It was then that he made the decision to tell her the truth. "I am DeForte!" he said. "Now, hush, hush, please! You must keep my secret for the moment, and I swear, I will protect you. Just tell me what happened."

And she did. Brokenly. She talked about Anne's determination to make her marriage work, and she also told him that despite whatever evil Jamison had done, he had loved Anne. The Lady Anne had died by pure accident. "But then the other one came," she said. "And he stabbed his friend without blinking an eye. It was awful. I was so terrified that I ran. And when I found out later all that had happened, it was too late."

Pierce nodded. He told her to stay at the bakery, that he would go to the king and give himself up— under the condition that she be protected.

But then he returned to the court, and discovered the uproar.

There had been a murder.

Beth! Jamison's onetime mistress.

Murdered in the rose garden.

Panic seized him. He searched the place high and low and could find no one. Finally, at the stables, he found Geoffrey, wandering around lost.

"Your Grace! Garth had me searching for you all day! Your lady was to meet with the woman who was slain. Now she has disappeared. And Jerome has, too."

"My God, man, Rose! Where would he take her? Why?"

Terror sizzled through him.

Because it was over. All over for Jerome. The man had killed Beth. He had grown reckless; there had been witnesses.

Perhaps he could feel the bars of a trap springing closed upon him. What would he do now, where could he go?

France? Escape across the Channel? Oh, God, yes, it made sense. Get far away from England. Anne had had family in Normandy—Jerome's family as well. He could find someone with whom to hide, and surely disappear for years if he was careful.

And he had Rose! Why? Why had he taken her? Pierce wondered with agony. Was she a human shield? Did he intend to take her with him all the way . . .

Leave her in England when she had served him? Or else . . .

Dear God, he didn't dare think any further. He had to be right about Jerome trying to cross the Channel, though. There would be no other recourse for the man.

"Get the horses, quickly," he urged Garth. "First

we ride for home. I must see that Woody is safe. And then . . .''

''Then?'' Garth said tensely.

''Dover. His only escape is France. We must beat him there! It is my only hope. Dear God, my only hope!''

And so they rode. Like the wind, like thunder.

They came to Castle DeForte.

Pierce could see a group of horses and men milling in the courtyard. He dismounted and spoke softly to Geoffrey. ''I'll slip past them. If I am seen, they'll not stop me in this robe. Pray God Woody is home, and safe. My father-in-law will protect him with his life, I know. If I can just assure myself that he and my father-in-law are safe now!''

Geoffrey nodded. ''Jesu, my Lord! Hurry!''

''I intend to,'' Pierce said huskily. And in silence, he slipped around to enter the castle.

Chapter XX

When Pierce burst into the great hallway of Castle DeForte, he was momentarily stunned into silence.

The king was standing there, before the fire, staring down at Woody in his little nap cradle.

He moved the cradle gently with his finger. Without even looking up, he addressed Pierce.

"He's quite remarkable, Pierce. And I can't seem to get myself one legitimate heir!"

Pierce cleared his throat. "Well, Your Majesty, you do have . . ." He paused, searching for some word to use other than "bastards." "You do have living children. I'm sure that soon enough—"

"Alas, I think I have been married long enough, to know that the queen will not produce a son. But she is a good woman. And I would not harm her, or hurt her in any way."

Pierce felt his muscles tightening. For every second that he lingered here, Jerome was moving farther and farther away with Rose.

He understood why there was such a gathering of horses and men in the castle courtyard. The king had not come alone. He was accompanied by his retinue. He could have him instantly arrested.

Pierce strode quickly across the room to him, bowing down on one knee. "By all that is holy, Charles, I swear to you! I have been guilty of sins in my life, but never murder! Jerome has taken Rose, and you must let me go after him!"

"Get up, my friend, don't beg. It never did become you, and you're wasting time. Go after him. I've men to send with you—"

"No, please!" Pierce interrupted him quickly. "I don't want him to know that I'm coming until I'm upon him. I have to go alone. With one man, Geoffrey. There's no telling what Jerome might do when he realizes that he's cornered."

"Then go," Charles agreed, while silently determining to send a number of men in Pierce's wake.

Pierce rose swiftly, his gratitude shimmering in his eyes. "I came back to see that the babe was protected—"

"He is my godchild," the king said flatly. "And he is protected. And his grandfather hovers just upstairs. Were anyone to come after this child in your absence, I daresay he'd make them very sorry, even if I were not here to see after this noble lad!"

Pierce flashed the king a quick smile and hurried toward the door once again, swirling his dull brown friar's cloak around him. Before he reached the door, the king called him back once again. "There is no longer any need for the disguise, Pierce. Jerome killed that poor little servant girl before a half dozen witnesses. You will probably still have to stand trial—but just to see that your good name is left entirely untarnished."

"None of it will matter a whit, Your Majesty, if I cannot return with my wife!" he said softly.

"Godspeed then!" the king urged him.

Pierce nodded, and hurried out the door. He could still see the riders huddled in the distance, and he almost shrank back into the shadows of the door.

Then he realized that truly, he no longer needed to hide.

He walked out into the coming dusk, and around to the side of the castle. Geoffrey awaited him there, ready to hand him Beowulf's reins. He leapt atop the stallion, nodded to his friend, and began to race toward the south.

How much time did Jerome have on him now? What would his plan be? Would he hold Rose just long enough to get him to the Channel?

Or did he intend to take her along . . .

And do away with her, as he had so many others, when she no longer served his purpose?

A cold sweat broke out on his brow. And he spurred Beowulf on to even greater speeds.

The man had Rose.

He could not let Jerome escape.

For if he did, he might well be damned forever, and it truly wouldn't matter in the least if they decided to hang him from the highest yardarm.

They reached Dover in record time, racing past the castle, riding straight for the docks. Geoffrey made the discovery that no ships had left in the last few hours; indeed, none had set sail since that morning. Two ships were due to leave with the morning tide; they would be boarding their passengers within the next few hours. The ships were the *Blue Hawk* and the Frenchman the *Bonjour*.

"That's her!" Pierce said softly. "A French ship! Jerome would definitely choose a foreign vessel, for he now knows himself to be an English renegade."

"So we wait?" Geoffrey said.

Pierce, as still as the dark night, shook his head

slowly. "I cannot wait. God alone knows what he will do to Rose, for she was the one to unmask him!"

"Then—"

"We search!"

And so they began a ride through the streets of the port town, stopping at each tavern, offering gold pieces for the information that they craved.

Time was ticking away. Time was his enemy. And they were getting nowhere at the establishments where they had stopped thus far.

He urged Beowulf out in the street. It was such a very still night. So very black, with dark clouds covering the moon. He stared up at the sky. There must be a storm brewing. A storm that made the air hover around them, thick and heavy, and covered the moon and stars. The ships might well be delayed in crossing. Perhaps the wretched night was buying him more time . . .

But what was happening with Jerome and Rose?

His heart catapulted and constricted in his chest so that he could scarcely breathe. He turned to Geoffrey. "We have to find her. Now! We go back to his last scurvy hideout, and search for him there!"

It had been so long since he had come there . . .

Tonight, he had to return.

Rose! Her name pounded in his heart and mind. Rose, take care, my beloved. I am coming . . .

And he fought that awful image of finding Anne, all those many months ago. When he got his hands on Jerome . . .

Pray God. It wouldn't matter.

Not unless he found Rose.

She came to very slowly. For the first several seconds, small things registered in her mind. Her fingers lay on rough material. There was an unclean scent in the air. There were cracks in the walls that she saw around her.

She tried to focus, tried to remember. She was alive! Her throat hurt. It pained her terribly. Swallowing was an awful effort, one she couldn't quite manage yet. But she was alive. He had not strangled her to death. He had brought her somewhere . . .

Here. Here to this little room with the cracked white walls, the rough-covered bed beneath her, the odious scent in the air. Where were they?

And oh, God, what of Pierce? What would he think? She had simply disappeared, vanished. Her father, her poor father! Oh, God, Woody . . .

She blinked, trying hard to focus in the dimly lit room. Then she would have screamed, except that she realized that a gag was soundly stuffed in her mouth and that her hands were bound tightly together. She lay on her side on the rough sheets, and now she was staring into Jerome's leering face. It was so very close to hers. The watery blue eyes with their cast of evil. The lank blond hair clinging to his forehead.

"Ah, my Lady! You're back with us! I'm so glad. I was afraid for a moment that I had killed you. And mercy, I wouldn't want that. Not yet. You see, milady Rose, I'm taking you to France. I've good friends there. And relations. We'll enjoy a little time together. We'll enjoy it so much that you just might perish there, life will be so wonderful."

There were so many things that she wanted to say to him. She couldn't speak because of the gag that bit cruelly into her flesh.

"What is that, milady?" Jerome mocked her. "You are awash with anticipation? Ah, so am I!"

She tried to shout back to him, but only muffled sounds escaped the gag.

Apparently he wanted to hear her words. He leaned down very close to her and loosened the gag. "I beg your pardon, milady?"

"You stupid, treacherous bastard!" she hissed to him. "Do you truly think that you will ever leave here alive? You will never be able to take me from here. Pierce lives—"

"And I have seen to it that the king has been informed that he is alive. He will not follow us, lady!"

"You sent a message to the king!" she exclaimed. "Just as you once sent a message to the lord constable in my name, telling him where he might find Pierce on the night when you murdered your best friend."

"Messages are very easy to send," he told her blithely. "A pity for you that your husband didn't die. You might have married anew in the colonies and lived happily ever after!"

She shook her head, her eyes fire on his. "I'd have pursued you until the day I die."

"Take care, my fair lady, for that may be very soon!"

She gritted her teeth, wishing away the sting of desolate tears. He was not a powerful man, not like many of the king's guards, not like Geoffrey, and certainly not like her husband. But that hadn't mattered. He had been stronger than she, and he had nearly killed her already. She could threaten as she pleased, but she was bound here in some tavern, and he needed only to slip the gag back over her face to silence her once again.

"You were seen! You were seen murdering poor Beth!" she reminded him.

"Ah, yes, well, that was a pity!" he agreed.

"You'll never be able to walk about England without constant fear. You'll—"

"Dear Rose! I don't intend to walk around En-

gland! I'm going to France—*we're* going to France—
just as soon as the ship sails."

Her heart sank. Never, except when she had believed Pierce to be dead, had she ever known a
deeper feeling of desolation. France! Pierce, the king,
and all his men might not be able to find her once
she had been taken to a foreign shore! She couldn't
let it happen! She couldn't.

He was touching her cheek. Stroking it with mock
tenderness. It made her feel as if her flesh crawled
with vermin. "I never intended it should be this
way, lovely Rose!" he told her softly, then shrugged.
"I really didn't kill Anne. Can you believe it? She
slipped! And then, Jamison Bryant was always such
a fool. He would have wound up betraying us both!
And really, if he hadn't been such a fool, none of
this would have ever come about! Anne would have
never died."

"I'm sure you were terribly concerned on that
point!" Rose spat out.

He shrugged. "Well, obviously not, not when her
holdings fell so sweetly into my hands. You see, I've
a dozen mercenaries in my employ this very moment, the best that my sister's money could buy.
They will protect us until we reach the ship, my love.
And then we will be Normandy-bound. It is a pity
about Jamison. He and Anne might still be man and
wife, happily raising their own brood, and you and
your dear Pierce would be raising a passel of brats
of your own. Alas, now there is all this tempest in
a teapot to get away with!"

"You're wrong," she told him earnestly. "You'll
not get away with anything like this again. I don't
care if you run to France. Or to Spain. Or to deepest
Africa. He will come after you. I know he will. He
will come after you tonight, I swear it!"

"Do you think so, little flower? How will he find me?"

Rose shifted away from him, her hair falling over her face. She couldn't say anything more to him, not until she had found a way to force him to release her.

He came closer, his fingers moving over her face, threading into her hair to clear her eyes. "How will he find me?"

She stared at him, pretending that she didn't really hear what he was saying. "I'm going to be sick!" she whispered.

"What?"

"I can't—breathe. Please . . . you've got to let me up. Just for a moment. I need air."

"I don't care if you're sick. I nearly strangled you, and if I had, well, things would have been different."

"If you're going to be with me and take me with you in a small ship's cabin," she warned, "you should care!"

He paused. "All right, little flower." He wrenched the gag completely from her mouth and eased off the ties around her wrists. Rose sat, looking at him while he straightened, smiled, and warned her, "I have men below, Rose. Well-paid men. If you scream, I might kill you myself. If you run, I need only give the order, and one of them will catch you, wrap his arms tenderly around you—and slit your throat. Do you understand?"

She didn't reply. She stood quickly, walking to the latticed Tudor window, and breathing deeply while looking down into the street. "Why?" she asked him.

"Why what?" he demanded.

"Why take me?"

His nearly colorless blue eyes fastened upon her.

"Alas, my lady! You are appealing baggage, as you must know."

"And you are simply smitten with love?"

He shook his head. "I am smitten with the idea of escaping your husband. Then there is the fact of knowing that he suffers, of course."

"You hate him so very much!"

He strode to the window to join her. Rose clenched her fists to remain still, to endure his being so close. She couldn't bear it when he reached out to touch her, lifting her chin. But she knew this man now. Knew that blood ran like ice in his body, that he thought no more of killing a man or a woman than he did of swatting a fly. She had to take the greatest care.

"Hate my good Lord DeForte! Lady, half of the nobility of England hated him for one reason or another. My Lord Perfection, he has been called. The king's favorite."

"For good reason," Rose reminded him. "He did ride with the king, endure exile with him, and fight at his back!"

"The valiant warrior! The perfect knight! Oh, indeed. But he had no power when he lost Anne. And he now has no power as he loses you!"

She couldn't let it happen. But how to escape him? The answer eluded her no matter how swiftly her mind raced, no matter how desperate she became with each passing moment. The time to escape would be when he moved her to a ship, she thought. But would he allow her to see or move—or even breathe—when that time came?

She idly touched the lattice on the window. What if she screamed now? If she called to the cutthroats and thieves below her, no one would notice, no one would care. But if she broke open the window, and screamed into the street . . . ?

Riders were coming even now.

Perhaps he would kill her. But he intended to kill her eventually anyway, she was certain. She meant nothing to him, except as a weapon against Pierce.

Yes . . .

Her decision was made. Her heart trembled with the terror as she slammed at the lattices with all her strength and determination. They broke and splintered, pieces flying into the street below. She stuck her head out the window, screaming. "Help! Please, God, help me! I'm being kidnapped! The king himself will—"

His hands were on her, wrenching her back. There was such a look of black fury on his lean face that she thought she was dead. He swirled her around violently, sending her flying back across the small room. He started to stride toward her, the evil and fury in his soul twisting his features. Then he stopped dead still as they both heard a cry in the night.

"Rose! Rose!"

She stared at Jerome. Incredibly, the voice in the night was Pierce's. The riders below . . .

Pierce. He had been coming for her!

She leapt up with an incredible speed, determined that she had to elude Jerome, if only for split seconds. She managed to reach the window. To look down to the street. To see him there . . .

On Beowulf. His ruggedly handsome face tense with anguish, staring up at her.

Dear God, but she loved him!

"Pierce! He has men scattered throughout the tavern below. Take care! He'll mur—"

She let off with a screech, for Jerome caught her again. His hold was a death grip about her ribs, cutting off her breath.

"I'll kill her, DeForte, before your very eyes. Turn around and ride away!"

Rose managed to bash her elbow against his chin. Hard. His hold eased for one second. "Get the king's men, Pierce. He'll kill me anyway. Don't let him sail, don't let him escape—!"

She gasped out, for his hands were around her nape, fingers crawling around her throat, cutting off the flow of her air to her lungs. And he was expert at this. She already knew that.

"You're the dead man!" Pierce raged from the street.

Then Rose heard him no more. She was struggling too fiercely against Jerome, trying with all her strength to break his death hold. She kicked, swirled, flailed. He had already robbed her of so much strength. She couldn't beat him, and she knew it. Unless . . .

She ceased to struggle. She went limp in his hold, falling.

He came down to the floor with her. His fingers remained knotted around her neck and he shook her several times. She was dying, she thought again. She couldn't see, the world was black. She couldn't breathe . . .

She had tricked him into believing that she was already unconscious if not dead, but he meant to be thorough. And now she really was dying, and she hadn't the strength to move.

The world went black again.

Jerome, satisfied, stood. He heard the shouting from below. He reached to the door for his scabbard and sword, convinced that he could flee the establishment while his hired army took on Pierce.

Pierce burst through the doors of the tavern he had come to so long ago, that same wretched tavern where he had come to try to discover where Jamison had taken Anne.

Where Jerome had now brought Rose . . .

For a moment, as Pierce burst through the doors of the tavern, he was blinded. Hazy smoke from the hearth rose all around him, and the creatures within the tavern were all somehow enwrapped in that haze. Barmaids, sailors, drunkards, pirates, and thieves, all alike.

Then his eyes focused, and he saw the rickety stairs that led to the rooms above. He started across the room toward them, but had barely taken a stride before two men sprang before him, their swords bared. One of them was a bearded, husky fellow. The other was taller and leaner. Both had deadly intent in their eyes.

Dear God! He didn't have the time for this!

But the silver blade of a sword was swinging his way. He had no choice but to fight.

"To the devil with you, then!" he cried. He raised his own blade with such a vengeance that his first opponent's sword met his, clashed, and cracked. With the thrust of his body against the bulk of the bearded fellow's, he sent the man flying backward and over one of the tavern's planked tables. He spun just in time to catch the leaner man across his sword arm with a serious slash. The man screamed and fell back, and Pierce stepped forward swiftly again.

More men were hurrying down the stairs now. Three of them this time.

And there was activity by the door. Geoffrey was busily engaged with a tall, redheaded combatant while a dark-haired man sought to take him from behind. "Geoffrey!" Pierce shouted the warning. His friend turned just in time to slice the second man in the side, then smash the hilt of his sword down on the other man's head.

Then Pierce could watch no longer, for he was thrusting and parrying against another man at the foot of the stairs, a very Gaelic-looking fellow with dark, curling hair and a fine swirling mustache. He dispatched him with the flat on his blade. The two others were rushing down the stairway. He darted and parried, and sent one man flying over the wooden banister.

Then he saw Jerome.

He had slipped out of the room, and was attempting to rush down the hallway, and escape by some other route.

One remaining man still stood between them, his sword drawn and at the ready, but his eyes wary. He was young, a platinum-haired man with strange dark eyes. There was a pulse ticking furiously at his throat. He was afraid, Pierce thought swiftly, realizing even as he did that Jerome was getting away. He looked back to the the pale-haired man and let out a roar while raising his sword.

To his great relief, the fellow simply fell back.

And he raced for Jerome.

He did so with such vengeance that he reached him even as he prepared to dash through a door at the end of the hallway. He spun Jerome around, slamming him against the wall.

He was ready to fight. By God, he was ready to fight.

But Jerome held his sword limply in his hand, staring at Pierce with his strange blue eyes. A very curious smile touched his lips. Then he spoke.

"Kill me! Kill me and be quick. Then go to your wife. Perhaps you can reach her in time . . ."

He stared at the man, incredulous.

"If you have harmed her, you will not die

quickly!" he promised. Then, frenzied, he turned away. The tavern was in an uproar. Geoffrey was close behind him.

Jerome wasn't going to escape. Geoffrey would see to it that he did not.

Pierce turned and raced for the door Jerome had come from. He burst through it.

And he saw her. Rose. Slumped upon the floor. She was wearing an emerald green dress. The skirt of it billowed luxuriously around her, too fine for these surroundings. Her hair was loose, a cascade of fire around her shoulders, covering her face.

"Rose!" He cried her name like a lost creature, his anguish rising in his voice. He fell to his knees, his heart thundering. Prayers flowed through his mind, his heart, his soul. "God, no!" he screamed. He lifted her into his arms. Her face was ashen. Beautiful, as clear and pure as porcelain, her dark lashes sweeping her cheeks. Her lips, even, were ashen. "Rose!" he screamed again, and the pain wracked him. He touched her cheek, he kissed her lips, he swore against God. He saw the faint purple marks on her neck.

And his rage burst within him.

"Rose!"

Miraculously, she heard the cry. It entered into the darkness that had swept around her. That held her. The darkness so very like death . . .

Someone was calling her. Calling her back to life. She had been tumbling into the black void. She had been ready to accept the darkness. But she could hear his voice, calling to her. She could feel warmth then. Feel his arms around her.

He was carrying her. Laying her out on the bed. She tried to breathe. Tried to speak. Tried to open her eyes.

"Rose!" He cried her name again, drawing her to

him. He kissed her forehead and her cheeks and her fingers.

She tried to say something, to assure him, but she couldn't. She had to concentrate, she had to summon her strength . . .

But he was suddenly gone. Swearing against God and heaven. Vowing to kill Jerome. Slice him from throat to groin.

Pierce burst out to the hallway, his fingers clasping the banister as he stared down into the crowded tavern below. Jerome was down there now, at the end of Geoffrey's sword point. Pierce leapt over the banister, landing deftly just feet before him. "God damn you! God damn you to eternal hell!" he thundered, his voice shaking.

Geoffrey fell back, fear dancing through his eyes as he saw the madman before him. Pierce raised his sword. Armed or unarmed, he didn't give a damn. He had to kill him. Had to . . .

But when it came time to lower his blade, something snapped.

He dropped his sword. Instead he sent a blow flying against Jerome's chin, and the man staggered to the floor. He looked up at Pierce, smiling over his bloodied lip. "It's too late, eh, mi-great-lord?"

Pierce reached for him, certain that he had the strength and blind fury to rip him right in half.

But then . . .

He heard his name.

"Pierce!"

He froze, unable to believe that he was hearing the voice. He turned, and there she was. Rose. Standing. Pale as snow, but alive, her hair a fire that tumbled all around her. Her emerald skirt fell beautifully about her. She was looking down at him so gravely.

God in heaven, she was alive!

"Pierce, give him to the king's justice!" she said softly. Her hand was at her throat. It must have pained her greatly. The bruises on it would soon turn black and blue.

He turned back and picked up Jerome. Literally picked him up, snatching him right from the floor. His body was rigid with tension.

"Pierce!"

Her voice, so soft . . .

He had killed men in battle, many times. But in all of his life, he had never committed murder. No matter how he longed to tear this man limb from limb, it would somehow be wrong.

"Pierce!" Her voice was soft, beautiful, entreating.

"Pierce, let him stand trial, I beg of you! You have now avenged Anne! She would not wish you to sacrifice your own soul. Let him have the king's justice, Pierce. For you, for me, for Woody!"

His lip curled slightly. He still held the terrified, red-faced Jerome in his death grip.

Rose didn't understand. Time had healed him somewhat. He didn't feel the desperate desire to draw blood for what Jerome had done to Anne, but for what he had nearly done to Rose. Perhaps it was a fine point. Perhaps explained by the very nearness of Rose's vivid beauty and unfaltering spirit. Perhaps it was the babe they shared.

Perhaps it was the future that lay before them, and the depths of their love.

His grip tightened. He could feel the cords in his neck standing out. Blood pounded in his head. It would be so easy to wind his fingers around this man's neck, just as Jerome had wound his own around Rose's throat.

Or he could draw his knife! After all that the man had done, he deserved it! If he could just slide that knife into his flesh and rip and tear and work away the anger and the hatred . . .

Jerome was looking at him. Jerome, who knew what his fate would be in a court of law. "Do it!" he commanded Pierce. He was nearly smiling once again, taunting Pierce to kill him. "Do it, and be done with it!"

"Pierce!"

Rose again.

Pleading . . .

Not for Jerome. But for them. For the son. For the future they might now share.

Slowly, slowly, his fingers unclenched. Jerome's trembling body fell to the ground. Pierce turned from him and bounded back up the stairs, to Rose.

Men rushed in to take Jerome. The king's men, Pierce realized. They'd followed him. Bless Charles.

He had reached Rose.

Pierce lifted her chin very tenderly. His thumb massaged her cheek. He kissed her lips. Softly. So softly. He touched her throat. "My God," he said, his voice breaking.

She caught his hand and held it, smiling. "It's all right! It's really all right."

It wasn't all right. It wouldn't be for a while. But she was alive.

And she would heal.

They would heal.

"Let's go home," he said.

He lifted her up, and into his arms. He walked outside, into the clear air of the aftermath of the storm. A cool breeze lay on the air now. Soft, gentle.

"You can see the stars," she murmured.

"And the moon," he agreed.

"All of the world. It's clear and beautiful now."

Someone came up behind him, clearing his throat. Pierce turned. It was one of the king's guards.

"They've taken him to Dover Castle, Lord De-Forte."

"Thank you," Pierce said. He stared at Rose again. The king's man seemed to melt away.

Pierce lifted her atop Beowulf and leapt up behind her. Geoffrey, and a number of the king's men, followed behind them, keeping a discreet distance. But Pierce was certain that the king had commanded that the duke and duchess be given an escort home.

And there was nothing that he wanted more than to go home that night.

So they rode, as safe as they might ever hope to be.

Therefore, he could throw caution to the winds and give all his attention to his wife, held so tightly in his arms before him.

"Did I ever tell you how much I love you?" he asked her.

"Just how much?" she mused. "No," she informed him, smiling.

"Never?"

"Never." She reached up and touched a dark strand of his hair. "A son and over a year of marriage. And you've yet to really go on and on about love."

"Well, I might have been too busy groveling," he told her, a smile curling his own lips.

"Pierce!"

He laughed, but his arms tightened around her. "I love you so much that I would welcome death rather than live without you. I do, my wild, rare little colonial flower, love you with all of my heart and soul," he vowed, staring down into the soft, exquisite beauty of her eyes.

She touched his cheek, and trembled. "My dear great Lord DeForte! You are, indeed, my very life!"

His eyes were grave for a moment. "So brave, my Rose! You nearly died for me tonight."

Her breath quickened and she caught it, staring up at him. She stroked his cheek, marveling at the hard, handsome planes, feeling the tick of life in his pulse beneath her fingers. "I nearly lost you once. I was not so brave. I simply could not lose you again."

Pierce reined in sharply on Beowulf. There, beneath the trees on the trail in the starlit night, he kissed her. Long and luxuriously and tenderly, he kissed her. The taste was infinitely sweet.

Behind them, the king's men slowed to a stop. Pierce drew his lips from hers at last, his eyes sparkling in the darkness. "Perhaps we had best go home for this!" he murmured. Then he frowned. "If you're feeling well enough to—"

"My love, I am feeling well enough to be cherished, I promise you!"

"Ah, lady, I am eager to cherish you! I so nearly lost you tonight! I was almost insane with it, Rose; I could have torn him limb from limb! But—"

"But I am alive!" she whispered. "You brought me back to life, you know! I heard you call my name."

He smiled and kissed the tips of her fingers. "So that is it, you see. We have to cherish all that we have, and look now to the future."

"To the future," she whispered fervently in return.

"So shall we hurry, milady?" he murmured.

She glanced down the path, to the men following them, and smiled. "Oh, indeed! I think so!"

And so they rode home. And when they came to Castle DeForte, the doors burst open. Ashcroft came rushing out, his features drawn, reaching for his daughter. "She's well, Sir Woodbine!" Pierce said. But he seemed to understand a father's love, and he handed Rose down to Ashcroft. Rose hugged her father fiercely, then smiled. "All is well, Father. All is well."

"Milady!" Mary Kate came rushing out next, with Garth on her heels. Then it seemed that the whole household was welcoming them back.

A droll voice suddenly rang from the doorway. "My dear Lord and Lady DeForte! I do not mind standing guard over my godchild, as any good godparent might do! But young Pierce is wailing away and does not appear at all pleased with my royal face. I am the king, mind you, not a nurse-maid!"

Rose and Pierce looked quickly to each other, and then to the indignant king. Then once again their gazes met. They both burst into laughter and Rose turned and rushed quickly to the king. She curtsied before him. "Your Majesty! Do forgive us! We've all returned, and we certainly shall not expect you to see to the changing of our young DeForte's pants!"

"Daughter!" Ashcroft cried out, horrified.

"In to your son, madame!" the king commanded her, smiling.

Then he saw Pierce, and extended his hand, a brow raised.

"Pierce, my good friend!"

Pierce clasped his hand. "Jerome was taken to Dover Castle to be held there, Your Majesty, until such time as he can come to trial."

The king nodded, lowering his head. Then he raised it, his dark eyes sparkling with Stuart care and charm. "I am glad, my friend. Deeply glad. Let's have some wine, shall we?" He clapped Garth on the shoulders. "Some of the finest from my Lord DeForte's cellars, eh, good man?"

Garth agreed. They all filed into the house. Before

the door had closed, Pierce hurried back out. The king's men had followed him home. They were hovering back by the gates once again. There were Sirs Neville and Paine, Lords Denoncourt and Mobley and a few men he did not recognize.

"Wine, my friends?" he asked.

They all looked somewhat abashed. But then Neville threw up his arms. "Aye, it sounds good all around, fine wine after long hours! You'll have us all asleep in your hall, DeForte."

"As long as you stay below with the fire!" he said, and the men dismounted from their horses to come in.

It was really morning, not night at all. But no occasion had ever seemed more festive. His best wine flowed freely.

Garth and Mary Kate and Geoffrey and much of the household joined the festivities.

Of course, the way that they whispered, it was becoming more and more obvious that Mary Kate and Garth were growing enamored of each other. Between the two of them, though, they managed the household quite beautifully, and both Rose and Pierce were delighted.

As dawn broke, the king determined to leave, accompanied by several of his men. Pierce shook his hand again; Rose kissed it in her gratitude, holding it fiercely. Charles, ever the courtly king, disentangled himself. "Nay, lady! Let me kiss your hand!" And he did so, then departed.

Half of the noble sirs and lords were asleep in the hallway, some of them snoring over their wine cups, a few with their arms thrown around the wolfhounds.

Mary Kate and Garth were tucking up Woody, Mary Kate giving Garth instructions on how to do so properly, and Garth, incredibly, as silent as a lamb.

Ashcroft appeared to be asleep in the chair at the head of the table.

"Should we wake him?" Rose whispered.

"I think not!" Pierce returned.

Then he crossed the few feet to her, and swept her up in his arms. He stared down into her eyes and smiled. "We needed to come home," he told her, starting for the stairs. "Here I can tell you just how much I love you once again. But I've done that already."

She wrapped her arms around his neck, a slow smile beautifully curling her lip. "I shall be more than delighted to listen again."

Pink streaks of the rising sun were just beginning to burst through the stained-glass window at the curve in the stair. It bathed them both. Pierce moistened his lips, watching her still as he walked. He paused halfway up the stairs and murmured dramatically, "I love you more than daybreak, more than light. More than the air I breathe, and more than life itself."

"Oh!" she whispered. "And I love you, milord! More than the world."

"More than the earth, the sea, the sky—"

A husky laugh intruded upon his speech. "I told you, daughter," Ashcroft called up pleasantly, "milord DeForte was indeed the most incredible catch to be had!"

They stared at each other, and then down the stairs. "Go back to sleep!" they commanded in unison.

Then Pierce smiled tenderly at his wife once again and vowed, "Just a few more steps and I can *show* you just how much I love you."

She gently smoothed back an irresistible lock of

raven-dark hair. "And I shall be just delighted to see!" she promised softly.

And so he proceeded up the stairs, and into their room.

And there he most tenderly and passionately set forth to fulfill his vow.

America Loves Lindsey!
The Timeless Romances
of #1 Bestselling Author

Johanna Lindsey

KEEPER OF THE HEART	77493-3/$6.99 US/$8.99 Can
THE MAGIC OF YOU	75629-3/$6.99 US/$8.99 Can
ANGEL	75628-5/$6.99 US/$8.99 Can
PRISONER OF MY DESIRE	75627-7/$6.99 US/$8.99 Can
ONCE A PRINCESS	75625-0/$6.99 US/$8.99 Can
WARRIOR'S WOMAN	75301-4/$6.99 US/$8.99 Can
MAN OF MY DREAMS	75626-9/$6.99 US/$8.99 Can
SURRENDER MY LOVE	76256-0/$6.50 US/$7.50 Can
YOU BELONG TO ME	76258-7/$6.99 US/$8.99 Can
UNTIL FOREVER	76259-5/$6.50 US/$8.50 Can
LOVE ME FOREVER	72570-3/$6.99 US/$8.99 Can
SAY YOU LOVE ME	72571-1/$6.99 US/$8.99 Can

And Now in Hardcover

ALL I NEED IS YOU
97534-3/$22.00 US/$29.00 CAN